Fairy Circle

Johanna Frappier

To Leo with love; you are magic.

***

To Carrie, who always encourages me.

***

To Laura, who accepts me and my demons.

Chapter 1

"Saffron, are you okay?"

Saffron tasted dirt and grass. She could smell the ocean and hear the waves. It was too much of an effort to answer her mother. Her eyelids were so heavy she didn't want to open them to take a look around and see where she had landed herself this time.

"Here," Derek's voice, "give me a hand getting her up. She's all right. We saved her again, like a couple of fricken heroes." He pointed up to the night-bright sky. "How come you didn't lock her door?"

Audrey looked up at the almost-full moon as she pulled Saffron to her feet. "I thought you locked the door." She said this softly, accepting the blame as they guided Saffron through the field and past the curious alpacas. Saffron was quiet on the walk back to the farmhouse. When her mother tucked her into bed, she felt like she had just graduated kindergarten, not high school. She was asleep before the bolt slid home on the outside of her bedroom door.

***

"And here he is." Derek leaned on the kitchen counter for a long look out the window over the sink.

Saffron stayed in her seat at the table. She looked down at her omelet when the heat rushed up the back of her neck.

"Awfully loud, what's wrong with his car? Is that a motorcycle?" Audrey gave the home-fries a scrape in the iron skillet and went to lean on the counter by Derek.

Derek snorted. "Yeah, it's a motorcycle. Saffron, come look at the yummy man-boy."

Saffron dropped her fork in her plate and rubbed the heel of her hand over her forehead. "I know what Markis looks like. He was only a year behind me in school. So stop staring at him Derek; that's gross."

Derek smiled. "You need to show the new lawn boy where the mower is, Saffron. And make sure he weedwacks around the fence."

"I'm not going out there. You do it."

Derek pushed off the counter. "Gladly."

"Don't scare him, dirty old man." Audrey whipped Derek with a dish towel, then went back to the home fries. "Aren't you going to go say 'Hi,' to him, Saffron?"

Saffron swallowed. "Never talked to him before."

"Speaking of school, if you're really not going to go to college, why don't you get a job to keep busy this summer? I saw a sign when I got the Half & Half at the Black Chicken. They're hiring."

Saffron sucked her next breath in through her teeth. "Mom, we weren't 'speaking of school'."

"It's not a bad idea." Audrey sniffed.

Saffron rolled her eyes over her cup of juice as Audrey came to the table with the home fries.

"And when's the last time you combed your hair? It looks like a pile of plop propped with chopsticks. Like red tide. I can tell you haven't combed it." Audrey pushed some potatoes onto Saffron's plate, and then some onto Grandmother's plate. Grandmother sat staring. She didn't seem to be in the room with them. The screen door slapped closed behind Derek just as the mower started up out back.

"Derek, you owe me rent." Audrey sat at the table, placed a wrinkled linen napkin on her lap, and buttered her toast.

"Put it on my tab, luv." He stared at Saffron. "Let me tell you something, honey." He went at his plate of mounded food like a bear dining at a toy table. When he started to talk, food went flying into the air, on the table, on his shirt, in his beard. "Listen to your mother. It's not like you hafta be queen of the fricken world right away. Just go do something. You hear what I'm sayin'?"

"How do you even know what we're talking about? You just came in the door." Saffron folded her arms across her chest.

"Well, let me see...." Derek shoveled in another load. "You've got a puss on your face. The sun's out. It's Tuesday morning. We're eating breakfast. And what else do you people hiss about day after day?"

Saffron stuck her tongue out at him.

He smiled and smacked his lips.

At least they weren't going to talk about her sleepwalking. They all treated it like bedwetting - she did it, they didn't talk about it, and they were all waiting for it to go away.

Grandmother's voice came muttering across the table. "Someone was here last night."

Grandmother always thought someone had come on the nights Saffron went on her nocturnal jaunts. Saffron assumed Grandmother was just hearing them all walking around during the hullabaloo.

Derek stopped mid-bite. "Well, Jesus H, Grandmother, you don't say." He shifted around without turning his neck to give Audrey a look.

"Derek..." Audrey's voice was soft. She had never quite perfected admonishment.

Derek picked up his coffee and slurped, avoiding eye contact with the old lady. Grandmother suddenly focused on Saffron. Saffron looked away, hoping her mother would handle it. Audrey's chair creaked as she leaned back. She grabbed her coffee mug. "What about the job, Saffron?"

Saffron made a disgruntled 'pfft' sound. "Why, Mom? What I'm doing's not enough? You want me to start paying rent too?" Audrey winced. "What?" "I mean, why do I have to get a job? You need some money or something? Why do I have to get a job? I have a job. I clean the house! I do the dishes. I wash the laundry and everything else. I dust till I gag, Mom. C'mon, since I graduated I pretty much do all of the menial chores. Inside and out. I do all the barn stuff, too. I feed the alpacas, I shovel their poop. I get the chicken eggs. I take the goats on their poison ivy binges."

"No, I don't need money, Saffron. And no, you don't do all of the work. And it's good for you to do work. Derek and I are working. A regular job would be good for you. I want you to feel good about yourself, about something you create or accomplish."

Saffron threw up her arms. "Oh, now we have arrived at our destination, folks."

"...and you never talk about your future. Nothing. Not even plans for this weekend." Audrey's voice crackled like a live wire skipping around in a puddle.

"Here we go round the mulberry bush on a hot and sticky morning." Derek bellowed, using his best Puccini.

"Saffron," Audrey gasped, "why do we have to keep doing this?"

Saffron looked down and wagged her head back and forth. "This isn't right, Mom. You're not being fair." Her mother was always the one to start this, and at least once a week since graduation. "Why do you always have to start this? I can't believe you just told me to go become a clerk." Saffron spat clerk' like clog from her throat.

"I didn't start anything. I only suggested you become a clerk." Audrey dropped her knife and the loud clatter made everyone jump. "I just mean you should find something, anything, to keep you occupied while you think things through. I just thought of the convenience store as an idea. Go become a brain surgeon. Go collect trash - whatever."

Saffron had to yell as the mower passed close by the window. "I am occupied."

"Doing what?" Audrey yelled back, even though the mower had moved on.

"Think what through?" Saffron gave the open window a dirty look when the mower doubled back.

"Oh, gee, look at the time." Derek hardly glanced at his watch, a shocking piece of jewelry graced with the Vitruvian Man, Davinci's famous anatomical. One rigid arm and one rigid leg kept time, sometimes at grotesque angles; his family jewel was a centered diamond. Derek used the table to push himself out of his seat. He patted Saffron on the head, and then went to peck Audrey's cheek. He rubbed her shoulders with his big paws, loosening her like a boxer between rounds. "Need help getting those canvases to my shop, honey?"

Audrey shook her head no, and dragged her eyes from Saffron to look up at him. She huffed. "No, but I need you to check Han Solo before you go. I think he only has one testicle." She bit her bottom lip. "I don't think I'll be able to show him at the Invitational." She reached up. "Derek, look at all the marmalade in your beard." She raked his beard with her short nails as he jutted his chin out.

"Yes, my love, I'll grope your alpaca. I'll call you. Then I'm going to go open up my shop. Because, you know, it's my J-O-B. I take great pride in clerking and so forth."

Saffron made the forced air out of her throat sound of disgust that women do so spectacularly. "You are not a clerk! You're the shop owner, the boss!"

"Oh, please, honey, don't start that bickering with me. You don't know who you're messing with. Now, I'm off to stand behind my store counter, aka, 'to clerk.' I need to know when my shipment arrives if somebody named Saffron could give me a call when UPS shows up. You owe me. I saved you again last night..."

Audrey rubbed her hands all over her face. "I know. I know, Derek. I'm sorry. Don't salt the wound. Thank you."

"Don't mention it, honey. Anyway, Grouchyrella, do you think you can do this for me today?" He was already grabbing his keys off the counter and checking his teeth with his tongue.

Saffron rested her forehead in her palm and waved him off with the other hand. "Yessss."

"Good. Ciao!" The screen door smashed behind him.

"I never said there was anything wrong with being a clerk!"

"Can't hear you." He yelled from the gravel drive.

"I never said there was anything wrong with being a clerk." She muttered.

"Then why don't you go try it?" Audrey studied Saffron while Saffron hunched over her cold breakfast dregs.

Grandmother was considering the blue veins on the back of her hand. The lawnmower moved around to the side of the house. Saffron and her mother listened as Derek slammed the door of his yellow bug and started the engine.

Audrey jumped. "And he already forgot to check Han Solo." She was out the screen door in two seconds.

Saffron perked up. Her mother was a brilliant painter but the worst actress in the world. Han Solo's testicles didn't warrant a two-second sprint. Saffron got up and hurried to the window over the kitchen sink. She couldn't hear what her mother was saying over the grind of the lawnmower. She saw Audrey yapping and flapping away like a jay bird and going on for way too long.

Saffron stretched her neck and flattened her cheek to the window, but Markis was out of sight. She took a step back and frowned at Derek and Audrey, then moped to her seat, her red hair slipping out of the chop sticks and streaming down her face.

***

That afternoon, Saffron straddled her mountain bike. Somber-eyed, she looked down the long line of the driveway to the country road at its base. She breathed deep for five seconds, held it for five seconds, and exhaled for five. Then did it again. It didn't help. Her teeth stayed clamped, her hands still shook, and the freight train still roared in her ears. She narrowed her eyes and scanned the farmhouse to see if anyone was watching. Her mother was probably still in the sunroom out back, working on her canvas. Saffron looked front and shuddered. Tears welled in her eyes as she held her breath.

In high school, the breathing technique had worked well. Used on a daily basis, the urge to chain herself to the quarry-stone foundation wasn't as strong as it was today when she hadn't left the farmhouse in weeks.

She got off the bike and let it drop to the ground. She lay down, and immediately got up, brushing the gravel off her back and butt. She got on the bike. Tears of rage welled up as she rammed her pedals around and around and forced herself forward.

She was at the bottom of the drive when she slowed to a stop and frowned at the line of mushrooms that marched across her path. Mushrooms that grew in gravel? The hot, sunny gravel? They had always been there, marching out of the field on one side of the driveway and disappearing into the tall grasses on the other side. Her paranoia piqued as she kicked and ground at them with both feet, then quickly got on her bike and pushed her way across the broken line.

You're nineteen and you don't have your license. Her eyes were narrow slits. This was all her mother's fault, making her do this. Freakin' convenience store clerk. She moved on in a daze, ignoring the cow-filled pastures and the rocky shoreline. The mountain bike had never been out of her yard.

After about two miles, she reached the business part of town. She passed the Happy Grocer, Gary's Old Thyme Wieners, which was in a pretty Victorian house with brightly-colored, scalloped edging, passed the post office and Frank's Diner, and rode around the corner of main street where the brick pharmacy stood. The Black Chicken was in the next little brick building. She pedaled into the parking lot and peeked out from behind her hair. She parked her bike behind a keeling evergreen decorated with faded candy wrappers.

Her lips started to get twitchy as she slunk past the sale signs that hung in the store windows. When she opened the glass entry door, a small man in a big plaid shirt and polyester slacks came charging forward, waving a lottery ticket in her face. She started swatting without thinking, as much to get the lottery ticket away as to dispel the smell of cabbage and smoky skin.

"This is it! The winner!" he let her know, then ran to the hood of his big, red Road Master to scratch it.

"Sweetie, you can't stand there all day, got the flies to think about. Food in here, you know." A sallow-skinned woman, fortyish, fake-smiled at Saffron from behind the register counter. Her brown teeth were not included in the ads of the good times you can have with Marlboros. She tilted her Michael-Jackson nose up. Clearly, she was queen of all she surveyed.

Saffron scurried across the threshold and presented herself at the counter like a terrified recruit.

"What can I getcha?" The woman smacked her gum.

"Do you need help?" White lights danced into Saffron's vision and blurred the image of the lady's cigarette teeth.

The woman reached under the counter, laughing. "Of course I need help! Who doesn't need help? I gotta kid at home that I need ta feed and keep in Wii games and music downloads. Now he wants a Kindle." The woman looked Saffron up and down, her lips still pulled in a thin smile.

The woman was at least three inches shorter than Saffron, but Saffron automatically gave her the upper hand by letting her own body shrink into a more pronounced hunch. She tried to fake-smile back at the woman, but just managed to look like she had shut her finger in a door. "I'm looking for a job." *I hate you, I hate you, I hate you,* she thought. *Ruh-row dumb ass; me need job.* She longed for the rough, brick outside of the building to rub her forehead on. Then she smiled wider, her bottom lip shaking as the woman smirked at her.

"Yeah, I get it." The woman presented Saffron with the one page form she had pulled out from under the counter. "Just fill this out. I'll give it to tha ownas as soon as they get back. They'll call ya."

Saffron's smile dropped and she stood up straight without realizing it. Her nostrils flared. This queen wasn't even the owner. Not the boss! Saffron could hardly believe she wasted her best mumbling kiss-ass routine on this woman. She snatched at the application and took it over to the lottery ticket station. There, amongst the shavings of a million 'winining' tickets she white-knuckled a half-chewed pen and quickly filled out some of the application, fretting over the other empty rest of it because she had done nothing in her life. Nothing.

Saffron walked the application back to Bea, the woman's nametag read, and handed the paper over with a grimace she was convinced, this time, was a nice smile. Bea squinted at Saffron, studied her like a moldy roll, and proclaimed, "Ya know, this job's not easy." Now she was sounding downright vicious. "It's not like you're gonna get hired, then come sit around here all day."

Saffron had no idea what to do with this information. "O...kaaay." She jerked her head around to look at the door. "You know, I gotta...." She sighed heavy. "I'll be right back." Then she took off through the door, jumped on her bike, and pedaled like the Wicked Witch of the West was after her all the way home.

Chapter 2

$\mathcal{S}$everal watchers came that night, always up for a game, just before two in the morning. They settled in the willow on the edge of the woods beyond her front lawn. But, they were too late - Saffron was already dreaming. They hung from the gnarled limbs until they became bored, and then scattered like a murder of crows.

Saffron dreamt of a rough woman who lived in a thatched hut on the shore of a different grey and raging sea.

The woman took care of everything - herself, her home, and some petty livestock. Everything but her own children who, in five years of marriage, had never come into existence. Her coarse, orange hair was windblown, its kinks dull and colorless from lack of attention. The skin on her hands was chapped and scarred from hard seaside labor. Yet, she was strong, and often when she rose with the sun, she possessed a warm light that marked her pretty to those who cared to search.

She was waiting for her husband to return from a holy war, a crusade she had never understood but supported blindly as his passions were her passions. She longed for the day when she could strip him of his mail to cast it to the white and foaming jaws of the sea. She cared not for war and the other vices of men, but thought only of her home, a family, and the sun on her garden, the moon on the water.

She had waited months for his return, then over a year. When two years had passed, she was one day out hanging clothes to dry in the briny air. The glare of the sun reflected off the white, salted grass, setting her eyes in a perpetual wince of which she was hardly aware.

The rider was obscured, wavering in the haze and dust of the path as his horse clopped toward her. She wiped her hands on her patched apron, breathed deep the wild-rose-scented air, and bit her bottom lip as she waited to greet the man she finally recognized as her husband's best mate. She let out a cry at seeing him back, and ran to receive him with hugs and babbled prayers of thanks. After several moments, he held her from him and looked sadly into her eyes. She asked harshly, "Is he dead, then?"

"No," the rider replied softly. "If only that he was."

She gaped at him, and stepped back, unsure of his meaning and stricken by the horrific statement spoken with such bland indifference.

He was brief - her love had found union with another and he would never be coming back. He, the revered friend, came only to tell her out of conscience. He knew she would otherwise wait for that Devil's whelp - that it would kill her to learn the truth. He hoped she could start anew, and with someone better deserving of her adoration.

He left her crumpled and crying under the dripping laundry. After a time, she sat up, her eyes as vacant as a doll's as she stared out to sea. She only half heard the crash of the waves, the cry of the gulls, and the wind that furled the clothes on the line. When the sun reached its zenith, she used the washpole to pull herself up and began to walk.

Her head was hot. She walked toward the pounding surf, to its heavy coolness, wishing it to surround her, to feel it chilling her toes, caressing her calves and crawling up between her legs, to her navel, to cover her breasts. She needed it to lap at her neck and, most exquisitely of all, she needed it to take her head in its arms and muffle the noise in her ears.

When Saffron woke up, there was a copper sting in her nose. It was the tang of snorting water, the taste of the sea, and of her tears. An abrupt sob bubbled up and out of her throat as she lay cloaked in the anguish of the dream. He had deserted her. It was a pain so raw, so real, that even now her shoulders ached from the strain.

Saffron realized she was huddled against her bedroom door. She had tried to escape again. Twice in one month. What was happening? Tears spilled as she crawled back to bed.

***

Later, Saffron heard her mother unbolting her door. Audrey knocked, then came in. When Saffron didn't answer, she chirped, "Yoohoo. It's a new day. Rise and shine."

Saffron wanted to scream. Why was her mother bothering her? Didn't she have anything else to do? A painting to finish? Derek to play house with? High school "friends" of Saffron's that she hadn't spoken to since fourth grade to hire? So those "friends" could come over and wonder why Saffron stayed up in her room all day... Saffron turned over and squeezed her eyes shut.

Audrey frowned at the back of Saffron's head, "What's the matter?"

Saffron would have to say something. Her mother could be persistent. She rolled over and yawned. "What do you mean, Mom? I'm fine." Then she stretched, tussled her red waves with the fingers of both hands, and scratched her scalp. Pretending nonchalance was almost unbearable. But it wasn't like Audrey to give up in the first few seconds.

And soon enough, Audrey spoke. "Did you look into that job?"

Oh, so Audrey was going to come around from the back, right? A little sneak attack, huh? Yeah, foiling with another subject ought to do the trick. As if Audrey didn't know Saffron had pedaled out of the yard yesterday. Saffron knew the whole world knew she had pedaled out of her yard yesterday. A thriving metropolis this town was not.

Saffron slapped the bed. "Mom! Yes! Now do we really need to talk about that? I'm waiting to hear back from them."

Audrey's eyes flashed, then she used her very low voice. "Saffron, what is wrong?"

As if. If she ever told her mother what was really going on at night, Saffron knew her mother would commit her somewhere. If she told her mother the truth, the years and years of truly disgusting truth, Audrey would have her straight on the bus bound for Club Wily Wackos for Wanton Ladies before another full moon grew. Or, maybe her mother would make her go to Sexaholics Anonymous class. Were you a sexaholic when you kept on having those kinds of dreams even when you didn't want to? Sweat pooled on Saffron's forehead, ready to trickle. It was already so humid out.

Jesus Christ, she would. She'd make me sit in a roomful of those people. That would be worse than a hospital. Saffron hated hospitals - the disinfectant stink of them, the wandering inmates of them, and the sickly green-painted concrete blocks of them. Hell no, no hospital. Saffron had never fessed up to Audrey and she wasn't about to give in this morning. Audrey would know nothing about the dreams, the little bits Saffron had remembered in vivid detail and the murky millions she could have guessed at.

The dreams had started when she was young. Without a single book, without a sneak preview of a stolen dirty movie with friends, without a school bus education, and before she really understood what the farm animals were doing, Saffron Keller knew about sex in detail. She couldn't fathom how you could learn so much from a dream, about a subject you had never researched or experienced. Saffron also learned about hunger, lust, betrayal, and how love can cripple you. It was all right there at night, played out like a movie.

She told no one. How could she explain such a thing? It was the one subject even Oprah hadn't covered, and Googling, which had provided help on every other subject known to man, was a big fat zero. Trying to Google for scientific evidence of the origins of your sex dreams always resulted in disturbing side roads. So, she didn't Google about that anymore. You couldn't Google 'Swiss cheese' without some perv taking you down a disturbing side road.

Over the years, she learned to deal with her dilemma much as most people dealt with theirs. She denied it. She ignored it. Time passed.

Audrey tried again. "You seem so different lately. Derek said you demanded the radio be left on all night, and the lights..." She reached for a lock of Saffron's hair, twirled it around her finger.

Saffron's face erupted red as she squeaked out, "Well, Mom, you were up all night too. Should we be concerned?"

Silence. Audrey wouldn't rise to the bait.

Saffron mumbled, "I want to get up, take a shower..."

After a moment, Saffron felt Audrey move off the mattress, heard the shuffle of her Minnetonkas and the clunk-clicking of her amber bracelets as she walked toward the door. She sighed from the doorway. "Breakfast will be ready soon."

***

"Mom?"

"What?"

"Why is it so important to you that I go to the school? I mean, why can't I go to school online? You've done online courses and look at you; you're a pretty smart chick. I'll get a degree online and you can get off me. Hell, I'll get three degrees. This is the cyber future. We can even get groceries delivered, along with everything else. No one leaves the house anymore." Saffron smirked and dug into her blueberry pancakes.

Audrey folded her arms across her misshapen hemp t-shirt. "Saffron..." it was the warning tone.

Still, Saffron pressed on. "I mean, what's the point of going to the college if you really don't feel like it. I really don't feel like it, Mom. I can get my doctorate even, over the Internet. Then I won't have to work that stupid job. I can do schoolwork all day." She blinked twice and waited for Audrey to answer.

Audrey manhandled the dish she was drying. "Saffron, I earned some online credits because I'm not afraid to go get them from anywhere. You are terrified of going everywhere, so that's where you need to go, anywhere and everywhere, until you see that it's okay, you're not going to get hurt, you're not going to lose your mind or whatever it is you think is going to happen."

"Oh, yeah. I won't get hurt. I'll get someone to lock me in my room wherever I go so I'll feel all cozy and secure. Who will be that someone? You? Everywhere I go? Or will we train some of my new college buddies to lock me in when the moon is full?" Now the pancakes felt heavy in her gut. They had never covered this angle out loud before - how she was going to become a world traveler when she needed to be in lockdown on nights approaching and during a full moon.

Audrey's usually-straight back curved. She didn't look at Saffron when she murmured her reply. "You can commute to the university from home." She cleared her throat. "Just come home at night."

Saffron dropped her spoon into her bowl with a clank, pushed herself up from the table, and brushed past her mother. She stomped upstairs and into the bathroom, slammed the door, dragged a comb through the rusty tangle that was her hair, and snatched her toothbrush from the holder.

The phone rang.

Terror sluiced up and down Saffron's limbs. Nobody ever called this early in the morning. It couldn't be good.

A few moments later, her mother knocked on the bathroom door, then opened it a crack until she was staring at Saffron in the mirror. "That was the Black Chicken. They said you can go in to train today."

Saffron held the toothbrush suspended in her mouth. She stared at her mother while the fear bore down and squeezed her chest. What kind of mother was she? Not helping your kid when she was obviously traumatized. Why did she keep pushing this?

Saffron shrugged her shoulders. "I don't want to go."

Audrey watched a drooley toothpaste string stretch down from Saffron's lips as she not so much as brushed her teeth but began scrubbing her gums raw. "What are you afraid off?"

Saffron spit hard, smeared her mouth with a facecloth, then chucked the cloth at the back of the sink. "I'm not afraid of anything! Okay? God!"

Audrey sucked in a deep breath and looked with bulging eyes at the ceiling. She blinked several times before she again leveled her gaze on Saffron.

"Just tell me, Saffron. If you tell me, you'll get it out and you'll be able to start to help yourself. I don't care if you tell me you're afraid of a holocaust, the dirt under your feet, or fat women's panty lines. Just tell me. I promise I won't laugh or lecture you or anything. I just want to help you. Tell me." Audrey huffed. Now she was whining.

A vision popped into Saffron's mind - squirming bodies, bruise-sucked skin, a leer that made her groin ache. She crossed her arms across her chest and blinked back hot, angry tears. She wanted to get past her mother but the woman was standing there in the doorway. Saffron didn't have it in her to push past, so she stood before her mother and grew angrier by the second. *Get out of my way. Why can't I just shove past her? I should shove past her. Why can't I tell her to get the hell out of the way? I can't stand here all day!*

Audrey sighed into the loud silence of the tiny bathroom.

Saffron pressed her lips. Why the hell was her mother always sighing? She was going to hyperventilate.

Audrey moved aside. Saffron scuttled past her mother with her if-looks-could-kill eyes cast down. Audrey followed Saffron to her room. "They said to bring a lunch, unless you want to buy something from the store. You can train six hours today and eight tomorrow with some woman named Bea. I spoke to her on the phone. She seemed very nice."

Saffron looked around for something sharp to poke the headache from her eye. She grabbed her bag from the closet. It was a gift from her mother - a caramel leather courier bag with antiqued buckles and dark red roses on the strap. A bag meant for people who were going places. It was three years old, clean and shiny. The leather was so stiff that it squeaked when she raised the flap to throw in a sweatshirt, some loose change and a couple of ones, some ChapStick so she wouldn't have flaky lips, some tissues so she wouldn't be caught with any hangers-on, and hand sanitizer to protect against getting a cold, which would cause flaky lips and hangers on. She ran down the sloping treads of the old farmhouse stairs and grumbled, "Fine, I'll go get my lunch for my glamorous new job."

She stomped to the kitchen, almost yanked the door off the Lazy Susan, grabbed a can of Spaghettios and threw it into her talking bag, the smell of leather wafting up when she ripped at the flap. Then she was out the front door, letting it slam behind her, and onto the farmer's porch, where she jerked to a halt.

She couldn't step off the porch.

She couldn't mount her bike and ride to that job. She couldn't. After two agonizing moments, she practically threw herself down the porch stairs and marched to her bike.

Her feet and lower back ached as she forced her way past the mushrooms that had grown back at the base of the driveway. She didn't slow down the whole first mile. When she did slow, she was so exhausted the bike started to wobble. Toward the end of the trek, she had to get off the bike, her legs so rubbery with fatigue, and walk the rest of the way down Main Street.

When Saffron arrived at the store, Bea informed her that after her training days, she would work second shift with a girl named Coco. Then Bea continued to talk, nonstop, for the next two days.

After the second day of training, Saffron was exhausted. It was hard learning how to dust the shelves (the proper way), stock the cooler, and learn the register program, while not being allowed to sit, ever. Saffron ripped the black winged baseball cap off her head and whipped it into the corner of her bedroom. Her jeans and t-shirt smelled like deli, so, even though it was early evening, she changed into a wife beater tank top and pink cotton pajama bottoms. She tipped, face-first, onto the bed. Somewhere around six pm she fell asleep.

Chapter 3

Saffron woke up nauseous and heavy-limbed. Above her, a wooden butterfly hung suspended from the ceiling, each of its brightly painted parts strung with fishing line. The wet night air that seeped in from the window moved it now. Saffron meant to stare at it until the grogginess cleared so she could get up and go to the bathroom.

Why was the window open? She had kept it shut the last few nights because the humidity was so bad. It felt better just to have the fan running. The fan was still.

There was a beat of vacuumed silence, followed by the loud tearing of a branch in the apple tree outside her window. She seized up and held her breath.

The air around her began to thicken as if it was gathering itself. It pushed on her neck, arms and chest. It felt like a heavy gas as she carefully took a few short breaths and exhaled frigid puffs.

Another resounding crack, then quiet except for the blood that pounded in her ears. After several moments of stillness, she sat up and grabbed the edge of the mattress. The waffle blanket slipped to the floor, leaving her shaking in her pajamas. She hunched down, drawing her shoulders forward. Her eyes reflected the waning moon as she stared out the window.

Beyond the window frame, in the black night, chaos started. The screeching of an owl joined the burp-croak of a bullfrog. The screams of small prey floated out of the woods. Dogs from near and far howled, and bats began darting in and out of her shutters, causing the weakly-bolted wood to clack, clack against the wall of the house.

She stood up, tiptoed toward the window, and gnawed on her

fingernails. As she moved closer, more of the apple tree came into view - the top of the tree, the next branches down. She was halfway across the wooden floor when she heard a thump on the grass outside. She stopped and stood poised, the heel of her back foot off the ground.

Then she leaned back, putting all of her weight on that foot. She pulled her other foot back too, and in this way, did a shuffling return to her bedside, both eyes still locked on the empty window. She eased back into bed and curled into the fetal position as she pulled the blanket from the floor and up over her head.

The animals bleated and hooted, screamed and croaked. The crashing of the ocean amplified, smashing at the rocks. She began to whisper to herself, a habit she'd had since she was a child.

And then, there was a voice.

Go to sleep.

The words were an edict which burst forth in her head like fireworks in a black sky. The voice seemed alien - not machine, and not human. It was commanding, and oddly enough, it was soothing.

Her senses dulled as she studied the blanket tented by her nose. Her lips went slack, her breathing slowed. She stared without seeing till finally, her lids closed completely and she lay still.

As quickly as the ruckus had started, it stopped, as if the animals had been cheering the start of a performance and now the show was to begin. A cloud drifted across the moon, leaving the house in momentary shadow.

In the undulating nebula of her mind, that dark place you pass through before you dream and never recall when you wake, she heard the far-off beating of many tiny wings. Then someone called her name, high and mellifluous, like a note puffed through a glass bird whistle. The wings came closer until the vibration was there, in the room with her.

Suddenly, both of her legs lifted and moved over, her torso rising and moving like a marionette. Her eyes remained shut as the blanket fell away.

A warm churning began in her stomach. It grew steadily, until it consumed her entire midriff, surrounded her hips and lower back. Invisible fingers of pressure rolled up her spine, over her shoulders and around her neck. As the heat moved past her ears, her head fell back. Her scalp tingled; she could feel every follicle hum as if each generated its own electrical current. The current lifted and separated the lengths of her hair and supported the roiling, red mass of it while it hung in empty space. She looked like a mermaid sitting under water, her hair waving in a ghostly tide.

From her belly she felt a tug, like an invisible elastic, pulling forward. It made her stomach spasm, and her entire body vibrate like a twanging metal rod. Then, three more pulls in rhythm with the pulsing of her hair. She dipped one toe forward, toward the floorboards, but quickly retracted. This was not the way. She responded on the fifth summons - the strongest pull yet - just floated up, a drowning victim whose body has expelled all air and makes its unconscious way to the top of the sea.

Behind her, her body slumped on the mattress.

Her entire soul levitated to the ceiling, moving as she rose so that she no longer was in a seated position, but hovered belly-down above the bed, seeing her stuffed panda in the rocking chair below her.

All of the windows in her room flew open without the usual moan of forced wood. Saffron coursed along the ceiling, then down and out into the waiting night. A gust of wind shrieked past her ears. She hung suspended above the crooked apple tree just for a moment before the pull in her gut strengthened, and soon she found herself coasting at high speed above the earth. Up ahead she saw a herd of deer leaping for the cover of the trees.

The voices that surrounded her told her to relax, to enjoy the ride, but not to be concerned with milestones or markers. She wasn't meant to know where she was going and therefore would never know. She flew across forests and lakes, mountains and oceans. She drifted in and out of semi-consciousness. Sometimes she rode the wave on her stomach and sometimes she spiraled slowly through space, her hair wrapping about her shoulders.

After an indeterminable amount of time - it could've been moments or hours - small hands grabbed at her fingers. She started to descend. Her feet drifted down until she was standing upright in the air, her hair snapping around her like crimson ribbons.

She touched down on a bed of brown needles surrounded by towering pines that crowded like stanchions. Lights swirled and bobbled in front of her, in back of her. All around her the trees sighed and grunted, moaned and snored. She blinked once, then looked sidelong at the massive tree to her immediate right. She took two steps away from it.

One of the phosphorescent globes stopped to hang in front of her face. Saffron heard a giggle, then the light zigzagged away. Some of the other orbs lowered to the forest floor. Their glow was soft, like tiny, solar-powered bulbs. Then the lights began to pop in showers. In the place of each little explosion stood a magnificent person - a fairy - with iridescent skin. Their glow came from the inside, and twinkled out from every pore. They were all taller than she was.

The one closest to Saffron turned to smile back at a friend. The being had great silvery wings, mottled as rice paper and veined with the same fuzzy radiance. The wings arched high over her head, curved down above her buttocks, then molded with the skin on her back.

Saffron couldn't decide if they were boys and girls or men and women. Their ages seemed to swim and change as she watched them. When they giggled at her, they seemed no more than five years old; but when they smiled at her, it was the proud grin of a parent looking down upon a cherished child.

Their lips were plump and red, pert as cupids, but their murmuring was sophisticated; their fathomless, bright eyes seemed at once silly, wise, and ancient. They each had different colored eyes, every hue, and shine. Some like jewels, some like metal. But the line of color was slim; it roped around the great black holes that were their pupils. Pupils so large they looked owlish.

The skin was completely transparent on some, while others had skin like the underbelly of a frog, milky-white and thin, so that in all of them you could see the network of veins and the lines of bones pulsing and working. Some had amber-bottle glass skin, some wild blue, and others, sea green. One even had licorice-black skin with golden veins vibrating in her wings, in her arms, across her chest and down her legs. The material that covered them wasn't like any material Saffron had ever seen. She couldn't figure what it was, but would later be told it was a weave of millions of tiny, impossibly-stretched filament taken from a "glass spider" that lived only within their boundaries.

More tall fairies came out of the woods, holding lanterns, radiating the gathering group in a cave of fluttering light. And everywhere Saffron looked, she made eye contact with the creatures. She felt a jolt and a ping each time. A flash of recognition. A nostalgic longing. Emotions that clutched at her throat and brought tears. In her life, she had never felt like this. She wanted to touch them, all of them, and be held by them.

She turned around, and in that moment there was no time, no air, no sound - only the man that stood ten feet away from her. He never spoke and never moved; yet Saffron felt her entire body react to him a swell of fury, a tightening of lust, an aching of loss. She became completely flustered, unable to think; and lacking a better reaction, she turned her back on him. When words finally fell from her lips, they came dry and hushed as if she'd been wandering the desert without water for a million years.

"What?" She addressed no one in particular. A woman in white walked forward. Or rather, a woman that was white, all white, walked forward. Saffron gasped. The fairy smiled. Long, white hair drifted like a cloud around her small, white shoulders, while glass lips held in check many small pearly teeth. Her voice was low and warm.

"Saffron. You are here because you have asked us to bring you here." She reached forward with a thin, bleached hand to pinch one of Saffron's fiery, banana curls. Her eyes were dominated by pupils so large, and so black that Saffron felt her consciousness start to slip as she stared into the creature's eyes.

"Shouldn't I remember that?" Saffron murmured. "I think I'd remember asking to come here. Where am I? And why are you all so tall?"

The white fairy offered her graceful hand to hold. "Come along, my friend. We will explain at the feast."

The crowd moved together through the trees. Saffron looked back over her shoulder just in time to see a fairy with gold hair and flecks of white and silver flashing around in her body as if she were a snow globe. The fairy shot her forked tongue out of her mouth to entwine a fat beetle that was scurrying up the side of a pine. Some sap stuck to the hairy leg she couldn't quite fit in her mouth and for a moment it formed a golden bridge between the beetle and the tree before it bowed and broke. She helped the still-moving leg into her mouth with one long finger, then changed size and became a small ball of light and moved off.

Saffron stumbled on a tree root and looked with wide-eyes at the white fairy, who steadied her. "That girl back there just ate something off the tree. A bug or something, I think."

The white fairy smiled down at Saffron and reached to pet her hair.

Saffron hunched while she walked and thought, 'whatever.' Humans ate bugs, big bugs. So it wouldn't have mattered if that fairy did eat that bug, which she probably didn't. It was dark on this path and it wouldn't have been the first time that Saffron imagined something so outrageous. She bit the inside of her cheek and kept her eyes averted from the movement in the shadows that they passed on either side.

They emerged into a wide glade. At its center was a bonfire. Full-sized fairies danced around the inferno and drank from golden goblets. They called to Saffron to join them. They flew into the trees and called from the boughs - their wings fluttering and drink sloshing from their cups. Flute players and horn players sat high in the boughs, playing in bursts and squeals. Throughout the trees and down the paths that disappeared from the center of the glade were strung hollowed-out gourds. They had been punched with tiny holes and inside, fireflies blinked on and off.

"Come dance with us!" the fairies cried.

She took a step forward, then saw the male fairy with the black, wavy hair coming straight toward her. He came quick and sure, alarming her and causing her to back away from him until she bumped into a tree. She pressed as far away from him as she could, but he moved right into her space and stood breathing down on her. He reached forward and grazed the back of his hand down the side of her breast. Her eyes flitted around. Thankfully, nobody seemed to be watching them. He pulled back from her but less than an inch.

"Do you know who I am?" He tilted his head, stared at her and she knew it wasn't long before he would reach forward, bite her face, and eat her while she screamed. She blinked in staccato bursts and looked away.

He murmured, "Ah, you do know. You know something." His voice was husky as if he was having her right then, in the middle of the party, up against the tree. He moaned, then spoke.

"I have known you as Rosemary and Iris. I have known you as Daisy and Lily, as Hyacinth and Violet. As Lotus. Sharon. Olive. I have known you as Suchamina and Locsunti - one an ancient flower and one an ancient spice - both long extinct. I have always known you." He fisted some of her hair and pulled, slowly, until her head tilted completely to one side.

She started breathing hard, snorting air through her nostrils as if she were a foaling mare. She looked at the other fairies - they were oblivious. She looked at the surrounding trees - they ignored her. She looked to the sky but couldn't see it beyond the black canopy of the trees. She wanted someone to help her, and at the same time, prayed no one was witness to her extreme humiliation.

He continued to stare down at her, to breathe on her. She thought about moving toward him. It seemed to be what he wanted. Panic bloomed and swelled her throat. She wanted to be away from him and quick, before he touched her again. She bit into her lip, her eyetooth almost slicing into her skin. She mustered every ounce of energy she could and took one step to the right. He didn't reach out to stop her, so she took one more step muttering, "No, thank you," as she stumbled away over the roots of the tree.

When she was five feet away, she stopped sidling and turned toward the fire. She saw something on the spit there. A small form, fat, with thick limbs and a big head. She looked away quickly, and back again. There was no spit. She hunched and clutched her arms over her breasts, her head feeling like a barely-tethered balloon.

Fairies grabbed at her hands, bringing her into their dance. She high-stepped and tripped and was totally unaware of herself. They laughed at her funny dance and tried to imitate her. Soon the whole crowd of them was high-stepping, bobbing and weaving to the music. She didn't even realize it. Once, she dared to look back at the tree where he had pinned her. He was gone.

The dancers joined hands and ringed round and round the fire. Then without preamble, the ring broke. One fairy became the leader of a long dancing line filled with glowing and winged creatures, and one human with wild red hair. The leader took them around the trees, in and out of shadows, by the inferno and circled back. They held fast to Saffron's hand, pulling her closer and closer to the fire as one by one they walked right through the flames. Saffron's haze lifted when she finally realized that they meant for her to traipse through the flames as well. In seconds, she found herself before the fire as it spit and roared.

"No!" she screamed. The flute playing ceased, as did the gay chatting of the fairies. After two drawn-out seconds of silence, murmuring started among the fairies, then some giggling. The white fairy came forward, took Saffron out of the line, and spoke to her gently, flames reflected in the shiny, black pools of her eyes.

"The flames will not hurt you, Saffron. You can dance with the rest."

Saffron pulled her chin into her chest. "No, thank you," she mumbled.

The white fairy rubbed Saffron's back, smiled as she looked down. "Saffron, I care for you deeply. I would never put you in the way of harm. I tell you; the flames will not hurt you. See here."

Saffron looked down at her stomach and screamed. Again, every single fairy in the glade stopped to stare. What she saw was the wiggling fingers of the white fairy as they poked out from her midriff. "Wha..." Saffron couldn't tear her eyes from the moving fingers.

The white fairy snapped her thumb and middle finger, then pulled her hand back. Saffron never felt a thing.

"You did not know I was going to do that. Therefore, you felt nothing."

"Great," Saffron muttered as she absently caressed her belly. "Great."

"It is like this. Your physical body is not here with us. Your physical body is safe in bed. You are here only in spirit. However, the memory of your body is still very strong within you. If you fear pain, you will feel pain. You will only as long as you want to."

"What do you mean, 'want to,' who 'wants to' feel pain?" Saffron sighed.

"Humans are defined by the pain they suffer," the white fairy whispered, and then she reached for Saffron's cheek and stroked it. "Do not fear the pain. Expect nothing, you will feel nothing.

Saffron blinked to clear her eyes. She murmured to the pine needles around her feet. "I think I understand. My uncle lost his leg, a long time ago, and sometimes he complains that he can still feel pain in his foot. 'Phantom pain,' he calls it. Is it the same for me?"

The white fairy inclined her head, "It could be. Yes, think of it that way."

"Huh. But I don't want to go through that fire." Saffron took another step back.

"No, of course not, sweet lamb."

Saffron smiled gratefully at the fairy and took her hand. They strode away from the flames.

"What's your name?" Saffron smiled at the fairy, could feel the puppy love starting, like the time she was absolutely in love with her first grade teacher, Mrs. Mulberry. The perfect woman who encouraged her, brought in homemade cookies for the class on Fridays, and always gave Saffron the biggest hugs.

The fairy's smile was brief. "I am Li." She didn't look at Saffron when she spoke but kept her eyes firmly on the path before her.

"You know what's weird? I feel like I should've known that, like I should know you." Saffron shook her head. "But I don't."

"And you were talking to my brother, Ny, over by the tree."

Saffron felt heat sear the back of her neck, felt her nostrils flare. She kept her eyes on the ground and said nothing. Her *brother?* No, that wasn't right either.

A large gong sounded and voices shouted, "Eat, eat! This human child cannot dance all night without a feast to fuel her!" There were hearty laughs and playful squeals. A banquet table appeared, covered by long swaths of silvery, billowing fabric. Two more tables followed and simple wooden benches. They accommodated everyone who swooped in, walked forward, and emerged from the trees. The tables set themselves with golden forks, spoons, and knives. Delicate plates clinked carefully into place. Great rustic vases filled with wild, dark roses, pine boughs, and twigs with red berries were placed every couple of feet across the tabletops.

Roasted turkeys appeared, brown and sizzling. Tender sides of beef and braised rabbits garnished with mint. Rosemary herbed potatoes and freshly baked bread followed brightly colored vegetables and fruit. The fairies were filling their plates, artfully too, arranging the brightness of the vegetables and the textures of the meats in beautiful display, but eating nothing. She noticed also that at any moment several fairies were missing from their places only to come back minutes later. Then another handful disappeared into the trees, like the kids who snuck away from class to smoke pot and slunk back in, quiet and glassy-eyed. Saffron frowned and looked down at her plate.

After the meal, some of the fairy girls gathered about Saffron, taking up lengths of her fiery hair, winding it and securing it with tiny, golden combs at the base of her neck. "Did you enjoy the food? The meat, was it cooked perfectly?"

"I couldn't really taste it." The fairy who questioned Saffron was freaking her out with her large, black pupils ringed in viscous gold. Before Saffron could say anything else....

"And, how was it on your tongue? Tell me how it felt - how all of it felt. Tell Li you want to come here in body."

Saffron sucked in a breath and quickly turned away from the odd request and the girl with the gold eyes who'd made it.

A gilded mirror was brought so she could watch them work on her hair. After, they tore apart roses from the closest vase and fit the petals on Saffron's scalp like a cap, her curled and pinned tresses flowing out behind. They kissed the top of her head and congratulated themselves on a job well done.

The gold-eyed girl moved close to Saffron's ear. "I will have what you have." Saffron frowned and shrunk away.

Li appeared behind Saffron, smiling wide. "Come with me."

They walked away from the dancers over to a dark chestnut tree with great, low limbs. It was difficult for Saffron to hop on the limb, so Li took her in her arms, flew her up to the widest branch, and held on while Saffron adjusted her balance. Then Li sat beside Saffron and stroked her cheek.

"You can feel this, can you not?"

Saffron nodded.

"It is the memories within your soul. You want to feel my hand against your cheek."

Saffron closed her eyes.

The white fairy continued to talk, hushed and sweet, in a foreign language whose sounds curled and rang. It was a language that sang like the wind in the treetops and was warm as the sun on a green spring afternoon. Saffron didn't understand any of it but the tone soothed her.

"I like being here," Saffron admitted. "But it's totally weird too."

The big, black pupils roped in purple settled on Saffron's lips. The fairy frowned for a fleeting second. "That does not exist here, that idea - *weird*. It is a human concept, invented to shame others. Why do you feel this shame?"

Saffron bit her bottom lip. "I don't know." She thought about the fairy tales she grew up on. She thought about changelings and lost time. She thought about that fairy that may or may not have eaten a humongous beetle off of a pine tree. "Are you going to let me go back?"

Li clapped her hands and threw her head back, her hair cascading like a fall of ice. She laughed. "We hold no one against her will." She added with a wink, "We only take infants; you're much too old!"

Saffron snorted. "Oh, yeah, that's right, fairies steal babies." She hugged her knees to her chest. "I just can't believe this is happening. It's too unbelievable."

"Yes." Li's upper lip twitched. "Many of the creatures you have read about exist, but they do not necessarily live the lives you have been led to believe they live. Some of the creatures you have read about do not exist at all, but were invented by humans to..." Li looked heavenward, trying to come up with the appropriate words. "...to name a fear. To be able to tame the unknown and give something horrible an existence, so that, in turn, this horrible thing, with a certain form, might be conquered and destroyed by useless potions and ineffective incantations. Or, at the very least, the monsters can be put in a little, symbolic box and tucked away in the mind."

Saffron leaned forward to speak, when suddenly, Li held a hand up to silence her. The fairy cocked her head to the side and turned to peer behind her. Her eyes became slits as irritation rolled across her face. She turned toward a small group of her kind that had been lolling under an adjacent pine.

"Take her home." The fairy's nostrils were slightly flared. "Do not dally in this; her mother is awake."

The fairies flew to Saffron's side and clasped warm hands around her arms. That was all it took for Saffron to collapse. It was as if she had just been injected with the most powerful sedative on earth. She had no muscle control and her mind dissipated into a haze.

Li stepped forward and caressed Saffron's cheeks with both hands. She smiled as tears filled her eyes and made the purple and black orbs shimmer. "How good it was to talk to you again. How long I have waited in the trees, watching you, wishing for the reunion we have had on this night. You must stay in your house. You must not leave the circle for any reason. You know this to be true."

Then she leaned forward and placed her lips on the petals that clung to Saffron's head and whispered in her strange language. She trailed her white fingers through the ends of Saffron's long, red hair one more time, then turned and walked into the black void of night.

Saffron struggled against the nothingness that pulled her down. Flashes of fairies dancing around a big fire, fairies laughing, fairies in fear roamed her skull. Ny, naked before her, his face filled with disdain. Then, he too, was gone.

"Sleep, Saffron. You will be home soon. "

She slept.

Ny watched her depart. He looked at the ground, his long, black lashes covering the pain in his petulant eyes. Li came across him as she wandered aimlessly in the shadows. She frowned. "What do you play at?"

Ny's eyebrow popped up as the blood ran darker beneath his thin skin. "What do we always play at?"

"Again? It is murder." Li hissed like a threatened snake. "It will not go unpunished. You infect me with this!"

He sniffed. "There are many words for such a deed." He held his hands before him in a placating manner and smiled his most dazzling smile.

She considered him for a moment, her eyes going dark with passion and a steely, possessive glint. She shook her head. "Murder." She shivered and hugged her arms to her body. "I will not stand by and watch your attempts quietly."

Ny laughed, chucked her under the chin. "Yes, you will. She is venturing out of her little nest. It is not our will she minds in this life.

Let us be done with it all and try our hand at her next incarnation. Who knows what will happen to her if we do nothing? Dear One, you will watch as I try my hand."

"What you are doing is not good. We will suffer here, longer." The deep, dark pupils of Li's eyes were cavernous and filled with a sadness that touched even him. He kissed her brow as she looked off at nothing.

Ny shrank into a ball of light and darted away from her, into the black woods. He returned short minutes later. He held a live rabbit kid in his left hand and offered it to her; its small velvety nose nuzzled his palm. The pain melted off her beautiful face and a faint smile tickled her glass lips. "But the sensation is so fleeting...."

Ny smiled wistfully. "Here. Enjoy him. Let him heal you, if only for a short time."

Li nodded as she reached for the small rabbit and cuddled him to her chest. Then she inclined her head and opened her beautiful jaws wide enough to clamp the head clean from his body.

"How do you do it?" Li swallowed. "How do you get inside her head?"

Ny smirked and jutted his hips forward almost imperceptibly, "She lets me."

Li's veins pumped black under her glassy, white skin as she chewed.

Ny listened to her teeth grind. So jealous. He rolled his tongue over his teeth. "Sister, you prance around the real issue. *Your* issue. You have placed my love in great danger. Yet, typical of you, you seek to reprimand me for uncommitted slights."

"Murder is not a slight, Ny. Mark me now; it would be worse for us."

"An uncommitted murder is nothing. And, if she walks off cliffs of her own accord...that is not murder either."

"You know it is."

He smiled. "And, what of your happy, night-lurking bedfellow? You have now *enabled* him to find our girl." Ny tsked.

Li couldn't look at him. Her large, dark pupils shrunk to steely pinpoints, making her look like a jungle cat caught in sudden light.

Ny sighed. "My love, if he claims her, who is at fault?" His lips twisted up. "Now that she has been here, she will have the sight. And whose fault would that be?" He twirled one of her white locks around his forefinger.

She wiped her mouth with the back of her wrist and punched his hand away.

Ny lowered his arm. "Now that she leaves her home again and has become a beacon, we must end this incarnation before he steals her from us. And who was it that brought her here?"

"You wanted her here just as much as I!" Li cried.

"In body!" Ny screamed back.

"You are selfish! In body! Does it never get old?"

Ny leaned right into Li's face. "I want to look at her when I touch her. I want to touch her body. Her *body*, so I can see her reaction, her mouth, her eyes. No, her worshipping me like a god does not get old. You are jealous. Now go away from me, sister, use your senses quickly before they fade."

Anger washed her beautiful face and, for just a moment, with her white hair flowing and her white skin glowing, she was more frightening than the black unknown of Hell. She spun around and disappeared into the looming shadows.

Chapter 4

Saffron woke up in her bed. Now she knew; she truly *was* a whack job. She had no proof of where she had been. There were no flowers in her big, bushy hair and no dirt stains on her feet. Of course not - her body had never travelled last night. It was just her soul. A maniacal giggle blew out one side of her mouth. Wouldn't her mother love to hear this story? Not. She knew mothers pretended to want to know things but they really didn't want to know things.

She heaved herself out of bed, then barefoot-slapped across the wooden floor to the door. She stuck her head out into the hallway and yelled, "Last night, fairies took my soul to their realm!"

There was a beat of silence, then up from the bowels of the old farmhouse came Derek's voice. "Oh, yeah, honey? Well, last night George Michael came to the door with flowers, a prenuptial agreement, and a teacup poodle that can fart out Viennese waltzes."

Saffron smiled and hugged herself. She sighed deep and shut the wooden door with a soft click. Was she crazy? She'd seen enough movies to know that people didn't always know when they were crazy. She knew people, honest people, honestly believed some things that just weren't true. Although the notion that she'd invented the tryst was ridiculous, in the end, she decided to sit on her secret for awhile and think it out. She wanted to shut herself away from the world and roll around in the memories. Already the sounds and images from last night were fading, just like a dream. And just like a good dream, she didn't want to lose the feeling that the visit had given her. That feeling of epiphany and of longings quenched. The only place for that kind of heavy zoning was the woods.

Flip-flops in hand, she crept out her bedroom door and tiptoed past Grandmother's room. Grandmother's door was open, emitting trails of Vicks vapor rub, saltines, and Jean Nate. Saffron held her breath as she slid by. She jumped down the stairs two at a time and hurried through the kitchen, grabbing a day-old raisin bagel and an almost-empty carton of orange juice. She didn't know where Derek had yelled from, but she hadn't run into him yet. Didn't matter. He wasn't the problem. She could stroll past him, but getting past her mother would be a different thing altogether. Audrey didn't like it when Saffron "loitered" in the woods. But Audrey usually painted late and slept late. Saffron and Derek were the early birds who had enough respect for each other to ignore each other.

She used her butt to back out of the screaming screen door and was just letting it back in its jamb when her mother's voice rang out, clear and concerned, on the still morning air.

"Saffron, what on earth are you doing? It can't be more than five-thirty yet!"

Saffron stood motionless, the door still in her hand. Did her freakin' mother ever sleep? She stared at the chipping paint on the side of the house and wondered again why her mother didn't get vinyl siding. They were forever scraping, priming, painting. In any given year, one side was done and another part was ready to be to be done over.

Audrey frowned. "Do you have to...."

"'Loiter in the woods now? Yes, Mom, I have to loiter in the woods now. It's called being a naturalist." Saffron raised her eyebrows and hitched up the corners of her lips.

"In your case it's called 'avoiding'."

Her mother's words were a slap. Saffron reacted physically,

snapped her head back and opened her mouth in protest, but remained silent. Her cheeks and neck flushed scarlet.

Derek's bushy, auburn hair came into view from down behind Saffron's mother; his curls sparkled shower-fresh. He was kneeling, picking through the herb garden with one hand, clutching a mug in his other paw.

"I mean really, Saffron, what's the rush? You need to get some sleep!" Audrey stood erect, weeds choked in her grip. "And stand up straight, you look like a used-up hippie. Did you comb your hair?"

Saffron straightened. Her teeth clenched beneath her pale cheeks. Who was Audrey calling a hippie? She reached down for the wide basket that her mother used to collect weeds. "You know what? We don't need to have this argument. I'll give myself a goal. Lemme fill this basket with blackberries." Saffron's last word came out at a higher pitch, almost shrill, as if she was trying to gather the attention of a deaf cocker spaniel.

Audrey began to drill her pointer finger into her temple.

Saffron backed away. When Audrey didn't say more, Saffron took off running for the trees, the hem of her nightdress gathering and getting caught up between her legs as they churned. She escaped the trim yard successfully and ran through the wild tangle of brush that fringed the forest. She picked up her knees to avoid tripping in the mess of white daisies and purple vetch, as grasshoppers leaped from the frill of Queen Anne's lace. She ran beneath the pines, the ground carpeted in brown needles, smooth and stretching out for miles along the rocky, and wooded shoreline. She passed the boulder shaped like a pumpkin, skirted the giant half-pine whose top was skimmed off by lightning in a long-ago storm, then slowed to a walk. She was almost there - a small clearing by the cliff where light shone down and cast a pool of forest floor in dusty gold. On the far side of the clearing was a prickly, green mess of wild blackberry bushes not completely ravished by little squirrel hands, skunk lips, or greedy beaks. Beyond the blackberry bushes a line of mushrooms disappeared into the thicket.

Saffron sighed.

Opening her backpack and reaching deep, she pulled out a bottle of bug spray. She anointed herself and the surrounding area with the poison. It was a strong brew, able to ward off most bloodsuckers, including the evil deer fly.

Next, she pulled out an old green tablecloth. Its weave had been worked in various directions so that the end result was a series of vines that shone faintly as it was moved around in the diffused sunlight. She shook it and lifted it high, guiding it as it fluttered to the forest floor. She lay down and stared at the sky, feeling like the Lady of Shallot.

The sun was already at least a foot over the ocean. It floated bright and glaring in a bath of humidity. A trickle of sweat ran down her temple. The coming weeks would become unbearably New England hot, and in two months, this early in the morning, she would freeze if she didn't bring a sweatshirt.

Better not to wait too long to pick the berries. Some of the fruit, too far gone, crushed and bled in her fingertips. Her hair hung heavy in the wet air, straight down her back like a copper stream. Once in awhile it became tangled in the berry vines; at which point Saffron swore while she tore herself free. She munched on her bagel and chugged on her juice. When the basket was filled half way, she decided it was enough. She was drenched with sweat and it was just too damned sticky.

She genuflected to the sun and flopped down on the tablecloth, arms thrown up over her head. A hot breeze came and blew a corner of the tablecloth over her face. She leaned over to stretch it back into place, then left her outstretched arm across the fabric so it wouldn't happen again.

She tried to dredge the memories from last night, but they wouldn't come without effort. Instead, she worried about the mundane things she always worried about. Although high school had been horrible daily to endure, at least it was somewhere she *had* to go, something she *had* to do. Even though she could hardly bear to get on that bus every morning, at least it provided better comfort than this going nowhere life that scared her with its big, open maw of choice.

Her cousin, Mindy the Beautiful and Proud, told her the other kids at school had called Saffron, "The Wax Doll," because she was always staring off into space and her skin had such a "faux" look to it, "like shiny and plastic." They said she walked around like she was dead already.

And now Saffron was an adult. She hadn't even kissed a boy. She winced. *A Boy.* It dawned on her that she had missed her chance. That another part of her childhood, of her life, had disappeared. When high school life was happening, she just wanted to get it over with. But right now, the ache of what could have been was sharp. The lower limbs of the pines were bones bare of needles. They clacked and cracked when the wind picked up.

She wouldn't be kissing any boys; they were men now, weren't they. She hadn't held hands with a boy, or talked to one since third grade. Nothing. She couldn't bring herself to do it. With each opportunity she had just seized up and moved her automaton-stick legs down the hall.

It was an undeniable force, this thing that made her act the way she did. Even on a good day, she felt the pressure of something guiding her. Her mother thought she was slightly retarded, no doubt. And Derek, the most wonderful of all of Audrey's not-lovers, helped her to the best of his ability. Although he wasn't quite clear on what he was helping with most of the time. They talked a lot, but she sensed he was suspicious of her.

She fell asleep.

Her mind woke, sharpened, while her body lay in hibernation. She sat up, looked down, and saw a fair face lost in dreaming. For the brief moment before she realized what was happening, before she realized she was looking at herself, she thought the girl below her was so beautiful with her soft hair that rolled like copper waves.

When Saffron realized she was looking at herself, she saw a zit by her lip and the way her skin was becoming oily in the ever-rising heat. She turned from her sleeping self and looked into the woods.

He was standing there, lounging as if he had been there for some time.

Her slumbering, physical self made a noise, a light moan as it lay flushed under the sun.

She looked at him again and he smiled. She couldn't help herself and smiled back. She felt different now, being alone here with him. She ached for him as she had ached a thousand times before, for the dream lover that couldn't possibly be real. She looked away from him, shy, and back at her supine body where she watched her hand rise to caress her neck.

In that moment, she knew; she would do whatever he wanted.

He grinned at her as if he understood her thoughts, then he cast aside the taper of wheat he had been rolling between his tongue and teeth. He walked away.

Saffron frowned. Why would he walk away from her when her

very existence depended on his attention? She yelled out to him, but there was no sound. She wanted to run after him - he was out of sight already - but she couldn't move her feet.

There was a sensation of pulling, of the need to respond. She realized her body wanted its spirit back.

She woke up inside her body to a smashing headache and an eighty-pound weight on her chest. She didn't move at first, couldn't move as exhaustion nailed her to the ground. With wincing effort, she shifted her legs.

She understood two things at the same time; there was no ground beneath her right leg and she wasn't on the blanket anymore, but lying directly on small twigs and stones which cut into her skin. Her eyes peeled wide as she gasped and took in her surroundings. She was on the edge of the cliff, her right leg bent at the knee and dangling over the precipice. Directly below her, ocean waves smashed on gray boulders. A wispy last bit of thought, of urge, trailed through her mind.

Fall.

Her blood curdled as she scrambled back from the edge, crawling on hands and knees. She was afraid to stand up at first, staying as close to solid ground as she could, her belly heaving against the pine needles while she fought to control her breathing. She looked up - the tablecloth was several yards away under the copse of pines where she had originally put it. How had she let that happen? There was no way she had *rolled* all the way to the edge of the earth!

Then it occurred to her, slow and jumbled in her shocked brain; she had fallen asleep *outside*! How did she let that happen? And, because she let it happen, she had literally almost rolled off the cliff. The enormity of it all punched her swift and hard in the stomach. She retched up her bagel and orange juice, and then moved away from the mess, still dry heaving and trying desperately to breathe.

She wasn't alone.

She turned, and through hot tears, she saw a woman. A girl really, dressed strangely. Her dress must have been beautiful once, but now the sky blue of it was soiled, the empire waist was crooked, and the capped sleeves drooped. The girl looked at Saffron and disappeared.

A pang of fear stabbed Saffron in the bowels. Above, the sky turned dark gray. Below, the sea raged gray too, so there was no horizon but an unending dome of lead, dense and pressing. There was no sound in the forest. The pain in her gut curled tight. *Oh, God,* she breathed, *what the hell is that?* Saffron quickly looked away from the tree where the wraith had emerged, but in doing so, she looked at another tree. The girl was there. She was staring at Saffron with vacant eyes. Saffron jerked away from the thing and started to whimper. Her breaths came in rasps; her eyes bulged as she stared at her flip-flops. *Don't look up again,* she told herself and immediately looked up.

The lips of the ghost moved. "Why?" the thing asked. It tilted its head to the side and stared at Saffron with bottomless, black sockets.

Saffron flinched. She hunched over to hug her knees to her chest. She stared without blinking as her hair whipped around her head in the wild wind that screamed up from the sea. She wanted to turn away, so badly, but she wasn't strong enough and continued to gaze at the thing, her eyes glazing over in shock.

The ghost turned away from Saffron and walked the few steps to the very edge of the cliff. The back of its head was a mess of pulp, hair, and ooze enmeshed with gray matter, flat and glistening, smashed in by something large. The dead woman's right arm hung at an awkward angle - a broken limb that would fall to the forest floor at any moment.

It caused the capped sleeve to pull with it, so both would soon be torn.

As it disappeared into ether, Saffron was washed in pain. The pain had a copper flavor, like a zap of electricity as it hummed through every pore. There was so much pain and confusion. Her hand shook as she automatically raised it to stifle the strange, animal sounds of grief which poured out from her. Suddenly, she heard a high-pitched scream tear through the air. As the scream faded, it gave way to the shrill call of the gulls. The sky became blue. The ocean turned back to green.

Saffron jumped up and ran. She ran so fast she didn't feel the brush scrape her shins or the pine needles slap her face. She also didn't see the stump that took out her right foot and sent her cartwheeling to the ground. She spit out some yellowed pine needles and dirt. She heard crying. When she turned around she saw the ghost woman, with her back to Saffron, crying into her hands.

Saffron jumped up and sprinted again. Blood from a scratch leaked into her eye and blinded her. She ran into the side of a tree, took it straight in her solar plexus, and lost her breath. She heard crying. She looked and saw the back of the ghost *again*.

Saffron tripped forward, holding her chest with one hand and smearing blood off her face with the other. Every time she turned around she saw the back of the ghost woman. The woman kept pace with Saffron. If Saffron ran and looked back, the ghost woman was right behind her. If Saffron walked and looked back, she saw the same, horrible sight.

Saffron barreled out of the forest, hurdling branches and rocks. She didn't stop until she fell face first into the green grass of her mother's manicured lawn. She sobbed, breathing in the wet dirt every time she gasped.

She heard her mother swear and Derek grunt about needing more coffee or a fricken Bloody Mary.

Saffron forced herself to be still and quiet. She had forgotten they were working in the herb gardens. She sat up quickly, her electrified hair taking a long time to drift down and lie fluffed over her freckled shoulders.

Audrey watched Saffron while she removed her gardening gloves one finger at a time.

Saffron knew her mother was waiting for her. She knew this time she had to give her mother something - Audrey wouldn't go away empty-headed. Saffron looked back at the woods. She raised her eyebrows. Why not use the ghost? People didn't place their children in treatment centers for seeing ghosts. Ghosts were super trendy right now.

And where would she start? *Well, I watch this guy screw these women in my dreams all the time, ya know? I think he's like, hot. When I wake up and want to vomit against my locked door I also feel crazy in love and wish I didn't wake up.* Nah, that's not the tone she was going for. And she wouldn't tell her mother she almost rolled off the cliff just now - her mother wouldn't let her go back into the woods. One who has a history of near-miss cliff-launches shouldn't nap by cliffs. She rolled her eyes. Maybe Audrey would like to hear that Saffron took a trip to Fairyland, to Neverland, to Santa's Land - that would surely clear everything up. She was so much braver when she was four. She would've told her mother everything.

So, a ghost was the best tidbit to give Audrey. It was a little morsel of truth for her mother's *I Need to Fix You* mentality.

"Yeah," Saffron halted, "when I was out in the woods...I saw a ghost."

And then the ghost woman walked by. Just beyond Audrey. Saffron watched the ghost woman glide all the way across the lawn. She didn't stop when she reached the edge of the field or when she reached the edge of the sea. Saffron cringed when the woman fell and started her screams.

A sudden sob leapt in Saffron's throat. She willed herself not to get hysterical. Willed and willed and willed. Like a ball in a balance maze, she felt herself rolling toward one black hole after another. She wondered if she was going insane. She realized she was grabbing at the grass, pulling chunks out by the roots, and had already uprooted several fistsful. She froze.

Audrey's brow furrowed as she continued to stare at her daughter. After a pause, she walked over and sat on the grass beside Saffron. She laid back, one hand behind her head, and reached for Saffron's icy fingers with the other. She held tight.

Above them, the clouds scudded past. The ocean wind picked up and whooshed brine across their faces. Saffron gave a nervous snort, startling Audrey.

"Look, I don't really want to talk about this because it like, really scares me. But I knew you wouldn't leave me alone until you found out what was wrong. So," Saffron sighed, "that's what's wrong."

Audrey looked at her daughter. Saffron locked eyes with her mother for a second, then turned away to stare at the peeling paint of the house. She shrunk even deeper into her hunch. "I'm scared."

Audrey sighed. "You know I lived with one before."

Saffron's eyes shot heavenward. She dug her fingers right back into the roots of the grass. Her mother was about to tell her that damned ghost story again; as if Audrey's experience would explain all.

Audrey thought her story would comfort Saffron.

Saffron thought her mother was just trying to one-up her.

Saffron cleared her throat, cut her mother off. "Have you seen *my* ghost? You know, around here anywhere?"

Audrey scratched her forehead, raised a foot and considered her chipped toenail polish, then adjusted her widening rear-end more comfortably on the lumpy ground.

"No, I haven't seen anything around here. Psychics say that ghosts don't come after people; that they're not trying to scare people. When people think ghosts are after them, really it's just that the ghosts are trying to communicate. But they're frustrated because they're dead or they don't know they're dead which makes them confused which makes them...short tempered. Psychics also say ghosts look perfectly normal...not all chopped up, bloody and ghouly like in the movies."

Saffron's voice was flat, "Ah huh."

Audrey shook Saffron's rigid hand. "Did it try to get your attention? Did it seem to want to communicate with you? Boy, girl, man, or woman?"

Saffron shook her head. "Woman. No, girl. I think."

"Oh. Well, if you see her again, see if she'll communicate with you."

Saffron's heart stopped. *If I see her again....* The flaccid balloon that was her throat filled all at once, as if someone had given it one great puff, leaving no room to swallow. Saffron was relieved to be sitting on grass, a base too great to shake as she shivered on top of it. She waggled her foot back and forth, back and forth, hoping her mother wasn't studying her as she vibrated with terror.

Audrey whispered from behind her, "How painful that must be."

Yeah, Saffron thought. That woman was very sad. Saffron had felt it. She felt the ghost's terrible, engulfing, wretchedness pull at her.

And, as the morning grew brighter and the sun grew hotter, the memory of the ghoul was enough to make her feel black and cold and lost. How could she possibly feel so much pain about that ghost, someone she didn't even know?

That spot in the woods had always been her refuge. Now, the ghost had ruined it for her. She felt violated, scared off from the place that called to her and comforted her like nowhere else.

Audrey was still rambling. "Don't worry about it anymore. And, believe me, I know, telling someone not to worry about something is like telling them not to think; it's impossible. But there is one thing you need to do, Saffron."

And as if Saffron knew instinctively what her mother would say, Audrey felt Saffron's hand seize within her own, felt her whole body go rigid. Saffron said nothing, just waited for her sentence.

"It's not fair for that woman to suffer. Call to her, Saffron. That's what the psychics say to do; let her know you're there. Then let her know she's dead. Let her know she doesn't have to go through whatever it is she's experiencing."

Saffron balked. It was a mixed-up noise, a snort of incredulity combined with the squawk of a kicked chicken. She rolled her eyes. "Yeah, okay, Mom. Great theory. But would you really want to be the person to tell someone else she's dead? Wouldn't a person kinda get pissed off if you tried to tell them that?"

Audrey shrugged. "Maybe. But are you going to avoid trying to help someone because you don't know how they'll react?"

Saffron shrugged back.

Audrey pinched the bridge of her nose. "Enough of this. I know what you need. You're going to work with me now. Oh, fantastic, physical fatigue. There's no better medicine. Derek's got the store to get to and I have the vegetable garden to see to. So, we're going to work very hard today, outside, in the garden. We'll get all nasty thoughts out of your head by working your body to exhaustion with physical labor. Won't that be fun?"

Saffron groaned. Her mother knew she couldn't stand working in the vegetable garden. She would reach down for the hose and it would be a snake. She would grab a weed stalk to rip from the ground and a fat slug would squash in her grip. There were spiders, mosquitoes, and unidentified aliens from the insect world. Or, her favorite, she'd turn over a layer of earth and find hundreds of wriggling grubs beneath the surface, yuck. Maggots too, in the compost. How she hated maggots!

Audrey yanked at Saffron's arm, pushed her over into the grass, and slapped her rear-end. Saffron gave a weak grin and quickly brushed the wet from her cheeks. Evading her mother had been easier than she thought. Now, if only the crap would stop escalating. She could avoid her mother's prying indefinitely.

Saffron walked to the shed to get the wheelbarrow. She met her mother on the right side of the house where the vegetable garden loomed. It was humongous and full of weeds – a whole day's work. She slouched to the tomato plants where her mother was bent over, working with her usual maximum efficiency.

Saffron squatted and poked at the earth, thick leather gloves on and trowel in hand.

"What are you doing with that?" Audrey had stopped to check out Saffron. "Trowels are for springtime. Fingers are for weed time."

With her sun-squint eyes, Saffron tossed the trowel into the wheelbarrow, but didn't move to take off her gloves. She stared back at her mother and said nothing.

Audrey knew to pick her battles with Saffron. If Saffron wanted to wear the gloves, let her wear the gloves.

"We have to pick all of these tomatoes too, then the lettuces and peas. We should start canning some tomato sauce. There will be tons more to come. You can take some over to Mindy's house later." Audrey resumed picking.

She didn't see Saffron snap to attention and cast her mother a sharp look. Why did mothers have to push relationships that didn't exist? When your sibling or cousin was some snotty, lying witch, why did mothers pretend that it was a good idea for the two of you to get together? "I have stuff to do later." Saffron mumbled.

Audrey looked back in Saffron's direction and threw her arms up into the air. But she never actually made eye contact and never said, "What? What could you possibly be doing later?" before she shook her head and turned back to her work.

They picked and weeded in silence for the next two hours. Saffron was working at the southeast end of the garden. She parted two thick, leafy vines to finish the end of a row, when, all of a sudden, she had to bite her tongue to keep from screaming at the sight that lay before her. There, on the ground at her feet, sunning his small, naked, and wrinkled nut-brown body, was a little man.

He was lying on his stomach, hair curled all over his back and rear-end. He was completely unaware of the giant girl who was in a contained frenzy just above him. He stretched luxuriously, reaching far out in front of him with his little knobby hands, and then raising his legs off the ground behind him, scrunching his toes and buttocks. "Mmmmmmwwwwwaaaaaahhhh." The yawn blasted out of his meaty, purple lips as he smacked them contentedly. He turned his head to the side, and now he was facing Saffron, still unaware, as his eyes remained shut. Instantly, he was snoring.

Oh, God, please, don't roll over. Suddenly, the air around her thickened, pulling at the tips of her ears, and drawing the skin of her face back.

The little man ceased his Mack-truck breathing. One eyelid shot open. Behind the lid was a beady black eye that stared at Saffron with a flinty intensity. Saffron gasped. The little man popped up from the ground like a shot and started to screech at Saffron in a language she didn't understand, but in a decidable that meant "screw you."

"Yuck, yuck! Ooooooh, YUCK!" She waved her hands frantically at him. Her chin pulled back into her neck, and wincing fiercely, she slapped one hand over her eyes. He screeched again, jumping up and down, his shrimp-sized penis ding-donging from its epicenter. She forced her hand away from her eyes to keep a watch on him. Who knew what he would do to her? He spun around so his back was toward her, bent over, and spread his legs so she could see his face as he hung his head between his thighs. And there, beneath his lumpy, dangling family jewels, he scrunched up his walnut face at her and stuck out his tongue. Then he stood up, grabbed his clothes from the ground, and ran off into the jungle of tomato vines.

"Oh, God. Oh, yuck." Saffron fell to a sitting position on the ground.

In the meantime, Audrey, from the other side of the garden had heard Saffron's grunts and shrieks and was making her way through the tangle of green to see what was going on. Audrey found Saffron still sitting, her eyes red and watering. "What on earth is the matter now?"

"Nothing, Mom. Oooh nothing. I just saw something REALLY gross."

At that moment, a high-pitched scream emanated from the other side of the garden, from the direction in which the little man had disappeared. Saffron was shocked. Could it be that the little man had heard her words *and* understood them? Quickly she looked up at her mother to see if she had heard the scream as well. Apparently not - Audrey was still frowning, still staring at Saffron waiting for her to explain herself. *That little runt can understand me!*

"Yeah, Mom, really it was nothing. Just a teeny tiny *maggot!*" And when she said "maggot" she yelled it louder than the rest of the words just to make sure he heard.

It seemed he caught her drift, as this time the scream was so shrill and so full of rage that Saffron felt a bit intimidated and decided that she had said enough. After all, what if it went Chucky on her and sneaked into her room tonight? She shuddered.

Audrey was more than a little perturbed. "Really, Saffron. All this drama over a maggot? They're harmless. (Another howl.) I think we'd better finish up. Let's do something else." As if Audrey could keep her going from project to project and outrun the crazies. "And I don't think it was a maggot, Saffron. Maybe a grub, they're a *tiny* bit bigger." She held her thumb and forefinger together to show Saffron a quarter-inch. "Maybe a little fatter."

Audrey bent down, amber bracelets clacking, and offered Saffron a hand to get off the ground. This was a good thing. Just as Audrey curved over, a rotten tomato sailed through the air where her neat and pretty head had just been. Saffron watched the tomato soar by and gave a weak nod of agreement.

Chapter 5

"Hi, I'm Coco. Welcome to the glamorous world of second shift."

Saffron watched Coco put on disposable gloves and start making a sandwich. She swiped at her nose after the ham, then the cheese, then the mayo. Coco had a little cold. Her body was long and thin, much like Saffron's. They were two beanpoles in the night.

Saffron studied Coco while the girl was busy making the sandwich. On her feet she wore leather sheaths with what looked like the heels of stiletto pumps peeking out of the bottom, as if Coco created her own boots by combining shoes with sheaths, which she did. The boot sheaths were decorated with grey feathers. She wore tight jeans and a t-shirt. The t-shirt had a bare-branched tree on it with the word "lunacy" barely stamped across the limbs. A rotten apple was in the grass at the base. The t-shirt had puffed sleeves. Netting had been sewed on where the regular sleeves had been cut off. It was another homemade item. Coco's hair was long, black, and straight with a knotted lump on one side - bed-head she had neglected to comb out. Her nose and face were long too – pretty, in a witchy, Cher sort of way.

"Hi, I'm Saffron."

"You got what on?"

Saffron raised her voice from a mumble to a little louder than mumble. "My name, it's Saffron."

Coco looked up. "Your hair's not yellow."

Saffron flinched and turned around to check her reflection in the window. She didn't know what else to do with this comment.

"Saffron, the spice, it's yellow." Now Coco was watching Saffron as she finished wrapping the sandwich. Saffron avoided her eyes. "Are you okay?"

Saffron's mouth opened, closed, then opened again. "What? Me?"

"Yeah, Sag-Ass Bea told me you were mental or something, like smiling all the time."

Saffron said nothing as her hands hung limp at her sides, their dead weight pulling her shoulders forward. She felt heat prickle her cheeks.

Coco put a Black Chicken sticker on the sandwich and threw it in the cooler, staring at Saffron the whole time. "Your face is baboon-butt red, but otherwise, you look fine to me."

Really? The dreadful weight in Saffron's arms lightened and she stood a little straighter. "I call her the Fried-Headed Lady." Saffron was still mumbling.

Coco cocked her head. "Wha...?" She opened her mouth and screaming laughter came pouring out. Her eyes opened wide. "Oh, my God, that's like wicked funny! What are you doin' workin' here anyway?" Coco wiped her nose. "You goin' to school part time? Help me toss these salads."

She gave Saffron a plastic long-handled spoon and together they began to stir the salads in the display case. She showed Saffron how to gently fold the congealed salads in on themselves so they would appear fresh. They were told to do it on every shift.

"I don't go to school."

"Savin' up for it?"

"Nah."

"You just graduated, right?"

Saffron looked up, stunned. Coco had remembered her from

school and she had been a year ahead of Saffron. They had never spoken before in their lives. "Yeah, I did."

"You hung around with all those snobs, that bitch, Mindy."

"Yeah, she's my cousin."

Coco stuck out her pointed tongue. She looked like a gagging bird. "Sorry. Sorry she's your cousin I mean."

Saffron smiled and worked at the tuna salad.

"So what are ya workin' here for?"

Saffron glanced away. She shrugged.

Coco swiped her nose on the back of her rubber glove, then wiped that on her apron. "I mean, what's your plan, dude?"

Saffron opened her mouth, but was saved by the ting-a-ling of the front doors, which meant a customer was coming in. Coco strolled up to the counter to sell a pack of strawberries-and-cream-flavored chew to a short, young guy with a baseball cap pulled low over his eyes.

"You old enough for this?" She wagged the pink bag in his face.

"Yeah." He sneered and slapped a twenty on the counter, then snatched the bag.

"I mean, dude, if you don't have a plan you're going to end up like Sag-Ass Bea. She's been here for like a million years now."

Saffron froze. She saw the miniature, angry, baseball guy looking in her direction. She bit her lower lip and felt the familiar roasting of her face. Saffron had assumed she and Coco would resume their conversation *after* he left. She looked helplessly at Coco, willing her to shut up as she watched Coco count out the angry baseball guy's change. In the same minute, his interest petered out and he walked out the glass doors without saying anything.

As he passed beneath the jingling bell Coco yelled, "You're welcome!" Then she muttered, "Angry little shit, that one." In the next second, as if nothing had ever happened, she looked at Saffron. "I mean, don't you have a plan?"

Saffron was even more petrified of getting into this conversation now that she knew Coco had no sense of decorum. She'd keep talking, probably say anything as the customers roamed in and out. *Why aren't you getting a life? What's your bra size? You've got something hanging out of your nose,* while all the while bored shoppers tuned their ears from between the rows of dusty canned goods and dusty condoms. Saffron grew hot and itchy just thinking about it. What the hell did it matter, anyway? Why was Coco bothering her about this? She didn't even know her!

"What are *you* going to do?" Saffron mumbled over the rush of water that couldn't move the congealed mayonnaise from her fingertips, then immediately regretted her mouthy blunder. Her eyes skidded over to Coco's face to see how pissed she was.

"What?" Coco yelled from the chip aisle, where she was choosing her dinner.

An old man came through the door, ting-a-ling, and behind him, someone else. Saffron bit her bottom lip - she wasn't yelling across these strangers to have this stupid conversation of Coco's.

Coco appeared alongside her. "*I* got a plan. I need this job for a short while, buy me some big jubs."

Three things happened at once. The Windex bottle Saffron just picked up dropped on the floor and bounced around, the guy who came in behind the old guy was getting beer out of the cooler and yelled, "Yee-ha!" loud enough to be heard three strip malls down, and the old man hissed from the counter where he had been waiting one second too long for his winning lottery ticket.

The big cowboy's head floated along above the deli counter,

looking for all the world like a lit jack-o-lantern as he made his way toward checkout. "C'mon baby, check me out. I got some celebrating ta do what with you on the rise!"

Saffron tottered, head pulled into her shoulders, toward the fuming old man. She thought she might faint. *Oh, God, Coco, why can't you shut your big mouth? Why are you so loud?* Then Saffron remembered school. She remembered Coco in the halls when classes changed, how Coco screamed and caterwauled with her friends, how the whole undulating sea of people yelled over each other, throwing their big voices around and around her head.

Saffron braced herself on the counter and said...nothing. She just stared. The old man wouldn't look at her. He glared at Coco with all of his seventy years of hardcore, praise-Jesus training. Saffron gingerly took the ticket he pushed toward her on the counter. It was a four-dollar winner.

"Wha...." She stammered and before she could get out more than that....

"Two more," he barked. He looked Coco up and down, up and down, his lip in a snarl. He grabbed the new tickets from Saffron's shaking hand and stalked out.

"Have fun, Roger! Lord have mercy. Christ have mercy. Mercy on your old gambling ass, I mean!" Coco snickered with the cowboy.

Saffron held fast to the counter, her face frying, and her gut wrenching. *Oh, Coco! Shut up!*

"Now you keep me posted," drawled the cowboy. He tweaked Coco's nose, tipped his hat to them both, and left.

"Definitely." Coco waggled her fingers goodbye.

Saffron couldn't look at her.

"My heart is all a-dither." Coco slapped Saffron on the back,

"C'mon, let's go stock the cooler."

Saffron sighed. It would be such a relief to get Coco's mouth into a small, insulated place. As they shelved milk from crates and Nesquick from boxes, Coco told Saffron about her big plan. Periodically they peeked between the cooler shelves for incoming customers.

"Ya' know Busties, right?"

Saffron shook her head 'no.'

"Yeah ya do; that's the strip joint down near the new green gas station."

Saffron frowned and put another gallon of 2% up.

"Well, those girls in there are makin' a lot of money. I mean *a lot.*"

Saffron wiped the sweat off her brow with the back of her sleeve.

"...but you know who's makin' more? Busty his own self!"

Saffron wiped down the next shelf, moved on to the Tropicana.

"I went down there to apply, for a job ya know, and Busty told me my jubs didn't cut it...go get the mop by the back door." Coco scowled at the orange juice Saffron just spilled all over the concrete cooler floor.

Saffron scurried out. Coco's frown cleared and she started to follow Saffron, to hold the cooler door open so she could continue her story as Saffron retrieved the mop. She had to yell, of course, to be heard over the engines in the back room. They were wicked loud. "So all I have to do is save enough money at this job so I can get the operation." Crash! Crash! Coco ran toward the noise. "You okay? What are you doin'?"

Saffron appeared from behind a stack of cardboard boxes.

"Lemme see that." Coco took the mop handle. She pulled, then pushed at it to roll it with its bucket into the cooler. Saffron picked up the juice jug and gawped at the cap that had blown off when she had dropped the thing.

"Bring that up front when we go, we have to account for it."

Saffron nodded.

"They don't mess with your nipples or nothin'"

Saffron overturned a milk crate, fell into a sitting position, and ground her fists into her eyes.

"You got itchy eyes?"

Saffron didn't answer.

Coco didn't care. "So if I have a kid later, and wanna breastfeed they said that's still possible." She snorted. "But then again, I know this chick that went down to South America to get it done cheap. Oh, my God, you shoulda seen what they did to *her* nipples..." Then Coco went on to discuss.

They moved out and on to sanitize the coffee pots. They made fresh Hazelnut, Columbian, French Vanilla, Caramel Cream, and Chocolate Raspberry brews. When the coffee was done, they each filled a cup for themselves. Saffron liked it with so much cream she had to put it in the microwave to bring it back to hot. Coco drank it black.

"Because Busty is like in his late seventies and he ain't gonna live forever, I figure," and here her eyes actually gleamed, "that I'm gonna do a real good job dancing, keep on Busty's good side, save my money...and buy the joint when he goes to sell! Pretty good, huh?" She smiled and she was beautiful, almost angelic. "I've got it all up here." She tapped her forehead. "I can support myself."

Saffron cleared her throat. Her pipes were rusted from having been silent for so long. She leaned forward and triple-checked to make sure the store was really empty. "Aren't you afraid of what people are going to say about you?" She whispered to make sure even the cockroaches couldn't hear her.

The corner of Coco's mouth pulled up as her eyebrows lowered. "I only care what I think of me. I'm not out there sellin' drugs, stealin', killin', hurtin' anybody." She poked her chest with one red, lacquered thumbnail. "I'm a good person."

Saffron didn't blink.

Coco gave her a funny look. "Anyway, we forgot to switch out the whipped cream - that entire row is expired. Be right back."

Saffron turned to even out the tails of the rolls of lottery tickets and restock cigarettes. While she was considering dusting the candy, a small voice scratched out behind her. Saffron made a little 'yip' noise and turned to see who was there.

It was a little, old woman. Her back was bent but there was a smile on her wrinkled-apple face. She pushed a can of tomato soup across the counter. "Ooo, hoo. Scared ya, didn't I?"

Saffron stared at the soup can and mumbled, "Yeah. No. It's okay. One twenty five, please." Where had this old biddy come from? Saffron didn't hear the ting-a-ling. She was mad at herself for zoning out again.

The ancient woman reached into a macramé purse.

In the cooler, Coco was just reaching for the last can of whipped cream. She happened to look at Saffron at the register counter, and saw her talking to herself and reaching out as if to take money from someone. Coco pulled her chin back into her neck and squinted, her hand stalled in mid-grab. She continued to watch as Saffron appeared to be making a transaction by taking money that wasn't there and giving nothing back to a person that wasn't there.

Coco shrugged. Saffron must be practicing. She came out of the cooler, her eyes on Saffron the entire walk back to the counter.

"Whataya doin? Practicin'?"

Saffron had no idea what Coco was talking about, so she did what she always did when she didn't want to continue a conversation - she agreed with a nod and a deer-in-the-headlights stare. Saffron never heard the old lady leave.

Chapter 6

When Saffron woke up the next morning, rain was pummeling the window. She'd had another dream, but this time it was different. Strange, because the dream took place in her room, not some obscure land in some far-distant time, and strange because she was herself in the dream and she was dressed and she wasn't having sex, watching someone having sex, or anticipating having sex.

She dreamed she opened her eyes, looked at the clock - the red digital display read 3:32am - and watched as an elderly, black couple strolled across her floor and straight out through the opposite wall. He was talking about the stock market crash. He was dressed in a pressed suit and derby and she in a flower-patterned, shin-length dress and straw hat. Saffron had blinked twice, then rolled over. The next thing she knew she was awake and remembering.

She got up and took a shower. It was her habit to dry her body with the shower curtain still closed, wrap her hair in one towel, and wrap her body in another before she opened the curtain to step out. She told herself she did this to preserve the shower steam and keep herself warm while she was drying.

She opened the curtain. There was a little boy standing before the toilet, dropping in pennies. She screamed and slipped to the tub floor. Slowly, she raised her head and peeked over the edge. He looked at her, then vanished.

Saffron heard Audrey come running and throw the door open. "What? What?" Audrey looked haggard and frantic.

"Nothing." Saffron ground through clenched teeth. "Mom, I'm naked."

"And underneath my Muumuu I am too, so what?" Audrey shot back and slammed the door.

Saffron didn't move. She bit her bottom lip. *I'm really not the kind of girl that could handle this,* she thought as she swallowed repeatedly at the walnut-sized lump in her throat. The air changed suddenly and she froze as she sat in the tub in her wet towel. Static zapped her tongue when the little boy walked through the bathroom door, straight at her, and through her. This time she held the scream in with both hands.

***

One day passed, and two more. There were ghosts everywhere. Gremlins or some little monsters just like them in the trash, gnomes in the garden, elves in the woods, pixies in the treetops. Whenever Saffron saw something otherworldly, she ignored it by letting her hair fall over her eyes. She'd scrunch her head up into her shoulders like a turtle.

Work became a little difficult because she was never sure if a customer was dead or not unless Coco talked to him first. Still, at least twice, Saffron got caught up in the moment and started interacting with things Coco knew weren't there. Then Saffron would wince and pretend it was all a joke while watching the disgruntled ghost out of the corner of her eye as he or she tried to press their ghostly money on her or persist in a conversation about the weather.

One night, Saffron had a dream about a woman who was to marry. The bride and the groom were both of patrician families and proud of their upper-class standing in society. *His* family knew Caesar! She was already rubbing elbows with dignitaries! She was content in this knowledge, knowing that their relationship with political powers would fortify her marriage.

Her step was light as she passed the formal gardens and geometrically-arranged hedges of his parent's property. She knocked on the sea-weathered door, drew her hand back and gingerly fingered her exposed collarbone with soft fingers.

She was a pleasant looking girl with strong facial features delicately balanced by fine, heart-shaped lips. Her obsidian hair flowed thick down her back, bound loosely by a few golden cords given to her by her love as a token of his affection. She was a bit tall and angular for the fashion of the time, but this did not seem to bother her betrothed. He loved her anyway, he always assured her. She was filled with giddy anticipation for this visit. She had decided to give herself to him before the wedding. He had been so patient with her these past few months. He had begged for her acquiescence on only a few occasions and with only a little anger.

He did not answer the door. She knocked again and waited, shivering with nervous, sexual energy. No answer. She waited. Should she search him out? Maybe he wasn't home. She decided to enter, just to make sure. She pushed the heavy wood door open and stood in the cool alcove. After a beat, she heard the squeals and giggles of several female voices. She stopped. These were not the voices of his sisters. Not the voice of his mother. And what was the strange smell in the air? She walked slowly, her fine-tooled sandals making not a sound on the stone floor. The liquid heat of anticipation melted away and left her with a sodden chill, chasing the warmth of the day right out of her bones. She frowned. She couldn't figure for the life of her who those women might be.

She walked past several doorways of luxurious rooms awash with vividly painted frescoes. His family's home was typical of the upper class, consisting of many rooms designed around an atrium open to the heavens above. She padded silently along the tiled floor patterned with the swirling blues of the ocean and sky.

Another giggle. A sigh. The voice of her love growling like a bear. She stopped again, frozen in time. Her hand flew to her throat and an icy dread crawled across her body like fouled trough water.

Leave!

She stood motionless except for kneading the skin at her throat.

Move! Find out!

She walked forward, toward the sound of the joyful voices, toward the bedchamber of her love. She adjusted her flowing, white robes, stood up straight, and rounded the corner.

There they were. Bodies. She couldn't count how many. Female bodies. They were jumping on his bed, rolling around in his bed, rolling around *him*. Flashes of twisted limbs and dark hair on snow-white skin. Him, wiping his mouth with the back of his hand as if he were a slobbering glutton. The stink of hot, perfumed skin and that something else. His dark blue eyes flashed under his long lashes before he slapped the naked rump of one of them. She was small, beautiful, and curvaceous. She turned on him like a ravaged animal, bit his cheek, and left a mark. All the while, they writhed.

The woman pulled her head from the doorway. She stood off to the side and backed herself up to the cool, stone wall. With wretched little choking sounds, she tried to catch her breath. She raised her hand to her mouth as if to stop an outpouring of bile. No one had seen her.

"No," it escaped her lips as a moan. She clamped both hands to her mouth and pressed with all her might. She began to heave and sob beneath her hands while the players continued to laugh and moan, drowning out what little noises escaped her.

The dream melted to black and Saffron almost woke, but not quite.

She didn't hear the sounds of the fairies tapping on her window. They giggled as they willed the panes to open and hushed each other as they flew to her bed, a thick, chill fog trailing after them. "Up, up, up! Open your mind to us and we'll fly you away."

Saffron sat up and opened her eyes. Heat flared and grew within her. A great force filled her with such rapture she almost fell back, but instead she was separated. Her soul levitated to the ceiling; her body crumpled on the mattress. Air currents moved her ghostly form through the open panes.

Her mother, snoring on a cot beside her bed, never moved. And, later in the night, when Audrey stumbled to the bathroom to pee, she paid no mind to Saffron, whose body was sprawled open-mouthed on the bed.

Saffron was hazy-minded throughout the ride, but every once in a while, a dim smile lit her face as she watched the shadowy night beauty all around her. They touched down in the center of the clearing. Tonight, small flames flickered in place of the great bon fire that had blustered at the previous party. Her entourage kissed her cheeks and lips and smoothed her hair. The veins under their skin and other innards rippled with pleasure, their pupils soaked her into their black depths before they suddenly departed in a flurry of wings and iridescence.

Slowly, strength and awareness returned to her limbs. She walked to the fire. There was snow here, but she wasn't cold. Just when she started to feel silly, standing there all alone, Li emerged smiling from the dark of the trees.

"I have had reason to retrieve you."

Through Saffron's mind, there flashed a picture of a golden retriever nosing in a marsh clotted with cattails, mouthing a duck with a lolling neck. *Retrieve?* She literally shook her head at the image, as if rattling her brains would clear her head. She smiled sheepishly at the fairy as a child to her mother, when she is unsure of her mother's mood. Li moved right up to Saffron and took a length of Saffron's dark red hair between her fingers. Her nostrils flared as she strained for the smell of human girl.

"You are disappointed to see me...it is Ny you were hoping to meet."

Saffron's smile faltered, and here, the child in her knew for certain that her mother's mood was tottering. She attempted to stutter around a response. But she had nothing to say and quickly closed her mouth.

"Do not look so worried, Saffron! Of course you wish to see him." But Li's lips pressed in disapproval, only for a moment. She reached for Saffron again, to run her thumbs along Saffron's cheeks. Under her own skin, Li's cheekbones were visible.

Saffron closed her eyes and breathed in the fragrance of the fairy's white hair and white skin. Pine and milk, honey and rain.

Li laughed. "Aren't we a pair? Sniffing each other like animals that cannot smell! Come with me." Li tugged Saffron's hand. "Today, we are working." She led Saffron out of the fire-lit glade and into a bright world full of lush, green foliage and the song of a thousand birds.

"Working? Why?"

"For pride."

"Why don't you just zap things to be the way you want them?"

Li laughed at this and shook her head. Finally, the fairy seemed to be relaxing, so Saffron did too.

"What would it all mean without accomplishment? Should we sit around all day and do nothing but zap, as you say, our lives away. It is intrinsic. There is no life where there is not the ritual of effort. Do I wish my friend to visit? Pow! Whether she likes it or not, she is in the chair at my table. Do we want to share tea? Bling! The pot is steaming before us. Are we too lazy to swallow our treats? Bam! It is already in our stomachs. We may as well skip straight to Kapow. Now we do not exist because we did nothing anyway."

"Oh." Saffron looked away, embarrassed.

"Come along, curious one. I will show you the work we do around here."

They turned right, through a copse of fragrant citrus trees and moved down a narrow lane crowded on both sides with swirling vines and hot pink flowers the size of Saffron's head, big hair and all. Every once in a while, the lane opened up to a yard. As they went along, the seasons changed, fading in and out at the edges of unseen boundaries. In one yard, it was spring in the morning. Down the road, it was fall at dusk. And though some had snow in their yards, it wasn't cold.

"It's not cold." Saffron realized she was hugging herself for no good reason and forced her palms down to the sides of her cotton pajama bottoms.

"Goodness no, we are fairies, not martyrs!" screamed a high-pitched voice from behind her.

Saffron spun around and there stood a stunning fairy with black, waterfall hair. The fairy dipped forward and pressed kisses all over Saffron's forehead. Her hair thundered and sprinkled water on Saffron's face and clothes. Saffron giggled and wanted to stick her finger in the waterfall hair.

"Go ahead," chimed the fairy as she took Saffron's wrist and made Saffron poke her finger into the torrent.

Li smiled her utmost patience smile and removed Saffron's wrist from the other fairy's grip. Li held Saffron's hand as she spoke, as they walked. "We do choose to work here, it is true, but we prefer not to suffer!"

"I've noticed that everyone is touchy-feely, too." With her palm, Saffron sluiced water from her face and shoulders.

Ny came strolling up the path, rolling a wheelbarrow, and looking like a god. His upper body rippled with muscle and sinew below his skin. Saffron frowned hard when she realized she was actually salivating.

He dropped the wheelbarrow, and with big strides closed the space between them. He held her with his eyes, challenging her in a hold of unblinking wills. He stopped so near she could feel his breath.

Saffron was confused. He looked younger than before, his skin changing even now until it was opaque, more human, so she didn't quite see the veins working underneath. The black orbs of his eyes were tamer too, showing more cerulean around the rim than she remembered. She swallowed hard and suffered through the dual sensation of wanting to fall before him so he could take her in the path and furtively searching for a tool with which to gut him.

"Ny." Li murmured, "I can see you have something pressing to tell our friend. I will leave you for a moment."

Saffron saw the warning glance Li gave Ny as she moved away - a glance Ny met with his own smirking lips and simpering eyes. Li turned her head, pretending she hadn't noticed.

Ny widened his eyes, narrowed his pupils, and stood staring down at Saffron from under his long dark lashes. He reached up with one big hand to comb the flopping waves back from his forehead. When he brought his hand slowly back to his side, the hair sprung forward, right back into his eyes. "And when will you come here in body?"

An intense heat swept through Saffron, flew up her neck, and singed her ears. She was so flustered she became angry. "I have to go now," she mumbled.

He made no sign of having heard her. She crossed her arms and studied a rock just off to his right. He didn't look away. His smile of complete confidence didn't dim. Saffron's muddle-headedness grew as he took several long moments to stand there, letting his eyes peruse her body.

She mumbled again. "I have a boyfriend at home, you know."

This caused a howl of laughter to explode from him and he threw his head back with glee. "What a little liar you are. Boyfriend, my foot." He grabbed a big handful of her rusty red curls and pulled her to him.

She stumbled, her face flushing in waves. Her entire body froze, her jaw clenched shut, and her mind screamed for him to stop touching her. Something about the possessive way he grabbed her hair stirred up a hornets' nest within her.

He released her hair and spoke low, "My joy at seeing you again, it is immeasurable." His eyes softened as if he were about to cry.

Saffron clamped her bottom lip with her teeth. She scratched the side of her neck. What was going on here? Why was he so freakin' dramatic? He couldn't have missed her *that* much since the night of the fairy party.

He bent at the waist and swept his hand through a profusion of roses that grew along the dirt roadside. He just reached down, grabbed, and pulled. Thorns pierced and sliced up through his skin like a whetted blade through ham. The blood ran down his wrist and onto the stems as he handed the bunch to her. "Here."

She sucked breath through her teeth as she watched his blood drip.

As if he only just realized what was happening, he looked down at his blood and simply said, "Oh." Then just as suddenly as the blood was there, it was gone from his hand, his wrist, and the stems. He took a rose from the bunch, filed its thorns with his thumbnail, and tucked it behind her ear. As soon as his knuckle grazed the skin behind her ear, her eyes closed and she tottered at the heady smell of the rose and the hot, dry touch of him. When she opened her eyes, he was gone.

There before her stood Li. She was not smiling. "Did he torture you too much?"

"Why does he do that?" Saffron's voice was rough, as if her throat had been brandy-soaked and massaged on a cheese grater.

"Ny has a great need to be the center of every universe. You do not have to succumb to his act. Do not look into his eyes when he calls for you, even if he begs. Maybe then you will find it easier to retain some self-control. And with that, some self-respect, I daresay. It is best you do not play his game. Eventually, he will tire and try someone else."

Saffron felt dirty. "Okay." She studied her fingernails. "Li, I've seen him before, you know, in my dreams...." Saffron fidgeted with the drawstring on her tank top. She felt so weird, as if she was having the "Birds and Bees" talk with her mother. Still, she decided to press on. It was time. She had to talk to *someone* about the dreams. She felt like she might be some kind of freak, a pervert, and she surely would never talk to her mother about it. She had the innate feeling that her mother couldn't handle any more of her weirdness. So why not talk to a fairy - you couldn't get any more weird or freaky than that.

"He's always with these women..." Saffron stopped. She looked around. *Those women* were probably close by, her with her big mouth. Now she was having second thoughts about telling a sister about the sexual acts of her brother, even if it was only a dream.

Li was looking away from Saffron. She had sat on a tree stump when Saffron began and was absently running the silken cords of her dress through her thin fingers. Li's face was strained. "It is most curious that you would have such dreams. Are you sure about them? Are you sure you saw Ny? His good looks are so generic after all."

Saffron hunched. She only really remembered the essence of him in the dream. Like when you dream about something that is yours, and you know in the dream that it's yours, but you've never owned it in your waking life. "Maybe it wasn't him." She crossed her arms over her chest.

In each dream, Ny looked slightly different. His skin shades varied. His features were always a little different, but somehow he managed to have a look somewhat the same each time. Maybe his blue eyes had more green in one dream, more hazel in the next. His hair was always dark and wavy or curly. His lips, always the same. His attitude - arrogance coated with a faint attempt at pleasantness, was steadfast from time to time. In each dream, Saffron recognized him instantly not by his looks, but by his presence.

Li smiled. "Sometimes, dreams are just dreams, human child." But now her wings hung low as if they were made of paper and someone had dumped a bucket of water on them.

Just thinking of the dreams made Saffron feel slick and oily. She sighed. She swatted a fly that had come buzzing around her ear.

Whether or not the fairy noticed the girl's discontent, she made no mention - but instead took Saffron's hand and once again led her down the lane, her white hair flowing out like a glittering flag behind her. She pointed here and there and explained those things that Saffron found curious. They didn't talk about the dreams again. The subject hung in the air as if it was smog, quiet and poisonous. With each breath, they drew it deep inside of them.

A fairy with golden hair and iridescent copper skin hung freshly laundered sheets on a line. A boy with flaming red curls, pert nose, and freckled cheeks mended his roof. A group of girls ran to Li and Saffron with cakes, buttered rolls, and sweet meats that they had just pulled from an outdoor oven. Some boys and girls sat fishing on the bank of a creek. Their wings glinted in the slanted fairy world light. Saffron looked again - maybe they were adults.

The skin, eye, and hair colors differed, but each fairy shimmered - their insides pulsed under their clear skin. Saffron barely thought of their see-through skin now - she didn't think it was so repulsive anymore. She saw beings she would describe as white, black, Asian, Mediterranean, Hispanic, and Indian – even alien with pitch-black eyes shaped like almonds.

Then there were the others. Sky-blue-skinned fairies with pink hair, and golden fairies with white hair, and ocean-green-skinned fairies with silver hair. She gawked at them openly. Some even had patterns on their skin.

Like the male she stared at now as he leaned against a tree, casting a devilish smile. He wore a woven hat that he tipped in greeting. The pattern on his skin was autumn leaves, striking reds and oranges, yellows and bronze. His skin glistened as if it had been rubbed with oil. His hair was jet-black, tied back with a piece of grass. The wings folded behind him were clear silver run through with many fine silver veins.

Another fairy popped out at him from behind the tree. The popper startled him and he tripped on his feet. He lifted off for a minute, wings pumping fast before he settled down again. They laughed together as he lunged at his playmate. She had striped skin, like a zebra. He took her hand and they walked off down the lane. Saffron turned to Li with a look of shock on her face.

"They choose such beautiful colors, don't they? They would love to live this way for their human existence, like proud peacocks. They are called *Vivids*." Li tilted her head. "Can you imagine if they were born on earth displaying skins of such hues and patterns? They would be annihilated, wouldn't they? The human race still has trouble with the few skin colors it has. What if that was walking among you?"

Li pointed to a being that was quickly making her way toward them on the path. Her skin was the pale aqua of the Caribbean Sea as it fringes the coast, glinting and reflecting the morning sun. Through her skin...fluids ran like waves from the roots of her hair down to her seaweed-green toes. Her eyes were electric violet and her hair was turquoise blue shot through with tendrils of lime green. She flexed her silvery wings and bared her teeth at Saffron. Saffron waggled her fingers, bewildered. Did she bare her teeth in greeting or in hunger? The fairy retracted her wings, stepped off the path, and disappeared into the wood.

"Come. Sit." Li showed Saffron a tire swing inside the thick greens of the forest. Her pupils bore into Saffron. Saffron hurried forward and sat quickly, never wondering why she rushed.

"Maybe," Li whispered, "you should stay close to home for awhile." And although she spoke softly, Saffron received the true message from Li's unblinking eyes and from the way the translucent skin of her face seemed to tighten up and pull back. It was a command.

A puzzled line creased Saffron's forehead. That was what she had always wanted to do - stay at home within the bubble of her family's yard. No one before had ever encouraged Saffron to hide. They were always telling her to *get out. Get out in the world! Stop hiding at home!* It was nice to finally meet someone who agreed staying at home was actually good for her. But why was Li saying this? Why was she *ordering* this?

For a second, Saffron felt all wrong. She felt like she was betraying her mother by listening to Li, and betraying her mother by just being in this fairy world. But then she narrowed her eyes as she remembered her anger toward her mother. Audrey was always push, push, pushing and nag, nag, nagging. Saffron was absolutely terrified when she had to leave her home. Why couldn't her mother see that and give her a break? What was wrong with staying at home? Society didn't agree; was that it? She was always outdoors, rain or shine, so she was physically healthier than most people. She read every book under the sun - history and sci-fi, biography and fantasy, memoir and how-to. Non-fiction, from animal husbandry to the start of the cosmos. So, her mind wasn't rotting. She cleaned the house from top to bottom - she was pulling her weight. Saffron couldn't see what the problem was. Not everyone needed a social agenda to exist. She knew there were still tribes in the Amazon that never left their confines. Yet they were born, they lived, they died, no problem. Saffron kick-started the tire swing again.

Here was Li, comforting her and telling her it was okay to stay at home. Agreeing with what Saffron had always wanted in the first place - to be cocooned within her space, to be left alone.

Li put her hands on her hips. "Your mother is a lovely woman, but she does not understand you as I understand you."

Saffron flinched. She wanted to argue that. A weak bit of defiance floated up her spine and fizzled out. The squeezing in her chest demanded she defend her mother. But Saffron only hung her head and waited for the moment to pass. When it did, she was left with nothing but shame. "Too bad I couldn't just stay here..." Saffron had no idea why she'd said that. She thought maybe it was because it was what Li would want to hear. She thought maybe she meant it. Why not stay and live in the fairy realm?

Li's eyes flashed. What Saffron saw there startled and unnerved her. It was greed in Li's black eyes, desperate greed. Then, just as suddenly, Li's eyes cleared and the big, black pupils were like that of a kitten begging for cream. "You cannot stay here after sunrise, my friend. Your mother will rise soon, reach to wake you, and think you dead."

Saffron gave a low gasp. "What do you mean, *dead*?"

"It is only your soul that visits us when you come - your flesh stays behind. That is why we had to hurry you back the last time. Your mother was up and about the house. Had she gone to check on you, she would have seen her child lifeless before her. Your body, right now, has no life. Its functions have ceased. Your body is suspended in time until you return. Were you to stay here for too long, your loved ones would think you most certainly dead. They would mourn you and bury you. Your soul would have no house in which to return to except for that body, trapped deep below the ground, available to worms.

"Listen, child. Your body has not let go of its soul. We took your soul. Your body is even now waiting for it to return. Should your people bury your body, your body will forevermore wait for your soul to return. Of course, you could stay here and live with us. But over the years, all joy would seep from you, as over the centuries you would watch others go off on human adventures. That would be a sport you would never again be able to partake of. Your body, sadly decayed, would be of no use to you, but since it hadn't properly released your soul - you can have no new body. You would not be able to be born again.

"You must go and quickly."

"So, I would be like that woman, wouldn't I, that woman from the woods who throws herself off my cliff every night." Saffron hoped the fairy would disagree with her statement. She wanted to be nothing like that woman.

Li frowned, and around them, the leaves shivered. "What woman?"

Saffron blanched, leaned away from Li, and though she was quite certain she had done nothing wrong, her body caved in on itself like a kicked dog with rounded back and tucked tail. "I dunno."

Li's voice changed. She growled and garbled like a demon, "What..." Then she clamped her teeth. Her nostrils spread for air and she said too softly, "woman?"

Saffron stuttered and stammered for a minute. "I don't know. I just saw her in the woods one day with this bashed-in head, the day I almost went over the cliff..."

Li squinted and shook her head 'no,' every vein red and raised like a map of welts on her fine porcelain skin.

"She just stood there, said, 'why,' then jumped off the cliff." Saffron watched confusion twist Li's face. She could tell the fairy was trying hard to figure something out, but couldn't come up with the answer. Saffron looked away, embarrassed, as if she were seeing the fairy fully exposed before her. "Now, she's out there every night, like, most nights. She just jumps off the cliff!" Saffron shivered. "Every night, just, 'Aaaaaahhhhh!' and jumps..."

Li seemed to be taking Saffron's measure. Finally, the fairy sighed. "She is nothing. A ghost. They are everywhere. You know this. She does not exist in such a bad way. Only, she does not know it. When she was alive and chose death for herself, her soul was released before her body was broken. Her body is not waiting for her soul to come back. She is not earthbound. She can be born again whenever she chooses...."

Li's eyes narrowed. "It is all a game, Saffron. If you lose your place, you must start at the beginning." She looked down at her pretty fist, where her nails dug in and sliced the thin skin of her palms.

Saffron was zoning out and didn't see.

"Has she asked you anything else, anything more than 'why?' Has she tried to speak to you again?"

Saffron shook her head no.

Li smiled, more satisfied than a fed cat. "What is happening to you is very different from her. Your body has not released your soul. You tricked your body while it lay sleeping. It does not know you have gone. So if your body is discovered and thought dead, your people will bury it. Then we will have to go through the trouble of retrieving it so you can get inside and walk away. But where would you go then?"

"Why are you worried about my ghost?" Saffron whispered.

"I am familiar with her kind. I want to be sure she is not frightening you; I know you scare easily." Li's wings hung still. Even the rivers of silver in the wiry veins were sluggish.

Saffron rested her head on the tire swing and let it slow to a stop.

Li walked over and kissed Saffron on the top of her head. The instant her smooth lips touched Saffron's hair, Saffron felt a tingling rush that shot straight from her head down to her fingertips and toes. Her whole body sparked.

"This kiss will remind you of our times together. It cannot protect you from harm but will serve to stay your confidence. Now stand so we can help you away."

Saffron stood, feeling that horrible lethargic sedation. She couldn't stop the images that swam in her mind like creatures in a swamp.

Chapter 7

Late the next afternoon, Saffron put on her black apron and black-winged hat. She was so exhausted her arms felt like noodles. She was getting paler too, as if that was possible. She turned from her mirror and didn't think about it. She thought only of the fairies. She couldn't tear her mind from them long enough to walk a straight line or to keep from stumbling down the farmhouse stairs and smacking her forehead on the newel post.

Derek was at the shop. Her mother was busy with her Grandmother in the kitchen. Saffron had to go through there to get her dinner to bring to work. She was torn. She was afraid to go to work and afraid to tussle with her mother, but also afraid to meet her Grandmother's glassy eyes and give a pretend-cheerful greeting.

She took a deep breath, forcibly straightened, and emerged from the beamed doorway into the kitchen, which was filled with afternoon sun and the smell of chocolate chip cookies. It was teatime. Grandmother didn't know her name most days, didn't know where she was, but she *never* forgot teatime. Saffron's mother was cutting slices of cucumber at the thick and scarred kitchen table, a long apron protecting her bright, swishy skirt.

"Have you come to collect clothes for the needy?" Grandmother rocked by the tall window that looked out on the herb garden. She had a ball of alpaca yarn in a child's sand bucket by her feet and was well into some intricate project. A spider sat unmoving in its web in the top corner of the window.

"I'm afraid I haven't much to give to you today. I'll go see what I can spare." Grandmother's voice was strong but clicking as if her throat was filled with marbles. It didn't fit her frail-looking frame.

"Oh, no, Mama. You can get those things later. Saffron is just here to say, 'Hi'."

"Can I get you some tea? A snack?"

Saffron scratched her head, gave her Grandmother's probing eyes a slight wag 'no,' then scurried to the fridge.

"The tea will be done soon, Mama. Please, just relax." Audrey cleared her throat. "How are your doilies coming?" She snatched at one of her own errant curls and pushed it back behind her ear. Her teeth were clenched behind her pursed lips.

"Well, I am tired, you know. That motor car broke down again and Edward and I had to walk all the way from town and didn't get back to the farm until dinner!"

"Oh, my! You must be exhausted."

The old woman tee-heed and nodded in agreement. Her blue-veined hands trembled slightly as she worked. Right now, she didn't know that her husband was long dead, her children grown, but she never dropped a stitch and could crochet an entire table mantle in a day, complete with curlicues and seashells and without missing a loop.

Audrey leaned toward Saffron behind the cover of the fridge door and whispered as she returned half a cucumber in a Ziploc bag to the produce drawer. "Derek's coming to bring you to work..." Audrey peeked over the top of the fridge door to check out her mother, then she dipped back down, "I don't want to move her right now."

Saffron nodded, owl-eyed. Fine, she wasn't too keen when her Grandmother came for the ride to work anyway. Yesterday, Grandmother leaned out the car window to tell two kids on bikes that the U.S. government was going to send men to the moon. But still, red-faced Saffron had gotten out of the rear seat thankful that Grandmother wasn't calling them *'little effers!'* That was a phrase her real Grandmother would never have used when she was with it; but these days she used it often when her eyes glazed and her shoulders slouched as if she were slowly morphing into a goblin and relishing the harsh texture of the bad words like candy on her tongue.

"Just let me run to the bathroom, I'll only be a minute." Audrey stopped and inspected Saffron for the first time that day. She reached two fingers toward Saffron's forehead and stopped just short of touching when Saffron jerked back a fraction of an inch.

"Saffron, what happened to you, your forehead, you have a humongous red welt there..."

"Nothing, Mom!" Saffron slapped a pale, freckled hand to the painful bruise and covered it as if it were a shameful part of her body. "Don't worry...just go to the bathroom."

Audrey quickly pulled her hand back. She contemplated pushing Saffron into a confession, but only for a moment. She would let this slide. She remembered the clunk she heard a short while ago and put two and two together. The next thing, and there always was a next strange thing with Saffron, the next thing she wouldn't let slide. Audrey trotted from the room.

Saffron shut the fridge door with one wooden arm. She straightened when she caught her Grandmother's eye, suddenly studying her with unnerving intensity. Saffron spun around and busied herself with slicing a piece of lasagna. She put freshly baked cookies in another container. Her fingers were shaking when she sucked the melted chips off of them.

Grandmother was still staring. It was unlike her to have such concentration, staring and crocheting at the same time.

Outside, something moved past the window above the sink, slow and unclear. It was very large. Saffron saw it out of the corner of her eye, but when she looked, it was gone.

Now another dread filled her. It drowned out the fear of her Grandmother in icy waves. Saffron crumpled into a chair at the kitchen table, giving her back to the window over the sink and whatever was out there in the dark, cloudy afternoon. She locked her eyes on Grandmother, who wasn't looking at her anymore.

"Who does she think she is, coming up to the house like that?" Grandmother dropped a loop, harrumphed, and corrected her mistake.

Saffron kept her saucer-big eyes on her Grandmother, never blinking, even though her insides rattled and shook like balls in a bingo cage.

Grandmother looked up at the window over the sink. Her eyes narrowed, focused, and followed movement. "Don't be playing cat and mouse with me, you."

Saffron shook in her chair and still couldn't turn to look. White noise roared in her ears and made it hard to understand what Grandmother was saying.

"You know, Missy, maybe if I had chosen to live in Arizona I wouldn't mind you so much. You're like a walking air conditioner. Sheesh. You're making my teeth chatter. If you cause them to chatter right out of my mouth and onto the floor I shall be very upset. Saffron doesn't do quite the job keeping this floor clean that I used to do, now, does she." Grandmother looked at Saffron, gave her one gruff nod in challenge.

Saffron eyed her Grandmother from between her fingers. She took offense to the cleaning crack and at the same time realized her Grandmother was right. The kitchen, which had just been warm, too warm in the aftermath of baking cookies and summer heat, was now cold enough to blow light plumes of icy breath.

Grandmother eyed Saffron. "Why is that one hanging around here anyway? She looks so morbid! She was never around before. Does she want something from you? She's looking at you."

Saffron sucked in her breath. Milky eyes, bashed-in skull, the trail of something gray and snakelike peeking through a rip in her back.

Saffron didn't answer. She watched her Grandmother's eyes refocus on the window above the sink. Grandmother slapped her crochet hook and the doily on her lap. "You *can* see her; can't you?"

Saffron never said a word, never moved her body. She stared at the cracks that traveled out from the crown molding high up on the wall until she felt her eyes cross from the concentration. Grandmother didn't remember her own daughter when she had left for the bathroom, but now she knew who Saffron was? Did that mean she was with it right now? Saffron forced her eyes to the cracks in the wall.

"Saffron?"

Saffron could hear pure joy in Grandmother's voice. *She must be so happy that, for once, someone won't think she's crazy.*

But Saffron couldn't do it. She couldn't admit to seeing that thing. She wouldn't look, wouldn't look. She wanted that dead woman away from the house. What was she doing here? The woods were bad enough, jumping off the cliff outside her window even worse; but what was she doing *here* now? Saffron just wanted to get ready to go to that stupid convenience store. This was exactly what Li had been afraid of, why Li had grown so scary last night. It was all about that woman out there, whoever she was. The other ghosts didn't bother with her; why did this one?

Came for you.

Saffron shrieked a low, frightened mouse hiccup. Whose voice was that? Where did it come from? Was it inside her head or outside? Saffron crossed her arms and began to rock on her seat - not far - only an inch back and forth very quickly. Her wary eyes met her Grandmother's expectant ones. She finally realized Grandmother was still waiting for an answer. She cleared her throat of the possessive little talons that held her voice captive.

"I feel sick."

Grandmother dropped her eyes, dejected. After a brief, tense silence, she resumed her crocheting.

Get out! Saffron screamed in her mind. *Get out! Get out! GET OUT!*

The cold left all at once.

"Well, good riddance to that silly cow." Grandmother scrutinized the limp doily in her veined hands. Her voice became harsh and deeply thoughtful, "Nobody uses doilies anymore. Am I dead?" She didn't look up.

Saffron didn't know if the old woman was asking Saffron if she was dead or asking herself. Her voice was so low.

"No, Grandmother; God, no." She found the strength to stand. "Now, please. Just stop this."

"Ah well, what a pity." With her perfect dentures Grandmother gave a rare smile.

Saffron rolled her eyes and used both hands to brace herself on the thick kitchen table. Where the hell was her mother? Who the hell not in high school took so long in the bathroom?

Saffron had known the ghost was real the first time she saw her. Saffron knew the fairies were real too, and the gnomes, the pixies, the other...things. She started gnawing on her thumbnail. Had she been hoping deep, deep inside that people were right? Had she been hoping she might be crazy? Crazy would surely have taken the pressure off of her. *Oh, she's crazy, she's seeing things.* And then it really wouldn't be her fault, right? She couldn't be blamed if her mind was going and she truly didn't realize it. She watched her Grandmother, braver now that the woman wasn't studying *her.* Saffron bit her thumbnail down too low - half of it was gnawed clean - but the other half was still mostly attached to bloody skin. She left off and started on the other thumb. She called her Grandmother crazy. What did it mean that they were both aware of the same ghost?

The tires of Derek's bug crunched over the gravel driveway. Audrey came breezing into the kitchen, showered and beautiful and smelling like fruity French perfume. The plastic, amber-colored bracelets clacked on her thin wrists and a new Mexican skirt swirled above her string sandals. She must be expecting company that evening. Saffron didn't like it when Audrey had people over to their cave. Audrey and Derek and their eclectic friends. Their favorite thing to do was play Wii Play. Followed by We Drink.

Audrey smiled wide. "Give me a kiss before you go."

Saffron winced at the pain in her thumbs, both bitten down to the skin, and quickly pecked her mother's mineral-powdered cheek. Audrey continued to smile. "Have a great night at work!"

Saffron fake-smiled in return and hoped she lived through the night.

Saffron was tossing salads when Coco's archenemy came strolling into the shop with a three-year-old child, his arms and legs spilling out of an Earth Mother body sling. The child looked odd, all heavy gangly in the sling, but there was something else Saffron couldn't figure. Finally, she realized that the oddness was the way the boy was bent and tucked...so he could snack on his mother's left breast. Saffron turned three shades of green and dropped the oily salad spoon. The kid burped some milk up on the floor.

It was widely thought that Coco's brother, Reginald, had sired the lad, but no one was positive. Reginald didn't know either, but he came up with money every month to help raise the child of his long since ex-girlfriend. Coco told all who would listen that she knew for a fact that the baby was someone else's, but never expounded further on her theory.

"OMG." Saffron muttered as she spied mother and child between the jars of sour pickles that sat on top of the deli case. 'Skin pickles' Coco called them because some of the clerks reached into the jars without gloves and there was always some unidentified cloud of something that swooshed up from the bottom of the green liquid when it was disturbed. Coco knew it was sloughed skin from gloveless dips past.

Currently, Coco was in the back of the store, stocking, and Saffron prayed she would stay there until this person and her child checked out. Saffron jumped over the dropped spoon, washed her hands, and then trotted to stand ready behind her register. She bit her bottom lip, scanned the parking lot, and hoped no one else would pull in. Where was the girl now? Over the tops of the rows, Saffron could see she had the cooler door open where the whipped cream was shelved. "OhmyGod," Saffron muttered as Coco came sauntering from the back. Saffron waved her away.

"No, problem, I got this one." Saffron mumbled.

"What?" Coco's voice rang out like a trucker's at a wrestling convention.

"I got this one; go back to stocking!" Saffron hissed even lower.

Coco came closer, holding her ear. "Girl, I can't hear a thing you're saying. Speak up for God's sake, scream it if you want. If you got something to say...LET IT OUT!" Movement caught the corner of Coco's eye. She turned to focus on it, on *her*. Coco's hands simultaneously went to her hips as her eyes narrowed. The girl and sucking child arrived at the counter just as Coco made it to Saffron's side.

"Holy Jesus, what do we have here?"

"OhmyGod." Saffron's face drained until she was potato-pasty. She hunched to a squat, feigning the dire need to paw at the paper bags that were neatly stacked on the shelf underneath the counter. She was too weak to stand, from spending all kinds of nervous energy on Coco, who had no idea.

Oh, shut up, please Coco, just this once, and don't say anything but thank you and good bye. Please. Saffron grabbed at the stack of paper bags, clutching them for dear life. She rested her head on the top of the pile. The stack started to slide. It spilled all over the floor, ignoring her squawk of protest. She never lifted her eyes to the counter top as she started reworking the pile.

For a hallelujah moment, there was silence while Coco rang in the girl's purchase, then counted out her change. Saffron held her breath. Maybe there was a chance?

"You know what, Charlemagne? You can wipe that baked-hippie-happiness smirk off your face – I wouldn't care if you had a kid hanging from each teat and one shittin' on your head – but I'd watch it if I were you – one of these days he's going to gnaw that nipple clean off with his wisdom teeth."

Saffron's eyes were squeezed shut. She leaned her sweaty forehead against the half-stacked pile of bags and started to hyperventilate.

"Screw you, Coco. And you can go screw your cheating brother too – go tell him I said that, that you can go screw him!"

"You damned nipple zit, go tell him yourself!" Coco roared as Saffron fell to a sit on the floor, holding her fire-hot cheeks and taking great lungfuls of air in through her mouth like a gasping fish.

The bell above the door ting-a-linged. The girl had left. Saffron felt Coco looking down at her. "Like I was telling you. You got something to say – say it loud, man."

Saffron squinted up at her.

"Girl, whataya doin down there? Get up." Coco offered Saffron a hand and pulled her up as easily as a Raggedy Anne doll. She gave the door a dirty look as if it had mortally offended her. "Bitch," she breathed. Then she smiled. "Hey, I was thinking, do you wanna come out with us some time? Me and my friends? You need to come out of yourself..." She looked pointedly to the floor, where Saffron was just hiding. "...we'll have a good time."

"No!" Saffron shot out so loud even the tails of the rolled lottery tickets shivered. Her nostrils flared as she stood and turned to hold onto the counter. She looked out at the parking lot, looked down the condom aisle, looked at her fingers.

Coco patted her back. "Very good. *That,* I heard. C'mon, coffee's stale. Let's get to work." She walked to the back of the store with Saffron slouching after her. Coco turned around, her eyes focused just above Saffron's eyes. "What in the hell happened to your forehead?"

Saffron raised her fingers to the welt from the newel post and shrugged.

"And what are you wearing today?" But Coco was smiling as she reached for a pod of Irish Cream.

Saffron looked down at her hot-pink-and-black, flowered, ruffled tank top. Then down further to her lime-green jeans which were rolled up once, till the long cuffs reached her knees. She wiggled her dark-purple-painted toenails in the holes of her peep-toe Maryjanes. She shrugged again.

Outside, at the intersection, a motorcycle engine revved. The deafening roar caught Saffron's attention. She started toward the windows at the front of the store. She watched as the rider passed through the intersection and drove straight on ahead, toward the store. When he started to slow down, and took the turn into the parking lot, she pulled her hands from the window where she had been leaning nose-to-glass, and retreated behind a tall Slim Jims display. She peeked out from behind the modified meat sticks. She couldn't be sure if it was him because the dark visor was down on his helmet. The cyclist shut off the engine, got off the bike, and set the kickstand. Here and now, under the buzz of life-force-sucking fluorescents, Saffron wondered if this could really be him, if it could be Markis. She couldn't hide from here, like she did at home when he came to mow. She tilted her head; the guy's rear-end was certainly correct. She pulled her winged cap low over her eyes and held her breath.

She crossed her arms in front of her and, as she did so, her knuckles barely grazed the Slim Jims display. It started to go over. She shrieked low and grabbed at the skimpy box, rescuing it just in time. During those moments, she never took her eyes from the driver. It dawned on her that she really couldn't handle seeing Markis face-to-face, if it actually was him, and considered bolting, running to the relative safety of the cooler under the guise of stocking milk. Then she realized that Coco had disappeared and was probably having a candy bar in the cooler and reading "People" under the guise of having bought them. Saffron stayed glued to the spot and frowned at the rider as he reached up with both hands to wiggle the helmet off his head.

It was Markis.

A rush of relief, of clean excitement, of vertigo, eddied and swirled within her, all the emotions pushing at the back of the other and threatening to erupt out of the top of her head. She turned to escape to the cooler, stopped herself, turned back to watch him come in. She stopped herself again, and decided to quickstep forward to stand behind the registers so she could hide behind the counter and restack the immaculately-shelved bags.

She didn't move.

He was a year behind her in school. He was going to be a senior this year. He was very popular and so nice to everyone. He was a soccer star, a basketball whiz, and the shining light of the baseball team. She had spoken to him once, in fourth grade, when they were picking teams in gym class. They had a combined class because, back then the classes were so small. He was a captain and he didn't pick her last. This had never happened to her before. Everyone took it for granted that when teams were picked she was left behind until the teacher sorted her to one unsmiling group and Bubble Butt Bernice to the other. Tico The Drooling Nose Miner, was even picked before the girls because he was at least a boy. But it was clear to all that Daffy Saffy and Bubble Butt Bernice were no use to anyone when it came to sports. Bubble Butt got in the way of balls and Saffron ran from them. When he chose her that day (and third pick, no less!), she thought her face would split from smiling. She had whispered thanks to him as she scuttled past to make her way to the back of the team. He had smiled too, patted her head, and said she was funny.

So that one time in gym class she had tried, just for him. She tried to catch the ball. And when she did, she was in awe of herself and in awe at the power of trying to excel at a game and conquering it. Realization came slowly through her haze of glory - that her teammates were swearing at her and the gym teacher was letting them. It was her cousin Mindy who pried the ball from her arms and hissed, "We're playing *dodge ball,* you moron." Then Mindy pushed Saffron in the chest, causing her to stumble and fall wobbly-limbed to her bony ass. Markis was cracking up as he pulled her to her feet. He kept telling her it was okay. But she was shaken and couldn't stop sniveling, so the teacher sent her to the nurse.

Over the years, Markis sometimes smiled at her in the halls. In her junior year, they had math together; he was brilliant, too. He'd smile and say, 'hi.' But she always looked away, embarrassed for him. She wanted him to know that he didn't have to do that - he didn't have to smile at her. She knew his friends didn't like her.

He carried his helmet under his arm as he came through the door, ting-a-ling, and squinted for a moment while he waited for his eyes to adjust from outside July-bright to inside-store fluorescents. Just before the door closed, something small and brown zoomed through to the outside, a bag of marshmallows tucked under its scaly armpit. Markis spied Saffron, not so well-concealed behind the Slim Jims. "Hi, Saffron." His voice was a little deep, but not too deep. It was full of humor, but not making fun, and it worked like a push to knock her out from behind the Slim Jims. She robot-walked the few steps and squared herself behind the register counter.

"Hi, Markis." she mumbled, then squatted down behind the counter and reached for the tower of perfectly-stacked brown paper bags. Suddenly, Markis's face appeared above her, which meant he was lying across the counter top.

"Whataya doin'?"

Saffron felt her face explode. She imagined his body stretched out on the counter, his jeans tight around his shapely rear-end, the front length of him pressed against the countertop... "I'm fixing these freakin' bags." Her teeth were clenched.

Markis smiled and backed off the counter. "Let me know how that goes for you," he called out as he walked toward the back of the store.

Saffron stayed where she was, swearing at herself under her breath. She heard the suck of a cooler door and next heard Markis moan, "Coco," in a bad ghosty voice, "where are youuuuuuuu. Come back to the land of the livingggggg."

Then Saffron heard Coco slam out of the cooler and come quick-clumping in her homemade shoes, high heels draped in a sheath of hot-pink feathers. "Little Dude! Where've you been? I haven't seen you in like, forever!" Two days was like, forever, to Coco. She gave Markis a quick hug and rumpled his hair. As they talked, they slowly made their way back to the register counter, she riding piggyback on him, her long taloned fingers gripping tight to his wide shoulders.

"I was with my mother's parents in New Mexico." He looked at Saffron. "I'm back for the rest of the summer."

Saffron snapped out of her daze and looked behind her. Was he telling *her* he'd be home for the rest of the summer? Or was he just letting Saffron know so she'd tell Audrey her mower was back? Or was he just saying in general that he'd be home the rest of the summer - was just looking in her direction because his bike was parked on the other side of the window behind her? She bent again behind the counter. There were bags to fix.

"Did you have a cool trip? Everything okay? Where's Saffron?" Coco strained to look over the counter.

"Yeah, the trip was great. Saffron's fixing bags."

Coco came behind the register counter. "Dude, those bags are already stacked and neat, okay? You need to stop fixing those bags. What is that, a nervous habit or something? Like a tic? Do you have OCD? Tourette's? My little cousin had scarlet fever, then got this tic for like, two years, scrunching her eyes all the time, but it went away. That was P.A.N.D.A.S. syndrome. You got something like that?"

Saffron gasped. She wanted to cry. She wanted to beat Coco about the head with Slim Jims. She wanted to disappear. She rose and placed both hands on either side of the register in front of her. Hanging on in quiet desperation, she said nothing. Something snickered. Saffron moved just her eyes to look down and around for it.

Markis watched Saffron look down and around for no reason. He smiled at her.

Coco was studying her. "Yeah, our girl Saffron is one nervous ninny."

Saffron's mouth dropped open as she stared at Coco. She didn't make a move or a sound as she wondered if she could lift the register and heft it at the other girl's face.

"What?" chirped Coco, all innocent. "So what, you're nervous; what's the big deal." She poked a red nail into her own chest. "I'm insane," now pointing at Markis, "and he's retarded. So what."

"You can't say, 'retarded' Coco, it's not PC." Markis wagged his finger at her.

"I didn't call a mentally challenged person retarded, Markis, I called *you* retarded."

Markis dipped his head demurely, "That's okay, then." He looked up at Saffron from under his lowered brow and winked. He crossed his arms across his wide chest, well defined under his thin, baby-blue t-shirt, and leaned his hip on the counter, perfectly at ease.

Saffron crossed her arms over her chest too, her back curving into a C, hair falling forward to cover her face.

Coco smiled, sly with dawning comprehension. "I told Saffron that she should hang with us."

Saffron perked up. *Markis* was the friend Coco hung out with? Absently, she uncrossed her arms and started running her fingers over the keypad on the register in anticipation of the rest of the conversation.

"That's why I came out to your fine establishment today, Mamas - to tell you it's time to start up the band."

Coco leaned on the counter on her pointy elbows and cradled her face in her hands. She looked at Saffron. "We've had a band going for awhile. Two years." She made a noise in her throat, a grunt. "We're pretty good. You should come check us out sometime."

Saffron didn't say anything.

Markis slapped the counter with both hands. "I'll take that as a yes, then," and he smiled widely as Saffron finally settled her startled wide eyes on him. "I'll also take this here chocolate milk, Ma'am."

As she took his money, his thumb grazed her palm. (Intentionally? Maybe not.) A smile forced its way from her insides where she couldn't trap it any longer. It was a genuine smile, the kind she seldom wore, it hung awkward on her lips and made the whole lower half of her face tremble with the primal force of it.

After he left, her smiled faded. Mumbling to Coco, who had started sweeping, that she'd be right back, Saffron went to the bathroom at the back of the store. As she waited for the light to flicker on in the small room, she braced herself on the small sink held to the wall by corroded, perspiring pipes. She checked her teeth, ran her tongue across them, checked her nostrils for any hangers-on, checked to see if there was anything on her face anywhere, checked to see if her nipples had been trying to bust through her apron, smelled her armpits and her long red hair to see if she stank (rightly assuming she stank like the store...a miasma of coffee, disinfectant, and deli), then dismissed this as okay since Coco probably smelled like store too and they probably canceled each other out, and maybe he wouldn't think anything of that. She sighed, her shoulders sagged in relief. Then she smiled. She smiled until her cheeks ached and did her work in peace.

Chapter 8

"Good morning, Sun Goddess."

Audrey yanked the coverlet from Saffron's face, causing a beam of sunshine to shoot straight through Saffron's left eye. She groaned and tunneled farther under her blanket. "I had a long night. Let me sleep in a little, would you?"

"Not today, miss. I need your help." Before she left the bedroom, Audrey turned, asked quietly, "Have you thought about what I said?"

Saffron stared at her mother. *She thinks you're crazy. She wants a shrink to peel it off you like an orange.* Her reply was almost incoherent. "Yes."

It had happened again, yesterday, when her mother picked her up at the end of her shift. Who the hell has such a crappy mother that they had that kind of talk with their kid at midnight? When she could not have possibly been any happier knowing Markis had come in the store, had smiled at her, and had invited her to hang out...here comes Audrey with her shrink talk. Again. Her mother had been trying to get her to go to regular shrink visits since the second year of cliff-walking. Sometimes, Audrey tried hard, and sometimes Saffron enjoyed a long, effortless hiatus from defending her privacy.

"I'll dig out the physician's directory. Why don't we try Boston? It'll be a beautiful ride and there are supposed to be good doctors there."

Saffron took her sweet time answering. The only sound in the room was the strange high-pitched squeals of two alpacas tussling and the tapping leaves in the apple tree just outside the window. Saffron brought her arms around herself, her shoulders rounded forward. This was entirely too humiliating. She wished her mother picked this morning to talk about sex or venereal disease...masturbation, for God's sake. Even that would have been better than this little chat.

"You don't have to feel ashamed, Saffron. Lots of people seek physicians when they are having trouble...inside. Like, troubling thoughts." She rubbed her palms down her embroidered skirt. "And you seem to be having more, trouble...."

Audrey lowered her head and frowned at the shirt in her hands; it was Saffron's favorite. There was a seam on the inside usually hidden from view. It was coming apart. Audrey wanted to mend it immediately. Today. Before it got worse. "I'm sorry I can't help you." She sighed. "Maybe if you tell someone else how you're feeling you'll find a way to...come around."

Saffron flushed bright red. Her ears rang. Now she felt ashamed *and* guilty. Her mother looked so beaten standing over there with her head hanging, playing with a loose seam in an old shirt. Why was her mother fidgeting with that shirt? Saffron didn't even like it. Audrey turned and left Saffron alone in the room.

Saffron checked herself out in her mirror. She was genuinely shocked at what she saw. She wondered why she was always taken by surprise at her image in pictures and her reflection in the mirror. She never ever looked like she thought she looked. She didn't know her eyes looked so sunken, that they were ringed in black.

She had been dreaming about Ny last night. Something about when people used horse-drawn carriages and wore big dresses fitted close to the neck and wrist. Something about him laughing and holding a woman in his arms in a carriage that bumped along cobbled streets. The streets were in a park. A park in winter. His face was flushed as his hands worked under a fur drawn over their knees. Her dress was up over her face, her bustle askew, and her feathered hat crushed as they fumbled wildly. Through a small window in the back, the Eiffel tower stood staunch and dark.

Saffron tried to stop the tremors in her gut that threatened to spread and vibrate throughout her whole body.

That day, she went mechanically about her business. When night fell, there was another dream. She was walking through the forest with a baby in her arms. Through the trees, she caught glimpses of the dark, pea-green. The wind was shrieking in her ears. She wore only a thin nightgown. Everywhere, there were thick shadows.

The baby was crying and her pupils were dilated as she stared into the darkest part of the wood.

Saffron came upon a puddle. Even though she didn't want to, she couldn't stop herself from bending over the water. She wanted to see her reflection. A raven screeched. Saffron looked up, then down again, as a hand shot out of the puddle, all slimy and gray. It snatched the baby from Saffron's weak grasp.

"No!" Saffron screamed as her knees buckled and forced her to the forest floor. She sat there crying while her mind told her to get up and do something about it. But, she would not get up. She was too afraid to move. She sat there and cried until the dream turned into another horrible scene.

This time she was at school. As usual, the kids were laughing at her. The school was dark and eerie, and the other kids didn't look quite human. Her cousin Mindy had some scales on her neck. One of Mindy's minions gimped oddly as she walked, as if she had talons. Her eyeballs were completely white. Another girl had tiny horns that were trying to break through her scalp; the skin there stretched white, waiting for the growth to split it. Blood ran down one side of her face.

The school looked ancient, decrepit. The cheap flooring was brown, cracked, and lifting. The floor itself was missing in some areas, and the holes led to complete black oblivion. The lockers looked punched and dented, and the doors were missing or hanging half off their hinges. There was dust, so much dust everywhere that Saffron began to choke on it. And there was dirt; she could feel the slime of it on her neck, see it brown and clinging to the walls and floor.

"Saffron!" It was Markis. He was at one end of the hall motioning for Saffron to come to him. "Run, Saffron! Run! I can help you!" She could hardly see him in the dim light of her dream. She started toward him, but the sludge of the dream bogged her down. All of her steps were in extreme slow motion. Tears streamed down her cheeks as she cried out, "I can't. I just can't."

"C'mon Saffron. Hurry!"

She tried and tried, but she felt so tired. Then all at once, she was by Markis's side and he was hugging her and comforting her. He cradled the base of her skull in his palm and told her it would be all right. He was going to kiss her. She could tell. He closed his eyes and slowly moved toward her slightly-parted, waiting lips. But there was no kiss. He savagely grabbed her neck. With his head, he shoved her head aside so he could get at her artery. He bit down into her flesh. To Saffron, it felt like two needles were piercing her skin and sliding into the muscles of her neck. She began to scream and scream and scream. Markis threw his head back, laughed, and then howled as blood dripped off his fangs and chin.

The vision began to dim and blur. Colors melded together like hot wax in a kettle. She heard Ny calling her. He seemed to be very far away. No matter which direction Saffron looked, all was pitch black.

She held her hand in front of her eyes and could not see it.

"Ny?" In her dream, she suddenly realized she was dreaming. She told herself she had nothing to fear. She told herself this wasn't real. Ny's calls sounded closer. Saffron felt her heart swell and she thought it might burst. She loved Ny. With every ounce of her soul, she loved Ny. With complete clarity, she realized she always had. She could feel him around her, could sense him in her heart, mind, and body. She could smell him now, fresh water and sweat, his freshly-washed hair. She didn't remember the women from her dreams. She didn't remember herself. "Ny?"

"I am here, Saffron. Come to me. Come to me over here."

Through a shimmering haze, she saw him. He was leaning on a cherry tree. It was in full bloom and in the middle of a meticulous Japanese garden. A fountain bubbled behind him; the water ran down to a clear pool. Small birds flitted in and out of the tree. Baby rabbits cropped grass at his feet. His smile was sultry, wicked. He winked at her and waved her over. He disappeared behind the tree.

She ran to him, as fast as she could. When she arrived, she was breathless. He wasn't there. She frowned and went to the other side of the tree. He wasn't there. "Ny?"

"I am here, Saffron. Do not keep me waiting! I want you with me."

He was several yards away, sitting in a field of daisies. The field grew to the edge of the sea where the sun hung like a white ball. His black, wavy hair glistened and his blue eyes shone. He had no shirt. The muscles in his neck and shoulders and chest were taut and gleaming as he sat straight and strong like a yogi.

"Please Saffron, come to me." He lay back among the flowers and vanished.

She ran so fast that her feet left the ground. She began to fly over the field. He was nowhere to be found, but below her she saw a woman with long hair. The world turned gray. She didn't know if she was the woman below or if it was someone else; the big hair matched.

"Saffron, I need you. I am waiting. It hurts." But where was he?

Saffron floated down into the middle of a desert. It was night. The moon was full. Except for the towering, night-blooming cactus on her right, she was completely alone. She knew there was no one around, not for thousands of miles. He had left her.

"Ny!" she screamed so loud her voice cracked. A gust of wind blasted past, followed by stillness so complete Saffron felt the entire world would shatter were she to expel her breath.

She woke up sobbing. Indistinct impressions of the dream lay in her mind like dirty rags. She lay sprawled against her locked bedroom door. She started to whisper, "Don't come back for me. I don't like this. I can't take it. Don't come back for me. I don't like this. I can't take it." She whispered those words over and over again, wringing her hands like a frightened child, her eyes darting and searching the dark room without seeing.

Outside, there were the strangled screams of the woman as she bounced off the cliff on her way to the sea.

Chapter 9

The dreams increased in number and in intensity throughout the rest of the summer. She didn't have to wait for the full moon anymore to dread the pain of them. They were with her every night, locked in her room with her. Saffron was okay with the bolt lock. She wanted the lock to keep her in, but begged her mother and Derek to respect her privacy and sleep in their rooms. When the moon wasn't full, they acquiesced. But when the moon was full, and her nights were a full-out rampage where she went raging about her room, screaming and tearing at the drapes, they insisted someone stay with her to keep her from hurting herself.

The dreams left her weak during the day. Sometimes, she was so tired the next morning she'd slur her words just to force out a sentence. She tried not to talk to anyone.

She fell asleep one afternoon, intending to take just a little nap before her shift. Another dream slithered into her mind like a snake into a hole. Ny was teasing her. She was watching him with wide eyes, actually salivating in her dream as if he was some kind of roast and she was a starving creature. With the dream came the pressing emotions she never experienced in daylight, the unearthly need and indescribable want. The intensity of the visions woke her twice but she never fully came to. She just sat up and cried a little, then fell back into a dead sleep, too far gone for the dreams to touch her. She woke up hours later, late for work.

She didn't eat and didn't shower. When her mother dropped her off at work, she showed up with dark circles under her eyes and frizzy unkempt hair. For reasons unknown, Bea was still at the store, nosing into some paperwork while Coco fumed, arms across her chest, in the back by the coffee pots. Bea lowered her brow at Saffron. Saffron stared back, unresponsive to Marlboro-Teeth's hostility.

On the ride over, Audrey had produced names and addresses of more doctors for Saffron to meet. With her eyes locked on the yellow line, Audrey missed how Saffron clawed at her temples and ground her teeth. Saffron had "considered" hundreds of doctors since she was twelve and had met seven, complaining to her mother after the torturous hour with each one. She was adamant; those doctors with their fish-eyed stares and monotone voices wouldn't help her at all. The other doctors, the overexuberant ones who patted you repeatedly and held you in a bug-eyed grip, and said things like, "let's talk about our truths," were even worse. Saffron thought that a doctor who couldn't have a conversation with a perspective patient without staccato blinking and stopping for breath every time she spoke in her high-pitched voice, then the doctor should get a doctor.

Audrey thought it was important that Saffron feel comfortable with the therapist she was to splay out her inner most feelings to. So, Audrey didn't push any one of the professionals on her daughter, but hoped that soon, Saffron would find someone with whom she felt comfortable.

Saffron suddenly realized there was a little blue thing on her shoulder, like a hairless squirrel. It wanted to dig its paw in her ear. She slapped at it feebly, but could never connect with its clingy little body. It used her shirt and jeans as a cat uses a scratching post to scurry down her body and lope away across the dirty linoleum.

"What is *wrong* with you?" Bea stopped fiddling with her papers. They were the lottery totals, and they probably weren't working out, or Bea, as head clerk, wouldn't have been called in. Now, because someone on first shift couldn't add, Bea was fast becoming Coco and Saffron's problem. Bea's right hand was caught in midair, holding a pen above the clipboard.

"Okay." Saffron waved her hand in dismissal. One of her knees was trying to give out so she lifted her leg to give it a good shake. She had no idea what Bea just said. "I..." And here she swayed, just a little, like a snake in a charmer's basket. "I gotta do the coffee." Saffron pointed one twitchy finger at the condom aisle, her lips as slack as a stroke victim's.

Bea watched Saffron swaying, had watched her slap at her ear for no good reason, and watched her shake her leg like a peeing dog. Her lips pursed over her Marlboro teeth. "If you're on drugs or somethin' you can just go home. Now!"

"Hey!" Coco raced forward on her stick legs and homemade boots. "What the frick, Bea? You can't send her home. You don't own this place. Just finish doing whatever you're doing and go home so we can do our jobs."

"You can't talk to me like that! I'm senior clerk!"

Coco's mouth dropped open. Her eyes blazed with 'you got it coming.' "Yeah, Bea, well, that's a title he only yells out when he's orgazmasizing. His wife hasn't officially given you that title, now, has she? Or are you screwing her too?"

Bea sucked in a strangled breath and her splayed fingers slapped her chest, causing her nametag to pop off.

Saffron watched the exchange without flinching, without ducking down to straighten the perfectly piled brown paper bags. A bit of drool formed under her tongue and with sloth-like reflexes, she finally remembered to shut her lips and swallow just before it spilled out.

Bea's eyes filled with tears. She grabbed her home party knock-off purse and ran out of the store, the lottery papers first flying up, then floating down to the floor, twirling and lilting like white leaves. Coco stalked to the cooler. Saffron loitered behind the registers.

When Saffron's cousin Mindy came into the store, Coco and Saffron were both leaning on the counter between the dual registers. The cereal shelf was dusty and the coffee thermoses were running low or empty.

"You look like a freak." Mindy always knew just what to say.

Coco's eyes slid down Mindy's fitted cashmere coat which was opened to show a leather miniskirt and thigh-high Italian boots. Mindy wouldn't even look at Coco. Saffron crushed her face in her hands. "Hi, Mindy. What's up?"

"Do you want to go to the movies with us tomorrow night or what?"

Saffron winced as she felt Coco's stiletto heel dig not so lightly into the toe of her Chinese slippers. To Mindy, on the other side of the counter, it appeared that Coco had never moved. Saffron felt a long-distance relief that Coco wasn't mouthing off for once.

"I mean, like, you haven't even seen your friends since you graduated."

Coco snorted. "Yeah, okay. Who are your friends, Saffron, hmmm?"

And here we go. Saffron thought about crouching down to stack the brown paper bags. Instead, she stared at the dirty Black Chicken floor and dreamed of curling up on it, covering herself with the lottery papers that they hadn't picked up.

Mindy leveled eyes on Coco for the first time. She spoke to Coco's flat chest, "Ah, I don't think you know them."

Coco stood up straight and tall, thanks to her stilettos. "Ah, yeah, *Mindy,* I think I do. We went to the same hick school remember? Remember there was like, ten people in each graduating class?"

Mindy expelled a short, forced breath, almost a cough, and refused to look at Coco again.

A level of discomfort started to course through Saffron's sluggish blood, just enough to wake her. She wanted Mindy out. "Mindy, can you just call me tomorrow? I'll go. Okay?"

Mindy turned on her heel, "Whatever," and strutted out.

"Do you *really* still hang around with them, Saffron?" Coco looked down at Saffron as if contemplating a sun-sat banana peel.

"No. I haven't seen any of her friends since we graduated and I haven't seen Mindy since a family Fourth of July party."

Coco snapped her gum. "She wants something from you."

"Nah, she's just like that. Sometimes she wants to do something together. She might seem snobby but it's just an act. She likes me."

Coco looked straight ahead, arched one brow. Her lips pouted way out into a feigned, "Oooooh." She patted Saffron's back. "C'mon, come with me, you're killing me standing there like that." They went into the back where the loud machines and boxes of surplus goods were kept. Coco took an X-acto blade and sliced at the tape on the seams of some large, empty boxes so she could lift their flaps and press the cardboard flat. Saffron stood swaying, watching her, until Coco took Saffron by her elbows and made her sit down on an overturned bucket. Then Coco took Saffron's sweater, rolled it up, and placed it on one end of the flat boxes that she had stacked. She left, then came back with her own long sweater jacket. "Here," she guided Saffron by the elbow one more time, helped Saffron lower herself to the makeshift bed. "I've never in my life seen anyone need sleep like you do. What's going on with you?"

Saffron smiled with her eyes closed as Coco covered her with her sweater. "I'm watching a fairy have hot, sweaty sex every night. Well, only most nights. He's making me insane."

"What do you mean a *fairy*? You mean, like, a gay guy? That guy that lives in your house? Oh, man, what are you talking about? You need someone to take care of him? What else is he makin' you do?"

"Oh, he doesn't make me do anything. It's all me. It's all me." She wagged her head with her eyes still closed.

Coco crooked one finger and removed a chunk of oily hair from across Saffron's eyelids. "Well, tell him to go do it somewhere else; you're starting to look like a zombie."

"...He still has time for me...can you imagine?" Saffron was quiet after that and soon started to snore.

Coco tucked the sweater in around Saffron's shoulders. "I could have sworn you were a virgin, in body and mind," she muttered as she got up and quickly made her way to the front of the store as the bell ting-a-linged.

It was Markis. He was smiling, expectant, and looking around. Coco came to the register counter and drummed her long nails on the laminate. Markis's eyes kept searching.

He made Coco smile too. "She's in the back, sleeping."

"What?" he laughed.

"It's not funny. She's so tired she's a little mental."

Markis looked toward the back of the store. "Can I see her?"

"I'm not her dang keeper; do whatever the hell you want," the smile still in her eyes.

Markis waited for the rotating camera to scan the other corner of the store, then slipped behind the counter and trotted toward the back.

Coco didn't follow. As he strolled past, she let him know, "She's goin' to the movies tomorrow with her bitch cousin and her bitch cousin's friends."

Markis saluted her. "Good work. I'll see you Saturday, right?"

"Yup."

He jerked his head toward the back of the store. "She workin' Saturday?"

"Nope, I make sure we work all our shifts together. She's a good worker, a good person. I'll make sure she shows up Saturday night, too, even if I have to put her in my trunk."

"Oh, Coco, you'd do that? For me?" He fast-blinked his eyes. "Shucks, you're like, wicked sweet, and groovy, and awesome."

She slapped his shoulder. "Will you go already?" She frowned toward the back of the store. *Having sex with a fairy.* She wondered if she should tell Markis. He *was* her friend. She didn't really know Saffron, not really, just had the feeling she was cool. But this, watching the gay guy have sex thing, shouldn't Markis know about it? What if they both got into something they didn't want to with this girl? Maybe none of it was a big deal. Then again, Saffron *was* a whole lotta weird. Did it matter?

Markis was already in back. He tiptoed to the edge of Saffron's cardboard bed and smiled down at all of the red hair haloed around her head. He reached out, stopped, and brought his hand back by his side. He squatted down beside her. He looked at her long and hard, from her hair and the fading bruise on her forehead, to her collarbone just under the stretched neck of her floral tank. He rolled his eyes over her breasts, down the line of her thighs, to her painted toes. Her roughed-up Chinese slippers had been kicked off to the side. He reached out again, his fingertips almost to her hair, then shook his head, retracted his itchy fingers and smiled. "Pretty soon." he whispered. Then he got up and left.

The next morning, in her own bed, Saffron blinked her dry eyes several times. She turned her stiff neck to look out the window and realized by the way the sun hung over the pines that it was already around noon.

A bureau drawer slid wood against wood and immediately the hairs on the back of her neck spiked to attention. What in the world was in her room now? Saffron dreaded looking over the top of her blanket. To her great relief and annoyance, she found her mother was in her room, putting away laundry. Saffron reminded herself that she really needed to take over that chore completely to keep her mother out of her room.

Saffron knew she had just been dreaming, probably even up to the point when she woke up, about something particularly nasty. Something she had enjoyed immensely but couldn't remember what right now. What if her mother heard her talking, or worse yet, moaning? It was way too embarrassing. Saffron fake-yawned and fake-stretched. "I'm going to the movies with Mindy tonight."

"Wow!" Audrey stopped and turned around with socks in her fist. She didn't restrain her enthusiasm at all. "You'll have to tell me all about it when you get back. I'm so happy you're spending time with some friends. It'll be so much fun!"

Saffron nodded as she unconsciously kneaded her hair, causing the big red mess of it to knot further. "It'll be great."

Audrey clapped her hands and walked over to pat Saffron's knee under the blanket. "Go get ready for your movie. It's going to take you three hours to comb out that head."

Saffron realized what she was doing and lowered her hands to her lap.

Audrey tweaked Saffron's nose. "I'm making chicken pot pie from scratch. I'll go start on it."

Saffron stared at the ceiling for a little bit, her hand back in her hair, twirling her fingers around her knots until they tripled and quadrupled. Finally, she got up, lurched out into the hall and headed for the bathroom.

The phone rang with a screech that rebounded off the high ceilings of the farmhouse, making her jump. They kept the ringer on high so they could hear the phone over the loud music any one of them might be playing at any time. Saffron stopped halfway to the bathroom when her mother called out, "Saffron, it's for you."

"I'll get it in my room." Saffron yelled down the stairs, then turned around and lurched back in the opposite direction. The old phone her mother had put in her room eight years ago was dusty with nonuse.

"Hello?"

"Can you like, (snort) can your *mother*, like, pick us up? Eve lost her license, Tamara crashed her ride last week, and Rochelle is still high from last night, so we need a ride. You need to go get your license."

So that was what Mindy wanted. And hadn't Saffron known that? Why had she defended Mindy to Coco? "Yeah, my mom can give us a ride." She looked at her mirror, where she found herself glaring back at herself.

"Make sure you get here by seven – don't be late." Saffron could hear the other girls laughing and screaming in the background. Mindy hung up.

Saffron took a shower and began to dress for her big night out. She breathed a long, heavy sigh. She sat down in front of the elaborate boudoir mirror, a heavy and ornate piece that Audrey and Derek had purchased at an antique store and lovingly refurbished for her last Christmas. Obviously, they had hoped she'd get a life and primp in front of it. It took Saffron forever to rip the knots out of her hair - no conditioner could conquer them - then another half hour drying her hair with a big round brush. When it was mostly dry, she pulled the long, unheeding tresses back and secured her hair at the nape of her neck with a tortoise-shell clip. One corkscrew at her temple popped out sideways.

The attack began during dinner. She didn't say anything to her mother or Derek. Her stomach twisted and pulled, twisted and pulled, till a sheen of sweat coated her forehead. And the burning! She wanted to rip her gut out and douse it in ice water. In half an hour she was riding high on the jitters. She had had plenty of anxiety attacks before to know what was happening to her. And always, it took just the smallest thing to set her off. She wasn't really panicking over the fact that her hair was atrocious. In fact, she had no idea why she was panicking. All she knew was she did not want to go out...not tonight. She began to concoct lies in her head, stories to tell Mindy and her friends, fibs to feed her mother - she was sick, she was tired, she forgot she had to work tonight. Anything to get out of this stupid girls-night-out-thing.

She trudged up to her vanity and sat down hard, slumped and dejected. She had some ideas earlier that afternoon about wearing a moss-green sweater, her favorite. It was a tunic with capped sleeves, which she tied off with a sequined, eggplant-purple kimono sash. Now that the time to leave was approaching, she wondered what in the world she had been thinking. Of course she wasn't going to wear such a color and combination. Mindy had always told her she dressed like a reject.

Saffron settled on an old high school standby - a black, fitted t-shirt and black cargo pants. She smoothed some lipgloss on her trembling lips, her jelly arms taking ten times the usual effort to do the small task. She inspected herself in the mirror and decided her lips looked greasy. She wiped off the lipgloss with her forearm. She sat for a beat staring glumly at her reflection, then picked up the tube of lipgloss and put it in her pants pocket. She took it out and slapped it back on the vanity. As she stood, she grabbed for the tube of ChapStick that lay on her dresser. She wouldn't take the gloss. She'd look stupid putting on makeup in public, she knew, better to reapply ChapStick; at least it was practical. Saffron now contemplated the concealing powder that she had fished out from her mother's stash. *Just a little,* she thought, *try and cover those freakin' rings under your eyes. You look like a raccoon.* The makeup wasn't very effective. Of course, this had much to do with the fact that she didn't know how to apply it. She wiped the powder off with a tissue and stared at herself again. "Man, Saffron, you have got to get some sleep," she breathed the words out. *Just tell them you're sick. Yeah, and how many times have you used that excuse? Do you want them to look at you one more time like that? Like you're the most pitiful moron on earth? Can you even stand it one more time? No.*

She decided the hairdo wouldn't do, too teachery or maybe too lawyer-like. But that wasn't it either. Something about the way she had raked her hair up in back was unsettling to her, though she couldn't imagine why. But it started her thinking about Ny. Then she started thinking about Li and how Li would not want her going out tonight. And wasn't this, in the end, the very reason why she was forcing herself to go? Just so Li wouldn't get her way? Was all of this tension worth that? Yes.

Why?

Quickly, Saffron let her hair fall free, and as soon as it curtained her neck and back, she felt somewhat better. She tried six other styles before finally settling on loose and flowing with just a tiny section pulled across her forehead and held fast with a tiny glitter clip. She crossed the room to the door, then ran back in front of the mirror and pulled some hair forward to cover the clip. It was too shiny. She tripped downstairs, grabbed her jacket off the newel post, crossed the hall, and went out onto the farmer's porch where Audrey and Derek were stringing up grapevine wreaths decorated with tiny pumpkins and ivy. Audrey stopped moving when she laid eyes on Saffron's whitewashed face almost hidden within the puff of her great red hair. The hair looked like it had suffered severe abuse.

She wanted to reach out to Saffron and hold her like she did when Saffron was little. But the child Saffron was always rigid in her embraces; this new woman before her seemed even less receptive. Saffron looked more stricken than an innocent in the guillotine. So Audrey didn't move toward Saffron, instead she leaned her weight on the support beam of the farmer's porch and let Derek have at her.

"Oh, good. The fricken commandant is back." Big, hairy Derek chewed his gum with his mouth open.

Saffron crossed her arms over her chest and stuck out her tongue out at him.

"Honestly, what happened? You were doing better for a bit. So much flair, such pissass! Now who the frick stands before me in all her midnight, bottom-of-the-pond, inside-the-gut-of-a-fish, blackness and gloom? Hm?"

"Mom, control your boyfriend."

"I don't know, Saffron...*are* you okay? You look...," Audrey indicated her own face with a flutter of fingers but said nothing more.

Figures, Saffron thought. All they could do on "the big night out" was to remind her that she looked like a wreck. When did mothers stop inspecting their daughters, anyway? When did mothers stop giving unwanted commentary about holes in jeans and bad bras? Too much makeup, bad makeup choices. This should be more, that should be less. If Saffron could have cried, she would have. All she could do was quake, her eyes bugging out like a marmoset's.

She could feel it coming, something coming. A freight train with no brakes, screaming toward her through the black, a smile on its grilled lips, ready to smash into her and run her through three miles of night, stuck like a bug to its cold, steel nose.

Out of the corner of her eye, Saffron saw an old man wearing overalls leaning on the rail at the other end of the porch. Through the man, Saffron saw the last of the sun as it sank into the ocean. She rolled her eyes.

"Let's just go, Mom, okay? Time ta hit the open trail!"

Derek swore as he stuck himself with a pushpin meant for the vine.

The old man crossed his boots at the ankle and smiled at her. Saffron curtsied and turned away from him, Derek, and her mother. She headed toward Audrey's Rav4, hysterical laughter bubbling up from her throat and blowing out like a plume on the chilly autumn air. She trotted her imaginary horse across the gravel drive and beneath the orange-leafed maples.

The garden gnome darted out from under the farmer's porch, ran between her legs, and howled with glee as Saffron stumbled and struggled to keep herself from smashing face-first onto the gravel and first-fallen leaves.

Audrey, who was watching Saffron's every move, gasped as Saffron suddenly stopped her horse play and tripped for no reason across the driveway. "OhmyGod," Audrey muttered, "I can't take this."

"Excuse me, sorry to interrupt..."

Saffron had one foot in her mother's car when she froze and turned toward the voice. It was a deep voice and one she had never heard before. Audrey and Derek stopped short too, he with his hands in the bag of tiny pumpkins and she with her hands on her hips.

"Hi, hello..." The man was coming toward them from out of the woods, their woods. He must have been six feet tall, with wide, wide shoulders, messy, dark hair and a five o'clock shadow that begged to be shorn. He carried a walking stick as he made his way toward them.

Saffron looked quickly to her mother, and then to Derek, who made no move. When the man got closer, Saffron gasped. First, his clothes were *so* weird. His pants looked like they were cut from some castle's dark tapestry, and his black top was long-sleeved, with no visible seams, stitching, or weave; like a sweater but not. It had a heavy drape and looked like alien sportswear. They couldn't accuse him of being some high-fashion European with a thousand-dollar ensemble because the clothes were clearly well-worn and faded, even tattered around the ankles. High-Fashion Europeans wouldn't wear *worn* thousand-dollar outfits.

But what she saw in his eyes made her clutch the car door for balance. As he walked up to Audrey he gave Saffron a good, long look; and in his eyes (they were light-green turquoise with a star of bronze shooting out from the black center), she saw recognition. Her bottom lip went slack.

"So sorry to trouble you. I'm searching for the Bucknell family. I heard they live here in this house?" He looked at Saffron again, as if he couldn't stop, while he waited for Audrey to reply.

Saffron turned away and fell into the passenger seat, shutting the door like a gunshot in the crisp, peaceful, golden afternoon.

"Bucknell?" Audrey's murmur was slow and troubled. "John Bucknell built this house...in 1860..."

The man frowned. He sighed. He looked down at the ground and slid his hands into his pouchy pockets. The walking stick rested in the crook of his right arm. He looked up quickly and grinned. "I guess I'm a little late, then. I'll try back later."

Now Audrey eyed Derek, and like a shot, he was by her side. "Is there anything else we can help you with?" Derek was all man, ready to kill for his wife and cub. (Since it looked like he wasn't about to get a date.)

"No, no." The man paused, looked up blankly at an oak tree. "Thank you! I'll be on my way, now." His head turned slightly in Saffron's direction but he never actually looked at her again. He started down the gravel drive toward the main road. Halfway down, he spun around and gave a little wave. Then, one hand in one weird pocket, the other on the walking stick, he hiked off.

Audrey and Derek never moved as they watched him walk all the way down the drive and out of sight. Saffron stared too, out the back window of the Rav4, biting her bottom lip.

"Is there some bylaw that says, 'You can trespass on anyone's land if you're hot.'?" Derek fanned his face.

Audrey nodded. "Do you think he got separated from his biking group? They're always on this road."

Derek scoffed, "Audrey, he didn't have a bike. And what was that stick; is he Jolly Old St. Nick?"

"Well, I don't know. What the hell was he doing here? What the hell was that all about?"

"I'll tell you what it was about. It's time for a glass of wine. I'll feed the animals; you get her to the bitches three. I'll guard the house in case Hot n' Crazy returns."

Audrey ribbed him with her elbow. "Don't call her friends that. They're young; they'll change."

Derek rolled his eyes. "Oh, spare me, Audrey."

"And don't protect the house in your birthday suit, armed with a bottle of Mumm." Saffron was in the car, checking her teeth in the rearview mirror. Audrey watched her. "If he comes back, it won't be for you."

When Audrey sat in the driver's seat she turned to Saffron. "Did you recognize him?"

Saffron shook her head, no.

"Huh. That was the strangest damned thing. He recognized you." Audrey's words untethered Saffron. And, while she wanted to float blissfully in that stratosphere forever, she hummed tunelessly to bring herself back to the uncomfortable place and time she was used to.

Audrey and Saffron picked up Mindy and Co. The other girls chattered nonstop, never saying a word to Saffron until they got to the movie theater. Audrey gave Saffron her cell phone and told her to text when they were ready to be picked up. Saffron frowned at the phone. Audrey sighed, put the car in park, and explained to Saffron how to use the phone. The other had girls snickered and walked off. Audrey gave Saffron a minty kiss on the cheek and drove away. If Audrey had noticed the pot stink and alcohol breath of "the girls," she said nothing.

Saffron slouched through the double glass doors of the theater and quick-scanned the lobby. Her face reddened every time she made eye contact with strangers, dead and alive, until finally, she found the group of girls. They were flipping their hair, talking animatedly, and coughing out greatly exaggerated laughs. To Saffron, they seemed so free and easy. They also seemed to be unaware of their actions, their bodies, and the attention they were gathering. Saffron ground her teeth.

"Saffron, are you really friends with those cackling hens?"

Saffron startled like a baby bird and turned around. She was face-to-face with Markis. She crossed her arms across her chest. He smiled at her encouragingly.

"Actually, I babysit them. This is our Friday night outing." She nodded and chewed on her bottom lip. She was trying to keep herself from grinning like a fool, her first genuine smile of the day, of the week. She felt her mind claw through the fog of sleep deprivation and carry her to a place where she could feel again - feel him warming the center of her.

She was so glad she didn't wear her mossy-green sweater tonight. It was too old-looking anyway, like she was thirty or something. But what about her ass? These were the pants that gave her wide-ass. But she had no choice! The other black pants, the jeans, rode so low they showed her coin slot when she bent over, admittedly trendy right now, but not her thing. She seized up, there was something else...she hadn't checked her breath before she left the house. Sure, she had brushed, flossed, used Listerine to kill the germs, and Scope to kill the Listerine, Plax, and her electric tongue-brusher. She had taken one last look/see in the rearview mirror, but she hadn't actually checked her breath. She took a step back from Markis.

He was still smiling. And looking good, too, wearing a t-shirt and jeans. He was in great shape, his new thing was mountain bike racing, and Saffron ached to just reach forward and manhandle him. She realized she probably looked a mite maniacal at the moment and tried in vain to tone her smile down.

"What are you and the kids going to see?"

Her cheeks burned scarlet as she answered in a mumble. Markis bent forward to catch the last of it. He frowned and said, "I wouldn't imagine that would be your kind of movie."

Heat prickled under her black t-shirt and she knew in a minute it would make her face look splotchy. He *imagined* about her? Markis Bryant *imagined* about her? She wanted to cry. She wanted to thank him and bring him gifts. While she hyperventilated, she caught a whiff of him, one of those water scents. Like "Bubbling Water" or "Man Water" or "Ravaged Ocean Man." Nothing in the world would ever smell better to her than this moment of cheap cologne, musky theatre carpet, and modified popcorn chemical number 5 as the scents mingled and rhapsodized her senses. She looked around to see if anyone saw them standing together. If anyone saw *him* talking to *her*.

Now, in a higher-pitched, more-confident mumble, she said, "I don't really want to see it, but I'm with them." She thumbed the cackling horde. "They're looking for sex and violence." Her throat erupted on 'violence' when she realized she had just said "sex." To Markis. *Oh, my God, you idiot - don't say sex!*

He leaned forward again, his manner intense, his voice husky, "What are *you* looking for?"

Saffron leaned back and made a noise somewhere between a bark and a hiccup. She turned red all over again and realized that the short window of opportunity that would have allowed her to say something cool had closed with a bang. Since there was silence between them, her mouth began working but no sound came. And so easily, he smiled again, his eyes bright and intense moving over her face.

A man and woman were walking toward Markis. The man was tall, burly. He had thick, orange hair and a beard, as if he drank much Guinness and said things like "lass," and "bairn." The woman at his side could not have been more opposite. She was small and sinewy, with long raven-black hair and dark eyes. Her nose was broad and prominent. Her hair was braided into one long plank which trailed down her back, almost reaching her bottom. She held the man's hand. Saffron backed off from Markis a little more. The big man and little woman smiled at her. The woman held Saffron with her eyes longer than was comfortable. The woman's eyes grew solemn. Saffron looked down at her shoes. The two older people turned to Markis.

"Who's your friend?" The man threw some popcorn at his mouth and caught some of it.

Markis moved closer to Saffron and touched her arm. "This is Saffron. Saffron, this is my mom and dad. We're going to go see *The Last Planet*." He watched people file into the separate theater doors. "Looks like everyone but you and the hens are going to see it."

Saffron nodded glumly.

"What are you going to see, Saffron?" Markis's father could sure chomp a lot of popcorn.

"*Psycho Carnage 2*." Saffron admitted shamefully.

Markis's parents pulled their heads back at the same time and winced.

"Dad, don't you think Saffron should come with us instead and see a movie that's actually going to be cool?"

Markis's mother laughed. "I would definitely come with us instead, unless your friends would miss you." Her voice was soft.

Saffron looked toward the corner where "her friends" had just been squawking and realized that the theatre was now quiet save for the low murmurs of the other patrons. There was no longer any cacophony from the Mindy-girls; they simply weren't there. They had left her behind. Not one of them, not even Mindy, had come to tell Saffron that they were going into the movie.

Saffron stiffened with the knowledge that she was completely alone in a room full of strangers. She looked at Markis, her eyes wide and unblinking. When she realized her mouth was hanging open and she most probably looked like a close cousin to the village idiot, she slammed her lips closed and forced a smile.

"I'd love to go see *The Last Planet* with you guys. I just have to go buy my ticket." Saffron was straining to hold on to a cool demeanor. Inside, she was raging.

"Mom, Dad, I'll go with Saffron to get her ticket. We'll be right back." He turned to Saffron, placed his hot palm into the small of her back, and guided her to the ticket counter.

Saffron could hardly believe this was happening! She thought she might be in a dream, just not her usual crappy dreams. This was a soft dream filled with warmth, wonder, and a positive energy that cradled her. She'd believe in fairies and vampires before she would have ever believed that someone like Markis, that Markis, would invite her to watch a movie with him! And OMG - he was touching her back!

Wait. Did his fingertips feel the fatty flesh where her pants pulled into her hips? She pulled herself up ramrod-straight as she laid her money on the counter for the ticket. Somewhere along the way, from the ticket counter to the ticket line, his hand had dropped. *So yeah, he felt you, fatty. Or was it your bones? Yeah, he felt you, boney.*

But what if there's chicken stuck in my teeth? What if there's something in my nose, just hanging there? I should have had mac and cheese for dinner. Yeah, right - with all of those carbs I could just stick a beach ball under my shirt; why wait for the fat to accumulate?

She blocked out the voices of the relaxed moviegoers that surrounded her while she rummaged in her tiny backpack for a tissue and a mirror.

Gum, too. Look for gum! Your breath probably smells like a camel's ass! Did you shave your legs? Make sure your pants don't ride up at any point while you're in the light, just in case...

She was completely oblivious to the buzz that had started up ahead, and was working its way toward the back of the line where she waited with Markis and his parents. Married women took a look and raised their eyebrows in pleasant surprise. They gave their husbands devilish grins. Husbands rolled their eyes *big deal,* and teenage boys were sneering. They didn't like the view and some of them actually moved their bodies in front of their dates as if shielding their territory.

Just in front of Saffron, gushes of delight bubbled from a group of fifteen-year-old girls. One girl craned her neck to look over the crowd and swayed as she came back to her heels. She whipped around to face her friends. Her jaw dropped in mock disbelief as she pretended to faint.

"Oh. My. God! He is Totally Hot!"

"I have found the man that is going to make me a woman," this from a girl no more than fourteen, sporting a constellation of pimples and enough brace-work to build a ten-speed.

"No way girl; he's mine!"

The banter went on. The exchanges became louder, and soon enough almost every female in line, young and old. was infecting each other with excited whispers and small shrieks.

Markis cast his father a look that said, "Oh, please," and fluttered his eyelashes.

Markis's father grunted, smiled with one corner of his mouth. "Who's up there, the goddamn Beatles?"

"Yeah, Dad, if it was 1964."

Saffron, existing in some obscure inner universe, dug harder in her purse. She grunted in dismay when she was only able to come up with an old, stale stick of gum and half a tissue. Could she clean her nose with such a little thing? *Not MY honker*, she sighed. She stared blindly at the back of the girl in front of her and concentrated. *No! Search harder! There must be a whole tissue in there somewhere!*

"Do you think he'll think *I'm* cute or is my butt too big?" Markis looked at his father with his most serious face.

"I don't know Markis, you're kind of lacking, you know...." His father held his hands in front of his chest and fluffed the air with them.

"Stop that! Honestly, you can be so vulgar sometimes," Markis's mother hissed. She nodded curtly at Saffron. "Remember, we are with a new friend tonight."

But Saffron could not have been more unaware. With eyebrows knit and cheeks fevered, she dove into the leather bag for the third time. She had dropped her ticket inside and she needed to fish it out.

The girls in front of them finally arrived at their personal, temporary Nirvana - the cause of the excitement, the featured act of the evening - the ticket-tear boy. He smiled majestically upon them, perfectly aware of his Godlike aura.

"Well, damn," Markis's father *was* impressed, "He's very pretty."

He was gorgeous. That, no one on earth could deny. None of the guys in line tried to deny it. They just looked away, very disgruntled.

Sensuality rolled off him as he kept up the banter with the girls. His voice was hypnotizing; it came in waves, washing over the girls until they quieted. He wasn't that tall, but his manner and the way he held himself made him appear much bigger. His skin was the color of coffee made light with a generous amount of cream. It was smooth and flawless. But it was his lips that the girls locked on, feasted on. They were so incredibly full.

As he spoke to the girls, he gestured with his hands. Sometimes he dipped his chin into his chest and tugged on his earlobe as if bashful at the praise he was receiving from his new fans. When he smiled, which was often, he did so without ever parting his soft lips. He had a kind word for all and often spoke in hushed tones as if to say, "Come closer, I have a secret, I can only confide in you."

"You should be in movies," gushed one of the girls as the others nodded in agreement.

"Why be in movies when I can go to the movies every night and be surrounded by such beautiful women?"

"Jaysus Christ," muttered Markis's father with one raised eyebrow as he scratched his ear and averted his gaze. They were now five people back and he just wanted to get past these cult-bound children. He was getting the creeps.

The ticket boy wore a thin, dark t-shirt, embroidered with the theatre's logo. Where his arms emerged from the short sleeves, he exposed more creamy brown skin and perfectly muscled arms. Where the muscles were under his t-shirt, you could see them, tight and thick in his shoulders, stomach, and back.

This, of course, was more than the girls could take. They had become silent, didn't even know what they were standing there for, just watching him as if he were a fine art exhibit. The ticket boy had to coax the tickets out of their sweaty hands as if they were invalids. The girls finally moved off as a unit, speechless and starry-eyed. When they were about ten yards away, and just at the entrance to their movie, the spell which held them mercifully quiet broke, and all at once they exploded into peals of laughter and animated chatter. This chatter between them would take them through the next four days. The topic of discussion varied little.

"He was definitely looking at me when he said, 'beautiful women'!"

"No way, he only looked at you for a second, then his eyes STOPPED on me and didn't move again."

"Are you out of your mind?"

"He brushed MY arm...."

"What a freakin' milk chocolate god!"

"Uh, yeah...I'll take a bite outta that!"

Markis handed over his ticket. He noticed the guy was probably a lot older than he was. Like four or five years or something, definitely out of college.

"Thanks, man." Markis stared at the guy for a second, then looked down the hall to see which theater was theirs.

"No, problem," said the ticket guy as his eyes barely grazed over Markis, then landed with interest on the red-headed girl who made a slow, unaware approach. Markis watched the ticket-tear boy watch Saffron with much more interest than he gave the other girls. Instantly, Markis was alert. And pissed.

Markis's parents handed over their tickets. They tried to let Saffron go first, but she was holding up the line with her spastic rummaging. *Chapped lips! And you left your lipgloss at home. Moron. Find the ChapStick. Dig!* The thoughts struck her like blows to the head. *Get some ChapStick on those scaly things for God's sake.* She finally pinched the small tube and in a half-daze, brought it to her lips.

Markis turned around. "Saffron."

He was amused. What the heck was she doing anyway? She seemed to be the only girl within a million miles that hadn't noticed "Mr. Wonderful."

Unused to hearing Markis say her name, his call cut through her self-imposed fog and her head snapped up toward the sound of his voice. He smiled broadly at her and motioned for her to give her ticket up. She nodded and turned toward the ticket guy.

He was a monster.

The train she'd been waiting for with sick anticipation had arrived. It rammed straight into her chest, causing the ChapStick to fall from her grip, where it clacked to the tiled floor and rolled around Markis's feet. Sound was sucked from the universe, creating a vacuum so great it pulled at her as well, dragging her toward him while she strained to pull back from this thing, this beautiful vision of death that clamped on her with his eyes and held her like an offering on an ancient table. And, as if the bloodletting had already begun, she immediately felt weaker, almost unable to hold her own head up, never mind the rest of her body. She took a deep breath in and held it for a million years.

She saw them like an x-ray; four long, spiked teeth behind his soft, extra-full lips. And now, just as she knew fairies existed, she knew this thing was a vampire. The snapshot of his horrible teeth hung in her vision like the burn of a bright light. A stench filled her nostrils. It was the strong tang of copper, and under that, she smelled dust, acrid and thick. A dizzy drone swirled around her head, shot down her neck, where it whipped up the acid that festered in her gut. She started to totter. Her mouth dropped open so that she stared at him as if recently lobotomized.

He grabbed her arm and frowned. His eyes widened and hardened. Then all of a sudden, he looked...victorious.

Don't faint. Don't faint. Don't faint. Saffron pleaded with herself. *If he knows you know, he'll probably kill you.* Saffron straightened up but her body still swayed like a nylon blowup at a car dealership. She let out a nervous giggle. She forced herself to lean close to his ear, hoping to indicate she needed to tell him a secret. Before she spoke, she realized how close she was to death, to destruction, to a monster that was probably hundreds of years old, and dead. He had probably killed thousands of people, maybe more. He was a walking corpse and she was close enough to take in his scent, which was something like her sweaters when they had been left in a box in the attic, not unpleasant exactly, but stale and dusty.

"I'm like, out with this really cool guy for the first time and I feel like soooooo light-headed," she whispered with passion. *Please let 'stupid girl' work.* She backed away from him and pasted a Cheshire grin across her face.

He fiddled with his ear lobe and considered her. Now that Saffron was eye-to-eye with him, she noticed the earring he played with, a diamond stud, just bigger than a green pea. Her eyes skittered down him, then up again as her face bloomed red. His skin was flawless, his nails, obviously manicured, and his haircut, well, it was perfect and clearly not mastered within fifty miles of their sheep-infested shores. She wobbled in her shoes and ignored the sensation that she had to pee, badly. She wondered why she was standing next to a vampire, and wondered how he could be so beautiful. She searched the dirty rug for her ChapStick, and hoped she wasn't about to die.

When he spoke to her next, he displayed two rows of perfectly beautiful, normal, white teeth.

"Your secret is safe with me." His Eclipse breath barely covered the copper scent of congealing blood. His lips closed over his teeth and, still grinning, he nodded her on. Her shoulders hiked up to her eyes as she slunk past

Markis picked up her ChapStick and trotted after her. A new set of girls giggled with the ticket-tear guy.

"What did you say to him?" Markis was bewildered. Maybe Saffron hadn't noticed Mr. Wonderful when all of the other girls did; but did she really have to almost faint when she finally did see him? It kind of crushed a guy. He rubbed at the pang in his chest.

Saffron started talking to her shoes. "I just said something stupid. I didn't want him to call the ambulance or anything. I wasn't going to faint, you know. I just felt dizzy. Strong perfume makes me dizzy. There's a lot of it in here."

Markis's mother lifted the collar of her blouse to her nose and sniffed. She let it fall back into place and sniffed the air. She shrugged. Markis's father sniffed his popcorn, then ate some more.

"Markis, I have to run to the bathroom before the movie - I'll meet you inside." Her knees felt like hot rubber as she awkwardly made her way across the plush, blood-red carpet and fumbled with the restroom door. The door was so heavy. At first she couldn't open it. She slammed all of her weight against it, and finally it began to give by degrees.

Markis watched her, his eyebrows drawn into a frown. He called over to her before she went through the door. "It's okay. I'll see what seats my parents pick out and wait for you in the hallway so you don't get lost in the dark looking for us."

She tried a smile for him. "Thanks, I appreciate it." When the door had given just enough, she slipped through the crack and out of sight. Inside the bathroom, she drew her hand across the painted concrete wall, leaning heavily on it as she expected to pass out any second. She walked all the way to the end of the room and locked herself in the handicapped stall, then leaned against the wall furthest from the not-pristine toilet. She took deep breaths in and out, in and out, to try to calm her frazzled nerves. *There's a vampire collecting ticket stubs at the movies. Oh, God, you stupid ass, why didn't you just listen to Li?*

She replayed the scene in her head to try and see if she remembered anything that would show that he knew she knew what he was. She didn't think so. But what was she supposed to do now? She still knew who and what he was! At that moment, she hated the fairies. She hated them because she'd been more afraid than ever since she'd met them - fighting with that rotten gnome and the freakin' gremlins, a bunch of small, scaly things she couldn't name, the ghosts that did nothing but still scared the crap out of her, that guy that walked out of her woods today. Who *was* he? He wasn't dead, her mother and Derek could see him and talk to him. But something about him made her feel really...undone. And now a vampire? Her breath caught in her throat, she wanted to scream.

She decided she could avoid the movies, indefinitely, or until he moved on. If she saw him anywhere, she would just look away. She shuddered, realizing she was alone in the bathroom and started to worry about *dying* alone in the bathroom.

What if he comes in here? What if he's looking for me right now? What if he rips open my jugular and I fall to the dirty, white floor and crack my skull? What if my blood runs gushing and streaming across these tiny, white tiles and drips down the rusted metal drain in the center of the room? Would he eat that blood too? Suck it off the floor?

Waste not, want not.

Saffron gagged on her thoughts as the restroom door opened and two boisterous girls came screeching into the bathroom. Saffron let herself out of the handicapped stall and washed her hands robotically, while the girls yelled to each other over their pee from their separate stalls. They were talking about the hot guy loitering in the hall outside.

Saffron turned off the faucet, dried her hands for a few seconds under the blower, then wiped her hands the rest of the way on the seat of her jeans. She looked at herself in the mirror, saw how she hunched, and forced her back to straighten. As she moved out of the room, her body curved back into the safe 'c' shape.

In the hallway, Markis waited as Saffron pushed out of the ladies room.

"Are you sure you're okay?" He looked doubtful.

"Yeah, sorry. Can we just go watch the movie?"

In the dark, while the coming attractions pulsed on the screen, he leaned over her shoulder and whispered, "We can just sit anywhere we want."

Saffron closed her eyes and nodded. He was alive, human, and whispering in her ear. She wanted to turn into him and feel what it was like to have someone hold her. She wanted to know if holding him would take away her fears. She was desperate for him to reach for her but they walked up the aisle instead. That was okay, too. PDA? She sure as hell didn't want to become the main feature. Just before the show began, it went through her mind that she hadn't even checked her teeth or nose in the bathroom. In light of all the newest developments in her life, things in her teeth and nose became supremely unimportant. Still, she leaned her head in her hand through most of the movie and hoped her palm held any bad breath at bay.

Chapter 10

After the movie, Markis's father boomed his goodbye and clapped Saffron on the back. Markis's mother told her that it was very nice to have met her. Markis stood between them and winked. Saffron smiled. They parted ways in the main entrance, which was crowded with the departures of many other movie-goers.

Saffron adopted her best poker face and slowly scanned the room. With a sigh of relief, she confirmed that the ticket-tear vampire was nowhere to be found. Then her gaze fell on something even more frightening.

Her cousin was sitting on a bench on the far wall under a poster for the newest and best action flick in the history of film. A suited, suave, and slick action star stared out in challenge. A car crash was taking place above his head. Just below his scowling face was Mindy's scowling face. She jumped up from the bench and pointed to the floor by her feet. Saffron rolled her eyes. Did her cousin think she would actually heel like a dog?

Saffron raised her chin, and taking her sweet old time, she strolled over to Mindy.

"Where've you been? I been sitting here for half an hour! I been asking people if they've seen you and everybody's like, duh, what, who? The other girls left, they were so pissed you dissed us like that, they took a ride with those freakin' DeMarco twins, they'll probably get raped. Don't ask me why I stayed and waited for you – you didn't do *me* any favors."

"Mindy, you guys went into the movie without me!"

"Well, where the hell were you?"

"I was standing in the middle of the room, where anyone in the world could have seen me, talking to Markis."

Mindy jerked her head back. "Markis? Markis who? Markis Bryant? From school?" She smirked. "Ah, Saffron...I don't know where you and Markis went for over two hours but I suggest you get off him and quick."

"What are you talking about Mindy? I'm not *on* him."

"Samantha just told me tonight that she likes Markis so I'm warning you now, cuz you're my cousin and everything; don't mess with her when she wants something."

"Jesus Christ, Mindy...he's not a freakin' dog. Samantha can't just act like she owns him." Saffron felt something vicious wake and squirm around inside her. *Samantha? Dexterous Whore of the East?* It was well known that Samantha taught yoga at the town gym, three barns down from DeMarco Auto Parts, and that she was a self-proclaimed expert on the Kama Sutra, and that her breasts could keep herself and a small village afloat in a flood. When Markis found out that Samantha liked him... Saffron whispered, "Markis can hang around with anyone he wants."

"No, *Saffron*, you don't get it, *Saffron*. You *need* to leave him alone now that I've just told you she wants him. It wouldn't be fair for you to continue, whatever, at this point."

"Well, what if *I* want him?" She tried not to mumble, but couldn't bring herself to say these bizarre, self-centered words any louder.

"Pah! Yeah, right! If you want everybody to think you're sneaky like that, that's your problem. Just text your freakin' mother so we can get out of here." Mindy plopped back on the bench, folded her arms across her chest, and glared across the now-crowded lobby.

Saffron fumbled with her mother's phone. She forgot if you were supposed to press the little green symbol before or after you dialed, was it before or after you texted?

Mindy's face contorted into another form of miserable. "And who were those *old* people you guys were hanging around with?" Mindy knew who they were.

Saffron's shoulders hitched. It wasn't hard to guess where this interrogation was headed. "His parents," she whispered.

Mindy sprung up, her perfect face twisting into something hideous under her blonde hair. "Dude! You went out on a date to a movie with him...*and his parents!* That's *so* not normal. You better hope nobody finds out about this. Markis better hope so too. Samantha won't even consider dating him if she finds out. You better not tell her."

Saffron's face blanched. "Why would I tell her? Why would I not tell her? When would I tell her? I hadn't seen any of those guys for months before tonight! Who's going to find out about us? Hasn't everyone gone on with their lives yet?" Now she was shrieking.

Two junior high boys walked by. They snickered at the women in battle. They hissed and howled like alley cats. Mindy reached over and managed to slap one upside the head.

"Hey!" was his only comeback as he reached to fondle his scalp. They scurried off.

Saffron's freckles stood out like cocoa powder on a sheet of white paper. Her voice came low and harsh. Mindy's words had hit her like a pile driver. She wasn't too far gone out of high school to remember how everything worked - the cliques, and how Markis's own friends had sneered at her. How, back then, someone like him would never ever go out with someone like her. She shrank inside her clothes. This night out had been too much. She scanned the lobby for the vampire again, but he was nowhere around; only a gremlin in the trash, and a fat woman floating on the ceiling. "Why would he even care if Samantha likes him?"

Mindy raised her eyebrows. "Oh, hunny," she grunted with overripe condescension. Her lips drew back; she made a click noise with her tongue and teeth. "You don't really think Markis *seriously* likes *you,* do you?" She reached over and gently patted Saffron on the shoulder. "C'mon, why would he like you?" She eyed Saffron without blinking.

Saffron said nothing. She was fighting to keep from blubbering here, in this busy room, in front of Mindy.

"I mean really, I'm not trying to make you feel bad or anything, but honestly...Markis Bryant? Does that make any sense to you, Saffron?"

"Hey, Saffron!"

Saffron and Mindy turned toward the entrance doors where Markis stood waving, something small fisted in his hand. He ran over.

Saffron could smell the cold, autumn night on his clothes. She breathed deep, and as the air moved inside her, it froze the monster in her belly.

"Saffron, I forgot, you dropped this earlier. I've had it in my pocket the whole time." He beamed as he took her hand, held it, and placed the tube of ChapStick in her warm palm. He stood back to look at her, then stepped forward and reached out with both hands. He locked his fingers around her wrists and slowly, slowly he slid his hands up her arms as he pulled her forward to touch his nose to hers. He looked straight into her eyes. "I hope you had fun. I did."

She nodded. Then he was gone, skipping through the lobby doors, and out into the world.

Saffron smelled strawberries. Markis had used some of her ChapStick. His lips had been on her ChapStick where her lips had been many times. Now she could put the ChapStick on where his lips had been. Right now, she could do it right now and know they shared that.

She smiled broadly at Mindy. It wasn't a malicious smile, or an 'I told you so smile,' not even a smile of conquest. She was just so utterly thrilled she needed to smile and share it with somebody.

To Mindy's dismay, she had to sit there and be the recipient of all of Saffron's glory. Mindy didn't say a word on the ride back to her house. She mumbled, "Thanks," to her aunt, slammed the car door, then stalked to her lighted front entry.

"Whew, what was that about?" Audrey glanced at Saffron.

"Humph. Guess Mindy *did not* have a good night. I, on the other hand, had a fantastic evening."

So Audrey had noticed. There was color in Saffron's cheeks – fresh, rosy color. Audrey just had to know what this was all about; this shining diamond was not the girl she had dropped off three hours earlier. "Well, c'mon. What happened?"

"Markis Bryant asked me to go to a movie with him!"

The statement, spoken with such happiness and wonder, was not what Audrey had expected to hear. How had that happened? How had Saffron jumped right over a good time with her girlfriends to a good time with her boyfriend? Like most parents, Audrey wasn't prepared for this little bit of unpleasantness when it first happened. Saffron had never uttered a male name until just now and, since it was the first time for both of them, Audrey was equal parts relieved and anxious. For years now, both Audrey and Saffron had been content in their space well away from men, except for Derek, who was to them a special kind of man, a safe kind of man.

There was silence for the next several minutes. After awhile, Audrey spoke. "So tell me all about it. Tell me everything!"

Saffron grinned as she told her mother all about it.

Later, after she washed her face, brushed her teeth, and dressed for bed, Saffron lay awake in the dark, still smiling. Markis Bryant. He was so hot. And he had touched her! Held her! He *liked* her! Mindy saw the whole thing, which meant the entire town would know by the end of the week. Saffron didn't mind that at all. Maybe if she was Markis Bryant's girlfriend she would stop being crap recipient of the year. Now, maybe the stupid dreams would stop. Markis Bryant wasn't about to rip into her throat. He liked her! He wasn't about to turn away from her, embarrassed. He had touched her!

The old house made a lot of noise. It groaned and creaked. The furnace came on with a boom. The faucet in the tub dripped. Everyone else in the house had gone to bed and had probably been asleep for some time.

Saffron stared at the digital glow of her alarm clock. 1:20 a.m. Her mind started to wander away from Markis, though she struggled to rein her thoughts and stay focused on him, he slipped from her grasp. Had that vampire suspected anything of her reaction to him or not? *Never mind. Think of Markis.*

The floorboards cracked on the stairway landing as if someone was walking there. Saffron pulled the covers closer to her face. She held her breath and strained her ears, but no further noise came from the landing. She exhaled slowly. *There's nothing out there, chill out.*

But what if that guy who came out of the woods earlier was still around? He seemed all right this afternoon, intriguing even, but he was still a stranger. What was he doing in *their* woods? And where did he go after?

She crunched up into the fetal position underneath her heavy comforter. If there were any dead people in her room, all she had to do was not look at them and she could get through the night.

She couldn't stand horror movies. They always went looking for *it* in those movies. How stupid could you get? She remained completely motionless. She breathed as shallowly as possible so she wouldn't make a noise. *Better safe than sorry* was really an ingenious saying.

Suddenly, Saffron was washed in a cold wave of fear. The air in her ears turned loud as her skin tightened. She couldn't have moved if she wanted to, not even her eyes. Someone was near. She knew that if she opened her eyes, poked her nose out from under the comforter, there would be someone standing right there by her bed, looking down at her. As long as she remained still, they wouldn't bother her. If she looked, if she called out, something bad would happen. Her eyes popped open. She jerked the blanket down and stared at the closet door. There was a shadow there. She stared at it so hard her eyes started to water and made the form waver. Then she realized, it was her dress - her mother had worked on a couple of stains and had hung it from her closet door to dry.

Saffron's eyes snapped to the chair at the foot of her bed. Someone was sitting in her chair. No, it was just a stuffed animal. But *something* was near. It was going to get her. She knew it. She could feel it. She jumped out of bed and reached for her light switch as demon fingers scratched at her calves and pulled her hair. Pop. The light was on, the evil was gone. Strangled air blew past her lips.

Just outside her window, under the apple tree, a man stood in the shadows. He looked up at Saffron's window. He saw her light suddenly flash on and he smiled. He knew she felt his presence, but, of course, was unaware of the exact *meaning* of her intuition. He stood there for a long time.

The animals that usually squawked and croaked and screeched in the night were absolutely silent. They hid in the woods and far out in the fields and eyed the shadow. They willed him to leave but he did not heed the will of the living. The pair of garden gnomes grumbled as they huddled in their hole but dared not move until that thing left. When would that thing leave? They all winced when they heard the screams of the woman as she flung herself from the cliff.

After awhile, Jethin turned and vanished into the darkness.

Chapter 11

Saffron slept. For a few hours. She was up most of the night, dropping into sleep and slamming awake. The vampire had not come to kill her, so she assumed he didn't know she knew. If he did know, he would have destroyed her immediately, right? Then he would not have to worry that she would expose him.

Before she fell asleep, she thought long and hard. She had had enough. She hadn't slept in months and it was obvious to everybody. She was sick of people asking if she was okay and she was sick of looking in the mirror at her own corpse-bride face.

She resented her visits to the fairyland. She was truly sick of Li and Ny. They were so weird, sneaky. She didn't want to go back there, ever. Now, all she could do was to wait for the magic to wear off. Then she wouldn't see things she didn't want to see. She wouldn't have to endure that woman screaming as she fell from the cliff. When it was over, she would consider herself normal. Relatively normal.

***

Her body was trying to wake up. She felt so groggy she let her heavy eyelids lie shut. She could smell that she wasn't in her room. There were green and growing things all around. There was the scent of roses, of pine trees and foliage, which tickled her nose and soothed her. She heard the gurgling and bubbling of water. She also heard the lilt of a flute; the player was beside her. She stirred a little, still not looking. Behind her lids, her eyeballs rolled back. She didn't know if she was dreaming or awake or maybe both. All she knew was this was the most spectacular she had ever felt in her entire life. Her body was heavy and sleepy but her senses were sharp, greedy, and soaking up this unseen exquisiteness with her ears and nose and emotions.

When she moved, the flutist ceased playing. Saffron felt a warm hand caress her cheek while fingers ran through her hair. The feeling was overwhelming. Her heightened sensitivities surged and she let out a small gasp of pleasure. Her eyes fluttered opened and there was Ny, his face so close to her she could feel his hot breath.

"Why do you deny me?"

Ny. She pulled away from his touch. In quiet panic, she took in her strange jungle surroundings. Alone? With him? Why was she here? Her mother would come looking for her if it got to be too late in the morning. She didn't want her mother to find her dead!

Saffron sat up straight. Here he was...available to her. Her mind filtered through some of the most erotic bits of her nighttime journeys, making her want to throw herself at him and live the moments she had only been able to watch him have with other women. She also wanted to slap him, violently, right across the face and make his entire head slam with the effort. Instead, she crossed her arms to protect her chest and looked away from him. "I shouldn't be here."

He crawled toward her like an animal.

"Whoa. That's far enough." She held her hand up in front of his face. It was like he was feral. She had to distract him. "Ny, why can't I see through your skin like before?"

"I do this appearance for you. I do everything for you and your happiness." He grabbed her thigh and rubbed his thumb under the line of her shorts. "Here, I will show you my best look."

Before her eyes, Saffron watched as Ny morphed into a more manly form. His face thinned out and became angular. He grew a heavy five o'clock shadow. His calves thickened and became muscular. Under his sheath, she detected movement and became extremely uncomfortable as his thighs bulged and rear-end filled out. She looked up, fearing she might see something she wasn't ready to see. The hair on his arms went from fine and downy to thick and black. She couldn't look at him anymore. She didn't want to give in to the insistence that pulled on the very edge of her consciousness.

Ny chuckled. "Saffron," he whispered, "I have changed back. Please, look at me. I am only truly happy when your eyes adore me."

She looked sideways at him. Yes, he was back. Looking around, she could see that he had definitely brought her back to his world. That was kind of like kidnapping, wasn't it? Just last night, she had decided she wouldn't come back. Why did he get her without her consent and bring her back here?

He sat Indian style as well, directly across from her, knee to knee on the dry moss.

She felt a jolt of electricity every time he touched her. She wanted to sit there, just a little bit. "I don't want to be here, Ny."

"My little liar. Humans tell so many lies and you, my love, are aspiring to be their heralded queen."

"What? Fairies never lie?" She tilted her head and waited for an answer.

"I could tell you many truths - one in particular, if you are ready to hear it." He squeezed her knees.

Saffron jumped, took his hands in hers to shove them back into his territory. He caught her hands and pressed his thumbs inside her palms. He held her with his eyes the entire time.

"Ny, please. This is a little freaky for me. You're like, a million years old." She could picture Mindy rolling her eyes. Mindy would kill to be in her shoes right now. Ny released her hands and fell back with a crack of laughter.

Sunlight streamed through the tops of the tall trees and sprinkled them with light. It sparkled off the water in the stream that was nearby, flowing over smooth rocks and cooling the minute pixies that were bathing in its pools and shadowed coves.

As his hysterics died down, Ny brushed unconsciously at the glossy, black hair that had fallen over his face. His legs were still crossed but his back and head rested on the forest floor. The long, long length of him was stretched out and languid. He eyed Saffron from this position.

She swallowed hard. He was so big, with so many taut lines.

He snapped his fingers and the pixies darted to Saffron. They spread out in flight all around her head. They gathered lengths of her hair and pinned it up at the very top of her head. One by one, at different points in time, they flew into the woods, returned with a wild blossom, and added this to the elaborate coiffure they were creating. Saffron forgot to be irritated for a moment and blushed as she turned to Ny. "Why are they doing this?"

Ny stared at Saffron without blinking. His pupils became dots as he settled his warm, ocean-blue eyes on the nape of her neck. "They do my will." He sat up and leaned toward her. Their faces were close together. She didn't know it, but she looked very much like the princesses she envied in her fairy tale books. Her hair cascaded down either side of her face. Here and there, multi-colored buds were embedded in the profusion of ringlets. Fairy magic.

He sent the pixies away and whispered, "Saffron, I think you are probably older than I am. But who could prove it? We are both millions of years old. I do not see a young human before me. I see the soul of an ancient being. A being that has been part of me since time began.

"You speak of truth. I am giving you the truth. The truth is you love me, Saffron...we are soul mates. You can search back and forth through time and you will realize I am the only one for you. The true one. Love is not a strong enough word. When you are not human, you are aware of our past and of how you are completely consumed with me. It is almost as if," he touched her lips with his fingertips, "you are my slave and I am yours. Do you not want to touch me? Even now, how can you sit there so prim? Do what you want...do what I want."

Saffron pulled away from the force that surrounded him and beckoned her. "That doesn't sound so great." Her eyes narrowed. Something felt suspicious, even sinister.

"I have chosen the wrong words, Saffron. Come, listen to me. I will try to explain better." He wiggled his eyebrows and pulled her back toward him. "Let me be more appropriate. I am your soul mate. We have loved each other for thousands of years. We are the greatest lovers of all time. We meet again in every lifetime. You cannot live without me. We are amazed by the unrelenting fire in our love and wonder at it. We say, 'My God, I think we were meant to be!' Each time we meet, we are instantly in rapture. We know without doubt that we know each other from somewhere else, from some other time. The way we fit so perfectly together cannot be denied. We worship each other."

His whispers were hushed and fervent. His hands were wrapped around her neck and his long fingers massaged the base of her skull. He stared into her eyes with such intensity that she felt he was burning a hole through her soul. She felt she was losing consciousness, that he was swallowing her.

She rubbed her face and kept her hands over her eyes. "Well, what about my dreams?"

Ny ran a finger down the back of Saffron's calf. He smiled vacantly. "What dreams?"

"Those freakin' gross dreams. What do you mean; what dreams? The dreams *you* keep sending me." She grunted. "Though I don't know why you make me watch them; you're not exactly Prince Charming in them, if you know what I mean."

Ny's fingers ceased. He was frowning as he pulled Saffron's hands from her eyes. "What dreams?"

Saffron was incredulous. "Duh, those dreams, about sex, with you, those stupid women...."

"Yes?" He smiled again, relaxed. He adjusted his hips just a little and rested one great paw of a hand on his lap close to his groin. His voice dropped deep, to an unknown bowel of the earth too dark and desperate to comprehend. "I want you to very slowly, and very carefully tell me about these dreams."

Saffron's eyes widened as she leaned back "I...I...you...with other women...always...all the time... They're so stupid I'm humiliated for them. God, it really pisses me off!" The last sentence came shrill. The gloss left her eyes as she tried to sear him with what she hoped was a really scary look.

"Saffron, just kiss me. Kiss me so you will know. You will feel it in every part of your being. The kiss will be so perfect, so all-consuming; you will feel you are close to death. But I will not let you go.

He came forward now, slowly, and frightened her with his intensity. Just before their lips touched, she could smell him - earth and male - and feel his hot breath tingling her upper lip. Lightly, just like a feather, they made contact. It was like a jolt of pure electricity had stabbed through her lips, sliced down her throat and exploded in her stomach. She could feel powers within her struggling to pull away and powers struggling to make her cling to him. She even swooned. With agonizing slowness, she pulled away and realized something wasn't right.

His eyes were black and furious.

She reddened and looked away. Something had been wrong with that kiss. It was nothing like she imagined and it was more than anything she had ever imagined in all of her erotic dreams. The first thing she had noted, and quickly, was his inhumanity. His body was firm, so firm it was completely unmoving under his skin. She gasped. He had no pulse! He was like a doll. He smelled good, he felt hot, he was hard and smooth at the same time but he didn't feel *alive*. And what was his problem? Why did he look so pissed off?

"Of course not, Saffron," he said as if she had spoken every thought out loud, "I am not the same as you. Not heart and blood as humans. I am a vessel of nature, nature's perfection." He smiled wide, assured of his place in the world, being nature's perfection and all.

Saffron quirked an eyebrow, "I just kissed a vessel?"

Ny's irritation came charging forward. "Really, Saffron, do you think you just kissed a vessel?"

She shrugged.

He reached for her with both hands. His touch worked on her like his kiss as she allowed him to lull her back into that feeling that was aching and swelling and wanting all at the same time. She felt like a tiny boat adrift on a stormy sea. Her mind blocked out the sounds of the forest. All she was aware of was a low rumbling deep within her.

This isn't right. That tiny seed of thought planted itself in her mind. It was nurtured with memories of lives she had previously lived but never remembered. The memories were of tears and anguish and pleading and desperation. And, within Saffron, these gestated into rich, shocking feeling. The seed became a frail tendril of green life searching for sunlight.

Her amber eyes grew dark. "No, Ny," Saffron blurted, "I don't want to be here with you." She shook her head.

A hint of panic crossed his face. "There is nothing but perfection between us! Saffron, we..."

A blast split the air, and with it came a sharp whiff of ozone. Birds, every color of the rainbow, with magnificent crowns of feathers and long, glorious tails, were flushed from the trees, flying straight up into the sky. A feminine voice sounded through the trees. "Ny, stop." It was Li and she sounded angry. She appeared before them in a burst of shimmer, taking Saffron by the hand and pulling her away from Ny. "I am sorry, Saffron. The fault is mine."

Saffron looked at Li's hand as the fairy gripped her none too gently.

Li petted Saffron's cheek and smiled sadly. "I have missed you so much, all of these years, that I have weakened. I made such a terrible mistake by giving into Ny and allowing you to come here. Last night, the wind brought your wishes to me. I vow to respect them. I will take you back to your world. One day, you will come back to us, to me. I will wait for that day with anguish as penance for the wrong I have done you."

"O...okay," Saffron stammered. What was she supposed to say?

"NO!" Ny screamed. Li and Saffron, stunned by his pitch and intensity, both jumped.

"Ny, for the love of all that is good and pure in the world, let her go. She has chosen to leave. Let her be." Li's tone was even.

Ny used his eyes to plead with Saffron.

Saffron could feel his pain. She was raw from her pain. She

wanted Ny. She really did. She wanted him more than any person has wanted another in a million life times. She didn't know what to do, what to think. She thought about listening to Li, letting the fairy take control.

As soon as she made this decision, that little tendril that earlier fought for life could no longer hold to the earth of her mind. It withered, and with it, the bane of Saffron's conscious went too, so she wasn't troubled anymore by her will.

Saffron moved away from Ny and slipped her hand into Li's.

Ny moaned and in an instant flew off as a tiny ball of light.

"Will you tell me what's going on?" Saffron's question was a forced whisper. Li had already put her in the hazy state so she could transport her soul home. Saffron's shoulders drooped.

Li put her arms around Saffron to give the girl somewhere to fall. "No, Saffron. It is better you do not know the truth. Go home and live the rest of your life. All too soon, you will become an old woman and you will die. I will see you then, and we will be happy."

"I assumed fairies didn't suffer."

"Well, I never told you that." Li closed her eyes. She inhaled, exhaled. "Let me take you home."

"But wait," Saffron couldn't hold on to Li's neck. She started to slide down Li's cool, hard body. Without strain, Li picked her up and cradled her like a baby. "...I saw one..." Saffron's lips rubbed on Li's neck as she spoke. It was like kissing glass. "I saw a vampire. I talked to him. And, geez, whenever I saw his teeth I was like, oh, my God. Ya know?"

"His name, Saffron!" Li bit out each word as she dropped Saffron to the rough ground. And underneath her skin, Li's face turned black. Her white hair stood on end and twitched like wet wires around her skull.

Saffron took one jagged gulp of air and held still. She was on her knees and terrified as Li loomed above her. The fairy was hovering three feet off the ground, her great wings wumping and stirring up half the forest floor.

"Oh, shit." Saffron cringed and covered her head with her arms.

Li came back down. A look of apologetic alarm spread across her face. The lavender rings once more outlined her pupils and her hair fluttered prettily back down to her shoulders.

Saffron whispered. "Li, I don't know his name." She lowered her arms and looked sheepishly into the fairy's eyes. "Honestly."

Li helped Saffron up, cradled her once more. She rested her chin on top of Saffron's downy-soft hair and stared blindly into the forest. A single tear, sparkling like crystal in sunshine, rolled over her perfect cheek. She whispered back. "What did he look like?"

Saffron swallowed hard, breathed in Li's vanilla skin. "Well, God. I don't know." How do you describe a monster? "He was perfect, gorgeous. I wish he wasn't dead." She sighed. "Long, straight hair to his shoulders. He was Italian, or mulatto, or Indian. One of those." One eyebrow shot straight up. "Gypsy?"

Li's eyes were squeezed shut and still a stream of tears poured out and onto Saffron's rusty hair.

Saffron's words were only slightly muffled in the spider-spun cloth at Li's shoulder. "I don't think he knew that I could tell what he was, you know? I think I got away with it!" She felt enormously proud. She nodded. "I totally kept it together."

Li opened her reddening eyes to roll them. Naive Saffron. Saffron couldn't hide an emotion with a paper bag over her head. Jethin certainly was aware of Saffron. Of that, Li was certain.

"Saffron, you will be fine. You will be strong. If... by chance... this vampire approaches you, under no circumstances are you to succumb to any of his wishes."

"What do you mean, Li? His wishes. What?" Saffron's pride flew away and panic oozed through her as she tilted her head back to stare at Li. "What wishes am I not supposed to *succumb* to?" Her voice was breaking.

"Look at me, Saffron. Come now; look at me." Li looked very pleased when Saffron obeyed. She petted Saffron's head. "You must trust in me. Everything is going to be all right. I will take care of everything for you. You will go home and leave it to me. Agreed?"

Saffron nodded miserably. She raised her eyes to the heavens and watched the birds swirl around and around and around. She'd leave it to Li. Why not? She was way in over her head.

Chapter 12

"That was a cool movie, wasn't it?" Markis grinned. It was a slow night at the store. No old gamblers, no drunken young studs rushing in for their alcohol buy before midnight. No one ever bought the dusty condoms. Coco was in the bathroom, sitting on the toilet tank. Her feet were on the toilet seat cover and she was giving her toenails a masterful paint job. Her homemade shoes had been kicked under the sink. Her arms were sheathed in the legs of black cut-off nylons.

Markis leaned against the register counter on one leg, scratched his calf with the other booted foot, and hummed tunelessly. Everything about him was relaxed. He was scrubbed clean and his dark eyes were bright. He wasn't hiding any secrets. He was who he was and happy just to be there with her.

Saffron stared at him blankly.

Markis's grin fell as he stared back at her. He tried again, but with less gusto. His booted foot planted itself back on the floor as he stood up. "*The Last Planet.* I thought it was a pretty good movie."

"Oh, yeah! It was the best." She was too forced, too cheery, and Markis was hurt, she could tell. She didn't want to deal with this right now. She turned her head and stared at the night-blackened windows. Suddenly, there was a vision there of Ny, hanging by his knees from the limb of a cherry tree in full bloom. He slowly swung back and forth. Back and forth. He blew her a kiss.

"Saffron, is everything okay?" She had managed to work Markis into a frown.

I'm poisoning this guy, she thought, and looked down at her hands. Her fingers were strangling themselves. She had to admit, she didn't even care that he was standing there. She wanted to zone out, to not think for a couple of years. She had already forgotten about last Friday. On Saturday she had backed out of meeting the band.

A car pulled into one of the spaces in front of the store. It was full of shadows, girls, and smoke. The driver's side door opened and Samantha's barely restrained breasts popped out. She pulled her wedge, then hen-strutted to the door of the store. Ting-a-ling. She walked up to the counter and smiled, her mouth so full of teeth she could only attract another piranha. "Pack a' Marlboro lights."

Outside, her minions struggled out of the car like corpses from their graves. They stumbled in one by one, ting-a-ling, their grins Bozo-wide under their heavy lipstick. One of them had a bright red smudge on her teeth.

"Hi, Markis," Samantha gushed and herded her breasts right up to his chest. Maybe he was supposed to shake them in greeting, pat them on the head. He seemed as confused as Saffron. Nimbly, he backed up before they could bite.

Samantha sneered and cast a withering glare at Saffron. Saffron rolled her eyes and slammed the register shut, firmly placed Samantha's change on the counter without counting it. To date, this was the boldest thing she had ever done. She didn't want anything to do with this. She just wanted to find a dark, quiet spot and scream Ny out of her mind. She was convinced he really was in there, actually in there with her and aware of her every move. He was violating her. She turned on her heel and walked away. She had work to do, pots to sanitize.

"What's her problem?" she heard Samantha spit at her retreating back.

"Maybe it's too crowded in here." Markis lowered his head and pushed his way through the gang of girls.

"Hey, Markis!" Markis stared at the ceiling, then squeezed his chocolate eyes shut. He wheeled around.

"What do you want, Samantha?" *To be worshipped? To pork half the east coast before 2020? To suffocate the life out of me?*

"We were just wondering what you were doing tomorrow."

"Do you mean 'we' or 'I'?"

Samantha winced at him, then shrieked with gale forces of high-pitched laughter.

"Ah, Markis. I don't think so. A bunch of us are going to the tracks and we were just being nice enough to invite you along. I really hope you weren't insinuating that I wanted you or anything because, to tell you the truth, that makes me a little queasy." Her slit eyes darted in Saffron's direction. "And to tell you the truth, I kinda, like, feel bad for you, ya know. I mean, what's going on with you at school? What happened to all your friends?"

Markis's jaw worked behind his cheeks. He shook his head, turned on his heel and walked toward the back of the store. He stopped at the coffee counter and watched Saffron abuse pots with a blue scrub wand while the water dashed against the bottom of the deep stainless steel sink and splashed up the walls.

"Phone!" they heard Samantha howl.

Saffron watched out of the corner of her eye while one of the minions fumbled to get the phone to Samantha. Samantha slapped it to her ear and monotoned, "Call the Bitch," obviously in response to a recorded command from within the phone. There was a quiet pause while everyone watched Samantha drum her Purple Plum Ho nails on the counter. She slammed one hand on her hip. "You know what,

Mindy? I don't care if she *is* your cousin. That little bitch isn't going anywhere with us ever again. Get it? What's she smokin' anyway? She's so like, *duh*." Then Samantha slapped the phone shut with a crack of plastic and yelled, "Get the hell back in the car!" The minions filed out and the store was silent.

"Saffron."

She didn't turn to answer him; she just kept scrubbing the same pot till the sanitizer grew thick on the walls of the glass.

Coco, aka Katy Perry, came screeching "Last Friday Night," from the back room, nail file working hard. She stopped behind Saffron and in front of Markis, who was staring forlornly at Saffron's back from over the counter and over two tiers of self-pump coffee thermoses.

"What the...what's going on here?"

The bell ting-a-linged. They all looked over at the door. It was 'Jack Black,' or rather, a woman that looked so much like him she could sign autographs. She always took exactly thirty seconds in the cooler getting cream cheese.

Coco looked at Saffron's back, then at Markis as he shrugged and crossed his arms.

"Okay, you know what? We're adults here. Saffron, Markis wants you. Bad. Markis..." she raised an eyebrow and watched 'Jack Black' make her way to the checkout counter, "I'm pretty sure you could take Miss Hot Pants out back now and have her any way you want her. She's ready for you."

Smash went the pot on the floor as Saffron shrieked, "Oh, my God, Coco!" and fled to the back of the store.

"Nice, Coco. Smooth."

Markis turned and headed for the door. 'Jack Black' put the cream cheese on the counter and cleared her throat, staring at the cigarette display directly in front of her.

"One minute Ja...Ma'am," Coco called over her shoulder as she eyed Markis with disapproval. Then her face flip-flopped as if she just remembered something. "Markis, can we get in an extra practice tonight?"

Markis threw a look heavenward. "Oh, my God, Coco. You. Are. Insane. You know I have school tomorrow."

Coco shrugged.

Ting-a-ling. Outside, Markis put on his helmet and got on his bike.

Coco watched him out in the dark parking lot.

'Jack Black' leaned on the counter and stared from Coco to Markis, then back to Coco.

Coco walked right up to the window and mouthed, "Are we practicing tonight?"

Markis shook his head, gunned the engine, and wheeled off.

Coco backed up to the register. "No dedication." She wagged her head.

"Pack a' Marlboros," Jack grunted as she pushed the cream cheese toward Coco.

Saffron came scurrying from out back with a dustpan and brush. Coco never took her eyes off of her as Saffron hunched over the mess and scraped the glass from the coffee pot into the metal receiving pan. Saffron swiped her eyes and nose as if she was crying, but Coco couldn't be sure.

'Jack Black' left. Slowly, Coco walked over to Saffron, bent down and picked up the brown coffee pot handle. It had a jagged shard of glass sticking out of it like buckteeth. "Okay, I coulda had more tact."

Saffron glared at the worn tiles. "Ya think?"

Coco shrugged. "Don't get pissy, missy. Why does this have to drag on like this? You guys like each other. Get together. Come to band practice with me next time. I tried to get your boyfriend to have a session tonight but he's all frantic about school. So come next Saturday...be his woman...see him every night, apply at his college, get in, shack up, get A's together. It's what you both want. I happen to know for a fact he liked you when you were still in high school, but he was afraid you'd explode if he got too near you. You guys have taken like, forever. What's the problem anyway?"

"What do you mean you, 'know for a fact,' he liked me?" Saffron's face was bright red. She looked down at her worn Maryjanes.

Coco looked coy. "Last night, when we were jammin', I was like, 'so when did all this Saffron stuff start up?' And he was like, 'She used to bite her bottom lip in school till it was red and puffy; I was mesmerized.' Shite! The dude actually said, 'mesmerized.' That's a fricken nice compliment, right? And sucking on your lip? Ooooh, so sexy." Coco sucked on her bottom lip. "Oh, yeah, baby, that's nice."

Saffron held her breath and scrunched her toes. The skin on the back of her neck shriveled. Just the thought of the reality Coco had painted filled Saffron with dread. Dread and guilt. How could she be with Markis? Every time she closed her eyes, Ny was there, waiting for her. But Markis couldn't want her that bad. Not, "move with me to college," bad. It would never happen. And as soon as she left this store, she would be safe at home again. Her skin relaxed.

Ting-a-ling. They both pushed off the counter where they were leaning and looked toward the door. It was the cowboy. Coco stood up straighter and smoothed her hands all the way down her apron. Saffron fretted.

The cowboy sauntered by. "Ladies," he drawled, but his eyes were glued on Coco.

"Why don't you just go jump him right now Coco, if you like him so much?" Saffron forced the words out, barely above a hiss. She thought she might have a stroke on the spot. She lowered her eyes to Coco's boots.

"Mebbe ah will," Coco drawled with a hack southern accent as she sashayed down the aisle toward the little break in the counter system that let her out to the main part of the store.

Saffron actually lunged for her, missed grabbing her wrist by an inch, then stood by, mortified, as Coco panthered up to the cowboy. She made him drop his Nesquick with her sly smile. Taking his hand, she led him back to the register counter, through the entrance slot, and down the aisle where Saffron stood rooted to the floor with the dustpan of shards still in her hand. Her mouth hung open as they passed. Coco smirked, winked, and kept on. The cowboy's eyes were starting to glaze. Was he drooling? Saffron slapped her hand to her mouth. She witnessed them like a traffic accident. She wanted to turn away, but the drama was too seductive.

Through another doorway, she saw Coco lean up against the wall to the right of the bathroom door. She nearly choked as Coco pulled the cowboy toward her. Saffron dropped the dustpan of shards as she saw the cowboy bend at the knees, squat, then push forward, pinning Coco's skinny-Levied pelvis up to the wall, grinding once, twice, one of his large hands yanking through her bed-head Cher hair, the other hand already sliding up her shirt.

"Oh, shit." Saffron shrieked low and ran to shut the door that separated the back of the store from the front of the store, blocking them from view. In a daze, she crunched back over the glass, back along the counter, turned herself like a marionette, and gripped the register. She covered her ears when the muffled moaning started.

Across the street, from the steepled church, five o'clock mass let out.

Four and a half minutes later, just as much time as it took her to get across the intersection with her walker, there came the first customer. Her blue hair peeked out from under her fur hat, her wool coat buttoned to her neck, and her galoshes firmly suctioned to her sensible shoes. She banged through the door, using her walker as a battering ram, threw Saffron a look that said, "I know you're a little whore," and step/step/clopped her way to the cooler.

The muffled noises increased. Saffron began to sweat.

Step/Step/Clop walked back to the front of the store as an elderly couple, also just released, greeted her with sugary smiles. They headed for the coffee station. Step/Step/Clop nodded at them, then turned to Saffron, her smile dropping from her face like dung from a donkey.

"You got something going on out back?"

Saffron stared at her.

"Hello? Out back, you got some noises. Like a machine breaking down or something." Her hands fluttered. "Bang! Bang! Creeeeeak. Sounds like something needs a new belt before the whole thing blows." She frowned at Saffron, shook her head. "Just this, please." She pushed a carton of Half & Half across the counter.

Saffron could hardly make her hand work to punch the keypad on the register. From far away, Coco started oooooing.

The coffee couple arrived at Saffron's register. They put their cups on the counter and spilled some. The old man leered, "Whatcha got? Got ghosts back there? *Oooooo!*"

Saffron felt bile creep up her esophagus. She dropped to her knees beside the pile of brown paper bags and started patting at them.

"No," said Step/Step/Clop from up above as she picked up her bag with the Half & Half in it, "She's got belts loose back there. Mark my words; somethin's gonna blow soon." She Step/Step/Clopped out the door.

Saffron pulled, then pushed herself up, using the counter. When she was standing at full hunch, she held onto the rubbed Formica for dear life. "Will that be all?" The couple wasn't listening to her.

The old man leaned over the counter, looked down the alley that Saffron stood in. "OOooooooooOOOoooo!" He put his hand behind his ear and waited for a response. But suddenly, all was quiet.

Saffron's shoulders sagged. She punched the keypad, told them the coffee total was four dollars, twenty cents. They paid with a five. She punched in the numbers and the drawer rang open.

Then, a noise from the back. "Unh, unh, unh, unh."

The man was still looking down the aisle at the closed door. Now his wife tilted over the counter to stare at the closed door as well.

Saffron's shoulders hitched back up. She slammed the drawer shut in time with the next, 'unh,' so hard that coins burst from their slots, and the drawer missed its catch, and popped right back at her. She slammed it again in time with the next 'unh,' and again, 'unh' crash, 'unh' crash, 'unh' crash; quarters and nickels, dimes and pennies kept popping free.

Sudden awareness crossed the dry wrinkles of the little old woman's face. Her hand fluttered to her chest. She gave Saffron the, "I know you're a little whore," look and yanked on her husband's arm. He spilled more coffee. "Let's go," she snapped. He didn't clean his mess.

Twenty minutes later the cowboy threw the back door open, adjusted his crotch, tipped his hat at Saffron, who noticed his fly was still open, and whistled out the door. Coco sauntered out. Her mouth and cheeks were red as if someone had sandpapered her. Her long, black hair puffed with knots. "Oh, God, I feel so alive! Don't you think he looks like Matthew McConaughey?"

"Owen Wilson." Saffron mumbled into her hands. She leaned on her elbows at the register counter.

Coco yelled over the splashing as she washed her hands in the deli sink. "You still mad at me?"

Saffron dropped her forehead on the counter. "No. I just don't know how you can be like that."

"Like what?" Coco opened her register to count out some bills and make a money drop in the safe.

"Never mind."

"No, really. Like what?"

Saffron was silent.

Coco stopped counting. She put her face down on the counter next to Saffron's. "Be rude and get it on while you're working out here alone? I know. I'm sorry."

"I don't care about working out here alone. That's not what I'm talking about. It's just, how can you do it at all?"

"What do you mean, you need a sex lesson?"

"Oh, for Christ's sake, Coco! Never mind!" Saffron turned her head over. Outside, twilight stars twinkled. "Coco? How come you never hung around with me before? You know, at school."

"Princess Fiona."

Saffron rolled her head over and squinted up at her.

"Yeah, did you know people called you that? All the chicks that hung around with Mindy and Samantha got princess names. The darling couple themselves? Well, Mindy was The Wicked Bitch of the East and Samantha was the Wicked Bitch of the West. I didn't want to try to know you, Saffron. Give me a break; who would? You hung around with them. I thought you were like them." She shrugged an 'oh, well.'

Saffron stood up straight. She never imagined hanging around with Mindy and Co. was making *her* look bad. She was always sure she made them look bad, and she had always been thankful for their scraps of tolerance, that they let her hang around them at all.

Coco chuckled at Saffron's wide eyes. "Girl, you need some confidence. If you were a self-induced moron with metal-bending halitosis I'd say, 'Sure, hide in a closet, you're scaring people.' But you're not. You're beautiful and I'm always laughing when I hang around with you. Look around, man. See things a little differently. You're getting old – yuh gotta get on with life.

"As far as I'm concerned, your only mistake in life was choosing that gag-me girly squad to hang around with. Your choices for friends, Saffron, P.U! C'mon, half of those freakin' coffee thermoses are empty; let's do another batch."

Saffron followed her like a puppy.

Throughout the night, Coco babbled on like rain on a tin roof. Saffron wandered with the duster, allowing Ny to stalk to the front of her thoughts. As she shuffled around the corner of the condom aisle, Saffron stopped and fell into a trance.

In her head, all was black. Then the black became a dome in which stars twinkled. The moon was full, every single crater magnified. She was encased in pristine silence as she saw herself standing barefoot on sugar-white sands on the edge of a black lake. The lake was surrounded on all sides by shadowed mountains with glittering, snowcapped-peaks. An empty glass boat glided toward her, across the inky waters, cleaving and moving the water as if it were yards and yards of obsidian air silk. She stepped into the boat and sat in the center, hugging her knees to her chest. Through the bottom of the boat, she saw flashes of tiny, glowing, neon fish. She hung her hand outside of the boat and dipped her fingers into the lukewarm water. The fish swam up one by one, kissed her flesh, and disappeared into the depths when they found her inedible. The boat was bearing her silently across the lake. She saw no one was waiting for her on the far shore. She strained her eyes as she searched the shore again. Her body became leaden. She felt her heart tear so wide she could almost hear it. Big tears welled in her eyes. She shook them away and searched again. The coming shore held only sand and the shadows of trees that swayed when the wind caught up in their canopy. A sudden gust of wind shrieked in her ears. Its scream amplified beyond her tolerance and the dream shattered around her.

Someone had come into the store. He headed for the milk cooler. Big round tears bounced off her freckled cheeks and plopped to the cracked linoleum. She couldn't catch her breath.

Coco appeared in front of her. "Saffron, look. I don't know you that well? But I've kinda been watching you because you seem to be acting a little...." Coco didn't say "strange," seeing as how Saffron was hypersensitive and always a little strange. But she also knew that Saffron, The-Gorgeous-When-Not-Hunched-Redhead, was weirder than usual today. Coco felt like she had to say something. Saffron was actually making her nervous. It was a strange sensation – nervous - that she had no use for. It didn't quite fit into the already emotion-filled saddlebag that was her mind. She scratched her head and looked around at the condom display. "Are you just trying to decide on which brand? These ribbed Trojans are overrated."

Saffron bit her lip to stop the tears. What was wrong with her?

What was Ny doing? *Was* he doing it, or was she really going insane?

Coco's eyes went flat. "Okay, definitely not deciding on condoms. Dude, what's going on up here?" Lightly, she tapped Saffron's forehead.

Saffron choked. "I'm okay. I'm so tired. I just need to sleep."

"Saffron, I can't keep putting you to bed in the back room. I mean, I don't mind workin' the store alone or nothin' like that. It's just that, why aren't you sleeping at home? If you don't get enough sleep, you'll go insane. It's been proven." Coco's head bobbed mournfully. "We're calling your mother. You need to go home. Maybe you're coming down with something."

Were all of her problems due to lack of sleep? Maybe she should go to a sleep specialist instead of a shrink. She could go to one of those sleep clinics she heard about on the radio station; the commercial after the 'breast enhancement' commercial and before the 'lose fifty pounds in a week commercial.' She decided Coco was right; she should go home, go to bed.

***

Markis came back to the store around ten-thirty. He was unusually serious as he craned his neck to look around the store.

Coco came from out back at the ting-a-ling. "Saffron went home sick." She reached into the cooler for the bucket of tuna salad. She put some on a paper towel and grabbed a spoon she kept behind the parade of scratch tickets. She took the salad from the reserves bucket, never from the congealed display tray. She cupped the paper towel of tuna and dug in, talking to Markis between bites as she leaned her bones on the counter. She babbled on while he frowned.

He stared out the black window. Was Saffron sick or avoiding him? He decided he was not going to hound her again. Maybe he was pressuring her. She was so upset when he left earlier. She wouldn't even look at him, like she wanted to avoid him. Maybe he would just give her a call to make sure she was okay. Or would she feel pressured? He decided to leave her alone. If she liked him...she'd let him know. If she didn't bother with him, except to give those forced polite smiles, then he'd know to give it up. He made himself listen to Coco.

"Mwah, mwah, mwah mwah, mwah mwah." She jutted her chin at him. "Yeah, I knew you weren't listening." She shook her head as she poked her cupped tuna salad. "You freakin' people. Just tell her how you feel. Believe me; she needs to hear that from you right now. She really was sick when she went home. She needs something to rock her world. You know what I'm saying? Rock her world, then give her a nap. That'll solve all her damn problems."

"Coco, you think that's the cure for everything."

She held her hands out. "It is."

On the ride home, Saffron's mother had gotten less out of her than Coco had. Saffron didn't want to talk. She wanted to get home to her bed. She wanted to go to sleep. No talking, no thinking, no dreaming. Just sleeping.

At ten-thirty, she was in bed, arguing with her mother and Derek, who stood in the doorway. They wanted her to pick one of them to sleep in her room with her even though the moon wasn't full.

While she argued feebly, Mr. and Mrs. Garden Gnome had a spat in the garden. Apparently, the Mrs. was sick and tired of the Mr. chewing on his toenails and spitting them about their spic-and-span, brand-new, underground lair. She screamed at him. She swore little gnome swears at him, flung gourds and other produce at his head. For a finale, she cracked a stick over his skull and pushed him face-first into a pile of fresh manure. He stormed off and harassed the alpacas by riding them and yanking their long silky locks. The alpacas skittered and rolled and hummed in dismay, trying to throw him off.

A few hours after she had passed out, Saffron woke up with a headache. She felt queasy. Maybe she really did have the flu. She sighed. She knew she didn't have the flu. She was making herself sick was what she was doing.

A bag of crackers and a can of warm ginger ale were sitting on her bedside table. Her mother left her a note signed with X's and O's. It said she could go down to the fridge and reheat dinner if she was hungry. Turkey, stuffing, mashed potatoes, and carrots with gravy. Or, if she needed help, to just call out and her mother would come.

Saffron got out of bed and walked to her window. She threw open the panes and gulped in crisp, fresh air. Autumn was her favorite time of year, even now when the nights were getting very crisp with cold. She could smell the apple-drops moldering beneath the apple tree and see every star in the sky as if they were crystals dancing on the inky surface of a black lake. She frowned. The inky blackness of the night sky brought her no joy this evening. She held herself tightly as the flesh seized up on the back of her neck and every little hair stood on end. Her eyes were drawn to the movement of a black shadow beneath her.

The vampire was smiling up at her.

He was right there, just below her, sitting on the roof of the farmer's porch, on the short decline. His feet were tucked up near his butt; his arms were wrapped loosely around his knees. He was so close she could reach out and touch him. She recoiled, reached to clutch the panes and slam them shut. Her intestines knotted and tried to slither away. All of the blood left her head, leaving her dizzy.

"Don't bother," Jethin said. "The old fables and folklore ring true.

I can't come in unless you invite me." He wiggled his eyebrows. "Hi. I'm Jethin." He could feel her fear. Each time it took a new form, her fear surrounded and fed him. He kept talking.

She didn't hear much of what he said at first. The blood had zoomed back into her head and was thumping like a bass drum in her ear canals. His words were muffled, but the sound of his voice was calm and soothing. Soon, it began to work on her. The thumping in her head faded away.

"...silly movies anyway. You know how it is, 'fear the unknown'." He snorted, "I'm just a big sweetheart." He had beautiful, full lips, big, fat lips that widened back to reveal big, beautiful, white teeth. His straight, dark hair was pulled back at the base of his neck. He wore a puffy black parka, black jeans, and black hiking boots.

She still gripped the window; her spastic breath frosted the glass. Her eyes narrowed slightly as she really focused on him for the first time. He sat there cozy enough on the slant of the farmer's porch roof, which was just below all of the second floor windows on the front of the house. When she was younger, had Saffron been a wild, fun-loving girl, or a mischievous hooligan, she could have easily used the roof as a means to sneak out at night. But Saffron had never had the heart for such a life.

Saffron didn't know if he, if *Jethin*, was mulatto, Hispanic, Hawaiian, or what, but he was hot. Li had warned her against such a creature. Saffron knew she would have to take the next few moments very carefully - even if he was giving her the most heart-melting grin. She smiled back, just a small smile. She couldn't help it. He already made her feel good. His teeth were completely normal except for the fact that they were so perfect, so perfectly white and shiny. "Could you attack me if I was walking around outside?" The statement was a poke, a jab at him to see what his reaction would be, as if she were a little girl at the beach who came upon a meandering crab. Maybe, if she was nice, he would be too; this monster below her that smelled faintly of decay. A scent his four-hundred-dollar cologne couldn't mask.

"Yep. I could rip your jugular out in two seconds flat and offer it to my mates as a door prize." He popped some bubble gum into his mouth, formed a string with it after a couple of chews, and twirled it around his tongue. He offered her some. He waved his hand to indicate the farmhouse. "But in your home, you are protected, by...something. The more loving the home, the stronger the charm; and let me tell you, your walls are like Fort Knox. They're absolutely impenetrable, unless of course, you allow me to pass." He winked.

She reached out to take the offered gum, then snatched her hand back to hold against her chest. "Why tell me that? I had no idea. You could have tricked me and done whatever it is you wanted to do with me."

"I don't want to rip your jugular out, Saffron. That wouldn't be any fun." He spoke so pleasantly and smiled so sweetly. He raised a heavy eyebrow at her and appeared to really look at her for the first time. "I'm a lamb. Listen, after we met at the movie theatre I was thinking about you. I mean, why are you glowing?"

She shrugged, and hoped she appeared casual, while every bone in her body clacked inside her skin. "It's no big deal. It'll wear off soon." Her head jerked involuntarily. "Some fairies took me to their home. Now, apparently, I glow like a firefly. To...some...people. It's only temporary."

He 'hmmmed' and cocked his head. "And why did they take you there?"

Saffron slumped against the window brace and studied the apple tree as it creaked in the cold November night. "Why?" She shook her head slowly. "I don't wonder why anymore. It just happened."

He snorted, "Nothing just happens."

She focused on him. "I can see these like, paranormal things. There are gnomes in my mother's garden."

"Cool; get the pesticide."

"And I can see you, your teeth. I saw you that night at the movies." Her stomach flip-flopped as she held it with both hands. She didn't think she'd get away with lying to a vampire, not for long anyway.

"So, you're covered in fairy flotsam. It exposes us – inhuman - to you."

"Yeah." She felt let down when his eyes drifted away from her. Maybe he wasn't really that impressed by 'fairy flotsam.' Maybe Li was totally out of touch and didn't realize vampires weren't hot for fairy stuff anymore. Saffron felt an inkling of distress as her courage scurried away. She wanted his attention back. "But, you know, whatever."

"It's more than, 'whatever;' it's a fantastic power." He cleared his throat. "I can make it so you would never lose that magic."

Saffron made the smelly cheese face. "You can?"

He suddenly sprang to his haunches and leaned toward her. "It would be easy."

She let go of the window brace and stepped back from the sill. "Yeah, no thanks. This fairy power has made my life crap. I know zombies exist because I am one. The sooner it wears off, the better." She was mumbling again, but didn't close the window on him.

Something about Jethin changed. His eyes seemed to clear against his will. For a few seconds, Saffron saw naked admiration there, in his eyes, as opposed to the bravado he had been showing up until that moment. Then the machismo came back, and Jethin fixed himself into a casual slouch. Saffron missed none of this and wondered what it meant. She knew one thing; he had thought she was interesting, at least for a moment.

"Saffron, you are absolutely the most fascinating girl I have ever encountered. I could make that permanent. Listen. That light around you is not just fairy magic - it's your youth. And it's almost gone." His lip twitched.

She looked down at her fingernails. "You're creeping me out." Her voice was trembling, "I mean, I don't think I even want those things."

"You don't want what?" he snapped. "Your youth? You don't want your energy? Your vitality? You don't want the very stuff that makes you interesting?" He shifted to look at her, his body expectant, his eyes intent, his voice low and demanding. "You really don't want that?"

Saffron shook her head emphatically, causing red waves of hair to ripple and resettle.

Jethin considered this at length. "Huh." He cleaned gum off his canine with the side of his tongue. He snapped a bubble. "Saffron, do you like going to see the fairies?"

Saffron made a grunt low in her throat. "I could live without it." But, then she felt bad, talking this way about Li behind her back. Yet, she meant it. She wouldn't mind seeing Li again, but she felt pretty sure she was done with the whole fairyland thing. It wasn't what she had imagined it would be. As bright and beautiful as it was, there was something wrong with it. Something off - repulsive even. When she was there, she felt she shouldn't be. The fairies pulled her soul there;

the world itself pushed on her until she left.

A look of high surprise stretched Jethin's eyes. Then again, "Huh." He changed the subject. He remarked on how cool and still the night was, and then went on to lull her with eloquent words and silly stories. After an hour or so, while Saffron sat on a pile of pillows she had gathered, he noticed her eyes were heavy and her attention waning. He told her he had to be off - an unbreakable engagement. He promised he'd be back. She hadn't asked if he would come back, he just told her he would return.

She hopped into bed and fell asleep. Just like that, as if it had always been that simple. She didn't remember any dreams, but there were circles under her eyes in the morning.

One week later, she had just come into her room from the bathroom (where the little ghost boy sat on the counter but didn't speak), when she felt a presence. She looked around the room; the strain in the back of her neck was painful. There was no one there. She moved her rigid arms out of her t-shirt and her rigid legs out of her jeans. She unhooked her bra and stopped. She had to use every ounce of effort to let the bra fall to the floor and not to cross her arms over her chest. She crossed her arms over her chest. She looked behind her, and then out the window. She saw her reflection - chicken body with wiry arms wrapped protectively. She swore at herself. She would have to remember to shut the curtains now. *He* could be out there. *He* was real. She grabbed her tank-top and jammed it on, then hop, hop, hopped quickly into her flannel pants. She slammed the light switch down, raced to her bed, tugged at the feather comforter, and clamped it down over her head.

Tap tap tap. The noise came from her window. Tap tap tap. "Saffron, it's me." Jethin's voice was dulled as it came through the glass.

"Well, duh." Saffron's giggle was sprinkled with hysteria. She lowered the comforter and stared at him. She whispered, "Have you been there the whole time?"

He heard her through the window. He was smirking. "You mean long enough to watch you clutch your breasts as if they were going to fly away? No, I didn't see that."

Saffron jammed the comforter back over her head.

"Come over here; talk to me."

She got out of bed and dragged her tuffet over to the window.

He was gone for the two nights following, but visited the next six nights in a row.

One night, just after the grandfather clock at the foot of the stairs chimed midnight, Jethin told her about how he became a vampire. It happened when he was just nineteen years old. When he told stories, he used his whole body, his eyes and his hands and his lush lips to make sound effects. Listening to him was like eating up a holiday meal; he satisfied every craving and left Saffron feeling full and satisfied. He spoke for hours. A few times, Saffron insisted he answer her questions. They both enjoyed themselves and laughed often. He was confident. He was affecting. And after these several long nights, she was completely attached to him.

Jethin glanced at the horizon. A pinkish light was gathering strength at the edge of the earth. "I'll need to be going very soon. Beauty sleep, you know."

Saffron hugged herself as she watched the first streaks of dawn fingering up from the back of the ocean. She knew her body was asking for sleep, but her mind was so exhilarated. Jethin was no monster. She could stay up with him forever. And, as a plus, she was able to mostly ignore the very faint, dead wood smell of him.

"I love it when you visit." Then, realizing her blunder, her eyes widened with shock. She had never told him how she felt before. What was she saying? Did she just cross one of those invisible barriers? Because she said that, would he be able to get at her? Close enough to hurt her? Her family? Quickly, she tried to cover her tracks. "What I mean is," her rushed words tumbled out on piggyback, "you can sit here again, on my roof, and talk. But, that's it; okay?"

"As you wish. I'll return to talk to you again and nothing more. If that's truly what you want. Either way, I promise you will never be one of my meals." He winked at her, then jumped down from the roof, quiet as a cat.

Saffron sat in her windowsill long after Jethin left. A trill of delight shot up her arms, across her chest and bathed her in delicate little quakes. This was different. He was different. She wasn't attracted to him in the same way she was attracted to Markis, which she could confirm was definitely puppy love; she didn't want him the way she wanted Ny, which bordered on obscene. She liked him because he was so confident. He was what she was not: strong.

She listened to the ocean. Over the cliff, she heard the waves crashing and booming against the rocks. High tide. As she shut the window, a cold wind came to blow through the naked limbs of the apple tree. She pulled the window shut and secured the lock, then dropped on her bed and snuggled with her comforter. The forecaster said the first snow would arrive tomorrow - two inches! Outside, it was lighter all at once. Saffron felt her heart beating. She felt her physical life. The rhythm matched the booms from the ocean. It made her feel strong. Was it because of Jethin?

Chapter 13

Li found Ny squatting by the stream where he had sat with

Saffron. He was teasing the tiny water pixies. The pixies were beside themselves. Here they were, minding their own business, bathing in the stream, when along came this form of male perfection who chose to spend his time with them. In the middle of their bath, wet and shining, they flirted with him with glee. He splashed them and they splashed him and flew about his face, giving out tiny kisses and rubbing their little bodies against his cheek.

"Now what have you done, Ny? Sincerely, you are the most wicked thing I know." Li waited for Ny to leap up and defend himself, as was his way. He didn't. She poked again, "Do tell, are you really a fairy or just some lower-rung demon?" Li gave up the lighthearted pretense. She put her hands on her hips. "Saffron moans in her sleep about you."

Ny smirked.

"She moans to be left alone. She moans for you to leave her mind." Li's black pupils dilated and shrunk like they were breathing.

Ny continued to play with the pixies as if Li were not there. The pixies looked from the female fairy to the male in bewilderment. When they saw him ignore the female with great concentration, they decided to snub her as well.

"Very well. If you will not leave her alone, I will be forced to go to her and tell her the truth. Although I know it will cause her to suffer greatly, I hope it will also make her wise to you, and give her the strength she needs to be rid of you. When she learns of the truth of our lives, I will then instruct her on how to block you out. Completely. No more journeys into her mind for you." She crossed her arms over her chest. "Please, we will all be back together soon enough. Do not drive her in the wrong direction."

"Your threat will remain a threat only, will it not? You have no intention of going against me, sister. Not with all of *your* terrible little secrets." He massaged his biceps, fully enjoying the feel of himself. "Too bad I know all of your secrets. You could get away with so much without me as your guide."

"Do not make light of this. It is not a game!" When she screamed, the water pixies scattered into the air. Some crashed into each other in the splashy confusion, then plopped back into the water. They dragged themselves to a rock, gathered their clothing of spider silk and flower petals, and then bobbed away like a flurry of butterflies. "Good, all of your admirers have left. What are you now? You are nothing without the Godly worship of females." She pumped her wings in staccato bursts, causing her long, white length of hair to get caught up where the wings grew out of her back. She picked up a stone and hurled it as hard as she could off into the sunlit forest. The veins pulsed with fire beneath her clear skin.

"You are nothing! Nothing to her without me*! You need me* to keep her around, keep her for you." He shot to his feet. "So behave and maybe I will let you stay." He jabbed his chest with his thumb. "I provide something for them to worship. It is what I expect. It is what I receive. If you commanded such from others, you would receive the same. You could have more than her, thousands more! But you only want your pet. Do not preach at me!" He bared his lips and clacked his top teeth to his bottom teeth. He had a delicious secret. If Li knew that he had shown Saffron the dark lake and the empty shore, her anger would indeed be immeasurable. The fairy world might just experience the first fairy murder attempt since the dawn of time. He snickered. He had been murdered before. Actually, he had been snuffed out in several lifetimes. Many a time, irate husbands had taken his life in a fit of rage. Once, he was even murdered by one of Saffron's husbands. Saffron was such an enjoyable soul. He would never give her up. She was like wild fowl - simple, but when prepared correctly, absolutely the most succulent flavor on earth. That never got old, no matter how often it was consumed. No, she would always be his, just as she always had been. Saffron wanted this, too. She just liked to cluck and squawk before she allowed him his way.

This was such a strange turn of events, the thing Saffron had gone and done, as odd as finding a toddler wobbling down a freeway. He liked to puzzle over it with his free time. Still, he felt confident that control was ultimately his. It was the way it always was. This was but a momentary lapse, this separation from Saffron - nothing but a sigh in the line of time. He was determined to enjoy this moment as a game. There was, after all, nothing else to do.

"Come, my Li, let us make up." He put his arm around her shoulder. "Be cheered. Although I play with Saffron in her dreams, she no longer remembers. Her days are filled with happiness. I have made it so."

***

Saffron was pissed. She was starting to have frequent dreams about Ny again. She slept a lot during the day and there he was - him and his gross girlfriends. But even worse, he'd show up while she was awake and give her visions...

At night, when Jethin visited, Saffron found she could keep Ny at a distance.

Ny felt the separation, but couldn't figure where she went during those times. He assumed she was in a sleep-pattern that he could not penetrate. It never occurred to him to leave the fairy world to confirm this.

Saffron was naïve to her power. Ny knew a human could open her mind to magic and knew too, that humans could close their minds to magic. He certainly would never let Saffron know she obtained the power to deny him. She was tapping into the power now, while she was with Jethin, which might have made her stronger, but tapping in unknowingly...that made her weaker.

Alas, poor Markis got nothing. Saffron tried hard to appear attentive when he came to the store to visit. They had long talks together. He helped the girls by mopping the floor before the end of the shift. He'd get takeout and he and Saffron would share it out of the same carton while he sat cross-legged out back, doing his school work.

But Markis often got the feeling that Saffron wasn't really listening to him, as if he was so boring her mind had to wander when they were together. The circles under her eyes were gone. So that was good. Her hair was shiny and braided in a cool way, but she seemed more out of it now than ever before. To make things worse, Saffron would suddenly realize what she was doing, perk up, and slather Markis with put-on, over-the-top sweetness. It was humiliating to Markis to chase this "preoccupied" girl; it hacked at his pride and left him with a cloying, pathetic feeling.

At night, Saffron cleared her mind of everything so she could relax and let Jethin's voice soothe her, restore her, and give her the strength to face another day. Jethin loved telling Saffron stories about his life, before and after the change.

He told her he was born in Ireland in 1698 and was the son of a poor farmer. Potatoes, of all things. He rolled his eyes. "Whenever I tell this story, I feel like someone should break out some bleeding violins." With an indignant sniff, he continued his tale. He felt his youth had been uneventful. Sometimes they had enough food to get by, and sometimes he was so hungry he gnawed at the corner of his blanket as he lay upon his infested, grass-stuffed mattress. But, that was only during the very worst of times. For the most part, his large family could scrape together something to eat.

Something had been bothering Saffron, so she interrupted him. He seemed irritated by her interruption and listened to her question with disdain. After he heard her out it was all he could do not to jump up and slap her silly mouth. She had asked about his origins, his skin color.

Saffron's face was twisted in confusion. "Irish? Ireland? Dude, aren't you like black or something? I thought you were from Puerto Rico."

Jethin ground his teeth as he fought for control. How he despised this stupid question, only the dead knew, for he had killed everyone who had asked him up until this point. "Saffron," he shook his head and raised his eyebrows as he stared at the apple tree. "I don't know why," he spoke slowly, as if to a child or an impaired person, "but you can find Irish aplenty that look like me. Go look it up."

"Well, don't you know your own lineage? I think it's cool the way you look. Don't you know why you look like that?" She had obviously missed his ill-disguised malice.

He clucked his tongue, looked at her in amazement. "I glad you find me fascinating in this way," lie, "may I go on with my story?" She shrugged. He saw fear dawning in her eyes.

He told her his family was devoutly Catholic. Every Saturday night, they went down to the river that rolled past their cottage and bathed in the frigid waters to rid them of the week's dirt. Every Sunday they spent at church praying, attending mass and celebrating whatever holy day was currently on the calendar. He moaned that there was always a holy day on the calendar.

"I know! Maybe you're a gypsy!" She smiled at her stunning thought.

Jethin spoke low and dangerous, "Saffron, do you think you can shut up now?" She sat back and pursed her lips.

Jethin readjusted himself on the peak of the roof, rested his forearms on his knees, and left his big hands dangling. He began one more time.

His brothers and sisters accepted the poor potato life, with little complaint. After all, they would say, what else could they possibly do? They accepted themselves as simple folk, trying to live a harsh life as simply as they could.

Jethin was not so accepting. He felt he was meant for something more. He would not accept this dirty, poor, heavily-burdened existence. He was constantly looking for a means of escape. He was a thorn in his parents' side. He was the most beautiful boy that anyone had ever laid eyes on - the meanest as well. He brooded, day in and day out, about their wasted lives, their embarrassing heritage. His mother never let him go into town if she could help it, for as soon as Jethin were to spy a gentleman there or someone well-to-do, his brooding turned into a white-hot rage of insatiable jealousy. His father took the belt to him on many drunken occasions, accusing him of ungodly and uppity behavior.

By age fifteen, Jethin felt he was man enough to leave home and change his life. In doing so, he would change the

lives of everyone in his family. Even though they appeared content with their miserable existence, he was embarrassed for them and determined to pull them from the muck.

He tied some potatoes and carrots up in a cloth, and with nothing but his bare feet and the worn clothes on his back, he was ready to set out at dawn the following day.

During the night, his father died. He had let himself waste away over the past many years, poisoning himself with drink. It was a family concoction - a vodka - born of his own potatoes. His father had once been a proud man of a well-to-do wool-exporting family. Jethin's grandfather had given his son half of his flock when Gethin's father married in 1697. One year later, their first son was born. Jethin, they named him, after an estranged uncle who, most surprisingly, had bequeathed them a fortune in pearls from his maritime adventures. In 1699, English Parliament passed the Woolen Act. It stated that Ireland could no longer export woolen goods to any country whatsoever. Within a few short years, Jethin's father had found himself and all of his relatives in complete poverty. Wool had been his family's trade for generations. They hardly knew what else to do. Jethin's father decided to turn to potato farming, hoping for the best. Until the day he died, a broken man with a broken heart, he never again experienced "the best." He left behind his wife and seven children living in a cottage that was really no more than a shack on the side of a rocky, sloping dale. Jethin's only brothers were four and seven years old. Jethin became the man of the family. He was miserable, and sickened at the thought that he would now have to stay and provide for his family from this barren, hilly land. His worldly dreams were dashed. Two years passed. Jethin toiled silently on the rocky farm. He worked from before sunup till after sundown, and took his meal only when the others had gone to sleep. He spoke very rarely.

One day, a peddler came along the rocky path that lined the sea. She picked her way carefully, so as not to stumble and roll down to the icy waves. She was young, voluptuous, and much too intoxicating for a mere peddler. She made her way under the hot sun, out over the dry dirt where Jethin worked alone. He discouraged his brothers and sisters from loitering around him and they heeded him without question.

Jethin was monotonously hoeing the parched and caked earth. When the tool slipped, the skin of his finger split from the nail. He cursed and stared at the wound as the blood mixed with the dirt permanently lodged under his nails. Her shadow fell across him. He did not look up. "Aye?"

She didn't answer.

Jethin looked up, annoyed, but immediately his quick temper was curbed. His dry, dusty mouth began to water.

The peddler could see why her mistress wanted this boy. Now that she got a good look at him, she wanted him for herself. But she knew better - were she to move on him, she could then welcome death with open arms. He had soft eyes, big, faded-pink lips, and ruddy cheeks. He was dirty, true, but the way his thick, black eyelashes closed over his flinty, dark eyes was so beautiful and perfect, that one could look far, far beyond the dirt. The peddler smiled provocatively. She threw her hair back over her shoulder and stood a little straighter.

Jethin was already half mad with too much sun; he had to look away before the sight of her healthy bosom put him over the edge. Her exotic beauty pulled at his eyes, demanded his attention. He had never seen such a woman before. But, unlike his brothers and sisters, Jethin was no country simpleton. "You are no peddler; state your business." He tried to give his voice a strong, deep edge, to seem commanding. He needed to get hold of himself and bury this sudden urge to throw the girl, whoever she really was, over his shoulder and carry her off into the woods. He knew just the tree he would put her on, too. *Don't be a fool*; he told himself, *the most beautiful blossom hides the bee.*

"I am a seller of wares, Sir. I wish to show you my wares." She had the voice of a siren with a little nettle and a little honey. She had no wares about her.

Jethin snorted. He was no 'Sir,' and she knew it. He hoped he appeared bored and annoyed. But his lust was growing. He wanted her to go away. He was afraid she would bring him trouble. Somehow, she meant to bring him trouble. He did not trust her, but he wanted her all the same. Out here on the farm, he did not chance any meetings with any girls, never mind ones the likes of this. He was losing his fight with control.

The peddler watched him squirm.

Jethin looked up and noticed her smug, satisfied grin. He jumped to his feet and loomed before her, snorting like a bull. "State your business or be off!"

Her bright smile lost its shine. The smirk remained all

the same. "I am here on behalf of my mistress, Jethin. She would like very much to meet you."

"Who is your mistress? How do you know my name?"

The peddler rolled her eyes and considered a distant hill. The wind, wet and briny, played with her dark hair. "Why is it they always believe it shocking that a person can find out their names?" Her muttering was almost incoherent.

Jethin narrowed his eyes. "Eh?"

"If you would like to be enlightened, meet my mistress in O'Donnell's tonight, upon the witching hour." She took Jethin's hand and placed it on the flat of her chest beneath her long, sun-kissed throat, and just above the swell of her breasts. "And do say yes, Jethin - you appear to be absolutely delicious." She laughed. Almost cackled.

Jethin ripped his hand away as if her skin had burned him and silently pointed her back down the path. He wiped his hand on his shirt as he watched her hips saunter off. He licked his lips and swallowed his saliva before he could drool.

As usual, he took his dinner late in the night. Sometime around eleven, he set off for O'Donnell's; two miles away across the moonlit moors.

His mother watched him leave but said nothing. He was a man and could do as he pleased. She rolled over on her sparse mattress, being careful not to jostle the children, and fell into a fitful sleep. She dreamed of blood and unending suffering and of corpses that walked in the gloaming. Pale and sweating, she awoke hours later, fearing for Jethin's soul. She prayed.

When Jethin entered the tavern, it was booming with men's voices and bustling with men's business. It was so crowded and smoky, Jethin could hardly see. It made things much more difficult that he didn't know who he was looking for. His feet stuck to the spilled muck on the wide, uneven boards as he limped through the crowd and suffered elbows and bumps from indifferent drunks. Just as his temper was about to flare, he saw her. It had to be her.

She was in a booth in a dark corner, staring evenly at him and smiling. She was out of place in this shady pub. She was exquisite - a rare flower in a barn among dirty beasts. Didn't she fear for her safety? Jethin admired her fearlessness.

He strolled to her table, pressed his thighs forward on the table edge, folded his arms across his chest and tried to stare her down. When she didn't waver, he held her gaze as he slid onto the seat across from her. They remained this way, as if in a trance, for quite some time.

One of the locals had long since taken notice of the crazy heifer in the corner. His drunken, fish-eyes were pale and mean. He swiped his thin hair off of his high forehead. The loud, red veins webbing his bulbous nose warned of a seasoned drunk, but Jethin was oblivious of him, wrapped up in the fascinating woman before him. The drunk was annoyed by the brazen action of the wench who had entered *his* pub and who was now staring gaily at the young pup - that impoverished slob - who lived on the edge of town. The drunk tripped over to the booth to have some fun with them before getting rid of them both.

"Wastin' your time with a little lad, luv? You look like you need a man!" He cupped his groin, jiggered his lumpy sack with his sausage fingers, then reached for her as his friends goaded him on, hooting and howling and jeering. Nobody stood to stop him. This was more fun than usual.

The woman broke her stare with Jethin in time to grab the man's hand before it could touch her skin. She looked into the eyes of the man, a coy smile upon her lips. Jethin was awestruck. She *wasn't* afraid! He watched her closely as she watched the foul-smelling man. Suddenly, her eyes widened and their color changed from green to black - a deep, dark black so solid there was no difference between her pupils or the rest of her eyes - just great, black orbs that seemed to bulge out of her head. Her grip tightened on the man. He keened and moaned quietly. He tried to pull his hand back, but she held firm. Jethin could not believe his eyes as he looked down at the growing wet mark at the man's crotch. Finally, the woman released him, and the man ran out of the pub and into the moonlit night, weeping like a child. She faced Jethin and folded her hands in her lap. The man's friends muttered and turned away from the two odd people in the booth. The men made motions with their hands to ward off the evil eye and the ancient gods of the pagans.

"Are you the Devil?" Jethin, having spent so much time listening to Catholic priests, knew a great deal about the Devil - all the townspeople did. Her laugh was soft and warm. She reached across the table for Jethin's hand. Jethin flinched and snatched his hand away. "Ah...no. I don't want to become like that chap who just left."

"I would never do that to you, Jethin, just as you would never treat me as that man did just now. True?"

"Of course, it's true. I would never do that to you. But, tell me, who are you?"

"My name is Cecilia. I live my life as I wish. Will you join me?"

Jethin took in her graceful hands, her long throat, her high bosom and inviting mouth. "Of course."

Saffron made a barking laugh. "You *are* kidding, right? I mean, she was the one, the one that made you a vampire?"

"Yes." His tone was flat. "What do you mean, 'you're kidding'?"

"My God, Jethin! Somebody asks you to give up your entire life and you just agree with them like they're asking you to choose between regular or diet?"

Jethin displayed great patience. "Saffron, tell me, what life was I giving up? A life of poverty? Of starvation? Of pestilence? Of disease? Of loneliness? Of failure? Which one of these things was I was supposed to deny her for?"

"And you *never* regretted your choice? Are you sure?"

He didn't look her in the eye when he answered. He turned his head toward the sea, where he saw nothing but blackness, then tilted his eyes toward the moon. "Never." It was only the faintest whisper. It was an odd sound filled with an unfathomable amount of sadness, which Saffron missed altogether.

She was wrapped in her own emotions; his subtleties blew by her like white noise. "I still can't believe you changed your entire existence over some fluttering lashes and a nice set of wahoos." She wondered if her own wahoos would one day hold such power. She ran her hand down the board and tennis balls that were her chest. She should Google when wahoo development stopped.

"You have it all wrong. Maybe I was somewhat attracted to her in the beginning, but our relationship quickly developed into something more complex, something more powerful. She told me she was the lonely widow of a dead count. She used his fortune to travel the world and hopefully bring light to her sad, desperate life."

Jethin continued to pick his way through his tale.

Countess Cecilia asked Jethin if he would be interested in being in her employ. She told him she would pay him well and reward his good work with ample prizes, money and jewels. Jethin agreed wholeheartedly. But, for once in his life, it was not the monetary reward that lured him, but the unearthly beauty of this woman.

She dipped her finger in her wine, which was cheap and soured. The barkeep told her she was lucky to get any such thing in his bar and not to complain. She ran her finger around and around in the liquid. It was as dark as blood. She tasted a drop by pressing it to her lips and darting her tongue to catch it, wincing at the bitter flavor. She pushed the glass away.

Jethin didn't notice the wince. He was lost back where the tongue darted to grab the drop from the lips. Lost in lust, lost in love. From that point on, he couldn't save himself. (He didn't tell Saffron this part.) Countess Cecilia reached below the table, within the flow of her robes, and retrieved a black velvet bag heavy with gold and silver and foreign coins. She beckoned Jethin to give her his hand, which he did now without hesitation. As she placed the satchel in his ruddy

palm, she stroked his wrist. Smiling prettily, she bid him adieu. She let him know that her servant, Claudia, would inform him on the morrow of some jobs he might perform for her.

He left the tavern in a haze of wonder and high spirits. His father had never accomplished such a feat without a drink! The hostile attitude Jethin had worn like a second skin seemed to have sloughed off and disappeared with the wind. He suddenly had an idea and giggled like a child as he stepped lightly along his way. He walked a mile further, into the heart of town, and banged on the carpenter's door. Bleary-eyed and grumbling, the carpenter answered his door.

Before the man could utter a word, Jethin commanded him to make three beds (as no more could possibly be crammed into the small shack his mother called "home") and the mattresses to match, and have them delivered to his home. Jethin grabbed the man's arm, startling him further, and poured a number of coins into his worn hand. "I trust that will suffice."

"Most certainly, lad. Tha'll do." The man stared at the coins in his hand like a hungry dog.

Jethin turned on one heel to head for home. The carpenter hailed him. Jethin turned to see him hobbling over. He offered Jethin, for a small fee, of course, the sale of his horse, which the carpenter proclaimed was a fine mount and agreeable working steed. He'd ready the horse - bit, bridle, blanket, and saddle - then present the snorting beast to Jethin a short time later. More coins clinked into the carpenter's outstretched hands and not long after, Jethin found himself riding home on a spirited, tall, black stallion.

In the morning, Jethin ordered his mother to hold out her apron. He dropped the remaining coins from the bag onto the worn cloth. His mother scowled. She cursed her son. She dropped the coins to the dirt floor and told Jethin she'd have none of it, this Devil's gold, and went off to cry. For certain her prayers had failed to save her son. That day, Jethin did not attend mass. (He had been in many a church since then. Churches, in the off hours, are an easy place to pick up prey. In the off hours, churches were where the sinners slunk, hoping to get a quiet pardon.)

Jethin called on his eldest sister. He pressed the coins into her hands and commanded her to follow him to market this morning, where he planned to buy the family a pony and cart and some food for the week.

His mother screamed, "Let it be known to all that I denounce the Devil's gold!"

The eldest sister, Patsy, glanced toward the corner of the room where her mother was huddled on a small stool rocking back and forth, and then turned back to Jethin with an imploring look.

"Never mind that silly, superstitious woman," Jethin barked. "We have lived in poverty for too long. We will not exist in this filth any longer; not if I have anything to say about it! I am the man of the family. You will obey me. Follow me to market this instant!"

He turned from his gawking brothers and sisters, the pitying look from his mother. He slammed the door of the cottage, causing it to fall from its frail hinges. Patsy hurried around the fallen door and struggled to keep at Jethin's heels. With his strong, farmer's body, he swung himself onto his stallion and reached to pull Patsy up behind him.

"Do you see how frustrating it is trying to save people, Saffron? They were too dumb to recognize how I was delivering us all."

Saffron frowned, was about to speak, then waved him on instead.

Patsy and Jethin rode to the market in silence. Patsy wondered how Jethin had come across the stallion and the gold and the silver but she knew better than to question him. They rode over hill and dale and along the edge of the sea and finally arrived to market.

At dawn, the carpenter had spread word in town of Jethin and his new riches.

Brother and sister were received in the marketplace like a king and queen. They had no need to dismount, for peddlers swarmed below them, holding on high their foodstuffs and wares. Everything they could possibly need, and many things that they wanted were offered up on platters and rough-hewn table tops. There were sweet meats and smoked sausages, fresh fowl strung up by their legs, exotic fruits just in off a ship from the Caribbean, vegetables, toys and wooden games, tools, hair ribbons and jewelry, great blocks of cheese, parsley, sage, rosemary, and yes, thyme, handy household devices... Jethin spied a cart and pony.

Claudia watched them from the shadows of an alley, the corner of her mouth hooked up on one side. It was always the same. Her mistress could lure anyone with her beauty and her little golden coins. Claudia often mused how she was caught in the spider's web the very same way! She looked down at her fingers – each adorned in rings of silver or gold - some with garishly big jewels. She mindlessly brought a sparkling ruby to her parted lips and licked the dust off it with her tongue.

"Jethin, how do you know she was making out with her rings at that moment?"

"She was always making out with her rings; it's a likely filler in my tale. Let me tell my story my way, will you?"

Saffron laughed and nodded.

When Jethin had filled the cart (almost over-filled it) with goods, he ordered his sister to go home. He stood in the middle of the market, searching for Claudia. His mistress had not instructed him how to find Claudia so he stood dumbly, his stallion snorting by his side, in the middle of the teeming throngs of market day. The hot, oily scent of sausages filled his nose and his stomach responded with a growl. He relished the fact that he could actually feed himself today! He could buy any food that his heart desired and stuff himself like a pig! He could buy a pig and stuff it for dinner!

Claudia watched him eat. She was crouched down now - he was closer to her alley and, if he turned just a little to the right, he would catch her spying on him. She winced each time he shoved the sausage in his mouth and ripped into the meat like a slobbering beast.

Her mistress had peculiar tastes. He was beautiful, true, but his manner was low-country. She did not look forward to coming out and presenting herself to him. At last, he finished breaking his fast. She could stall no longer. She walked up behind him and tapped him on the shoulder.

When he spun around, he silently appraised her. He was not exactly sure what had changed, whether it was he or Claudia, but she did not appear today as she did the day before. Where there used to be a flowing of dark hair, today he noticed her hair hung in greasy lengths on her shoulders. The soft skin of her face was not the shine of youth, but the oil of a long overdue washing. Even her bosom, which had played such a promising role last night in his long hours of fantasizing, was not so much "full" today but "fatty," and painfully pinched by her broad corset.

As moments became a whole minute, Claudia's eyes burned with a growing hate for Jethin. She saw him. She knew what he was doing. He looked at her with disgust! Well, she thought, pity him. He has no idea what hell awaits him. But this did not calm her as she stood before him, he the sacrificial cow, ridiculing *her* with his eyes as if she were a dirty commoner. But she couldn't let it go. "Aye, Jethin. You think me ugly today. No doubt twas the beauty of my mistress which hath blinded you to all else. Just you remember - I was good enough yesterday, and one day soon you will realize that I am quite a prize compared to some."

Ridiculous, he thought, *what is she bleating about*?

"Indeed," Claudia continued with a fiery conviction, "the fruit which is already rotted on the inside may still happen to wear the most beautiful, ripe skin."

Jethin didn't appear impressed by her prophecy. He

stood erect, his face the essence of disdain. His eyes flitted from her head, down the length of her body, to her toes and back up again. *Jealous wench.* "As fascinating as I am sure you find yourself to be, I do not wish to stand about this rank market all day listening to your incoherencies."

"You great snob, I am learned, and I do not believe "incoherencies" is a word! Listen to yourself. You are an embarrassment. Look at you, the dirty potato boy trying to crawl from beneath the plow and into society. You *Sir*, are a mockery!"

He would have liked to slap her then.

She would have liked to slap him then. "I have nothing more to say to you."

He scoffed. "Nor do I, you. However, we do have work to do; do we not? Please, let us try to get it done so we can be away from each other!" Jethin made sure he had the final word.

Claudia spun about on her heel and shoved her way through the congested crowd. She halted once, Jethin ramming into her back, and impatiently they waited for a mother to move her three mewling children out of the way.

Claudia was relieved Jethin did not stalk off. This had happened before, several times. Her mistress's "boys" were all smiles and hungry eyes for Claudia until they met her, The Countess Cecilia. Then they turned on Claudia so quickly she could hardly believe what was happening. What did her Mistress do to them? One perfect specimen had walked off after a tussle with Claudia and her Mistress had let her know, in no subtle terms, that it would mean Claudia's death were she to run off another. But sometimes, even in light of death, it was so hard for Claudia to control her temper in the face of these arrogant, hell-bound boys.

Now, she and Jethin began the ritual that started over every several months, ever since The Countess had met Claudia in that rat-ridden brothel so many years before. The boys - in this case, Jethin - would help Claudia with odd tasks too difficult or impossible for a woman to do; whether the barriers be brute strength or the dictates of society. Then, when all was completed, the Countess would take the boy for dessert, and she and Claudia would move onto a different town, a different country.

What Claudia did not know was that this time would be different. This time, her relationship with the Countess would come to an abrupt and ugly end. For Jethin would not cower before The Countess when it was time for his death, but would stand before her proud, virile, and glorious in his youth, and the Countess would decide another fate, something special, just for him.

Each day, Jethin snatched uneasy sleep for a few hours at dawn and a few hours at dusk. During daylight hours, he performed odd tasks for his new mistress. At moonrise, he raced to the side of the Countess.

The Countess played him softly, smoothly, and thoroughly. Within a matter of days, he was completely smitten with her. She professed a great love for him and he believed in that love without question - her gentle touch on his arm while they shared a late dinner, the soft kiss on his forehead when she bid him adieu before dawn. He yearned for so much more. At moments, he pressed himself upon her to let her know that it was okay to express their love, to let her know that he needed to express his love.

With a coy smile and firm grip, she always held him off. He was almost driven to the brink of insanity with unrequited desire for her, but each time he felt he could not possibly wait for her any longer, she whispered soothing nothings into his burning ear and was able to hold him off for another day. He was, after all, her employee, she reminded him. When his work for her was done, he would be a rich man. He would be her equal when they came together.

He never questioned her. He never pressed her on the fact that it was odd, this request of hers, for him to build her a velvet-lined casket (She felt she needed a fresh bedstead.) He never asked her why they only met when the moon was high. He didn't ask Claudia, as they were not on regular speaking terms. He took his orders directly from his Mistress, and in fact, had not seen Claudia in several days.

He worked happily on his own. He whistled a ditty while he labored and thought only of the moment when he could finally claim the Countess and make her his.

One night, yearning for new surroundings and a new boy, Cecilia decided it was time to shock Jethin with the truth - something that always gave her such a rush of pleasure - then devour him. Maybe it was only in her grandly delusional mind, but the more in love with her they were, the sweeter their blood tasted on her tongue.

It was early spring. Jethin and Cecilia sat on the banks

of a swollen river. A lover's moon hung fat above their tipped-together, stargazing heads.

"Jethin?"

"Yes, my love?

She turned to face him and shyly took his large, callused hand with her two delicate ones. She shivered with delight; this was her favorite part. It was the culmination of all of her arduous feigning – she would be rewarded with the sweet, warm, flavor of fresh blood spiced with just a dash of fresh fear. "I must tell you something, Jethin. It is something I can no longer keep inside." Her eyes widened with the excitement she felt.

He reached to smooth a curl behind her ear and stroke her cheek. In hushed tones he tried to soothe her. "Never fear, my love, what is it? You can tell me anything!"

"The truth is..." she stopped. It was just too difficult for her to continue - the burden of the secret too great!

"Come now, my lovely. You can tell me." Jethin sat up straight and proud, so supportive of his delicate woman. The moon splashed his face and revealed such a tender countenance, a look filled with so much love.

"What I must tell you is this. I am a vampire, Jethin. I am of the Order of the Undead. I drink the blood of men and have never regretted it."

Jethin did nothing.

Cecilia watched him do nothing. She watched in fascination, as that silly enamored stare clung securely to his face! It was she who was shocked tonight. She found herself quite speechless.

"But, my darling Cecilia, I have known of this for quite some time. I had guessed as much awhile back when the moon was just waning. I have waited patiently until you felt comfortable enough to tell me yourself." Then, sheepishly, "I have waited patiently for you to change me. I wish no longer to remain a virgin looking in on your world as a ridiculous human outsider."

Cecilia lost all composure. She gawked at him openly.

He smiled at her. It was nice to see her finally free of that mask of the "gentlewoman."

It suddenly became clear to Cecilia that Jethin thought she intended, all along, to make him a vampire when the moment was right. He had no idea of her gleeful plans to rip him to shreds. But, of course, he didn't. He fancied she was in love with him. Disgusting! She turned from Jethin's adoring eyes and contemplated this turn of events. While watching the river run, her gut gurgled and rolled in much the same turbulent manner. She needed blood. Swiftly, she came to a decision. *Hmm.* Why not? Why not make him a vampire and add some entertainment to her sometimes-dull existence. She was over a thousand years old – she would always be stronger than him. She could easily be rid of him should she choose to do so later on. Trap him outside as the dawning sun burned his flesh; drive a stake through his heart as his lay dreaming of her in his silken coffin. Yes, this was a wonderful idea! She clapped her hands in girlish glee and jumped up from the damp grass. "Come, Jethin. Let us convert you right now, on this, the finest of all nights!" Her voice was sweet, as if offering to buy him cotton candy at the

fair.

"I was thrilled with my new life, Saffron. I enjoyed the odd induction ceremony and loved the benefits of my new existence. I have the strength of one-hundred men. I can fully dilate my pupils - a little trick that always sends the natives running in fear. I can grip a man's body and transfer an electrical current, which provokes the heart to stop."

He smiled at his memories of people opening their mouths to scream, at the barely audible "pop" that came from the chest when he applied pressure just so. When it was done, he would shove their slack bodies away from him in repulsion. It was too much trouble to suck the blood out when the heart wasn't pumping it. He'd then have to expend the energy to go look for dinner.

"Vampires also have night vision and miss nothing that walks, crawls, or slithers in the dark."

Jethin didn't tell Saffron that he felt his passion for Cecilia vanish. Her beckoning lips, her shapely rear-end, her taut, high bosom no longer excited him as they once had. It had made Jethin feel just a little sad. Worse than that, Jethin lost the function to urinate – and something frightening had happened to him - the man below no longer stood for his morning salute! He lay there in Jethin's lap, limp as a poor, dead soldier. When Jethin fully realized that Cecilia could not have wanted him as she pretended - for he knew now she had absolutely no urge - he fell into a great depression that started the third week of his new life. He now understood, like a slap in the face, that most of their relationship was built on lies, Cecilia's lies. She didn't want him. Not in body. She had never wanted him and that shook him to his quickly-vanishing primal core.

Cecilia knew exactly what was bothering him but felt too bored to get into it with him. He would get over it - they all did. He would recover in time and forget what it meant to be a physically-functioning human male. Jethin could take all of the time he needed; he had all of the time in the world! And she was right. In time, Jethin came out of his slump and the two monsters began their new life together. As a consolation prize, Cecilia offered Claudia to Jethin, to destroy as he pleased, in the hopes that he would perk up a bit. His moping and whining was making her edgy. Not quite used to this consuming lust for blood - which seemed to simultaneously replace his lust for all things sensual - Jethin was shocked at his fervor when he took Claudia to death's door. He ripped into her body like a savage wolf. He was messy and panting and covered in gore when he was finally satiated. How she would have hated him one last time with his disgraceful show of mastication! Later that evening, he cleaned his teeth with an ivory pick and contemplated his new passion. His thoughts were interrupted by a tickling on his hand. He reached down and removed some straggling bits of Claudia's oily hair from his lap with disgust.

Jethin smiled at Saffron, who could never have guessed at his musing. It was unfortunate he couldn't tell her the details of the disposal of Claudia. He wished he could make Saffron understand. When she became a vampire, she'd understand his joy in the act, the ecstasy of finally quenching fires seemingly too big to contain. She'd understand without explanation. It was like explaining sex to someone who had never had it. There was no explaining an orgasm. He frowned, realizing *he* couldn't quite remember an orgasm. He had the fleeting urge to reach into Saffron's window and strangle her for being what he was not. He had to get away from her.

"Jethin," Saffron seemed sad, "were you and Cecilia *a couple* after you became a vampire? Did you finally...get together?"

"This life is not like that of a human life, Saffron. We do not need to debase ourselves in animal activity since we do not procreate in that manner. I am no man. Man is always searching for the Universal Whore. Do you know what that means?"

Saffron bobbed her head yes, like a girl who is trying to fool her teacher. Her wide eyes registered that the "not man" before her was clearly insane.

"The Universal Whore is the one who performs all tasks with pleasure. Is this what you want? To be some man's Universal Whore - it is what every man desires..."

Saffron waved him away. "Am I supposed to be able to answer that?"

"I can answer that for you. No. You do not want a man. No man has been truly happy since man first came into existence. I am above man; you could make me happy."

"OMG, I've never gotten such a beautiful proposal before." Her hands flitted nervously to her hair, where she entangled longs strings of it round and round her finger. She thought about how many times she had imagined herself and Jethin as a couple. Now, she was just plain embarrassed. Obviously, he was *not* thinking along the same lines as she was. *He's right; I'm just like an animal. Just like freakin' Coco and her pig cowboy.* She was suddenly so mad at Coco she could have spit.

"Proposal...You're funny. I just want you to know you don't have to succumb like those around you. The sex, the drugs, the smoking, the drinking, the binging, the fighting, do you know why they do it? Do you know why they can't stop? Because they are searching, Saffron. They are searching for a way out of their fears, a way out of their lonely lives, a way out of their memories, and a way to live life on a higher level.

"Vampires are slaves to no hormonal command. I am in complete control of my body. I don't need *anything* to make me feel better! I have it all. My need is simple...to feed. And I do not feed my emotions, only my thirst; this makes it impossible for me to become a slave to the outside world." Jethin smiled pleasantly.

Saffron was completely stunned. She sat back a little on her tuffet and rubbed at the angry, red welts dug into her forearms from leaning on the window ledge too long. If they didn't have sex, did that mean they didn't have love? "You don't even kiss?" She was so embarrassed to keep asking these deeply personal questions. Her cheeks flamed like two poinsettias. But the nagging thoughts wouldn't let her be still.

"Most certainly not. We don't need to. Please understand that the urge leaves you, utterly and completely, when you are transformed. Life is so much better without all of those complications. Believe me. There is no jealousy among us. We do not rape. We do not believe our greatest power lies in our pants. We are above all of that, and proud to be such."

"Can you love?" She saw him flinch, saw black hate in his dilated pupils, and finally realized he was probably a little pissed off.

"Saffron, I have to go. It's late. You'll never understand me until you stand in my shoes. You just have to take my word for it; my life is perfect!"

"Jethin, wait! Don't be mad. Please?" She looked down at her fingers twined in her lap. She muttered, "I'm just curious. I.... I believe you. I believe everything you told me." She smiled weakly. "I hope you're not upset."

As soon as she finished speaking, Jethin gave her the biggest smile as he wiggled his heavy eyebrows. "It's okay, Saffron. I could never be mad at you. Till next time, okay?"

Saffron nodded, tears of gratitude filling her eyes. He really was wonderful. He lived on blood – so what? Everybody had flaws. You couldn't hold those flaws against people. She caused the murder of cows every time she went to Burger King. Her inner thoughts rambled on, searching and digging for ways to justify her friendship with Jethin.

Later on, in the small of hours of the morning, in that endless gray that seems to drag on for eternity, Saffron wondered why she had been so quick to placate Jethin. Why had she been so panicky and in fear of losing his admiration? Did she *really* accept the life he lived? *No, no, no.* She viciously rubbed her eyes. But she did envy his courage, and his relaxed devil-may-care attitude. And his complete self-assurance. How she longed for those strengths. Jethin never had to face the "cold light of day." He was protected by the dark. Something came knocking at Saffron's mind, an important thought that wanted to surface. Vaguely, she knew it was there, but gave it barely a moment to show itself before sleep took her.

Chapter 14

Jethin walked across the field at human speed, away from Saffron and her quaint farmhouse. He could have moved faster. He could have zipped faster than a hummingbird. But he chose this slow pace to ponder. When he came to the edge of the forest, he crunched through the dried, dead leaves, absently brushing at the twigs that poked his clothing. He decided not to return home. Not yet. He would feast again tonight. He didn't usually eat twice. On the nights he visited Saffron, he dined before he saw her so that she would see him in his glory, his cheeks glowing pleasantly, calculated moments after the slaughter.

He remembered her naked admiration, her empathetic expressions as he told his "story." He snorted. What a crock he had offered up to her. Some of the story was true sure, then some of it was left out, some exaggerated, some completely fabricated.... He smiled. He had told her nothing of trickery. Nothing of hate and murder, and oh, how she had eaten it all up. How she cast those angel's eyes upon him as if he were the biggest, saddest treasure on earth.

She would never change, he decided. She was the same in this incarnation as she was when he last knew her. She trusted him so completely. He could do no wrong, poor Jethin. He felt a bit of remorse, just the tiniest bit, as if a grain of sand was working its way into the wound that was his heart. This mess was not Saffron's fault. She was stuck in the middle, now, as she had always been. He shrugged. Oh, well, he'd just try to do what had to be done and forget about it. She was a slightly annoying girl. He focused on this thought and hoped it would get him through his scheme's fruition.

Now he could move faster. He was a blur shooting forth under the pale light of the crescent moon, weaving through the trees and cold streets of the sleepy town. When he arrived at the theatre, the late show had already let out. He knew Tammy would be inside, shutting down. Tammy would be alone.

He didn't see her, but didn't need to see her to find her. He sensed her heat as if he contained a built-in infrared seeker. That's how they would describe it these days, in the 1700's, he was simply the Devil.

She was kneeling down behind the candy counter unlocking the safe. He neared her without a sound on well-practiced feet. No one could hear him approach, not even an animal, if that was what he desired. His inhuman attributes had guided him effortlessly through many a quiet murder.

He was behind her and upon her and reaching for her long neck before she could take half a breath. "Oh, Jethin! You scared me." Tammy grabbed her neck in surprise and shook her head.

Jethin could see by the rise under her thin t-shirt that she was very well pleased to see him. As usual, he used this to his advantage. He reached forward, removed her hand from her neck, and grabbed it himself. He rubbed her throat as he murmured to her.

She relaxed under his practiced hand, and let her eyelids drop. He had spent some years with snake charmers - he found them delightful, and adored the way they soothed the snakes in their baskets. Apply the right stimuli and any animal would respond. He considered himself akin to a butcher, tenderizing the meat for consumption. The pressure of his strokes grew. He watched her, released one hand from her neck, and slowly rubbed his fingers along her collarbone, then down to one breast which was mashed into and muffin-topping her too-small bra. "Did you shoot up yet?" He tried to keep the disgust out of his voice.

Her eyelids were stretched shut, enjoying his caresses. "No," she gushed back, her voice thick with sexual tension. She couldn't form another coherent word after that, just sat there making animal noises of satisfaction.

He studied her further and decided she might be telling the truth. He certainly hoped so. God, heroin made blood taste like shit and he wouldn't appreciate it if she was lying to him.

Tammy's eyes snapped open. Unfortunately, she found her voice and whispered, "Are you going to give it to me tonight, Jethin?" She spoke using her itty-bitty-baby voice.

He wished he was capable of retching. "Give me what I want first. Then, we'll see." He smiled at her, revealing neither fangs nor disgust.

"We been goin' out, foreva. I'm so ready for you."

"We've been courting for three weeks, Tammy."

"Yeah, and you're like, so awesomely kinky." She giggled and moved her long, ash-blonde hair from her neck. There were two small pricks in her skin, scabbed over from the last time he partook of her. He felt her freeze up when his teeth sliced through the old wound. She bit down on her bottom lip and tried not to scream. The sharp pain was quickly followed by sweet, sweet ecstasy. She fell back against the candy counter, he going with her and supporting her weight so his teeth didn't rip out of her neck. He had learned long ago that if you didn't support the falling body you'd wind up with a jugular dangling from a fang and blood spilling everywhere.

She started to moan and pant as if in the throes of outrageous passion. Jethin took deep pulls on her; she was a perfectly primed pump. Apparently, the exquisiteness of their coupling wasn't enough for her. Tonight, she wanted more and chose that moment to try something she would never try again. Usually, when he ate at her, she lay limp - shoulders slumped, arms hanging, hands resting palms up on the dirty candy floor, and her legs splayed wide as he knelt between them.

But tonight, she suddenly raised her hand to grope at his crotch. Jethin's nostrils flared in alarm. He chomped into her with all of his teeth, crunching past muscle and tendon. Her arm froze in midair, and her eyes widened and began to water at the impossible pain he was inflicting. He growled once, like a lion gnawing a gazelle. He sucked at her neck with such sudden strength, her breasts very nearly inverted. Her arms flailed only once before she was completely drained of blood and fluid.

He was that quick.

His fangs retracted as he withdrew from her. He knew she was dead, but slapped her face anyway. Had she been able to reach him, she would have realized his impotence, the soft mass at his crotch that for one shining speck of time in his long-drawn-out existence had been his everything. Not only his source of pleasure, but of his pride and strength, prowess and power. "How dare you!" he screamed at her dead and staring eyes. He fell to his rear-end on the dirty candy floor, breathing heavily, and slumped on the side of the freshly-disinfected candy counter. He swiped at the strand of ooze at his mouth and continued to eye her.

Her mouth was agape, her limbs sprawled, and her eyes glazed, forever reflecting that final moment of shock. Mostly, he relished taking prey. In life, Tammy had been as dumb as a cluck and just as harmless. But she lied all the time. She had lied tonight. He had tasted the heroin in her blood with the first pull. The vile bitterness of it burned his throat now. From terrible experience, he knew he could look forward to a night of cramping and tearing, excruciating pain in the region where his intestines nested and, once upon a time, functioned properly. He didn't know why drugs affected vampires in this way; the government hadn't gone that far in their testing. But he knew if he could destroy every drug on earth and everyone who had ever touched them, he would. Then he could feed without fear of gas pains. A sharp pain ripped through the small of his back and he gasped. Mentally, he added this to *the list*, the list of everything in his life that had gone wrong.

And he blamed it all on Li.

In total silence, he slunk out into the night and hid in the obscurities of the dark and the ambiguity of the shadows.

Chapter 15

The next night, Jethin didn't go to see Saffron. He hid in his limestone cave to pout and ponder as he watched waves crash below. It was a funny place, his cave. Every half-century or so, people or creatures would materialize from the white wall in back. He'd eat them and throw their carcasses in the sea before they got two seconds to 'ooh' and 'aah' at the fantastic new world they found themselves in. Sometimes the carcasses caused a great stir on the news. The footage played over and over again as the skeleton was explained by a fever-eyed cryptozoologist. But he didn't think about those things tonight.

Tonight he was back in Ireland. When he used to be human. When Li was human too, and her name had been Molly.

Tammy's dirty blood boiled within him at the mere memory of Molly. In fact, Molly had been with him since last night, ever since he told Saffron the edited edition of his becoming a vampire. He easily talked around her existence - not so much as an "ahhhhh" or fumbling silence as he smoothly cut her from the portrayal. Her face had swum in front of him the entire time, still jeering and laughing like a fiend. Everything that had gone so terribly wrong in his life was entirely Li/Molly's fault.

Molly was the little girl who lived down the lane when Jethin was struggling through life on his potato farm. Molly was the girl of Jethin's dreams. She was the only child of well-to-do parents. Her mother was a quiet, easy woman with thick, dark red hair always precisely pinned. Her father was gregarious and debonair, an Earl or some such thing. He was never around. Molly was more like her father, which

Jethin, blinded by infatuation, refused to see.

Molly was Jethin's friend. He discovered her when he was very young on a barefoot hike through the lowlands of bracken and gorse, long before his Da had keeled. It was high summer and the gorse was blazing. The sun slanted down the western sky and stabbed through the shafts, making the world look like it was on fire. The gorse plant had served Jethin's family in their desperate life of need. When they had sheep, they used gorse for dying wool. Now that the sheep were gone, they still found many uses for the hardy plant. They used it to light their fires; it could ignite with a single spark, and they used it to brush the chimney. Jethin used it as a tool to till the soil.

In the very old days, Da used it to flavor his whiskey. Back when he felt moved to flavor his drinks. Back when he could afford whiskey. Later, Da took whatever drink he could get, as raw as it was, as long as it was alcohol.

Jethin had found Molly beyond the gorse and on the far side of a little stream sitting among the wildflowers that dotted bank. She was weaving a wreath of flowers, working rapturously and never taking her light, violet eyes from the task at hand, as drowsy bees droned round her head. Her golden hair, made almost white by the summer sun, trailed down her back and cascaded over her shoulders.

He loved her instantly.

She was younger than he was, by three years, but her father's money allowed her to be worldlier than Jethin. She became his teacher. She was a wild girl, mischievous and always into other people's business or places where she didn't belong. They were sly, the two of them, as quick as the little people, they were never caught doing their sheep-worrying, or milk-spilling, or wash-stealing as the sheets and clothing hung drying from someone's line or fence. At first, they spoiled their stolen treasure (she especially loved to have great, rousing fires) till he finally told her his family really could use the things they stole, and from then on she gave over with a smirk.

Over the years, Jethin begrudgingly spent less time with Molly. He had to assume more and more of the role as head of household while his father, like a fleck of something impure, drifted lower and lower to the bottom of the bottle. His sisters took Molly for their playmate, which sparked Jethin's jealousy and made him surlier. His love for her, however, did not wane, and he kept an unblinking eye on her when she was in the yard with his sisters.

Molly grew. Her body plumped under her dresses and petticoats. She had a milkmaid's line of breast and waist and hip, and enjoyed stuffing her form into clothes that were just this side of too small. She drove Jethin mad with longing.

A few days before he met Claudia, and then Cecilia, before the whole horrid thing happened, he went to Molly. He found her within the grape arbor, shaded by heavy leaves, huddled in a corner under an ill-kept mess of vines so thick the sun could not penetrate. She had her little sketchpad with her and was doing an unlikely illustration of her father in jester attire. She didn't look up when Jethin entered, but continued to draw furiously.

Jethin observed her in silence as she slashed a crooked

line for her father's mouth and shaded heavily his mocking eyes. "Do you know where he is today, my father?" She fisted her hand around the pencil and slashed again, so hard the paper tore under the pressure. Jethin said nothing. He knew better than to offer words of condolence or advice when Molly was in a fit about her father, which was often, as her father was usually doing something wrong. His wife gave him no discourse for his pusillanimous actions. It seemed it was only his child who held such disdain for his sins, and she, so very much like him. "I believe right now, at this very moment, my father is mounting the Widow Murphy." She slashed the drawing again. "And probably her dog as well."

Jethin's eyebrows rose in surprise, and although he had olive skin made darker by the summer sun, his cheeks grew pink. He cast his eyes aside and feigned interest in a rodent hole at the base of the arbor post. She had never used such crude words before and it immediately drove him to imaginings of doing very much the same to her. But not her dog. He couldn't raise his head on account of the shame of it.

Silence.

He felt her eyes upon him, boring into his skin. His flesh began to tingle as if her glance was actually searing him. "Jethin." Her voice was low and smoky, quite different from the squeal of rage not three minutes earlier. "Do you want me, Jethin?"

His head snapped up. "Yes, of course!" he blurted without eloquence. He would marry her right here, right now, if only she would say yes. He had waited all this time just for her.

Her eyes were half-mast, and clouding with desire.

Jethin felt himself respond. The work-worn and mud-stained cloth that barely passed as his pants grew unbearably tight. It was all he could do to restrain himself and not close the space between them, to not smother her with all of the love he had been caging for these many years. He had rutted with many a willing slut, but to have Molly would be to express his love. This was the first time Jethin felt joy swoop into his heart and hope lift him high. She wanted him! He could see it there, in her eyes. She wanted him as he had always wanted her! He bit his tongue to keep from crying out.

Molly shifted. Slowly, she leaned forward to place her ravaged sketch in the sparse grass. As she did so, she tugged almost imperceptibly on her bodice, pulling the cloth down just a little more to give Jethin a better view of her bosom; those two perfect breasts as high and round and hot as melons ripening in the afternoon sun. She enjoyed the way Jethin's mouth hung in naked awe. "Come to me, Jethin," she whispered as she reached for the ties on her bodice.

Jethin felt his limbs go weak. He fell to his knees and scuttled forth. He didn't feel the stones pressing into his kneecaps as he went. When he was directly in front of her, he sat back on his heels.

She had finished with the last tie. She opened the cloth and the most glorious breasts Jethin had ever laid eyes on tumbled out; massive and creamy-white, with two perfectly hardened nipples. Molly smiled like a Cheshire cat and arched her back so her breasts would stand higher.

Jethin sucked at his teeth. A million thoughts rammed through his head as he thought of the many things he could do with those breasts.

"Do you want to touch them, Jethin? Suckle at them like a little pig?"

He began to sweat; the ache in his groin was growing painful. But, before they began he had to know, had to hear the words of love from her own mouth. He would have chosen a better time, but she gave him no choice. "You will marry me then, Molly?" He decided he wanted to kiss her first on her soft, petulant lips before grabbing those breasts.

Molly frowned. "What are you saying?" Her words were sharp and flat.

Pop! Gone was the amorous bubble of his love. It was as if the world slammed to a halt. The breeze vanished, the noise of the crickets in the lawn hushed, and the church bells ceased tolling.

Molly noticed the subtle change and looked around to see what the disturbance was. Was someone coming? Was it about to rain? What? What? It was the sun. The sun hid behind a massive and churning cloud, and caused the air to chill by measurable degrees. Her shoulders drooped, her nipples now pointed south. "Marry you, Jethin? *You?*" she hiccupped.

Jethin didn't know what to say.

Molly let out a howling laugh. She leaned back against the arbor post, and in vulgar display, kept laughing as her breasts jiggled. She wiped her eyes and stared at him. "My God, Jethin, when did you come up with that idea?" She fanned her face, tried to calm her hilarity.

Jethin didn't move, just kept staring and staring at her. His pupils had constricted.

"I just wanted to have some fun with you." A curious look crossed her gleaming eyes. "You don't suppose this is my first time, do you? That you are my first?"

He didn't answer.

She took that as a yes and laughed again, a forced sound that was wry and full of bitterness. Still, she didn't bother to cover herself, but sat before him splayed like a Jezebel. "What a fantasy world you are living in. Fancy that, *me*, a virgin. Me, your wife!" The words were harsh. Her expression changed in a split second; it hardened and became grotesque with spite. "I was with child before my thirteenth birthday. I lost, it of course, and have been careful since not to repeat that vile scene. I have been sullied these three long years, Jethin. Marry you." She sniffed and flicked a fly from her breast. "I just wanted to have fun with you, teach you tricks as I have always done."

A single tear slid down Jethin's cheek. His face was placid.

Molly eyed him coldly. "Did you really suppose I would marry you, Jethin?" Lilt sprang in her voice. "I am the daughter of an Earl. An *Earl*, Jethin!" She spat his name out so hard that strings of spittle came with it, illuminated for a fraction of a second in the beams of the setting sun. "You are a potato boy, for God's sake." She looked him up and down. Disdain made her lip quiver. "And a dirty one at that."

In one quick movement, Jethin was upon her, having

leapt from his docile position with blinding speed. He grabbed for her smooth neck. As black rage blinded him, he found her throat and pressed, his elbows pushing on her breasts for leverage.

She started, her arms flying like the spastic flapping of a bird's wings. Fear replaced the sardonic cruelty that had been in her eyes.

He could see nothing as the black blinded him, but he could hear her and he listened to the sound of her gurgling lessen and weaken till at last she was still. When it was over, he slumped on her perfect breasts and sobbed into her shiny, corn-silk hair.... He didn't move from the spot for a very long time.

Besides the acid burn in his gut, Jethin was also suffering from his memories. He hated Li. He hated thinking of her and remembering that time, hundreds of years ago, when she caused his life to become a living hell. Funny thing about time, when you had it in limitless supply, you took it for granted, and it became a non-entity. What happened over three hundred years ago may as well have been three days ago or three thousand years ago. When time had no meaning, the pain lay always available.

Under the shadowed arbor, Jethin waited for some measure of control while Molly lay unmoving before him, her lips parted, eyes wide with disbelief, and a trickle of spittle running out of the corner of her mouth. He raised his head, and wiped frantically at his snot which was sliming her perfect breasts. He looked around. As usual, there was no one about. Her father was off mating with the throwaway of the moment, and her mother was stuffed deep within the walls of the stone mansion on the other side of the hedge.

She never came out of there. She was a strange woman, Molly's mother, and she was often the subject of discussion at the pitiful meals Jethin's family shared around their rickety table. Closed-in and protected by stone and mortar, Molly's mother whiled her days away in silence.

Jethin stood on shaky legs. He struggled to lift Molly and her breasts. He carried her to the old well. It had long since dried up and was kept neat and pretty for show. He shifted her body to his shoulder as it lolled and pulled at what little strength he had left.

This was the most shocking afternoon of his entire life, he thought, as he attempted to stuff her into the well. She didn't fit. He made the mistake of bending her in half and tried to shove her rear-end first. Her body filled the hole like a plug, her head bent forward, her legs sticking up, her swirl of yellow hair obscenely catching the last of the afternoon breeze. With Herculean effort, he grabbed her under the armpits and hauled her out again. He decided to tip her over, grab her ankles, and shake her head-down into the well. Her hands and skull thudded on the old rock. Her arms kept getting in the way. So he brought her back up and tucked her hands into her sash. He ripped the hem of her dress and tied her legs together. Now she couldn't cartwheel down the well like a starfish. (She was aerodynamic, he thought, when he considered the scene in modern times.) His arms were just about to give out as he stood in the moment of final decision. He shook with fatigue as he held her by the ankles. He let go, and gave a small, strangled cry as she shot down the black hole. He made the sign of the cross.

***

Molly's mother stood before Jethin. On the threshold of his dilapidated homestead, she stood cowering, ringing her hands as she told him mournfully of her child missing these two days and nights. He listened to her story in stony silence as her frightened eyes flitted round the inside of his shack, seeing nothing. Her missing child had forced her from the protection of her home. He imagined she was panicking, being out and so exposed, and wishing only to crawl back into her hole to hide and cry and pray to her strict God for the safe return of her only live-born child.

Such a waste, Jethin thought, as she babbled on. Her hair fell in an unruly tumble, cascading over her shoulders and glowing like waves of red fire, sparking and glossing in the afternoon light. "You are such a good young man, Jethin. Such a good friend to my girl. Might you know, perhaps, where she is?"

Jethin screwed his face up. He wondered, as he gauged his facial expressions, how best to get rid of this pathetic woman, and fast.

"Rosemary! Why, you look just terrible! Whatever is wrong?" Jethin's mother had come in from the fields, and entered through the hole at the back of the shack. She approached the two standing in the front entrance, her cracked and dirty hands clutching at her filthy apron heavy with potatoes.

Jethin's mother stared at Molly's mother in plain shock.

Never had she seen this woman out of her home. Jethin's mother had been to Molly's home on many occasions offering homemade recipes and medical concoctions for a fair price. Rosemary had always treated Jethin's mother well and took care to make a purchase every time, though Jethin's mother had a queer feeling that Rosemary never really made use of her purchases. Rosemary was a sweet woman, so quiet, yet friendly to the extreme to the few that came peddling at her doorstep.

"My girl," Rosemary rasped, "she has been gone these two days and nights. Do you know nothing of her whereabouts?" Her hands were still kneading and pressing; the fingers seemed to strangle each other with unfathomable distress.

Jethin's mother stared at her blankly.

Just then, a bird flashed past Rosemary's head and flew into the shack. It bumped against the opposite wall, fell to the dirt floor, flew up again, crashed and bashed into walls and beams, and finally fell into a crude bowl of potato soup on the wooden oddity that the family used as a table. Then it swooped yet again to continue its desperate, bumbling search for a way to escape, all the while scattering feathers, which floated down to the dirt floor.

Jethin's mother watched the flailing creature with burgeoning horror. Rosemary's mouth formed a large 'O.' The women knew what this meant, the bird entering and crashing about the premises. It was an omen of death. The two took it as gospel that this small, trapped creature confirmed the fate of the missing girl. Rosemary let loose a

howl and fled down the lane, back to her walls of stone and mortar.

These were Jethin's real memories in as much as memories can be real. These memories were tainted as well, of course, as he envisioned Li/Molly, after so many centuries of brooding, to be something akin to the Antichrist. When Saffron was Rosemary, he had no idea what kept her confined to her home; maybe it was her fool husband. He vaguely wondered what kept Saffron now. It didn't matter. He would use her as he saw fit.

Chapter 16

In time, the sun warmed the earth. Tender green shoots shot up
and tiny blue speckled eggs appeared in the robin's nest in the tree
outside Saffron's window. It was warm enough to leave windows open
all day and throughout the early evening. Infrequent gusts of wind
rifled throughout the house, setting the curtains to dance and papers to
fly.

On one such windy night, Jethin said, "Saffron, I want to talk to
you about something very important."

They were in their usual seats in their usual poses. She rested on
her tuffet next to the window, her feet poking out of her thin cotton
pajama bottoms. He sat perched on the roof, his feet supporting his
weight on the downward slope. She had once asked him if that hurt his
butt, sitting there that long. He remarked that her company made all
his pains unnoticeable. She had blushed. He always knew what to say
to her; he always made her feel so special. He listened to her talk. She
felt like she could tell him anything. Her mother was wrong; she didn't
need to leave the house to have a social life.

Sometimes he got a little moody if she steered the conversation
toward the rocky cliffs of love and emotion. As long as they weren't
talking about these things, he was fine. Saffron found she could easily
avoid those subjects. They had always embarrassed her anyway, why
not drop them completely? Sometimes, she still felt guarded. Her
caution made her feel foolish. He would never hurt her. Even though
he got mad at her sometimes, she just knew he would never hurt her.

"Here goes." He was picking rocks out of the sole of his shoe.

"Hmm?" Her eyes were locked on the green star to the right of

Venus as it twitched and sputtered.

"You're *so* amazing."

Saffron frowned. Whenever Hollywoodites were asked to describe their peers they always said, "he's *so* amazing," and "she's *so* amazing," as their go-to cop-out phrase. She suddenly felt very uncomfortable and equally unamazing.

"You mean so much to me. I would hate to lose you." He gulped once and gazed at her. "Oh, Saffron. If you only knew how wonderful my life is...I am like a god. Don't you want that? Don't you want to live...without fear?"

Saffron moved back from the sill and wrapped herself in her arms. After that totally awkward night in November, he had never mentioned this again. Just the idea that she should become what he was... She realized now that she had been kind of dumb to think he would never ask again.

Her squeamish actions inflamed his irritation, but he masked his feelings and quickly recited words to sway her back to him. "When you die, I won't know who you'll be born as or where you'll be. It'll take forever to find you and wait for you to grow up... Then you'll be afraid of me all over again," he pouted. "I'll miss you."

"Won't I become a fairy when I die? Won't you come see me there?"

His attempt at pathetic melted into a sneer. He stared hard at her, as if to figure if she was very naïve or very dumb. "Go to the fairies? Why? Who did you murder? Did you molest a puppy? Have you worn white shoes after Labor Day?"

Saffron hunched on her tuffet. "What are you talking about?" And then she figured out what was going on; he was jealous. He had been sarcastic about the fairies before. She cleared her throat. "I see no problem with our continuing our friendship in the fairy world."

He looked at her for a long time. He cleaned his teeth with his tongue, making little tweeting noises. "We would not be allowed to...be together in the fairy world." He held her eyes and gauged her reaction.

She tilted her head and waited for him to go on.

"Saffron, look. I have the power to end all of your misery. You've expressed the hard times you've had in your life - being forced to go to school, being forced to become a..." He winced. "...a clerk, being forced to go out into public. You would never have to do these things again. Indeed, as a vampire, it would behoove you to stay out of public consciousness. And when you are out in public, you would never have to feel bashful or embarrassed or inferior. The blood that will move through you will fill you with such confidence. Believe me, it is a feeling like none you have ever experienced before. And this feeling, Saffron; it never goes away. Always, for the next thousand years, you will feel powerful and confident. You will never fear harm...be it intentional or accidental. You will never suffer death. But you may die terribly in this life if you do not heed me. There is no need for that! There is no need for such pain!" His nostrils flared. He was outraged at the way humans lived. They were worse than animals. He sniffed...and it was him they called a monster. "I take only what I need to live. When I take, I don't hurt anyone. What does your government do? What do kings, and dictators do around the world? Go to war? No! Go to slaughter, I say! They encourage thousands, hundreds of thousands of children to get together and kill each other. So they can play their games. No. I am not the monster.

"Saffron, being human, especially being a human woman, means you can't even walk a city street at night. C'mon! Don't you deserve to walk wherever you want, whenever you want, without getting mugged and raped?" He flung his hands up.

"Jethin."

Why was she speaking? She was breaking his stride, like a mosquito in his ear. "If your way is so much better, why isn't everybody doing it?"

He smiled. It was the most beatific smile she had ever seen. "This is an exclusive club, my darling. You've got to be invited. Don't you know why? Most humans are a bunch of simpletons. They're too stupid to live, never mind graduate to all of this undead perfection." He used his thumbs to point at himself. "Only when your soul has reached its zenith are you good enough to let it go and become...*vampire*."

This statement, of course, was worth less than the manure stuck in a goat's cloven hoof, but he found himself caught up in the moment, sowing incredible lies with ease, imagining himself a marvelous raconteur. It was his passion that had always made him believable. With passion, you can convince anyone of anything.

The time was now, he needed to hook her or lose her. And there was a bonus to be had out of this. He was so, so bored; he wouldn't mind the company of such a pretty puppet. He completely understood why Li kept her tethered. Another bonus - she was still full of fairy magic. What if they tapped into *that* a little more; what would they find? And of course there was the point, the coup d'état - wouldn't Li be pissed! He was going to have *his* way this time.

Saffron stared down her nose at him. "Congratulations on your Zenith Soul; it sounds like a Lady Gaga album." *What In Thee hell was he talking about now?*

"It's true, Saffron. It's true! Consider this: most humans can't handle the power of love. Right? Love is the absolute most basic of the primal powers. But love is too hard to master, so people turn to another basic power - hate. Hate is easy. Hate has limped along through the centuries, always striking out, but always being tempered by love. Yet, in each lifetime, humans grab onto hate as if finding a shiny pot of power for the very first time. They try it and it fails them. Their grandchildren try it and it fails them. Their great-grandchildren try it and it fails them. Do you see the pattern here?

"But, ah, love.... Most humans can never learn to wield it. They don't want to wield it because it takes constant attention, and cleaning, and polishing, and updating - too much work.

"Believe me when I tell you, very few in humanity could ever handle this power that surges through *my* veins." He shook his head sadly. "If they cannot even grasp the power of love, my power would make their heads explode."

"So, you became a vampire because of your great capacity to love?" Huh. *That* sounded...off.

"Yes, Saffron. The greatest love, love of oneself."

"Okay. Now I see." She checked to see if he was looking at her. He wasn't. She rolled her eyes.

"Saffron. You can handle this power. Within you, I see a great capacity for love. Please, don't be alarmed at what I am about to tell you. I have notified my counsel of your existence, of your unique qualities. They are excited to meet you. You will be greeted as a dignitary among the vampire race!" (They knew nothing of her, and if not hidden well, she would be taken immediately after he changed her.) "And I, Saffron," he reached for her hand and she gave it to him. He kissed her palm. "I will treat you like my queen." It was the first time she had physically touched him. Cold washed beneath his smooth skin.

"But Jethin," she wrinkled her nose, "I don't want to drink blood."

Laughter exploded from deep within him. Saffron jumped and glanced back at her bedroom door. "SSsssshhh!"

"Don't worry about them, Saffron. They will sleep for as long as I wish. I have seen to that."

Saffron pulled out of his icy clamp of a hand. What had he done? What had he done to her mother and Derek?

"Relax." He held his hands up in a placating manner. "They're fine. They're only sleeping."

"Yeah? Sleeping how? I sleep in my bed every night but we had to put my dog *to sleep* last year. What did you do to them?" Saffron discovered that he could really annoy her. She had never given him permission to exercise some kind of mind game or whatever he did over her mother and Derek. He never asked. She thought he didn't have power inside her house. How much more was he capable of?

"I didn't do anything to them. It's just a sound barrier trick. The fairies know it, everyone knows it but the humans and the gnomes."

Mr. Gnome had eavesdropped on every conversation between the two idiots, that vampire and the human, since they had started. He kept himself well hidden in the brush by the antique tractor that Audrey never got restored. He ate sunflower seeds and garden contraband while he reclined and listened.

"As for the blood, you develop a thirst for it. You will find, in time, that you crave it, worship it. You can still eat regular food, you know. It's true. It's a little-known fact that vampires can eat any food they want. It just won't keep a vampire nourished like it would a human." *And you won't enjoy it*, he thought but didn't tell her. She didn't need to know that all food would taste like glue when she became the undead. Gooey glue, crunchy glue, slippery glue, hot glue, cold glue.

That about summed up the vampire food experience.

"The food goes in, it comes out. As a vampire, if you want to rejuvenate, feel incredible and alive, well, then you must drink blood. This is not so strange. Do you know what *humans* eat by *choice?* Listen, in many countries people eat bugs. Humongous, burst-when-you-crunch-'em, live bugs. If you can't take them straight, how about some chocolate covered cockroaches? That'll help them slide down. Have you ever heard of Casu Marzu the Sardinian cheese? Sometimes it's called "maggot cheese." It's goat cheese with fly larvae. The larvae eat the cheese as it's fermenting and they are growing. Their waste gives it that special flavor.... I once went into a specialized market in Asia. They served a drink with a frog hopping around the bottom of the glass. It is customary to consume the drink in one pull, then munch on the frog. Let's go to Alaska where we can eat fermented salmon heads; they've been rotting in the ground for a few weeks now, let's have Puyuk dig them up and mash them into a pudding for us. Let's drink coffee made from beans regurgitated by weasels. Yummy preserved ant eggs? Jellied moose nose? You look like a lamb-brain-with-rice-and-yogurt-sauce girl. No, no, not brain. Lamb's eye in a vodka shot... Or Hasma, made from the fallopian tubes of frogs. Finish it all off with musk-flavored Lifesavers."

Saffron had gasped at every delicacy.

"People eat the feet, tongues, intestines, cockscombs, brains, and organs of animals. Around these parts, *in your own home*, people munch on the still-filled stomachs of mollusks! You love your pizza; am I right? Do you even know what you're eating when you eat every day? Did you know that there is pus in cheese? MmmMmm. Yummy yummy cow pus.

"In desperate times, people eat the corn from their own waste.

And there are even blood drinkers, human blood drinkers. Not the kids playing around in basements with expensive pointy-teeth dentures, but in South America, in Africa, in Asia, they eat the meat of their kill and drink its warm, collected blood from their earthen jars. For them, it's not fantastic. It's not for shock value or intimidation. It's life. It's the same for me - just life." He shrugged.

Saffron's face was yellow. She dry heaved, once.

"So now you're enlightened. Vampires prefer blood. It's warm and clean, fresh and fragrant. It's not such a hard concept to grasp." His eyebrow rose. "There are much worse things than blood."

"I guess." Saffron's hand was covering her mouth; she was breathing through her fingers.

"I really must go. Think about what I'm offering you. Think of all that plagues you just suddenly...disappearing. Think of burdens lifted and hardships flying away with the wind. Think of questions. I can give you a satisfactory answer to anything, because there is no more perfection in the world than this." He indicated his chest. "Later." With his customary eyebrow wiggle, he left.

***

Markis wasn't happy. Something weird was going on with Saffron. Granted, he didn't know her that well. But he'd been after her for months and they never seemed to get anywhere. She was so...preoccupied? He wasn't quite sure. People never acted bored around him before, but now he wasn't so sure. Was he boring her? It wasn't like that in the beginning. She had liked him. He was sure of it. What had changed? When did it change?

When he had finally made a move to go over and talk to her, really talk to her, that night at the movies, he felt so *on*. He had always thought she was pretty. In school he often thought about bumping into her at her locker or dropping something near her table in the cafeteria. But he was always with his friends and she was always with her friends and the two groups didn't mix. And she was always looking down, across, or up. She was always looking *away*. When he was able to snag her, lock eyes with her, her face would turn ten shades of red. Then she'd actually *run* away. It was fun at first, that he could get such a reaction from her. But, after awhile, he gave up. When Jeanine told him she was working at the Black Chicken he thought he finally had a chance to approach her slowly and without all of the high school drama to separate them.

At the theater, he saw the look in her eye. She was *thrilled* to see him. Her smile really did light up her face. It made his insides jellyfish and wiggle. He had had girlfriends before. He had crushed on loads of girls. In first grade, he used to lure girls into the coat closet and see how many times he could kiss them before Mrs. Walker pulled him out by his ear. On one such occasion, his parents were called in for a parent-teacher meeting. That night they discussed "propriety" and "discretion" with him. When his mother left the kitchen, satisfied with the verbal hand slap, his father waited until she was out of earshot before he clapped his son on the back. And while the great big, redheaded man stifled roars of laughter behind his large hands, Markis sat grinning, his legs swinging from the dining room chair. His father wiped the tears from his eyes. He smiled at his son, his little stud, his virile guy. Markis's parents were called in at other odd times and told to corral their young stallion. His mother would pin both father and son with her evil eye, so they would keep their giggling to themselves. But who didn't want such a confident little boy who was in love with the entire world? His mother was secretly proud.

Markis was in awe of Saffron. For the first time in his life, he felt neither smooth nor in control around a girl. She seemed almost...magical, like she wasn't even human. He wondered if he was good enough for the girl that he wanted so badly. For all of her timidity, he felt she was almost too overwhelming.

Now, over the last couple of months, he saw a transformation come over Saffron. A change so swift and total, it stunned him. She smiled all of the time. She held her head high when she worked with the customers. She yelled to him when he came in through the convenience store door - yelled clear across the long space that separated them. And she smiled at him. They were special smiles. The kind that grabbed you and held you until you couldn't breathe. She would look right at him over the deli case, without blinking, and hold his gaze over the rows of congealed salad and fat-free bologna. She liked to giggle. She flirted with him all of the time. She'd sneak up behind him from the rows of Corn Pops and Stouffer's Stuffing and slap his rear.

He could never get her to be serious. Conversations flip-flopped and contained no real substance. She was so sweet to him, *sickeningly* sweet. Always calling him "sweetie" and "uh-huhing" everything with a big smirk stretched across her lips, the stars permanently in her eyes. This wasn't Saffron. This was not the girl who had always intrigued him.

Chapter 17

Saffron invited the band over to the farm. It was Derek's idea, a "Coming Out" party for Saffron because she was starting to come out of her mother's house on a daily basis, what with her job and the few trips to watch the band jam. When Derek first mentioned the idea, Saffron had gone to work that night complaining to Coco, who thought it was a great idea. Coco proceeded to call the band members and let them know about the party.

"What night?" Coco blinked rapidly as she held the receiver to her chest. She was on the phone with Iggy. Saffron chucked Coco the bird and walked away. "Saffron says the first. Yeah, duh Iggy, that's Saturday. God, man, you're thick...." She hung up the phone and called Markis. Then she called Hippo, telling them all about the great jam session/party they were going to have at Saffron's house by the sea. Coco even called Bernice and left a message. Bernice never answered his phone.

On that warm June night, under the azure sky with the air smelling new and green, Saffron begrudgingly hosted her very first party. The ocean heaved against the cliffs, the alpacas grazed on the tender new grass, and somewhere off in the distance, a faraway neighbor gunned his mower to start cutting long expanses of lawn.

Saffron and her mother worked all morning on hors d'oeuvres and canapés, salads and meat marinades, chips and dips. Audrey didn't know if she should supply the beer and tell the parents, or supply the beer and pretend not to know what was going on, or to not supply the beer and pretend not to know what was going on. She decided on the latter with the intent to make everyone sleep over if she had to.

"Derek, set up the ten- man tent."

Big Derek halted as he crossed the kitchen. His arms were full of condiments; he was balancing a bag of charcoal on his head with a bundle of wood pinched under one arm. He mumbled behind the tongs in his mouth. "I'm not setting up the fricken ten- man tent."

Audrey blubbed her tongue at him and went back to the salads. She tried not to grin too much, but couldn't help it. Saffron had come a long way. Derek disagreed. He said there was something up with Saffron; he didn't trust Saffron's poor-me drama, and he didn't trust her 'happy girl' drama. He would tell Audrey, "We haven't got to the root yet." Audrey pooh-poohed him. Fricken Scorpio - he was so suspicious. Audrey finished stirring the potato salad, licked the spoon, then threw it in the sink and covered the bowl with its lid. "Hey, Saffron, have you been thinking about colleges?" Behind her, there was a kafuffle; a second of silence, then the smashing sound of what Audrey rightly assumed was the jar of relish. Every muscle in Audrey's body seized up as she raised her eyebrows.

"Mom, aren't you happy that I'm working at the Black Chicken? I thought you were all set with everything. Look at this," she indicated the counters littered with party prep, "I'm socializing. So, we're going to drop it; right?"

"Saffron, it's not about what *I'm* all set with. I was just wondering what you're thinking. If you think you're ready to take the next step."

"Because you want more."

Derek came gliding into the kitchen on roller-sneakers and carrying lawn chairs. "Oh, lucky me, I get to walk in on the volleynag game." He set down the chairs and waggled his fingers at them. "No, thanks, ladies. Call me when you're ready to start the grill." He turned on his heel and rolled right back out.

"Yeah, Mom, call me when you're ready to start the grill." She hunched out of the room.

Audrey picked up the potato salad spoon and throttled it. She felt her blood pressure rise deliciously in her head and muffle the sound of the neighbor's lawn mower. "I'm doing the grill myself!" she yelled at the empty room. She had never lit a charcoal grill in her life. "Screw that." She started slamming through the cupboards, grabbing the pink grapefruit juice, cranberry juice, cranberry vodka and champagne. She sloshed the ingredients in a pitcher and poured herself a Mason jar full.

Later, when they were all sitting around the fire pit, with Bernice and Iggy plinking their guitars, Saffron opened her "Coming Out" gifts. The gifts were Coco's idea. There were suitcases from her mother (she shoved them away with a wan smile to the confusion of the others); a polka-dotted bra and panty set from Coco (which made her burn purple while everyone laughed); a fairy figurine from Markis, that was so finely detailed and so beautiful he was shocked when her face turned deathly white and the little thing slipped from her hands. Markis looked helplessly at Coco. She shrugged.

Thankfully, the band members and Derek got her more mundane things. A Star Wars t-shirt from Iggy (gently used and all the more valuable he demanded); a recording of their band from Hippo (Hippo always gave homemade gifts); a set of maracas from Bernice (so she could play in the band; she welled up); and a George Michael CD signed by the artist himself (from Derek who was so proud he was crying, tear dollops splashing onto his rotund belly, until he took a deep pull on his Mason jar and several cleansing breaths). Around the bright fire in the dark night, everyone started to get slap-happy and rowdy.

"I know this is your prized possession, Derek. Wow, thank you."

She was sincere in her thanks. She liked George Michael and hoped one day to attend George and Derek's wedding, but she was especially thankful for Derek's ability to clear the air and make a place fun again.

Bernice plucked some flamenco and inspired the rest of the band. He always did that, talked with his guitar. Saffron had never ever heard him speak. Suddenly, Bernice stopped plunking and sat up straight. He looked toward the cliff just as Saffron heard her suicide ghost start caterwauling. Bernice looked around the group. His eyes settled on Saffron. She looked bug-eyed back at him. But still, he said nothing. He looked down at his guitar and started plinking again.

For the next couple of hours, they jammed badly and loved every minute of it. It was only ten o'clock when Saffron yawned outrageously loud and said, "Whew, that was fun! Let's do this again!"

The band members frowned. Audrey, who didn't leave when Saffron hinted because she *just loved these kids(!)*, frowned. Derek, who snored chin-on-chest on the lawn chair, frowned. Was Saffron dismissing them? They were ready to go all night. They always went all night - she knew that.

She got up and started to pick up paper plates with half-eaten food and the beer bottles that Audrey had ignored. The others grumbled as they slowly packed up and made their way to Bernice's van. Coco was the designated driver. Poor choice. Coco talked too much when she drove and was a menace to society even if she didn't drink.

Markis followed Saffron around as she cleaned. Maybe she was getting rid of everyone else so they could be together? He trailed her to the kitchen where she dumped the trash from her arms into an almost-over flowing bucket - the trash bag sliding off one side. When she turned, he was right there in her face, looking hopeful. He took her hand and moved into her space. "Do you wanna hang out tonight?"

Saffron felt everything in her body lock up. Jethin would be here soon. She pulled her hand out of Markis's and edged away from him. "Markis, I'm sorry. I don't know what it is, maybe the champagne... (He knew she didn't have any; he studied her every move as if she were a theatre performer) ...but I really don't feel good. I have to go lie down."

"Do you want me to come with you?" He hooked his fingers into the belt loops on her jeans and pulled her into him. He wasn't going to give up, not tonight. She was taking *forever*.

Saffron coughed, backed up, and tripped on the extension cord they had used for Coco's keyboard. "Ah, yeah, not with my Mom in the next room, know what I mean? That would be kind of weird." She looked really strained.

"So come with me, we'll go someplace and hang out." He pulled her to him again and rocked them back and forth, his face coming closer to hers.

His breath smelled sweet and she actually swooned like a broad from a 40's movie. She turned away and looked out the dark window. She bit her bottom lip. What if Jethin was watching? Was he here early tonight? She and Jethin weren't an item, and they weren't about to be, but Jethin gave the impression that he was one of those not-sharing types. The, 'I don't want it but you can't have it either,' type. The idea of Jethin's rage scared her so much she jerked away from Markis and placed both of her outstretched hands on his wide shoulders. She didn't blink. "You have to leave with the rest of them, right now, okay?"

He shook his head once and grabbed her. He pulled her body with one hand, securing her hips against his, and the base of her skull with the other. He put his lips on hers and spoke through his teeth. "What's going on?"

"Oh, my God..." she laughed nervously as she wrestled her way out of his grip. "Markis, go home."

He flinched. It made her sad to see confusion eat at his confidence. He was slumped now, just like she used to stand. He turned around without another word and stalked out of the house. Coco closed in behind him, walking forward but looking back at Saffron and mouthing, "Why? Why?" until she walked into the doorway, swore, and then was finally, mercifully - her and her mouth - out into the night.

Saffron heaved a sigh and ran upstairs. She passed Gram's bedroom where her mother sat on the side of the bed reciting Yeats.

Outside in the van, Markis fumed. As Coco backed up, he saw a light come on upstairs on the second floor. He squinted to look inside the room and his breath caught when he saw Saffron sit in front of her mirror and put her hair up. It wasn't styled that way five minutes ago when she dismissed him. Is that how she got ready for bed? He watched her apply something to her lips. "What the hell?" he yelled into the silence, causing Coco to yank on the wheel, go off the driveway, and *screeeeee* along the alpaca gate. The band members shrieked like little girls and Coco squawked like a chicken.

Markis's thoughts raced. It looked like Saffron was getting ready to go on a date! Maybe he wasn't all-knowing of the ways of women but he was pretty sure they didn't do up their hair and apply lipstick or whatever to go to bed sick on the champagne that they didn't drink! And she had been afraid! He thought of it now as the diss played in his head, just like it would a thousand times before he went to sleep. She had definitely been afraid when she was trying so desperately to get rid of him. At first, he thought she was nervous about what was going on between them, about how close they were getting, and about the thoughts of what they were about to do. But some little inkling told him her fear didn't match that of being nervous about the first time you touched someone you liked. Which left him thinking what? That Saffron had pushed him out of the house to get ready for a date she was afraid of? Who? It was just too bizarre. He couldn't be right. Suddenly, the van felt too small. The cracked leather seat was pancake-flat and painful to sit in. He rubbed the back of his neck and squinted at the dark road ahead.

Unwanted puzzle pieces came clunking into his brain. The entire ride home, he juggled the memories of odd things that Saffron had done. Not long after the movie "date" he had gotten her phone number and had started calling her almost every day. They talked and talked and talked. She was always so animated. He imagined her sitting there in her room on the other end of the line, lying on her bed, laughing and twirling all of that red hair between her fingers. Sometimes they talked for hours. But she would never talk long after dark.

He counted. Besides seeing her at the Black Chicken, he had contact with her after sunset only tonight, at the party she didn't want to have, three times at band practice, and that first lame-ass date, if you could call it that, at the movies. His gut told him that if he proposed a movie to the group, this time she wouldn't go. He wanted to test his theory but there weren't any good flicks out right now, so they'd all say no.

His heart dropped like a rock, rattling down his ribcage, and landing with a dull thud onto his lap. *Was* she seeing someone else? After dark? Who was he? A damn vampire? Markis shifted and bounced his knee. Then he leaned forward and heaved his body back, trying for an elusive bit of comfort in the stiff leather seat. He stared without seeing into the blackness of the starless night as the drunken band members sang, "Forget You."

Chapter 18

As Saffron sat on her tuffet waiting for Jethin, she wondered; what would her life be like if she was a vampire? She felt a little ashamed just thinking about it but she couldn't help it. There were pros and cons. She would never see Li again. Jethin had said something about him and Saffron not being allowed to be together in the fairy world. What did he mean? Why? She'd have to remember to ask. So, if she was a vampire, she could never go back to the fairy world. That was okay. Most people never saw the fairy world once; she had been there three times. She didn't like it the last time, and she didn't like seeing magical critters. They scared her. She was all done with the fairy world. Could Li come visit her in the regular world? Even if Li brought Ny with her, Saffron would have nothing to worry about - she'd no longer be attracted to him. He could try all he wanted but he wouldn't be able to affect her anymore. She wouldn't have to feel herself giving over to him, like a dog in heat, just to be repulsed by her actions later. Who did that? Who lost control like that? It wasn't right. She needed to get away from him. She was so afraid she'd give into him, and soon, lose herself completely.

It was interesting to consider those things. But, then she thought about her mother and started to cry, as if her mother had already grown old and died. She made herself sick. This wasn't fun to think about at all. *But,* as a vampire, she could protect her mother and protect Derek. She could make sure they were always safe. The way she was now, she was no help to her mother at all. Her mother was the biggest dreamer on earth; she would never go to college. If she was a vampire, she would be strong. She could annihilate anyone who threatened her or her family. She would just go to her mother as a vampire, show Audrey she was okay, and show her all of the great things she could do. She would prove how smart she was, how confident. And she'd be a *rich* vampire. So Audrey could buy more acreage and make her alpaca farm bigger, and have a store built right on the land. Besides, weren't mothers always saying they didn't want their children to grow up? Her mother wouldn't have to worry about Saffron losing her virginity, being tempted by drugs or any of those other *human* things mothers worried about. Saffron could walk down the most dangerous street, in the middle of any city, at any time of night and never fear attack. Saffron stilled. She wondered when she had crossed the line from musing about it to justifying it.

Where was Jethin?

She waited another hour and went to bed. She was half asleep when she heard the very sound she didn't want to hear. But she was between sleep and dreaming and she couldn't stop them. The tinkling of tiny bells and slapping of tiny wings heralded their arrival. Her puppet soul responded to their unspoken commands. Her body stayed behind and rested peacefully.

Chapter 19

The fairies knew something was very different about the girl tonight. They exchanged looks of alarm. It disturbed their ultra-finely-tuned fairy senses. It was almost as if she was...*disappearing*. They carried her into the clearing, dropped her, and blinked away.

Ny was there, on his knees. He gathered her in his arms. The full moon splashed across her face, lighting her cheekbones and her thick, golden eyelashes. No matter how hard she tried to hold a firm expression, he saw how she instantly melted in his arms and soaked him up. He grinned. He would never lose her. She would never leave him. She could run away from him, run to the human world, and leave him behind. But, even in the human world, she chained herself to him in her dreams. He licked his lips and breathed her in. So desired to breathe her in. His blue eyes roamed the contours of her skin. He smoothed back her hair. She was his little treasure, always and forever.

Saffron's lips were parted, her cheeks flushed. She was waiting for him. She had been with him for only two seconds but she knew. And he knew. She would give herself to him. Not Jethin, nor Markis, nor any other man for all of her existences, because no man but this man mattered. She reached up to graze her fingertips along his jaw line, and then pressed his bottom lip. She reached up with her other hand and raked her fingers through his hair. An eddy swirled through her brain, gathered strength and, in only a moment, became a thundering tornado that whipped her blood. He pulled at her without touching her. She had no choice but to respond to his gravity. The sensations in her were, by measure, both excruciating and sublime.

Then into the swirl came a picture, an image of pain, a sight so crippling, it would prove to be her savior. It was the strangest fleeting vision. She was at his feet, weeping. It was some other time, some other place. Her hand froze in mid-stroke as her eyes widened with a burgeoning knowledge.

"Ny!" The shriek shook Saffron's entire soul. The fog that Ny had created to dull her senses blasted out of her mind. She jumped out of his arms, sobbing. Why was this happening to her?

Li stepped out of the shadows. "And now she will learn the truth, Ny. Before I allow her to give herself to you one more time; I will tell her the truth. Maybe she will protect herself with it and find some might to deny you."

"Why would you do this, Li? Why will you not leave this business alone? It does not concern you. It concerns only Saffron and me. We will decide our paths."

"You are wrong! It has everything to do with me. I will not watch my friend suffer. I will not stand by and watch her sacrifice herself to you. And I will not watch you destroy her one more time."

Ny's eyes narrowed. "You will undo our lives? But, sister, I am not the cause of her grief, but of her pleasure. I am the answer to her desires."

"What's happening?" Saffron shrieked and started to run. But run where? There was nowhere to run. This was their world. She collapsed into a heap on the forest floor.

With tears in her eyes, Li watched her friend. She dropped to her knees beside her. "Saffron," Li whispered, "I must tell you now. I will not leave you in the dark any longer. You may not want to hear what I say, and indeed, it is much easier to hide from the truth than to face it. But face it you must, and if this truth does not destroy you, you will grow stronger for knowing."

Ny scowled at his sister but made no move to stop her. What could he do? Saffron would know all when she died anyway. What did it matter if she found out a few years earlier than expected? What did it really matter? He could take Saffron again. He had done it a thousand times before and he could do it again. After she cried it out, she would be his again. He leaned against the trunk of an ancient oak and watched his sister soothe her favorite pet.

The girls sat side by side. Li's wings glinted and flexed. Ghostly wisps of Saffron's red hair had escaped her up-do and moved in the breeze. Li placed both arms around Saffron and held her tight. She spoke very softly. "Do you not yet know who I am, Saffron? Can you not feel what I really mean to you? Close your eyes and feel me. Feel what passes between us and tell me what it is that washes over you."

Saffron sighed and forced her breathing to even out. Her eyelids fluttered shut. At first, she felt nothing but the pain, confusion, and desperation that plagued her. Then slowly, the pain and confusion and desperation seemed to separate and take on solid forms. They were like odd shapes in her mind with piercing colors and jagged edges. Her breathing slowed to a stop. Waves of soft color floated into her mind, and with each pass a color first washed away the jagged shape of pain, then the scribbled block of confusion, then the downward spiral of desperation. The waves kept coming; they cleansed her and massaged the fatigue out of her muscles. They cleared her mind.

After awhile, Saffron opened her eyes and started to breathe. She felt light and free. "Oh," she gasped. She had been staring straight ahead, but now she turned to Li. "I love you." She thought her lips would split from smiling. She hugged Li. They held on to each other for a long time.

"Yes," Li crooned as she wiped away her own tears. "You and I, before we enter our human lives, we choose to be best friends or mother and daughter or sisters. We are always together. We had never been apart, until now. You left me, Saffron."

Saffron started to shake her head no. She would never have done that.

"It is true, Saffron. One day you begged off from a fairy feast, promised to be soon back, then never returned. You became human alone."

"No." Then louder, "No! I would never leave you!"

Li lowered her head.

"Oh, no, Li. I know nothing would cause me to leave you. My God, I can *feel* that. How come I haven't sensed you all along?"

Li didn't raise her head. "Because you were only sensing him."

Ny crossed his arms over his chest. He glared at his "sister." "Come now. So melodramatic. Must you?"

Li looked over at him, her expression blank. She stared at him for some time. He pretended nonchalance.

She was still watching Ny when she said, "Your bond with Ny is also very, very strong. In the fairy world, he and I call ourselves "siblings," as it is the best description for the platonic relationship we most usually share. The three of us, and several others, always enter the human world together and take parts in a play that is somewhat predetermined. Of course, the path of our lives is not set in stone. We are free to make our own choices. What kind of fun would the human adventure be if we could not make our own choices?"

"So, sometimes you are my best friend and I, I marry Ny, and he's your brother, right?"

Li turned away from Saffron to tear fungus from a rotted tree. "Marry? Yes, sometimes."

Something tugged within Saffron - it wouldn't go away. It was the force she sometimes felt when the fairies first took her, when she wanted to stay in her bed. It had made itself known to her on other troubling occasions, but she had always ignored it. "I know what you're not telling me. It's Ny. He doesn't love me."

As Li opened her mouth to speak, Ny leapt from his tree. He just sprang like a wild jungle cat, all of his muscles pumping. Saffron didn't see him cross the distance but suddenly he was right there, by her side. He pulled Saffron to him with tears in his eyes. He clutched her head to his chest. Saffron was wide-eyed, but made no movement to get away from him. She lay as limp as a frightened mouse between the paws of a cat.

"I will not have this, Li! I will not have you leading her to believe that I do not love her! You *know* that is not true. Will you now start another chain of lies to protect her from the truth?"

"Pah, truth. What does truth mean? Fine. Yes, Saffron, Ny loves you very much. Just look at that display of crystalline tears. But come now, Ny; you do not *respect* her."

Ny took Saffron's head in both of his mannequin-like hands, warming his palms for her. He looked into her eyes. "Only love matters, Saffron."

Li scoffed.

With very little patience, Ny ignored her. "Saffron, sometimes you cannot handle the nature of our relationship..." He flipped a hand imperturbably at the air, "...you get yourself very worked up. But I tell you now, I love you. This relationship that we share. It is incomparable."

Li walked a little away from them as Ny continued whispering, holding Saffron's face. "Ny, you say Saffron cannot handle the nature of your relationship. Should you not explain what that means? By the moon and the stars, Ny! The nature of your relationship is like that of a violent storm, or raging bull, or any number of destructive things!" Li's eyes blazed. It was coming. She could feel it, the first fairy throttling since the dawn of time. But what would that accomplish? It would be as fruitless as choking the wind for scouring, choking the rain for drowning, choking the sun for burning...

Saffron spoke very softly but her voice was firm. "What, exactly, is the nature of our relationship, Ny?

Ny released Saffron. "Well..."

Li beckoned for Saffron to sit with her on the mushroom-covered log. Wild flowers grew there too. Wherever the sun could break through the trees and nourish the seeds, the tiny flowers grew, though their roots were relatively weak. Li plucked several flowers of white and fuchsia and red. She wove the stems around and around. Silently, Saffron watched her. When Li completed the crown, she placed it upon Saffron's head and petted the rings of fiery curls that fell down Saffron's back. In one of the trees above, worker bees slaved for their queen. The drone of the males could be heard even though it competed with the wind, the rustle of leaves, the bubbling of a brook, and the far-off, forlorn bleat of a deer.

Li smiled and continued stroking Saffron's hair. "The fawn searches for her mother. We are in much the same situation."

"You are *not* my mother."

Li's hand stilled, then continued stroking a little more stiffly. "Ny is all things male to you. I am all things female. It is what we have chosen."

"What does that make me, the eunuch?"

"Saffron, sshhh. Listen."

Saffron leaned away from the white fairy.

"You were lucky to receive your mother." Li chuckled and shook her head. "Although, the poor soul would give her life for you now, you did scare her upon the declaration of your arrival." Li tilted her head like a mischievous puppy. "She thought of killing you, you know. Something I had never considered in all of the times you were in my womb."

Saffron sucked in her breath and instant tears welled in her eyes. "Did I do something wrong to her? I mean, did I cause her trouble?"

"Oh, yes, Saffron." Li's laughing bubbled over, and Saffron wanted to know what was so hilarious. Causing her mother grief should not be so funny.

"Your mother was very young when she learned she was with child. In that era, she was too young." Saffron nodded. She knew this. Her mother was only sixteen years old when she discovered she was pregnant. Saffron, who was now nineteen and no closer to sex than Vlad the Impaler was to pleasant, couldn't fathom being several months pregnant at this point in her life, never mind *sixteen*. Saffron squirmed on the log. She definitely did not like talking about this. Her mother + sex = disturbing.

"Do you know why birth control pills are only ninety-nine percent effective? Because of fairies! Sometimes we want to get born.

Saffron looked impressed.

"At that time, you decided for everyone that Audrey should be your mother..." Li sniffed. "I'm really not sure why."

Saffron shot her a warning glance.

"It was not her chosen destiny to have you. Her soul, deep down inside, knew that what had happened was very much...off its destined path. Your mother fought through terrible times of great confusion, and with confusion comes depression. But, as I have said, our lives are not set in stone, and remarkably, stranger things have happened. Your mother is...a special soul, so she was able to overcome her predicament." Li's mouth curved into the same and too-frequent smile. The smile didn't reach her eyes. "That is the wonderful thing about our destinies; they can change," She sat so erect, she looked painfully prim. She shot a sly look at Ny, who was tossing acorns. "You can meet new souls and new people to love."

Ny was unusually quiet. He was sure something was amiss. He had been suspicious for some time now. What was she up to? Beautiful fairy she might be, with her hair of spun sugar and flashing, violet-rimmed eyes, but she could be a mean spirit too. It wasn't uncommon for her to be into some secret business. His eyes softened as they settled on the long, curving form of his naïve love. "Saffron, the meeting of true lovers is not common. Do not expect to have such a great love life this time around - nothing like what I have given you." He tilted his head back to catch some of the sun's rays.

Saffron wanted to touch him, just once, everywhere. She wished she had the power to stop time and take off his clothes without anyone knowing, not even him. He could stand there like a museum piece while she admired him. As long as he didn't know. He was so freakin' arrogant.

"Ah, yes, Ny. And what is it that you usually give our Saffron?"

"More than she has now. She can feel that she does not belong, that something is amiss in this life. She does not belong in this time, with these people. She will never feel right until she leaves this life and comes back to us, until she returns to me."

"There is time, Ny. Things could change for our friend, Saffron. She could change things for herself, customize life to suit her needs and wants. Meet people who can help her." Li had a Cheshire grin.

Ny ground his teeth. "What is it? What do you know? You will not make me salivate over your secrets."

Li sprung from the log and stood toe-to-toe with Ny, both of their wings pumped. Saffron looked from one to the other. She saw the determination in their stances, the look of defiance in their eyes. Yeah, they were just like brother and sister, and a bratty pair at that. "Ny." He didn't seem to hear her. She spoke louder, more insistent. "Ny, what is the nature of our relationship?"

His shoulders drooped, just a little. He wagged a finger at his sister.

Li nodded. She had won. "I will tell her, Ny." She brushed his wagging finger away. "Ny will never love you the way you want him to love you, Saffron. As for your part, you chain yourself to Ny. You give of yourself until there is nothing left to you but an empty shell of desperation and misery. One thinks you would, after a time, leave him and search out other loves. We all have many true loves. Sometimes we intentionally create chaos by entering a human life with two or more of our true loves. As human, there are absurd ways we learn to handle that. But most of us, most of the time, agree to enter the human race with one chosen love. Someone we can navigate the world with. Then there is you, Saffron.... Ah, well. You choose Ny over and over again. You give no one else a chance. And over and over again Ny cuts your heart out of you and laughs while its pulse slows and weakens in his hand."

Saffron fell backwards off the log. She scrambled up from the leaves and yelled, "What?"

"Oh, I do not mean that in the literal sense, Saffron." Li's laugh tinkled like Christmas bells. "You would be much luckier if he did just kill you."

"Come now, Li." Ny put his hands on his hips. His fine tunic clung to every edge, hill and valley of his torso. "Watch yourself. Or you will chase her away too."

The warning scared her. Ny could see. Saffron saw the flash of fear as well. Li blurted, "Saffron, we do not have much time left. You must leave soon. Be done with Ny. He hurts you, Saffron. Over and over and over again, he hurts you so terribly. You are married to him and you find him in your bed with another woman. In other lives, you have affairs with him, and even though he promises, he never leaves his wife for you. He promises the moon and gives you less than the fodder of a worm. You cry for him. You beg at his feet. You commit suicide....."

Li finally fell silent, satisfied with the horror in Saffron's eyes. Saffron clutched at the log on which she leaned, pressing her fingers into the soft, mossy rot and crushing the fungus. Black spots formed and danced before her eyes. She broke out into a cold sweat and knew she was going to faint. She flopped and sprawled unceremoniously across the top of the log, passed out, only to come to a moment later. When she opened her eyes, she saw nothing but the woman on the cliff on the edge of the sea. She had felt every little last bit of that woman's agony when she jumped. Saffron hadn't known why she empathized with the woman, but she knew now. In a way, she *was* that miserable wretch of a soul. She was that woman so set on snuffing out her existence. She knew what it was like to live in such pain that the body wanted to dash itself like glass on rock.

"It *was* you..." Saffron raised her arm up until her index finger stretched out and pointed straight at Ny. "In my dreams. Always cheating on me. In Rome, in China, in the tenth century, in the twentieth century...in bedrooms, in wide-open fields...all those women." Saffron held her chest. "Oh, my God, those awful, awful dreams."

"Not dreams." Li whispered. Her voice trailed in the breeze like a length of silk over smooth, cool marble. *"Memories."*

Not dreams, memories. Not dreams, memories.

This was all wrong. This wasn't like the reincarnation stories she had heard and read about. People who were hypnotized and asked to describe a past life always discovered that they were Cleopatra or Hercules, a king, a queen, an emperor, a celebrity. Even Jesus! Here she was, in what should have been her shining moment, reincarnation of all things, just to discover she was wretched, pitiable, and weak. But the humiliation was only one thing she couldn't swallow.

She had been able to tell herself to dismiss the pain. It was only a dream, nothing real, nothing to consider. Now to discover that all of the feelings were real was too much to bear. Every horrible moment came rushing back in the clearest of details and this time she crumpled and folded under the agony, knowing that the visions were all true. All true.

Suddenly, everything happened at once. Saffron jumped up and flew at Ny. She thought of nothing but clawing his perfect skin and mocking smile from the bone of his skull. She wanted him to live while she ripped him to shreds. Li jumped after her and Ny blinked into a ball of light just as Saffron was about to lay her hands on him. She was running at him at full force when he disappeared. She tripped and flew face-first into the dirt and decay of the forest floor.

Ny flew to a low branch on a nearby tree. He was low enough to keep an eye on Saffron but high enough to stay out of her reach. He stared at her in wonder as his body trembled; he had never seen her act like this. Where was his gently-cooing dove? Where was his mewling kitten, his weepy maid? "Even though you did not touch me, you hurt me, Saffron." He was pouting.

Saffron started to scream. She screamed until her throat became ragged and she could taste blood on her tongue. Then she raged some more.

Ny looked to Li, who was wringing her hands as she stood over Saffron. Li wanted to touch the girl but was afraid to.

"She must leave now or her rage will spoil our land. Take her away."

"Oh, ho, so you make a mess of her and I clean it up. Does this ring any bells, Ny?"

Other fairies started to arrive. They told Li to take Saffron home. They told Li never to bring her back. Her human hate was hurting them. Hate, the only thing they could feel on their skin, with its crawling and biting like scorpions, burning them with its poison. It reminded them of their punishment, of why they were there. It was unbearable to them.

"Yes, yes. Here..." Li put her hand to Saffron's brow and instantly Saffron was silent and staring with glassy eyes. "Please take her. I will take my leave and lessen her struggle." She turned to Ny. "She will be done with you now." She looked very sure of herself. "There is one with her. One who has loved her from afar. I had long known of his feelings for Saffron and I decided it was time to urge him forward, help him against you. And he will allow me to be near Saffron when next we take our human lives. He has promised me this. His now mother calls him, 'Markis.' He is from another tribe. He went to that tribe many ages ago. But he once belonged to our tribe. He was here for murder...yours." She adjusted her tunic. "When he was here he watched how you continued to abuse her love. He tried to approach her. You blocked his way, and Saffron chose not to see him. He went away. He quickly ascended in the other tribe and was able to choose rebirth after a short period.

"When Saffron left us, I discovered early on what had happened to her. I have always loved her better than you, Ny. I have always been concerned for her welfare, truly cared for her pain. I easily realized what had happened and what she had done. I acted on my hunch and found the truth; Saffron was better than both you and I. Her only crime was in not protecting herself, so her sentence here was short. We were both too selfish to notice that she was not our equal. She is better. She stayed with us in the fairy realm after our other incarnations because she *chose* to, not because she was imprisoned like we were. Like we are.

"I set out to find the soul that would be Markis. I found him. I found him still greatly in love with our Saffron. Of course he was; true love doesn't go away. He went after her and was born not many months after she arrived into the human world. I told the rest of you so many years later, when it would be fruitless for you to give chase, when she would consider you just a baby and give you no audience. You had been looking for her among the tribes all that time, with never a thought to what she had really done. You have underestimated her. And, although his human body is not aware of what a great chance this is, Markis's soul will lead him home to her. True love cannot die, Ny. But I think obsession can fade if Saffron will let it."

She stood tall, towering over him, her chin lifted in victory, her hair flapping and furling around her like a long, white flag.

Ny sneered. "You think it so easy to keep her from me? She thinks it so easy to keep from me. You are both wrong! I did not know of Markis. So what? It does not matter. I have my own secret...*I have shown her the lake!*" Right then, he didn't look so beautiful. Even to Li, who had always been proud of his good looks, he was like a creature neglected - ugly and vicious.

Li wasn't expecting to hear anything so terrible. Her wings seemed to fail as she stumbled toward a tree; her clear skin turned a sickly gray. "Oh, Ny," she breathed, "How could you? We'll be chained here for eons. How could you?" Through her tears, Li summoned the wind and sent a message to Saffron. "You are in danger, but I will help you. Do not leave your home. Allow no one in. Do not make contact with the creatures of magic. Do not speak on the phone. Pull your shutters. Do nothing at all until you hear from me again."

Li raised her hands to her mouth and held back a scream of frustration. That was why it was no good to have humans there. Humans left residue. Hormones flying around freely in fairy air were like an airborne disease. Too many little bugs in the air could make fairies sick. And Li felt ill now. She knew what the lake meant. Dreaming of the lake told the soul to prepare for death. The dream came to all humans just before death. It was like the final announcement before your train left. Ny had sent the dream and tricked Saffron's soul. Saffron did not know it, but inside, in the blackest and strongest part of her mind, she had been preparing for death. To prepare for death was to justify it, to give in. If Saffron died now, her shameless soul would be reborn somewhere else and they'd have to find her and wait for her all over again and still she wouldn't really be with them. That was the best-case scenario. The worst case would be if something caused her to break the circle...

"Ny. Ny! Jethin has developed a relationship with her! If he tricks her well, she may not die! Did you not know of her meetings with him?"

Ny looked doubtful. "Oh, please. Not Jethin again." Was this another ruse of Li's?

But Li saw him falter. "Did you really not know what was going on with *your love* all of this time? Of course not! This is what I mean. You care nothing for her! Why do you not release her? Thanks to you, her soul fears death, it may cause her to make very rash decisions, decisions that are probably being offered to her with sugar and cream and blood! Ny, our Saffron would never entertain a vampire. You did this; I am sure. I am sure her defeated soul accepted Jethin only after you showed her the lake."

Ny's face drained of color; even his long, sooty lashes changed from black to gray. The veins under his rice-paper skin turned gray. How had everything turned into this? How had Saffron become this creature who caused him such pain? It was not fair! It was not their way! The way they had always chosen...a simple way, each acting a role, fulfilling basic needs. He half-fell and half-jumped from the tree. When he landed on the earth, his legs were splayed beneath him. His palms were before him, on the ground, supporting his weight. His fingers dug into the black earth. So that was the mystery; that was why he could not ease into her mind in these past countless months. She had saddled herself to one of the undead. Jethin had found her. How had Jethin found her? His head snapped round to stare at Li, his eyes like white-hot flames as he glared at her from under his dark brows. She stared off into nothingness, her hand still over her mouth.

Jethin's persistence was entirely Li's fault. Ny had barely known Jethin back in Ireland. Li was Molly and Ny had been Molly's father. Usually, Ny liked to laugh about those times. Li, as Molly, had formed herself into such an angry slut that it was comical. And, when Jethin had killed Molly, then spiraled down into the world of the undead...well that was a story Jethin never tired of telling around the bonfire. He was not to blame for Saffron's dalliances!

If Saffron became the undead, barred from his loins for all eternity, then Ny felt most certain he would snuff Li for it. He'd be branded a demon but it would be worth it. He could work at being a demon. He roared with fury and actual fire burst from his orifices, singeing the tender growth nearby.

Li's whisper was hoarse. "Who was waiting for her on the shore?" Li knew she, herself, was certainly not there. Had Ny convinced any of the others to join his scheme? Souls soon to depart their human body have a dream just before death. It is a vision of a dark lake in the shadow of tall, dark mountains. All is blanketed by a black-domed sky pricked with a million stars. The moon is so large you can see every detail of the craters on the visible side; it glows with a light of such brilliance it illuminates a glass boat and the lake around it. There are neon fish that swim just below the surface.

When a person is about to die, that person has a vision of the lake, of themselves seated pleasantly in the glass boat being propelled forward by an unknown force toward the glittering moonlit sands of an unknown shore. As all the loved ones of that soul are notified of the impending arrival, they all gather on the beach to show that they are happy to see their beloved again. This is why humans are entranced by sandy beaches, why when one walks the beach at night his steps are as inspiring as a trek to forever.

This is the only way to die a peaceful death, to accept the inevitable without fear. When one has a vision of the lake *and* the crowded shore, they know at the very core of their heart, soul, and being, that they are loved and therefore have nothing to fear.

But Ny showed Saffron an empty shore.

Li felt fear creeping all over her. It was so unusual to feel fear again, like a coat of slime over her body; a sentient slime that tried to probe every inch of her. Anger, fear - these were not the emotions she so longed to feel again. She wept bitterly. Like a demon, she thrashed at the tree and gnashed her teeth.

"The empty shore was no fault of mine, Li. Saffron pulled out of the trance before I could complete the message."

"A thief is not excused from breaking a window by accident when he only meant to rob the bank!" Her hands found her hair and pulled.

"There was no one waiting on the shore, Li. I am truly sorry for that." He rushed on. "At first I wanted her to see no one was on the shore. I wanted her to panic, just a little. Then I wanted her to see me, coming out of the mist - her savior. Then when she died, her soul would know.... She would believe.... She would think no one cared for her as I have cared for her..." It was no use; the last part of his speech did not come out as strongly as he had wanted it to. He had made a grave mistake, and now he knew it. "Her soul would know I was the only one there for her." This last, he whispered without conviction.

"What do you mean, 'when she died;' have you not stopped trying to coax her to her death?"

He shook his head like a naughty three-year-old, black waves sweeping back and forth over his forehead. "I have lessened my efforts. Those with her guard her very well on the full moon, and we both know I am not as effective on any other occasion." He put up a finger. "She did fall asleep in the forest once. I almost succeeded then. But we were not alone and I think the dead may have helped her."

Li looked at him sideways. "You will cause our sentence to lengthen by a hundred years."

"Who are you to speak? Consumer of rabbits. That too, condemns us."

"It is a lighter sentence, to consume the lower creatures. I cannot live without sensation. I need those rabbits. The sensations that their essence brings are exquisite, even if it is only for a short time. You only require to be fondled in dreams, but I want it all here, in our waking world - the smells, the tastes...." Li lay back on the earth and stared up into the growing dawn. Now, not only was Saffron's soul preparing for death, it thought no one was waiting for it on the other side. Deep down, so deep that goodness and light could not reach it, Saffron's soul felt utter despair and loneliness. And, as was natural for a soul to do, it would search for a way out of the pain.

Chapter 20

As Saffron flew toward her home, she felt the fury within her bubbling up and burning off the fog of fairy flight. Each time a wave of anger rolled through, she felt the tiny fairy hands grip her more tightly and pull her up to keep her afloat. Apparently, anger made souls heavy.

They pleaded with her. "Saffron, let go your rage. It is weighing you down. It is hurting us. We will not be able to keep you up if you do not let it go. You are going to fall and crash to the earth, Saffron...."

Suddenly, Saffron felt herself free-falling. Her gut rolled into her throat, ready to fly out through her lips. Terror replaced anger and Saffron's descent accelerated. It sent her spiraling downwards like a falcon. The fairies flattened their wings against their backs and nosedived after her. They worked their magic on her terror-filled mind. Anger was able to burn their magic off, but terror was what they longed for. With terror, the fairies could easily slip inside and soothe her with their ancient and hypnotic magic. Saffron came to an abrupt stop just before she was impaled on the steepled point of a church spire. She bobbled clumsily in the air. All at once, the fairies were there, gathering her up again.

"Let us help you," they whispered. "Think of something peaceful. If you were to remain angry any longer, you would surely have plummeted all the way down..."

"What does it matter?" Saffron brought her hands to her face and rubbed hard.

"It matters, human." A pink-skinned fairy fluttered directly in front of Saffron's face. "You will feel the pain of the crash because your mind expects to feel the pain. Your soul is only temporarily out of your body. Your mind isn't above making certain assumptions. Did Li not tell you this? Help yourself here, human child. You must not be guilty of making yourself suffer, lest you find yourself caught in the fairy realm."

Saffron looked hard at the speaker. Confused, she nodded. She started to shake, aftershock from her near-death experience. She opted not to look down upon the little chapel just several feet below. She focused on a small mountain peak off in the distance. It was illuminated by the full moon. It reminded her of the chain of mountains that surrounded the lake full of the glowing fish. She concentrated on keeping this in her psyche. She hadn't thought about the daydream since that weird day it happened, but now every detail was full and lush and wholly in her mind. She found that thinking of the velvet black waters and ring of solid ancient mountains soothed her.

Now her soul became so light that it flew up instead of down and just as quickly. She bulleted straight up into the sky so swiftly, that most of the fairies lost their touch on her. They gasped as they watched her fly up and away and out of reach. The others still adhered to her throttled-through open space as if they were clinging to a shooting star.

"What is she doing?" one of them shrieked, "Is she thinking about what I think she is thinking about?"

"Stop it...STOP IT, Saffron!" begged another fairy. "Your soul thinks it is dying. For the love of all that is good in the universe, think of something else!"

Saffron felt wonderful. Then, in a blink, she was terrified at the way her soul was ascending into black space, without anything to stop her. How could the image of the lake do that to her? She barely heard the fairies screaming at her to clear her mind. It was difficult, but she thought of home. She thought of her mother and Derek, of Coco and Markis. She thought of alpacas being born in the field in the early morning hours in July and puppies and kittens and Christmas presents.

She slowed to a stop and hung in black space. The fairies wouldn't look at her as they guided her back down. Sometime later, travel-weary and human-weary, the fairies deposited Saffron through the window and onto her unmade bed. They shook their heads. They assured themselves that when they became human again, they would not pull such abominable stunts and good riddance.

Saffron rolled over and closed her eyes. She heard the fairies leave, the "ppfffft" sound of their wings and their fading bells. She lay in the fetal position as tears slid slowly across the bridge of her nose and down onto the sheets. She heard Li's voice from far away warning her against leaving the house or doing something with her shutters. "Screw you." She turned on the radio to disrupt the "Li Channel."

She stayed in bed all day. That night, she got up to watch Raising Hope with Derek. Even Maw Maw couldn't make her laugh. She said nothing to Derek until she grunted, "Goodnight," then trudged her way back up to her bedroom.

A short while after midnight, Li made her descent over the house and felt anger come to greet her. She opened Saffron's window and slid inside to sit on the edge of Saffron's bed.

Saffron rolled over and looked sadly into Li's eyes. "I just don't understand. I *do not* understand how I could have lived a hundred lifetimes. I *do not* understand why I'm pathetic in each one of those lives. And how come you never tried to help before."

Li's long lashes swept down over her cheeks. Waves of white, windblown-curls rolled over her shoulders, between her wings, and just barely touched the sheets. Her expression was unreadable. "You always choose to be as inconspicuous as you can in each of your lives. You hide much. You hide things from your family...your friends...yourself. When it comes to Ny, you choose to suffer alone. Right now, I have memories of all of my lives. When I am born again, I will not have these memories. When and if, as human, I come to realize what it is you are doing, I either step down and respect your need for privacy or, less often, try to interfere for your sake. The outcome of interfering varies from life to life. Sometimes you simply ignore me, sometimes you get mad enough to distance yourself from me, and sometimes, you leave me completely and let me wallow in my own misery of losing you. I believe some essence of each of our lives builds up inside of us. I believe this is called intuition. So, when I discover your dark, secret life with Ny, and my intuition tells me to let you be or lose you...I let you be."

"So fine, you respected me and tried to help. Why am I so dreadful to begin with? It's so mortifying! It's like watching a this-is-your-life episode, and instead of finding out you did good things in your life, admirable things, you find out you're just a big loser!"

"No, Saffron. No, no. You are wrong there. You are wonderful in all of your lives. You are an incredible mother. You are book-smart, and earth-caring. You are a good listener and your family and friends always adore you. I adore you. You are just so precious."

"But I'm miserable!"

"Yes. For all of your kindness to others you are never kind to yourself. You are beyond appalling to yourself. You are destructive. And Saffron, I do not fully blame Ny."

Saffron's chewed-up fingernails cut into her balled fists. So it was all her fault, was it? She was too weak to resist Ny? Well bring that dumb ass here, now, and she would show him what it would be like to screw around with her these days!

"I know you are distressed, Saffron."

Saffron's eyes widened. Distressed? "Distressed! It's not like I left the house forgetting a freakin' bra!"

"You must listen to me, Saffron. You must hear me. It is never too late to change. In this life...in the next. You have all the time in the world to stop the grief, and rage, and desperation. You can choose to live the life you wish to live." Li paused. She watched Saffron's back, and waited for a response. "Saffron, in all of your lives you never tried to be with another love besides Ny. You have no idea what wonderful adventures await you. I know of many that have tried to be with you. You know none of them. You chose to keep them out. Your happiness depends on you. Your soul depends on you. Even if you choose incorrectly or unwisely, it does not matter, choose again. But choose, Saffron. Act, Saffron. Do not sit back and drown in the storm."

Saffron remained rigid as death.

"Saffron, do not fool yourself. Jethin does not hold the key to your release. In a way, he is no different than Ny. In a way, Jethin is much worse than Ny."

Saffron kicked her way out of her sheets and rolled away from Li to get out of the bed. "Don't you compare Jethin to Ny. Don't say Jethin's worse than Ny because the truth is Ny could never have the goodness, he couldn't have one one-hundredth of the goodness that lies in that quote, unquote, monster's heart!" Saffron's chest heaved.

Li spoke softly and firmly, as if Saffron had never spoken - as if Saffron was not looming above her with fairy execution flaming in her eyes. "Jethin is like Ny in that he knows exactly what to say to you to trick you into doing exactly what he wants."

"Oh, so now I'm stupid? Are you trying to say that I'll believe anything anyone tells me? Think again, because I think you're lying now and you've been lying all along!"

"And," Li calmly continued, "Jethin is unlike Ny in that almost all goodness and happiness had been wrung from him from having spent too many years on this planet as the same person. That is why he wants you, Saffron. Your youth, your freshness, your beauty, your strength, and that bit of fairy magic you so despise - these things render you almost goddess-like in his eyes. But in time - granted it may take hundreds of years - you will yearn for your youth, for change. Jethin will have no use for you then. He will find you, too, were unable to deliver him. He will not keep up the pretense of kindness.

"It is about being born, Saffron. That is the magic we all seek. You and I can be reborn for eternity. Or, at least until the human race destroys itself, then we'll all be stuck as fairies with no planet, but that is a different matter. Think. Think of why they call his kind the "undead." His soul has not been released from his body – yet it no longer exists as it did when he was human. He walks around at night, in blackness. His heart has been blackened by the cynicism that has grown within him century after century. He experiences everything with the same tired eyes, the same perceptions. He can never see things a different way. He is filled with the doubts and prejudices of 'Jethin', the human he used to be, before he became the undead. And since he can never be born again, can never change - he can never be truly happy again. He cannot escape."

Saffron stared at Li for a moment, then turned around and gave the fairy her back once more.

Li looked down at her fingers. "Saffron, there is something you need to know about Jethin."

Saffron rolled her eyes. "Oh, what are you gonna tell me now?" Saffron dropped back on her chair, on her panda. "You're driving me insane; do you realize that? You're literally making me crazy! Look at the knots in my hair!" She was whispering in a high-pitched hiss.

Li continued to look at her fingers. She had a ring of symbols around both middle fingers, like a tattoo. They were ancient fairy symbols and minutely etched. They spelled out her fairy name. Names were always the same in the fairy world, not that she was banished there *that* often. She would leave Saffron now. The girl was too walled up in anger. She would try again tomorrow.

Saffron saw Li make that, 'sitting forward and looking at the exit' motion to leave. "What?" She leaned forward, her elbows resting on her knees, "Had enough?"

Li took in a large breath, forced it back out. She should not leave this matter to another day. "Jethin is not who you think he is. He is not what you think he is."

"Yeah, okay. What are you saying? He's not a vampire? Sure."

"I did not say that, Saffron. Please, let me talk."

Saffron threw her hands up, muttered incoherently.

"Saffron, Jethin is the reason why I have not incarnated in several hundred years, why I did not follow you after you jumped back into the human world." She rubbed her arms as if suddenly chilled. "Jethin murdered me in my last incarnation. Murdered me and threw me down a well in Ireland. It was soon after that that he became a vampire. I went to him one night hoping to show him that I was not eternally dead. I wanted to tell him that I forgave his monstrous deed." Her voice caught before she continued - how miserable it was to relive this again, how traumatic even in memory. "I was not ready for the depth of his hate and anger. I did not realize how I had fanned his rage with my claims of everlasting fairy life. He was not happy to learn what he had given up when he became a vampire." Li went to sit on the floor by Saffron's chair. "He tried to kill me again! When he discovered he could not kill me, he vowed to kill me in my next incarnation. He vowed to kill everyone I loved as well, to punish me for driving him to his fate.

"I tried to protect you, Saffron. Throughout your life, I tried charms to seal you from his knowledge. For many years, I succeeded. I went to you in your dreams as a black shadow to ward you from public places when he was nearby. I placed a fairy ring around your property, a line you felt too uncomfortable to cross. It worked, for a while. I protected you well."

"What?" Saffron spat like a cat, her back arched. "You were sending me those feelings? That awful darkness that sat on me like ten tons of crap? I could hardly get out of bed in the morning because I was so afraid. That was *you*?" Saffron lurched out of the chair and went to stand by her window. She bit down into her lip; she didn't want Li to see her cry. "That was you?" she whined.

Saffron remembered morning upon morning of waking up in tears, so many mornings she felt herself nearly slip over the edge into lunacy. Li's sick idea of protection had really worked. Saffron was perpetually afraid of leaving the house. There had been so many sick days that kept her from school, from life. Saffron's voice was barely a squeak. "You were controlling me with fear? You, who loves me so much? You?" Then Saffron jabbed an accusatory finger and roared, "People treated me like I was crazy! I treated me like I was crazy."

"I was just trying to help," Li lamented.

Saffron scrunched up her face. "I don't believe you."

Li panicked. "But you must, Saffron! You must open your eyes and realize what is happening to you! Do not run headlong into the same misery as Jethin!"

"Maybe you should stop pushing me there." Saffron walked out and left Li in the dark room.

Chapter 21

Saffron stood in the shower and let the water roll across her skin. She dripped some fruity bath gel on a sponge and, without much effort, dabbed at her body. She got dressed. Underwear, bra, low-riding jeans, tight white T-shirt, black v-neck hoodie, socks, hybrid hiking sneakers. Hair clipped up.

No. Wait.

She sat before her mirror and wrenched the clip from her hair. It rained red all over her shoulders. She didn't want to be like them. Like those fairy women. How they loved long hair. She thought of how Ny had stroked her hair and stared at her hair and pulled her close to him by tugging on her hair. She pulled her hair into a ponytail and reached for the scissors in her drawer. She stared at her face in the mirror for a moment, then reached back and crunch, crunch, crunched the scissors through the hank of hair. The lopped-off chunk fell to the floor. Saffron turned around, picked it up, and deposited it in the trash. A short stump of hair stuck out of the elastic that remained close to her scalp. She took the elastic out, parted her hair down the middle, marveled at the light weight, and styled her hair into two pigtails just behind her ears. She waited upstairs in her room until it was almost time for work. Then she ran down with her Black Chicken ball cap firmly on her head, her short hair hidden within the thick hood of the sweatshirt. Audrey, with a paint smear on her cheek, was taking a break from her canvas to wash the breakfast and lunch dishes that she, Derek, and Grandmother had left behind.

From the hall, Saffron called out a quick "G'bye," then ran through the door and onto the farmer's porch. She threw herself on her bike like a cowboy on his horse, pedaled furiously down the driveway. She sneered at the withering mushrooms that grew across the gravel. She pedaled back to the base of the driveway, then jumped off her bike and smashed every single mushroom. With their power revealed, their power was gone. She felt fantastic as she crushed each one to crumbled, powdery pulp. Today, she had no fear of leaving her mother's house.

Audrey held a sudsy pan and watched Saffron from the kitchen window as she disappeared down the drive. A black hoodie...in June? It was almost eighty degrees. And the ball cap? Saffron bitched about having to wear that ball cap. Maybe there were Suits evaluating the Black Chicken today. Maybe Saffron was going to rob a bank. Did she really have *all* of that hair in her sweatshirt? Audrey walked out into the hallway and considered the stairs to the second level. She started up. On the bottom step, she looked up with apprehension at the vacant landing above. Her mother was at a craft session for the elderly, Derek was at the shop. The grandfather clock ticked and half a mile away, their neighbor's lawn mower thrummed. She hoped he received the Shorn Lawrn Award at the county fair this fall.

She mounted each stair, and tread softly on the wide pine flooring that led to Saffron's room. Inside, she touched nothing, but roamed around the bed and the chair. When she got near her daughter's dressing table, she looked down. Something in the trash caught her eye. Audrey gasped and did a double take. Was that Saffron's hair? All of it? She reached down and pulled the almost two-foot-length out of the trash. Tears welled in her eyes as she stared at the rejected coil of hair. She looked out Saffron's window at the lush apple tree, running her hand over the hank of hair. Her eyebrow arched. If Saffron didn't want it, there were others who did, others who needed it.

She held on tight to the hair and made her way to Saffron's phone.

At the store, Saffron refilled the cup dispensers while Coco babbled on about her cowboy. They ignored the three boys stealing condoms for a water balloon war, and ignored old Mrs. Thatcher at the other end of the store, who bitched about burnt coffee. Outside, at the intersection, a motorcyclist gunned his bike so all the bored pedestrians would look and fail to be as impressed as he was with himself. Saffron's eyes slid sideways - it wasn't Markis. It felt like it was a million years ago, when she used to get excited at hearing an idling motorcycle at that light. She barely remembered her happiness that day when he pulled off his helmet and stood before her, his dark, wavy hair curling under the stuffy helmet. It was no use brooding about it now - things had gotten so awkward between them that she tried not to think about Markis at all.

Whump. A condom balloon blasted against the outside of the window and made her jump. She hadn't realized they left the store. Mrs. Thatcher was gone too. Coco left off at, "and then he said what if we did it on the roof of Wal-Mart," to go out and scream at the boys, who each chucked her the bird and ran off hawk-screaming with laughter. Saffron wondered if she should eat them when she was a vampire. She bet they tasted better than a lamb-eye vodka shot.

They had just finished tossing congealed salads when Coco sighed. "Dude, what in the hell is wrong with you? And don't you even tell me 'nothing' cuz I just told you a new nether-region technique that you could take notes on, copyright, and sell...and your little cheeks didn't even get pink. So, *what the hell is wrong with you?*"

Saffron put down her spoon with the congealed stuff on it. She turned and considered Coco head on. A mother and toddler ting-a-linged in. Saffron crooked her finger at Coco. "C'mere."

Coco pulled her chin into her neck. "Since when do you tell me to 'c'mere'." Her head jerked from side to side. From Goth to Harley to Urban Youth, and sometimes all in one day, Coco left no trend unmolested.

"I'll tell you something even you've never done." Saffron nodded solemnly, and leaning toward Coco's ear, she began to whisper.

As she spoke, Coco's eyes alternated between wide and study-hard squint. "...and then you take your leg...."

Coco's hand went to her mouth, first time she ever she tried to hold something in.

"...and then you work it, don't slow..."

Coco's eyes started to water.

"...and then pull it until you can't stand it anymore..." Before Saffron could finish speaking, Coco pulled back from her and shut Saffron up with a look.

"Saffron, that's totally...oh my God...you're full of crap; nobody's that flexible." Coco swallowed hard before she shrieked "How would you know that?" She looked at Saffron like she'd never seen her before.

Saffron didn't blink. "I've done it before."

"I thought you were a fried-chicken virgin!" Coco was completely indignant. She looked Saffron up and down, up and down, not knowing, for once, what to say or do.

"I am."

Coco's hands went to her hips. "Well, what does that mean?"

"It means stop giving me your Goddamned, unasked-for sexual advice...I obviously don't need it." Saffron picked up a feather duster and made for the cereal aisle.

Coco stood rooted to the spot. She looked down and considered her crotch and the space to her knees. Her eyebrows rose. She smiled and looked at Saffron again.

From the aisle, Saffron gave a cool smile in return. "Tomorrow, everything will be better."

Coco's smile fell. "Yeah, that's not creepy." Being somewhat of a B movie aficionado, Coco was quite sure that there was the possibility that Saffron's mind had been taken over. How else would squeamish little Saffron utter the spew she just poured into Coco's ear? What Saffron had just told her, it was like, archaic or something, something that chimps might do. A new feeling started to gel in Coco's blood. She felt helpless. She stood by her friend throughout the shift and wished for the night to be over.

***

When Saffron got into her mother's car at midnight, Audrey tossed the hank of hair into her lap. Saffron jumped as if it was a ferret, then quickly settled back into her gloomy glass-eyed mode. "So you know."

"Yes, I know you cut your hair off, Saffron. And it's only hair; it's no big deal. But I'd like to know why you did it. Why did you sneak out this morning?"

Saffron shrugged her shoulders with a look of complete disinterest.

Her mother let the silent seconds go by, then gave one curt nod. "Well, it turns out this was a good thing. I have been in contact with some people who can help me find other people who will turn this into a wig or wigs for cancer patients. It's way more than ten inches, and that's what they need."

With an ice pick jab of shame, Saffron realized she should have thought of that herself. It was just last year that the "hair drive" was the big thing in town with half the girls she knew going into the salon and getting their hair cut off. They were doing it for some cancer drive, for wigs for little kids. At the time, Saffron had considered jumping on the bandwagon but quickly decided there was no way she could cut her hair off. Where would she hide? When things got really embarrassing or hard to handle there would be no sheet of hair to hide her face behind.

Wasn't she telling herself she was going to become a vampire to *help* people? She wasn't helping anyone today. She was living in such a bubble she couldn't even see what was going on around her. When she was a vampire, everything would become clear. It was one of the vampire gifts – clarity - something most humans could never grasp. Jethin said it would most certainly happen. Her mind would become sharp, her senses keen, and she would be one hundred times stronger. When she was a vampire, she would help people all of the time, kind of like a superhero; she would make sure only good prevailed.

That night, Jethin didn't come.

No fairies came.

There was only the ghost on the cliff and her strangled cries that disappeared into the waves like rain.

Chapter 22

The next morning, Saffron took her cup of coffee out onto the farmer's porch to be free of her mother's prying eyes, and Grandmother's instability, and Derek's crabbing.

She planted her butt on the steps and hunched over the steaming mug. She was so lost within herself that she didn't notice Mr. and Mrs. Gnome until they were standing below, looking up at her and waiting for her to notice them. She pulled back with a start and eyed them wearily. Then she relaxed. She didn't care what he did to her today. Nothing on earth could make her feel worse than she did right now. She watched as Mrs. Gnome stepped up behind the Mr. and shoved him in the back. He tripped forward, then glared back at his ample-bodied wife. The miniature woman set her jaw firmly and lowered her brows; she jutted her finger at Saffron and commanded him forward. He released his arms from behind his back and Saffron was startled yet again when she saw him awkwardly climbing the stairs, one by one, with a wilted daisy in his sweaty, hairy, little hand. When he got to the step just below her, he offered up the flower. She didn't take it right away; she just stared at it for a moment in dumb wonder. The gnome's cheeks flared red; he had never been so emasculated, so humiliated. Then he saw it - one tear formed in Saffron's right eye and threatened to drip over. The little gnome immediately curbed his emotions and shook his hand at her, the daisy flopping this way and that.

Saffron took the flower as her tears started flowing freely. "It's a truce," she whispered and the man nodded. She continued to weep. The gnomes left quietly.

The thick, sweet scent of lilacs hung in the still air. Saffron had always loved the heady scent of lilacs in bloom. The smell calmed her and brought memories of past summers. Would she still be able to smell lilacs as a vampire? Would they smell the same, evoke the same feeling? Saffron felt her body preparing to heave. She fled inside the house and ran up to her room.

She padded quietly around her room, looking at her things, then she sat before her mirror and arranged her new 'do. It felt so awkward, the way it fell against her neck and brushed just the very tips of her exposed shoulders. It felt so light. Should she put her hair up for Jethin so he wouldn't get a mouthful of hair when he bit her neck? Did they really do it like that? Like the movies? Tiny rivers of unease began to flow through her at the thought of it. She took a deep, jagged breath and tried to force herself to calm down. She cleared her mind again. She would not panic, not now.

The ring of the phone shot shrilly through the air. Saffron flinched and reached to read the caller ID. It was Markis. That was the fourth time this morning. Last night, she saw Coco jump on the phone as soon as she had left. So, it must have been Markis she called. Saffron felt guilty. Coco did look shook-up over her. But it didn't matter now. Saffron meant to protect Coco, too. As a future dancer and owner of a strip joint, Saffron felt pretty sure Coco was going to need protecting. Saffron shut off the phone. Her hours as a human were numbered. She would get through them as best she could.

She flopped on her bed and was suddenly aware that she was not alone. The fear she didn't want to live with anymore charged under her skin and made every hair stand painfully on end. In her peripheral vision, she caught movement and knew there was someone in the room with her. The shadow came nearer. Saffron jerked her head painfully to the side and took in an eyeful, up close, of the ghost who threw herself from the cliff every night. She had been across the room but was now making her jerky way toward Saffron. The long gown left a trail of wet on the wood floor like a slug. She stopped her advance, looked at the panda in the chair, then sat on it. The ghost folded her hands in her lap and stared out with her milky, unblinking eyes.

Saffron just lay there, breathing low and shallow, and ignoring the pains that started in her hip and leg from holding herself immobile. The ghost stayed where she was. Saffron stayed where she was, wishing the thing away. There was a soft knock on the door.

Saffron reached for the doorknob, as if she could open it from ten feet across the room. Her mouth opened and closed without a sound but the light smack of her tongue on the roof of her dry mouth. She heard her mother walk away.

The ghost stood. She started toward Saffron. The blood rushed to Saffron's ears; her bladder gave out. She made a small keening in the back of her throat, a noise so high-pitched it hardly carried across the room, never mind to someone outside. Saffron held her hands out to tell the thing to stop. But still the entity kept coming, her head wound glistening, her right arm hanging.

Saffron moaned. Tangled up in her sheets, she lifted her butt and did the crab walk until her head was jammed up against the headboard. She started flailing as the ghost moved right in front of her face. The ghost leaned close enough for her rotted nose to touch Saffron's nose. Then it moved closer still, her face into Saffron's face, her shoulders into Saffron's, her breasts into Saffron's, her hips into Saffron's...until her entire body disappeared inside Saffron. Saffron's eyes popped so wide they could have easily left her head and rolled around on the floor. She reached out one more time before she seized up and went completely still. Her eyes were open and unseeing as they reflected the slow swirl of the ceiling fan blades. Swirling went all through her head. Swirls of sun and blue sky and green field on a summer day.

The ghost woman searched the field. Her hair was shining, her skull was perfectly formed. The woman called out a man's name and felt the tall grasses at her fingertips as she kept walking.

Saffron swam somewhere above the woman as she roamed. Calling and calling and calling. The woman stopped abruptly and screamed, as if there were a snake at her feet. Saffron floated over to where the woman stood in a patch of swaying daisies and wild lavender.

Saffron saw what the ghost woman saw.

There below them, in a circle of crushed grass, was another woman. She was clad in nothing but sun-kissed skin and long, long, flaming-red hair. She sat atop a man and writhed. He smiled up at her with beautiful white teeth, his black hair curling softly around his temples. His deep blue eyes shone like a little boy's. He bucked one more time while he watched the ghost woman watching them.

Saffron stared at the naked girl's body, too stunned to look anywhere else. She forced her eyes up to the girl's face...and saw her own face. Her own smirking face, there, looking up and mocking the pain of the woman above her. The ghost woman turned and ran screaming to the other side of the field. Straight to the edge. And straight over the side. Her screams scattered the gulls.

Saffron came to with a harsh intake of air. She dug her fists into her eyes as she cried. "Oh, God, tell me that wasn't true. Tell me I wasn't like that." No one answered.

***

The sea swallowed the sun. Saffron prepared for Jethin's arrival.

A thought crossed her mind; about how this night should go.... She dug through Grandmother's closet and went out into the twilight gloom.

Jethin appeared. With no forewarning of cracking twigs or swishing grass, he came from the forest and now stood perfect and pressed in a gray-blue button down shirt, butt-hugging jeans, and ostrich cowboy boots. A smile lush with wry amusement caught up the lower half of his face. "Saffron, what are you doing?" He leaned over her.

She was laying poker-straight on a cold, flat rock out in the field. The ocean wind blew the gown of ivory lace that lay flat against the peaks and valleys of her rigid form. The nightgown, lacy and beautiful as it was, looked like it might belong to her Grandmother. It did belong to her Grandmother. She had stolen it out of Grandmother's closet that afternoon. She removed it from a yellowed box full of yellowed tissue paper and snuck it into her own room

Jethin covered his mouth to hide his glee while he took in her petrified limbs and startled eyes. He cleared his throat and contorted his facial features to resemble compassion, then sat beside her. There wasn't enough room, so he nudged at her with his hip until she relinquished some space.

By small measure, she began to release her stiffened body. Now she felt stupid. What was she doing anyway? Out here in the dark, stretched out on this rock like a sacrificial offering. An hour ago, she wasn't sure how to greet Jethin on this, the last day of her human existence. How did you go to your vampire death? Shouldn't there be some kind of ceremony? This was, like, a big deal.

Jethin kept his arms held tight around his bent knees and rocked on the stone. "You look...beautiful."

"Oh, shut up." She backhanded him in the thigh (but not *too* hard.) "I've been waiting for you every night. You wouldn't believe the scenarios that have been going through my head. Tonight," she indicated the dress and her alien-autopsy presentation, "you get this."

"Oh, my God, you have to chill. Listen; when I change you I won't be killing you. Your life is not ending, you know. You'll still be Saffron, Saffron on a diet that you want to be on...till later." He brushed her cheek with one very hot finger.

Saffron looked up at him. "You know what happened to me this afternoon? I just found out I caused this woman's death...suicide...she found me with her husband and jumped off a cliff.... I was smiling at her when she found us...." The deep breath she expelled came out rushed and jagged.

"Oooo. Not nice! Tsk, tsk. You should forgive yourself, Saffron." He chuckled. "Now c'mon; you're such a creepy girl sitting out here performing your sacrificial-lamb gig." He stood up. "Let's get you back inside, you to your room and me to my perch, so we can have a sense of normalcy."

His gaze fell to her mouth. His pupils dilated wide, then snapped to pinpoints. Her blue blood showed underneath the thin skin of her lips. He would never have blue blood again.

After tonight, neither would she.

"Let's go, get up," he grumbled and stalked off. She popped up behind him and ran through the wet grass. The lace caught like froth between her pistoning legs.

They walked without speaking.

At the corner of the great gabled farmhouse, he made off to the right to climb up to the roof of the farmer's porch. She went around the back of the house to enter through the kitchen door, being careful to guide it back slowly to lessen the squeals of the springs. The door was just about closed when Jethin suddenly appeared on the other side of the screen. Saffron gave a 'yipe' and jumped back, causing the door to slap.

Jethin jacked his thumb toward the upper floor. "Go ahead, get up there. You don't need to go so cautiously...so *slowly*. No one will wake up."

Saffron frowned. *Why? Why won't anyone wake up?* But she said nothing and followed his order, resenting her obedience even as she did so. In her room, she grabbed her robe off the panda on the rocking chair and covered herself with it. She skulked across the wood floor and sat on her tuffet by the windowsill.

He was waiting on the shingles, running his tongue across his teeth. He cast her a reproachful glance and indicated with one swift point of a finger that she should join him on the little roof. She jumped up and moved outside the window, all the while telling herself not to do it. "Man, I'll be *thrilled* when you're not this slow anymore." He grunted, "When we're done, I want you to crawl back inside and go to bed. It'll take three days."

"Why do I have to be out here with you?"

"If you don't do exactly as I say, this can get a little...messy. Better the mess be outside on top of a black roof than in your pretty bed." He flicked her robe. "If you get any on your clothes I'll take care of them."

Saffron looked down at her clothes. "Oh, my God. Should I go change?"

"Saffron, you're wasting my time. And if you could've changed you would've done it by now...."

She scratched her ear. What was *that* supposed to mean? And what was going to happen if she spent three days in bed with the vampire flu? Would she be in pain? What would her mother be in for?

A morphing freak, screaming like a maniac? "What's going to happen during those three days?"

Jethin shrugged. "You'll be sick. On the second day, I'll follow you all to the hospital. And on the third night, I'll get you out just before they declare you dead. If I miss you, I'll pick you up at the morgue. Do you think you're the first person to ever become a vampire?"

Saffron was shaking. Jethin ignored her. The sickle moon glazed them in mediocre light. For the first time that night, Saffron got a good look at his face. Under his heavy brows his eyes were large and bright and fringed by lustrous, long lashes.

"What's up?" His question was clipped.

Saffron blushed and looked away, but soon enough her eyes crawled back to his face as if it were the scene of an accident. His cheeks were flushed. They were *very* red. And his mouth...he had a smear of blood near the corner of his mouth.

Saffron tilted her body away from him, repulsion making her face pucker. She turned her head to stare at the farmhouse wall. This was much worse than noticing your friend had a little Bar-b-cue spare ribs caught in her front teeth.

"What, Saffron? What is it?"

Her eyes fixed once more on his lips. She gulped down the vomit in her throat.

He sat up straighter, his nostrils flared. He was thrown by her intent scrutiny. He knew he looked perfect. What possible cause could there be for her sour expression? The final pretense of his accepting demeanor shifted like ice breaking on a river. His eyes turned liquid black as they bore into her.

"I...I'm sorry, but you have some...." She didn't want to say, "blood," she would just as soon say "crotch rot." Instead, she took her fingers and brushed at her own mouth to simulate cleaning.

Jethin licked two fingers and worked the skin near his mouth where she had indicated. He looked at the greasy smear on his fingertips and under his finger nails. He licked them clean. "It's just blood, Saffron. No big deal." He smirked. "I just ate."

She clutched herself in a hug, shut her eyes, and leaned her forehead on her knees. The sinking feeling in her gut told her that today she had made one stupid mistake after another. Dressing up like a pitiful heroine from a 1960's vampire flick! Did she expect Christopher Lee to come visit her in all of his black-and-white glory? What had she been thinking? Placing herself so carefully on that rock. Had she really planned to act out the scene all the way to her death? No. Until this moment, she had never thought of her actual death. She only thought of the incidents leading up to it. Now she felt awake and sharply in tune; it was awful. She had gone out there to greet him, serve herself up. He could take her now - she had no more protection from him - she had traded it all in for a couple of romantic notions.

Earlier, she had felt so ashamed about the woman who threw herself from the cliff...and fantasized about being a vampire. She saw Markis and his longing eating away at him because of her...and fantasized about becoming a vampire. She saw Audrey nagging her about cutting her hair, going to college, making some friends, getting out of the house...and fantasized about becoming a vampire. She saw Ny harassing her and Li treating her like a brain-dead child...and fantasized, fantasized, fantasized. Where would she escape to when she didn't want to be a vampire?

Her heart beat erratically. Her whole body quaked and sweated. What if he grabbed her right now and ripped her throat out? The skin along the back of her neck and tops of her arms crimped uncomfortably.

Her fear wafted over to him. He felt it like a cool breeze in the desert and he smiled. This was good; he could use her fear to control her. It was so stimulating. He remained calm and adopted a soothing, familial behavior. He moved over to her side and put his arm around her. "It's all right. I know this scares you."

She felt his body alongside hers. He was so hot; his skin felt like beach sand in August. She tried to pull away.

"Don't worry. It's just fresh blood. It won't harm you. Everything will seem so unusual to you at first. But you'll get used to it. You'll get used to your power and the important place in this world that you are about to accept. You'll be catapulted to a level so fantastic - to a place you can't even comprehend right now." He chucked her chin. "But not until you try." He smiled encouragingly and kissed the top of her head. "You know, we should just get this over with. Later, I can show you wonders greater than anything found in the entire universe. Hidden intrigues, all for us." Fear, fear, and more fear, washing off her in tidal proportions. He drank it in as it poured almost sweeter than blood. The fear would dull her senses and make her pliable.

Saffron's breathing came in short, shallow gasps puffed through her lips as her throat tightened and locked. She clamped her teeth.

"C'mon... I know you're anxious. But listen, we'll just do it quick and end your indecisive agony." He smiled encouragingly, like a father to his child. "I envy you. I remember when it happened to me and I wish I could do it all over again!"

Saffron held herself tighter, braced herself, when she blurted, "Yeah, right! I don't freakin' think so."

Jethin blinked hard. He looked around dramatically. "I'm sorry, what was that?"

She bit her lip shut.

He clicked his incisors. "Excuse me?" What was her problem now? He wondered if he should just kill her. Leave her body like a calling card for Li. He could murder Saffron for the pure joy of it, like smashing eggs at Halloween instead of cooking them up for egg-salad sandwiches. It wasn't frugal, but, meh, he'd try again next time. This incarnation, this body, this girl was a pain in the ass. Yet, if he retained control, he could have more fun toying with her in the long run. But hey, sometimes one can't ignore one's impulses. He would ruin everything. By breaking her body he would set her soul free. But, oh, that first smashing bite - how fabulous. Larry Goile, the vampire from Provincetown, always drank the blood *and* ate the jugular. He claimed there was nothing finer. Jethin wasn't into jugulars though. When he went to town on Claudia, on all the others, he just threw her "stuff" in the ocean along with the creatures that came through his cave walls. But what to choose now? He held himself back. He shifted to sit on his fingers; they positively itched to grapple Saffron's swan neck. *Visualize the win. Li will be crushed if you take her beloved toy away for all eternity. Don't let Saffron have the luxury of returning to the fairy world. She might plop herself there and wait with them again. This is your golden opportunity. They will hide indefinitely this time, for sure. In the meantime, some fool might turn you to dust. Then they can come back at their leisure, play their silly human game, and laugh at you. It's nothing to them, the passing of time. And it's everything to you, the dragging of time. Take a moment to relax. You can do this.*

Jethin swung his head round to face Saffron. She had no idea how beautiful she was, stupid girl. She could never imagine how he had admired her in her past life. After he first became a vampire, he used to linger in Molly's yard. He did this often in the early days. He contemplated the meaning of life, while the wafting scent of Molly's decomposing body curled up from the black hole of the well and tickled his nostrils. It was a few months before he could drink the blood of humans, so repulsed was he by that lingering odor that he gagged on the blood of sheep instead.

He had been sitting on the edge of the well for hours when suddenly, he realized he was being watched. Nothing more than the tightening of the skin on his neck let him know this, but he knew, and looked across the lawn to a little window in the house that Jack built (Jack was Molly's father). There Rosemary hid, peeking at him from behind the heavy brocade of a dark curtain. Saffron peeked just the same way when she was afraid. Only Saffron hid behind her hair so she could take her cover everywhere she went.

Rosemary and Jethin had stared at each other for several seconds, then she lowered the curtain and disappeared. After that, Jethin found a lamb waiting for him when he went to Molly's yard. He didn't know how Molly's mother knew, but another lamb was there each night he visited. He watched her window as he fed but never saw her again.

Rosemary and Saffron had some things in common. In some ways, they weren't alike at all. Rosemary was aware that she was beautiful. She feared other things... But Saffron was all hopped up on this 'fat and ugly' trend that was the zeitgeist of her generation. Jethin longed to see the end of this era with its diets and plastic surgery. It was such a bore.

Saffron was splendidly built with hair that shone like molten metal even in starlight. And what did she do? Hunch and gape. Blanch and bite at her fingernails. And every time she crouched back into that spineless, simpering bit of blob, he felt the blood within him curdle. Oh, how he wanted to dispose of her. "Sit up!" Jethin snapped. His eyes probed her as he ravaged the tip of his tongue with one elongated incisor. Why was this proving to be so tedious? Maybe he should have consulted a shrink before the big night. This was grueling. He felt their close rapport, built with careful attention over these last few months, had been blown away like clouds on a rising wind.

"I'm going to bite my wrist," he pointed "here. I'll pierce the veins so my blood will flow smoothly and make it easier for you."

"Make what easier?" She knew what he was talking about. She was stalling. But she felt him, his pressure. It would be too hard to push him away, and so much easier to give in. She was so exhausted and sitting on the roof was giving her vertigo. She imagined rolling off the roof and drifting to the ground.

"Biting my wrist makes it easier for you to drink, Saffron. Don't you watch vampire movies? I love the movies. That's why I bought the Cineplex. I watch the sheep flock in for the horror movies. They bleat and scream at all the right moments. I watch them leave. I feel their 'just a movie' relief, and laugh. Sometimes I even pay one or two a little visit."

Saffron frowned. "You told me you only took the bad people. You told me you "cleanse the earth of scum." Is that what 'scum' is to you? A bunch of teenagers screwing around?"

"Au contraire, Saffron. Not all teenagers are innocent. I assure you, mine are well-chosen and well-punished, each for his or her particular sin."

Saffron sighed and brought her hands up to cover her eyes. This was so bizarre. What was she *doing*?

Jethin pulled her hands from her face and began to croon soft words to calm her. "Never the innocent, Saffron, you have my word. Your life will be perfection. You can have anything you want! There's a shop in Ogunquit. It's small and dusty and hushed and they sell exquisite jewelry. Antique diamonds as big as your eyes and set in platinum. Do you want one? Do you want them all? Do you want to visit Mindy one night and show them to her?"

Saffron hissed. "You leave her alone!" She didn't like Mindy but she didn't want her tortured! "Stop talking like that. You don't know what I want. When it's time *I'll tell you* what I want."

Jethin clapped. "That's my girl!" His smile was sweet and brimming like a four-year-old before his birthday cake. He put his wrist to his lips and was about to pierce the skin when they both heard a low moan on the wind. They listened, and after a few moments the sound came again. It was louder. The sound was familiar to Saffron, but Jethin had only heard it once. Then promptly forgot it.

"You have a banshee here?"

"No," Saffron whispered, "it's her." Her face reddened as she crossed her arms protectively across her chest. "Look," She mumbled and pointed toward the cliff.

Jethin searched in the direction Saffron had indicated, and finally found the woman. Well, the dead woman. A moaning spirit. Disdain crept across his perfect features. He felt no pity for them. He had no idea why they would choose that existence. The vampire life was the most admirable, the fairy world had its perks, being human wasn't the worst thing. But, being a ghost? Just plain deplorable.

"She doesn't matter. Let's go; we have work to do."

Since the very first moment Saffron laid eyes on the ghost, all those months ago, she had feared her. Not now. Tonight, she watched the woman with a mixture of great sorrow and empathy. Saffron felt the woman's ache and wanted to reach out to her, to soothe and help her.

"Don't you feel her pain? Can't you tell? She matters."

"I don't feel anything. It's just a defect of that fairy dust you've got clinging to you. C'mon, now. I don't want to spill this all over my jeans. Drink up." He had since bitten himself and was keeping the flow of blood back by pinching the punctures with his thumb and forefinger. He held his wrist before her and smiled. "You won't like it at first, but give it a couple of seconds and you'll find you become addicted very quickly. Drink away. Enjoy. I'll stop you when you've had enough." He moved his wrist closer to her mouth. "Open up, Saffron."

She shifted her position. She screamed inside her head to tell him, "No!" She closed her eyes. He shoved his wrist in her mouth, forcing her lips open until they split at the corners. She heard a crack in her jaw and screamed with the pain. The blood was spurting from his wounds. It was hitting the roof of her mouth. It was pooling near the back of her tongue. She took a great big gulp of it. It was heinous. It tasted like copper and.... She didn't know what else. It tasted like metal. Like charred metal. Like sickening, sweet, cloying spice swirling all together, thick and black. Her gag reflex was triggered, and she gulped down another dose of the wretched liquid.

Her eyes widened with fear as her body recoiled from it. A chill rushed through her limbs and froze her bones. She thought of old things and dead things and things unchanged and ignored since the dawn of time. All around her, it smelled like a mildewed antiques barn. She shivered. Cold overtook her entire body, and she knew that if someone were to poke her, she'd shatter into a million frozen shards.

Just as quickly, the frigidness rushed from her body and she discovered her mouth was full again, full of the viscous fluid, a thickening draught which threatened to force its way down her throat. Saffron actually felt it pushing to go down as if it were *aware* of what it was doing. This time, she spat it out. Everywhere, she retched and spit and blew.

"No, Saffron. No! You're so close, quickly, drink again! You are on the edge of need! Just drink it and you'll see, you'll crave it! You won't be able to get enough! Hurry!"

"no." The tiny two-letter word was firm and sure. "I will *not* drink it!" She swiped the back of her hand over her mouth and felt the oily blood smear between her fingers. This wasn't going to be easy, but she didn't care anymore. She knew what he was; she had figured what he was hiding. "I will not become what you are. I will not exist forever as one person. Look at you." She leaned back to take a look at him. "You're like a block of ice at a New Year's parade. Yeah, you're cut and you look like a piece of art, but there's nothing else there! You have no pulse! And you love nothing! Remember the greatest power on earth? 'It's love.' You don't love anything, Jethin. What do you do with yourself every day, every week, every month, year, and century? If I were you, I'd fill my time up with loving people. I mean, what else is there? But I can't love them when I'm a vampire; can I? I'll just want to eat them." She shook with the effort of her speech.

"You realized too late that the true beauty of life is..." she fluttered her arms wildly. She frowned, her mouth twisting with the pressure of quick thought and exasperation. Burning blood dribbled from her chin as she struggled to understand. "...ahhh..." She slapped her forehead lightly, several times.

Jethin watched her fumbling in surprised annoyance. Luckily for Saffron, it made him pause.

"To be born again!" Saffron yelled, causing some wild turkeys to fly from the branch where they had been roosting. Was that what she meant to say? All of the puzzle pieces were so confusing. It was true; there were two sides to every story. And anything could be justified. "In your search for the most envious life, you messed up. Instead of getting more, more, more; you denied yourself. You denied yourself the prize most humans take for granted. Change. You truly are dead." Her mind popped with epiphanies. "You want that life back. You want a chance to be what you used to be. Man, you reek of jealousy. My God, what was I thinking?" She rubbed her knuckles into her eye sockets. "I was going to throw my life away because it was the easiest thing to do." Her eyes burned like an evangelist's one hour into the sermon. "But I'm not dead. I can start over any time I want! You have absolutely nothing to give me."

Not a blink or a twitch broke the stare that bound them. She waited for him to attack. Her intestines spasmed and she doubled over. She groaned and hissed when she spoke. "How dare you!" Her nostrils flared and her eyes narrowed as the blood continued to drip from her chin. "You were tricking me in the same, exact way that Cecilia tricked you. Why? Weren't you mad at her for doing that to you? Didn't she hurt you so bad you could never be happy again? Why would you do that to someone else? Why would you do that to me? Jethin, I would *never* do something like that to you."

He had been sitting there, all this time, watching her work things out. He could have slaughtered her ten times over; he could have walked away. Yet, he sat there and watched in amazement at the transformation that sped through her like pure energy. He felt a grudging admiration for her. Did *he* cause her to change like this? He was more powerful than he thought...

She was mostly right in her accusations. She had the wrong person though...the Countess hadn't thrown him over the edge. Li had, when she was Molly. He couldn't tear Saffron's steaming organs from her lily-white belly now. How could he enjoy it? She gave him no incentive. After all, she wasn't afraid anymore. He could feel it, the fear draining from her as water from a sieve. Now she felt...pity. And pain. Blek. What a waste of a night. How would he piss Li off now? Maybe if he got Saffron to marry him... He sniffed. Like a dandy perturbed before his cold afternoon tea, he actually sniffed with great disparagement.

"Fine, Saffron. This is all very well, but I should let you know. If you don't continue the process within the next few seconds, you are going to become very, very...unwell. My blood flows through you. Your blood will reject it as a foreign invader. If you don't allow me to drink of your blood and break down its defenses, you will enter a world of such extreme torture the likes of which you and your kind could never imagine. Do you think you've had nightmares before? They will not compare to the inescapable hell you are about to enter - a black death that will eviscerate you and leave you delirious with pain. That doesn't sound very good, does it?" He tilted his head. "And just when you think the pain couldn't possibly get any worse, it does, and it leaves you begging for the easier pain you had just wished away.

"We must continue what we have started or, simply put, my blood will attack you." He sniffed again, "it will probably eradicate you." He raised his eyebrows and shrugged as if to say, *Oh, well*. In fact, he said nothing and watched to see how this little bit of terror would affect her. He was being fair; he had warned her. He was going to have a lot of dancing to do after this fiasco to get her to marry him. Just the thought of it was exhausting.

Saffron gave him nothing. Her face was screwed up in shifting grimaces of pain, but she just stared at him. She had nothing more to say.

This was crap. He wanted the last word. He stood up, casually dusted off his clothes, and stretched luxuriously like a cat emerging from a sunbath. "Have you really never wondered how it is that we were fortunate enough to meet?"

Saffron ignored him. She pretended to study her flip-flops as she bore the pains in her belly.

"Li, Saffron. Li is the reason why we have met. As a matter of fact, Li knew this moment was coming all of your life. Yet..." He looked around; over the lawn toward the sea, through the ghostly branches of the trees, and into the alpaca field. "...where is she now? In your hour of need, where is she?" He spoke as gently as a lover. "Is she leaving you to die, Saffron? Because you will, you know...die. That pain you're feeling is the foreplay of death." He continued to smile pleasantly. "I'm here. I can help you. No matter what you say, it hurts me to watch you suffer like this." He stretched his arms above his head and tilted his head to get a crick out. Saffron heard the crunch and shuddered. He shifted his legs. "She might thank me for your death. I'm sure she has been wishing for your death since you were born. Have you suffered many accidents in this life? Any repeated incidents of near-death calamities?"

Saffron gasped.

"Ah, hah. I see *that* means something to you. I only point it out because this gasp of, 'Hhhgggg,' denotes shock, whereas the other gasp you made earlier of, 'Wheeeeew,' was clearly from pain." He smoothed his eyebrows with his fingertips. "I'll take the blame there. I should've told you. Li is *so* possessive."

Saffron jerked her face away from his line of vision. Her eyes rolled back in her head as the pain mounted and squeeeeezed her gut. How she wanted to cry, but couldn't even take the breath to moan.

Jethin leaned on her back and put his mouth by her ear. She could smell his fetid breath. "If you won't let me help you, there's nothing left for me to do. Goodbye, my Saffron." He stood up and bowed to her. "See you next time."

She felt the wind at her back. He was gone.

Her eyes began to glaze with the pain. Her feet scraped down the slope of the roof as hot waves of cruel, spasmodic stabbing pierced through her lower intestines. Her breathing came in pants as she fell back against the wall of her home. She wanted her mother. She didn't know what to do to reach Audrey beyond the sound barrier that Jethin put up. Low, guttural sounds poured from her lips, sounds she wasn't even aware off. Then, "Ma, Ma, Mommm...." so weakly, that the gnomes only heard, "Mm, Mm, MmMm," and went back to catching nightcrawlers.

Saffron was foaming at the mouth. Her body began to convulse. Just before she passed out, she heard the tinkle of one tiny bell. Her head lolled to the side and that was the way Li found her, a limp lifeform in a pool of black blood. Li assessed the scene, and then crouched beside Saffron, careful not to slip in the blood. Was Saffron becoming a vampire or was she dying? Li prayed for Saffron's death. How had this all happened so quickly? She didn't want to believe Saffron would rush to Jethin so soon. She had assumed she could keep her safe. She had made a grave mistake. She ran her hands over Saffron's inanimate form. A small smile of triumph crossed her lips. Saffron was not a vampire. It occurred to Li that the gore around Saffron's wasted body was a telltale sign. Li could see that he had tried; but he wouldn't have left a new fledgling in such a way. Saffron would have been weak and sick as a newborn vampire; he would have stayed very near during her three days. Something had gone wrong here. Saffron had been left to die.

The fairy looked around. This was a lot of blood to clean. There was blood splattered on the side of the house, blood sticking and running down the roof, blood dripping off Saffron's chin and soaking her robe, blood stuck in her (short?) hair, congealing in dark clumps. Li sat on the roof and pulled Saffron's boneless, sticky body into her arms. "A fine mess you have left for me, little girl." Li retrieved a gossamer cloth from among her robes and gently wiped at Saffron's face, then neck and arms, and hair, and finally her clothes. Wherever the cloth touched, the blood was wiped clean away. The cloth itself blackened but it didn't drip.

When Li was done, there wasn't a trace of blood anywhere on Saffron. For a good while longer, Li worked on the mess that had splattered all around. Soon, the walls of the house, the shingles on the little rooftop where they sat, and any tainted surrounding areas were all spotlessly clean.

Across the field, and deep within the shadows, Jethin watched the fairy work. He leaned, arms crossed over his taut chest, on the trunk of a massive willow that stood on the edge of the forest. Its drooping limbs and tender, knifed-edged leaves swished back and forth in the gentle night breeze. The branches hung low and obscured him from human sight, but the animals knew he was there. They could smell him. Li knew he was there. She could feel him.

His lush lips were pressed together and his eyes were squinted in thought. It wasn't often he could lay eyes on her like this. Her beauty still touched him. The grace in her movements filled him with an agony that was too much to bear. He could move at her but she could move more quickly and leave him even more angered for his embarrassing try.

"As always, my beautiful girl, I rush to your side to help you. Oh, what would you do without me?" Li smiled pleasantly while she worked, overjoyed to be of such great use to Saffron. "We don't want people wondering why you were dining on blood this fine warm evening, now do we? You have learned your lesson; have you not? No more associating with vampires." She looked at Saffron's limbs and cocked her head. She adjusted Saffron's arms so they folded over her belly, straightened her legs so they wouldn't be skewed, brushed her long bangs to the side, and hooked them behind her ear. "There. Now you be good and watch me clean your mess.

"I will not speak harshly to you about all this. I know why you did it. Ny confessed he sent the dream to trick your soul. That dream was a fabrication. Your soul can rest knowing the shore will never be empty for you, Saffron. I will always be waiting for you on that shore. Not the frozen tips of the earth or the fire within could keep me from you. I will always be there. There will be others, too, always there for you." Li looked through the window into Saffron's bedroom. "Would you like to see it? Hm?" Her voice was lower than a whisper, cooler than the bottom of an iceberg. Her lips were so close they grazed Saffron's ear. "Would you like to see me waiting on the shore for you? Would that help?" Her voice was slithery. "Go look, Saffron, go look for me on the shore."

Li sat up straight, looked around the dark night, and squinted her black eyes. She felt Jethin still. When would he go away? She raised her head proudly. She refused to blame herself for this mess. Jethin could blame her for the senseless life she led as Molly all he wanted.

But the fact was, she was Molly no longer. He had no Godly right to hold her actions unforgiven. She persisted in ignoring his presence and continued to chant to Saffron's unconscious form. "Now Saffron, Ny will be there on the shore as well, and hundreds of others. Each and every one of us has a crowd waiting to receive us on the shore when we die. That was a dreadful trick Ny played on you, but how could you have believed it? Since the dawn of time, the shore has been empty for no soul! Why do you always place such trust in Ny? It is ridiculous! Try loving him as I love him - as a playful soul with boundless energy and a zest for adventure. But don't give in to him; he can never give back."

She looked down at Saffron's pale, clammy face, and watched her eyes move rapidly beneath her eyelids. Li knew Saffron could hear her. "You are in a bad position right now. You will be in pain for quite some time, I am afraid. Then again...you don't have to be..." The movement behind Saffron's eyelids slowed, then stopped. Li knew Saffron had left her body.

Chapter 23

Saffron floated in a sea of black. Luminescent colors drifted past her and soft breezes washed over her skin, soaking her in the essence of warm, night-blooming flowers. She saw a light. The light grew. It was the full moon, one hundred times its normal size, suspended over the snowcapped mountains of her dream. Her body started a slow spiral. It drifted down. She landed in the glass boat and found herself opposite her beaming Grandmother.

Only, her Grandmother didn't look like herself. Grandmother was now somewhere in her twenties; her figure perfect, muscles toned, skin tight, smooth and beautiful. Her hair was jet black and hung like ribbons over her shoulders. She peeked out from under a heavy fringe of black bangs. She had large eyes, almond-shaped and the sparkling color of cognac. Her full lips spread open to reveal beautiful white teeth. She laughed with a joy so pure Saffron could feel the sound loosening her own heart and chasing away the darkness.

"Grandmother, what are you doing here?"

"Darling, I died just a little bit ago." She tilted her head. "You didn't die, did you?"

Saffron shrugged. "Li told me to come meet her at the shore."

Grandmother stretched her eyes shut and used the voice saved for very naughty young children. "So, she's found a way to be with you in this life, has she?"

Saffron nodded glumly.

"And she's told you to come meet her at the shore?"

Saffron looked down at the neon fish.

"Well, you'll do no such thing!" Grandmother slapped Saffron's knee. "You just went ahead and did what she told you to do, didn't you?"

"Grandmother, I was in so much pain."

Grandmother softened. "Oh, my darling. There will be more pain to come in this life. Go back. There is more love than pain waiting for you."

"How can you be sure?" Saffron wanted to cry, but no tears came, as if it was impossible here.

"God is telling me. He is telling me to tell you to go back. You can't hear Him, can you?"

"I only hear the boat in the water."

"Then it's not your time to be here." Grandmother gathered her dark hair and pulled it all over one shoulder.

"Why do you look like you're Chinese?"

"I'm trying this on for next time. What do you think?"

"You're beautiful." Saffron smiled. "Enjoy yourself with the fairies."

Grandmother balked. "With the fairies? Did I murder someone?"

Saffron frowned. Jethin had made the same comment, "Did I murder someone?" He actually *had* murdered someone; but he found a loophole. When Jethin said it, she thought he was being facetious, he didn't like the fairies. Why was her grandmother saying it? "Li told me..." Grandmother rolled her eyes. "...that we all become fairies when we die."

Grandmother chuffed. "Lies. We don't *all* become fairies...only those of us who have caused great grievances against mankind become fairies when we die. Then those souls wait out their time steeped in nature and denied some pleasures, while they contemplate their actions. Without tactile senses like touch and taste and smell, they are free to put more effort into their other studies...like how to be a good human. To smell again. To taste and touch again. The desire for these things inspires us to be better souls. Some of *us* don't wait too well in the fairy world, and get stuck there longer. If a fairy absolutely refuses to evolve, he devolves. That's where you get into your hobgoblins and demons and such. They're just fairies that revel in their rot until they become scary little monsters. Which brings us to angels; good angels are good angels and bad angels are the ones who collect and set to task all of the demons.

"When one is allowed to be reborn after one's stint in the fairy world, one must be born into a strict, religious lifestyle. Religion is the lowest rung on the ladder to understanding God, so that's where one begins." Grandmother grinned.

Saffron sat in stunned silence.

"Saffron, I was thinking. I know you must have made agreements with others who are to become your children, but I was wondering if you would consider having another. Could I come back as your youngest child?"

"Well, yeah. If I marry a Chinese guy, I guess."

"Oh, you! The looks aren't set in stone. What do you say?"

"Sure, why not? Anyone else over there on that shore want to jump on the bandwagon?" Saffron squinted at the nearing coastline.

"Good Lord, girl. Do you want to become 'The Old Woman That Lived in a Shoe?' Counting me, you've just agreed to have seven. And the one you agreed to have them with? Well he's pure spitfire, and so will his children be. I don't think it's too soon to begin mental preparations." Grandmother hooted and leaned forward to slap Saffron's knee again.

Saffron hugged the delicious sensation of the conversation close to her. "And who am I to have these children with, Grandmother?"

Grandmother wagged her finger. "Ah, ah, ah! Not my place to tell. But, I think you've met him already."

"Already? Like what? I've met him once? Or, I've met him, and you know, I'm with him?"

Again, twenty-something Chinese Granny smiled. "Not my place. But I'll tell you about me as your darling child. Why, I'm an absolute pain in the ass! I don't listen, I throw fits, I'll dump your expensive shampoo in my bath water, I pee my pants when I don't get my way..."

"Oh, great! Sign me up!"

Grandmother tapped Saffron's nose. "But I'll love you more than the sun, and the moon and the stars...just like I do now."

Saffron's face softened, along with her voice. "Great. Sign me up."

The boat cleaved the black water. The neon fish were fat and plopped when they jumped.

"Grandmother?" Saffron's voice caught in her throat on barbs of guilt.

"Darling, it's okay."

"No, it's not. I mean, I feel awful. I didn't even try to talk to you or to help you. I'm so sorry. It's just that..." Saffron sighed, "I was so afraid of you." Shame pressed her head down.

Grandmother leaned forward in a scented swirl of sweet and foreign spice. She tilted Saffron's chin up with two silky-skinned fingers. Saffron looked into her cognac eyes and found them to be like mirrors, reflecting her sad face and wild red hair. But then Grandmother smiled, and so did Saffron. And that's what was in Grandmother's eyes – herself, beaming and beautiful.

"I know." Grandmother whispered. "It's okay." She pulled

Saffron close into her small, strong arms and wrapped her warmly. "Don't be afraid." Grandmother leaned back against the bow, her arms resting on the sides of the little glass boat. She shifted and crossed her legs, then tilted her head to continue studying Saffron. "So now, what do you think of this go-round?"

Saffron shook her head. The full moon behind her wore a skirt of clouds.

"I'm sure there was a sonic boom in the world of fairy when you snuck away from your friends." Grandmother's tiny smile never left her soft lips.

Saffron grimaced. "How do you know about that?"

"Oh, posh. Everyone knows of you three, inseparable since the dawn of time. And that last life time! What a doozie!" Conspiring, Grandmother leaned forward. Saffron met her halfway. "Did you hear what happened during your Ireland 1600's incarnation?"

Saffron looked down. "Some." The question was if she really wanted to hear any more...

"Well, Li, who was Molly, had poisoned her father, who was Ny, and he expired just as he was having his jollies with that slutty widow in town...he died only minutes before Jethin threw Molly down that well. What a soap opera those three are!"

"So that explains why Li is stuck in the fairy realm. But what about Ny?"

"How do you think the old slut became a widow?" Grandmother's eyes sparkled. She was enjoying herself.

Saffron hung her head. "And I didn't do anything, did I? I just followed them like an idiot later on...right?"

"Saffron, give me your hands." Grandmother spoke earnestly. "You are not what they are. I'm not laughing at you. I can't figure out what you're doing here now. But what a joy you were to live with. Thank you for choosing us this time around. For whatever reason, thank you. And while you're at it, congratulate yourself. Always did say it wasn't good, what you were doing. Never saw a creature chain herself the way you did. We all do it, while we're human. But you? You did it while you were in other realms as well." Grandmother shrugged. "Why'd you do it?"

Saffron began to shake. If only she knew why. If only she could remember. "I don't know."

Grandmother sniffed. "Not important. What matters is that you left. That you did something for yourself instead of for them." She winked. "Good for you, honey." Then she looked hard at Saffron, and nodded. "Yes, I think it has worked. You seem stronger. Your essence, you feel stronger." Grandmother threw a casual glance back over her shoulder and straightened. "Oh, look! There they are! Can you see them? Hellooo! Hello there!"

Saffron saw forms of light walking forward on the beach. She couldn't make out the forms very well. They were vague, gesturing images, making not a sound. Grandmother was so ecstatic, Saffron wished it was all happening to her. But she couldn't force a tear; she had left them with her body on the rooftop.

Grandmother turned around. "Now, honey, one more thing. Remember, you have control. The only time people go around controlling others is when people forget they *have* control. You need to remember you have effort. Effort will cure you. But you have to *sustain* the effort. It's hard, but you can do it." Then she patted her long, black hair, and ran her fingers through her long, black bangs, "How do I look?"

Saffron opened her mouth to answer, but Grandmother cut her

off. "Hey, you need to get home before you give your mother a heart attack. I've already done enough damage to the poor girl today. Go home to her. Be with her through her troubles."

Saffron nodded and willed herself back to her body. It took only the thought to start her spiral upwards and away. As she ascended, her Grandmother gave her the 'Queen's Wave.' Grandmother's smile lit up her body with a pulsing light that surrounded her and the little boat, and reached for her loved ones on the shore.

Saffron had never seen such a happy recently-deceased person. She drifted through the black abyss for only a few seconds, then felt her soul squeeze itself into her stiff body.

Inside her body, she was not alone.

She could feel him. Everywhere. She could feel his impatience. And his determination.

She was possessed.